the
Painter's
Apprentice

A novel of 16th-century Venice

Laura Morelli

Published in the United States of America by The Scriptorium.

Library of Congress Control No. 2017915226

Hardcover ISBN 978-1-942778-96-7
Paperback ISBN 978-1-942778-92-9
EPUB ISBN 978-1-942778-91-2
mobi ISBN 978-1-942778-95-0
Audiobook ISBN 978-1-942778-93-6

Cover design by Kerry Ellis
Interior layout by Shannon Bodie, Bookwise Design

The Painter's Apprentice / Laura Morelli

Venetian Artisans series

www.lauramorelli.com

FREE TO MY READERS

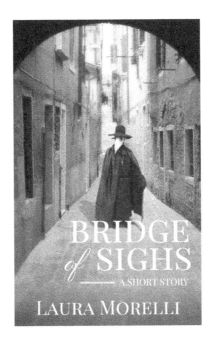

Join my Readers' Group and get a free copy
of my Venetian short story, "Bridge of Sighs."

To get started visit
www.lauramorelli.com/bridge-of-sighs

Go behind the scenes of

THE PAINTER'S APPRENTICE

To see videos and pictures, and to learn more about the research behind this book, visit www.lauramorelli.com/TPABonus.

There you will find bonus material available exclusively to my readers.

Visit:
www.lauramorelli.com/TPABonus

Thank you for reading!

Laura

Dedicated to those whose hearts
propel their hands

The Lazzaretto Vecchio seemed like Hell itself. From every side there came foul odors, and indeed a stench that none could endure; groans and sighs were heard without ceasing; and at all hours clouds of smoke from the burning of corpses were seen to rise far into the air. Some who miraculously returned from that place alive reported, among other things, that at the height of that great influx of infected people there were three and four of them to a bed.

—From an account of the plague houses by the 16th-century
Venetian notary Rocco Benedetti

Venice, Winter 1510

Chapter 1

I am scraping golden flakes from my palette knife when I learn that the pestilence has reached the quarter of Our Most Serene City where my father's workshop lies.

"Caresini the baker says that planks have been nailed across a half-dozen doorways along the rio de la Sensa." The painter's wife bounces her drowsy infant in one arm as she paces from one side of the workshop to the other. The baby's soft, round head is barely visible in the crook of her mother's woolen sleeve. With the other hand, the painter's wife works a lace-trimmed twill into a tight twist, winding it around her fingers. "Crosses nailed on the doors—*Dio*!" She shakes her head vigorously as if to rid her mind of the image. "How long might it take to reach us?" She sets her wide blue eyes on her husband.

From my tottering stool in the far corner of the painter's workshop, my eyes track the lady's nervous pacing, and I wait for her husband's response. The painter's journeyman stops grinding pigments in a marble mortar and stills his lean body as if suddenly frozen, gazing wide-eyed at his master from across the room. For a long moment, the workshop falls silent save for the gentle crackling of the fire in the hearth. The air feels stifling even though delicate ice crystals have formed on the window glass.

All of our eyes settle on the man seated at the easel.

The painter's face remains placid. His eyes never stray from the sanded poplar panel propped before him. I see his mouth twitch left and right, weighing his wife's question before responding. The movement makes his thick beard shift and roll as if it has come to life. Finally, he removes his brush from the surface of the panel and suspends it in midair, but his eyes remain focused on the Madonna and Child on the easel before him.

"It is a long walk from Cannaregio to San Marco. The pestilence would have to get very much worse before it reaches us here, *amore*." He touches the panel with his brush again. The journeyman resumes scraping his pestle across the bottom of the mortar, pressing small cakes of pigment into fine powder.

I watch the painter for a few more moments. His hooded eyes regard the indigo pigment at the end of his brush, which he applies in a slow, meticulous motion. He appears composed, I think, but sometimes, what appears on the outside is not what is on the inside.

My father taught me that. Deception is our trade.

The gold we apply to the surface of an altarpiece is designed to fool the eye, to convey a feeling of sumptuousness, to bring an appearance of precious metal to what is only a hollow wooden core. That is what we do. It is my trade, my father's, and his father's before him, as far back as anyone remembers.

The painter's wife moves to the window and peers through its icy, leaded panes into the canal. The dull winter light creates a soft, glowing halo around her wisps of fine curls. "When we were children our father told us of a time when the pestilence descended on Our Most Excellent Republic as no one could remember. He was only a boy but it seemed, he said, that half of our people were dumped into the mass pits at Lazzaretto Vecchio. I have never been able to banish the image from my mind." She places her handkerchief over her eyes for a moment, then addresses the ceiling. "The worst outbreak of a generation, he said. *Che Dio ci aiuti!*"

God help us, indeed, if what the painter's wife says is true. I shudder, picturing the bodies thrown five deep into stinking pits on the lagoon island whose hazy outlines we can see from the Giudecca but do not dare to visit. The Lazzaretto Vecchio; many will not even utter its name for fear of conjuring the black hand of disease. It is where our people are sent when purulent boils appear in their armpits and groins, or blood flows from their mouths; where they are whisked on black ferries before they infect their families and neighbors. All of us have heard the stories from the old people.

The last plague that struck down large numbers of our citizens occurred before I was born. Only the elderly remember that ghastly time but there have been outbreaks more recently, too. Each of us knows at least one person who has perished of the Black Death. It strikes without warning, unfurling its ugly hand to clutch anyone—the young and healthy, the thriving, the rich, the poor, the old. It grasps babies from their mothers' breasts. Just two months ago, it took our own beloved Giorgione, the only member of our guild of Saint Luke who seemed to paint not with the hands of a human but with those of an angel. Though Giorgione's house lay only a stone's throw from our own, my father and the other *indoradòri* of the quarter have been spared. But I am not naive enough to believe that any one of us is immune.

"*Tesoro.*" The painter turns to his wife as he wipes his long, wooden-handled brush on a rag. His face remains calm and reassuring but an exasperated sigh escapes his mouth. "Do not unleash a storm from a glass of water. As far as we know it has not gone farther than one or two streets in Cannaregio."

"Better them than us," says the painter's journeyman, pinching a square of indigo pigment between his fingertips and dropping it into his mortar. The painter's face turns dark, and he casts a stern-looking glance at his journeyman, then at his wife. All three of them suddenly turn their gazes toward me in the corner of the studio, as if I have only now appeared.

Have I been that invisible? With my freckled nose and cascading curls the color of fire, I am accustomed to standing out, not disappearing into the shadows. Could it be that they have only now realized that I am here in the room, that it is *my* home, *my* quarter of the city where the pestilence has begun to steal people from their homes?

Heat rises to my cheeks. I study the knots in the wooden table-top and try to become as invisible as I believe I have been all along. Ignoring their gazes, I scrape my knife again and watch the gilded flakes drop into my ceramic bowl. Dust-flecked winter sun reflects from the canal and filters into the room. Each gold flake catches the light, flashing brilliantly and briefly before falling into a dark heap at the bottom of the dull brown bowl. There I will collect them and mix them again, pressing them out into thin gleaming sheets and setting them aside for another picture.

"Stefano!" The painter's wife comes to my aid, reaching toward the journeyman and shaking her handkerchief at him. "You forget that young Maria's family lives in Cannaregio. You must not be so callous," she says.

The journeyman shrugs, then presses his palms together in a gesture of prayer. He wags his hands in my direction. "Forgive me, signorina," he says, casting me a sheepish glance as his soft Venetian inflection rolls across the room. "I had forgotten." The young man's face is the picture of innocence and I cannot find it within myself to reprove him.

"*Niente*," I say. "You meant no harm."

The baby begins to fuss and gnaw her fists. "Shh," the painter's wife whispers, pushing the swinging door with her toe. They disappear into the kitchen. The three of us return to the work of our hands: Master Trevisan the painter at his easel, Stefano the journeyman at his pigments, and I at the gold. We fall into a companionable silence, but the words of the painter's wife ring inside my head.

The worst outbreak of a generation.

I wipe my knife along the edge of the ceramic bowl to remove the last flecks of gold as the words turn over in my head. This act of reconstituting the gold leaf does not require my full concentration for I have done it thousands of times. It matters not that I am a girl; I am as much an *indoradòr* as my father, as competent as any man who is a full member of our guild. In all of my nineteen years, I never wanted to be anywhere else but at my father's side, laying and punching the gold into the poplar panels.

But instead of punching gold in my father's gilding studio, I am learning the ways of the colored pigments in the workshop of Benvoglio Trevisan. I am told that Master Trevisan is one of our guild's most respected masters of color and light, that he is one of the best painters of altarpieces in our territories and beyond, and that I am fortunate to find myself at his side. I do not doubt any of it, but it does not change the fact that I feel a stranger in his home. How I ended up here is still difficult to fathom.

Everything is new here. The peculiar, pungent odor of egg yolk and wine from *terraferma* used to bind the tempera paints. The ringing of the brass bell at the canal-side door. The late hour of the morning meal. The countless images of saints, ancient heroes, and mythical beasts cluttering the walls from floor to ceiling. The warble of the baby girl, the footfall and screech of the painter's young son in the corridors and on the stairs. The taste of fish stew made with spices I have never sampled before.

It has all taken some getting used to.

It is not for lack of a welcome. On the contrary, ever since they brought me here a fortnight ago in a fine new gondola, the painter and his wife have done what they could to fold me into the rhythm of their household. They have fed me and housed me under their own roof, in accordance with the agreement that Master Trevisan made with my father and our guild leaders. Though it is only a short distance as the pigeon flies, I feel far removed from Cannaregio, from that place where my childhood home lies and the pestilence has now begun to unfurl its indiscriminate claw.

The painter and his wife believe that I am here to help with a new altarpiece commission that requires a significant amount of gilding. That they will not have to pay me the rate established in our guild for apprentices. That instead, I will learn the colored pigments and secure the future of my father's name. That this arrangement will benefit all of us and strengthen our painters' guild.

But just as gold leaf can make something seem what it is not, my place here in the painter's studio is not as it appears on the surface.

The truth of the matter is that my father has sent me away.

Chapter 2

On the mantel in the painter's studio there is a small, exquisite gilded box of a kind I have never seen. We make gilded boxes in my father's workshop, to be sure. From my workbench in the corner of the painter's studio I can make out the decorative patterns across the lid, the kinds we make with metal stamps that have been handed down to us over generations.

But this box is different. Nearly all its surfaces are decorated with delicate, white molded figures and animals in relief. Women in flowing dresses, men in exotic costume, a lioness, an elephant.

Beneath the box on the mantel, I watch the servant woman, Antonella, sweep ashes from the great stone hearth. She gathers the gray powder into a pan, then pours the ashes into a copper bucket. The fire has been out for nearly an hour. Winter's breath sweeps through the cracks around the canal-side door. I draw my woolen shawl tightly around my neck. Upstairs, the children have been tucked beneath a pile of blankets. The painter and his wife have also retired to the upper floors. The house is silent except for the gentle brushing of the broom on the stones. Flickering light comes from a pair of flames dancing in the draft near the door and a large bronze lantern on the worktable. In the candlelight, the gilded box above the hearth glints like a dull beacon.

I wipe my paintbrushes clean with a rag and I feel desperate to sing. In the foreignness of the painter's studio, I do not feel at liberty to lift my voice. I have not anticipated this problem, for it has never occurred to me that I would not feel at ease to sing while I work. It is a popular *frottola* in my heart now; I feel like a muzzled hound, as if the song that has welled up inside my throat will burst out of me. My hands and my voice have always worked together as one. Singing is such an integral part of my gilding work that I doubt if I will be capable of fashioning the gold with my hands without lifting my voice at the same time. Sometimes my voice hums quietly, sometimes the words come out loudly, but I make a noise all the same.

Now I have fallen silent.

Some of my melodies are the ones we hear on feast days, those melodic chains that echo through the streets once a year and become lodged in our collective minds. Others are songs repeated over years in our parish church. Still others come out of me, sequences of notes of my own invention from someplace inside me that remains uncharted.

My father says that I sang even before I could talk, inventing melodies from the time I was able to open my mouth and make a noise. "To the joy of your mother's ears," he told me, before a shadow passed over his face and he fell silent.

Outside the painter's studio, the boughs have been laid in the stalls and the convent choirs fill with the melodies of the Christmas season. I wonder if they have seen or heard any of it back home.

"Master Trevisan has agreed that you may come home every second Sunday for the midday meal," my father had said to me as I closed the latch on my trunk and prepared to board the painter's gondola. It was no consolation. "*A presto, amore,*" my father had said when he squeezed my hand and helped me step into the rocking boat. Only fifteen days ago. It feels like a lifetime.

"Are you coming up?" Antonella straightens her plump body, one hand on the small of her back as if it aches. I judge that she is not many years older than I, but her hands are dry and cracked, and she moves as if she is already an old woman.

"I have almost finished," I say.

"Extinguish the lamps by the door before you leave the studio." She gestures toward the canal before picking up the pail of ashes and pressing the door with her other hand. "You will need the one on the table to find your way upstairs." She walks crookedly from the room.

As soon the swinging door to the kitchen comes to a halt, I feel the song well up in my breast. Quietly, I begin to hum. At first, the lyrics stay inside my head, a story about a man who tries to capture a woman's heart by luring her with a small, soft dog. The words then begin to fall quietly from my lips in the flickering light. The knots in my shoulders and neck begin to unfurl. My hands seem to move effortlessly now, returning the small pots of pigment to the shelf.

As I hum, I imagine Antonella in the servants' quarters tucked high up under the roof of the painter's tall house. She is trading her worn housedress for a nightshirt and tucking her aching body under the stack of woolen blankets spread across the narrow, straw-stuffed mattress I will share with her. The family—the painter, his wife, their young son and their infant daughter—are asleep in a large room on the *piano nobile*, a gracious floor overlooking the bricked façades on the other side of the canal.

The rest of us—the painter's journeyman, the maid, and now I, too—are lodged in rooms cramped under the eaves of the tile roof. I suppose my father discussed this arrangement with Master Trevisan, for he would not have wanted me in a room by myself on a floor filled with men, especially under the circumstances.

I share a well-stuffed mattress with Antonella in a small room with a single window overlooking three crooked chimneys. At first, something in her flashing, dark eyes made me crawl under the covers with her only with trepidation. But my unease has lessened, as Antonella has proven an agreeable bedfellow. She rarely tosses in her sleep and only snores a little.

I wait a few moments to make sure that Antonella is upstairs, then I lift my voice a little higher in song, a tune that I have known since I was a girl. It sounds loud and hollow in the giant candlelit room. The painter's studio is several times larger than my father's. A hundred pairs of eyes—those of saints, nobles, satyrs, nymphs— peer out at me from the painted panels hung on the walls and propped on the floor, a still audience for my reticent song.

It is these colored pigments that I have come to Master Trevisan's studio to learn. I am to practice how to mix them on a palette, how to apply them with various brushes to the poplar surfaces, to fashion trees and rocks in the background of the great holy figures reserved for Master Trevisan himself to paint.

But the gold has brought me here, too. That is another story.

Before the painter and his wife came to fetch me from my father's workshop, my father reminded me that we have worked together already for years. That is, the picture-maker Master Trevisan and my father, the gilder, have worked together for as long as anyone can remember. My father is a master of gold, while Trevisan the picture-maker is a master of the brightly colored pigments that magically transform into the serene faces of saints, into drapery, into fantastic landscapes. Put together with the carpenter and armature maker, all of us guildsmen make and restore some of the most beautiful altarpieces in Our Most Excellent Republic.

The timing was perfect, Master Trevisan told my father. He had just been given a commission for an altarpiece in the abbey of Santa Maria delle Vergini, the very convent where my aunt has spent most of her life. The patron asked for a large amount of pure gold leaf. Master Trevisan would need a gilder to work with him on the altarpiece for several months. The notary scrawled a brief contract, and the next day I was handed into the painter's gondola with my trunk.

In addition to my meager belongings I have brought a large stash of gold leaf, stored in a dark wooden cabinet in my corner of the painter's workshop. The nearly weightless sheaves of gold were flattened by the *battiloro*'s own hands.

My lover's hands.

In my mind, I see him hammering the gold ingots in the courtyard behind my father's house. I close my eyes and feel a tremor run through my body. It is his hands that I miss the most. I wonder what he is doing right now, if he is thinking of me as I am of him.

I bring my lantern to the hearth and raise it to get a closer look at the gilded box on the mantel. Though I have never seen one like it, it brings me comfort to see the familiar glistening gold patterning around the raised figures. I run my fingers across the figures. There is a woman in a roundel, a man with a sword, and two elephants in a procession. I try to raise the lid, but it does not budge. I press the small iron protrusion where a key must fit. It is locked.

My song comes to an end and my heart feels lighter than it did just minutes before.

From the empty hearth, a cold draft swirls around my ankles. I extinguish the flames by the door and grasp the lamp, heading to the creaking stairs. As I pass the hearth, my single flame makes the gilded box flash for a fleeting moment before disappearing into the shadows. I push the hinged door open into the kitchen then find my way through the dark to the back stairway that leads to the upper floors. I feel my way up three flights of the sagging wooden stairway to the long narrow hallway at the top of the house.

WHEN I STEP into the room, Antonella is already snoring, a soft, rhythmic wheeze emitting from her mouth. I blow out the flame in my lantern and creep across the planks so I will not wake her. In the darkness, I feel for the wooden trunk wedged under the window. My fingers lift the lid and run over the two work dresses, the two smocks I wear to protect the dresses from stains, two nightdresses, and a comb that is nearly useless in my tangled mass of curls. I brought along a pile of gold leaf books, enough for the altarpiece that we will make at Santa Maria delle Vergini. That was the agreement with my father. Apart from the small collection of my own gilding supplies now downstairs in the painter's workshop, this trunk holds everything I own.

My trunk is a failed marriage chest, a fitting container, I think. My father, and his father and grandfather before him, were applying gilded decoration to these marriage chests long before I was born. This one was abandoned in my father's studio years ago, left behind after an engagement did not proceed for a reason that was never fully explained to me. When I had asked, my father, a man of few words, had only shrugged. My father never felt that it was his best work, but as a girl I loved to run my hands over the glittering repetitive designs that decorated the sides.

For my entire life this trunk has sat in the room of our house that serves as my father's workshop as well as our dining, cooking, and gathering space. Until the day I left, it held the meager table linens made for my mother's dowry. As a child I loved to pull out the lace-trimmed cloth and careful needlework to examine them. We never used them for they were my only connection to the mother I barely remembered and could no longer visualize in my head. It seemed the most sensible thing to put my own things in the trunk, so my father and I had emptied its contents onto a shelf and repacked the chest for my transfer to the painter's house.

I run my fingers across the bottom of the trunk to feel for one of the nightdresses, an old linen shift that I have worn ever since the summer when I grew taller than my cousin. In the darkness I pull my smock and work dress over my head and push my arms through the nightdress. Then I slide into bed alongside the housemaid.

Above the sound of Antonella's breath moving in and out, I can hear my own heartbeat. I close my eyes and immediately I see his broad face, feel his hands on my hips, inhale his musky smell. It has been less than a fortnight since he pressed my forearms in his palms and said, "I will wait for you." It feels like years.

Tomorrow. Friday. It feels like it will never come.

In frantic whispers, we promised to meet every Friday night when the *marangona* bell rings. "There is a small garden behind the church of San Giovanni Elemosinario," he had whispered quickly. "The one with the tower near Rialto market. I used to live near there with my mother before I was apprenticed. Halfway between here and San Marco," he said. "The monks never use the garden. Open the back gate on the market side."

Then my father entered the room and both of us cast our eyes back to the worktable littered with tools and shreds of gold leaf.

The moment I arrived in Master Trevisan's house I looked for an excuse to leave the house on Friday evening. With some finesse, I convinced the painter's wife that a certain baker on the edge of the Rialto market made the best yeast rolls, but only on Fridays. The painter's wife raised her eyebrows and nodded. "Antonella will go with you," she said. "Much safer than walking alone. Besides, you should make a friend of Antonella. She is capable and will help you in many ways. I trust her with my own children, after all."

"Thank you, signora," I said, and I was left to consider how I would break away from the maid in order to meet Cristiano in the garden behind the church.

If only my father knew.

My father. God help him. I press my palms to my face and the back of my head to the pillow. How are the men managing without me? It is during the winter months that my father's ailment strikes with a terrible fury, when his breath comes raw and ragged, and he wakes us in the night coughing and gasping for air. I am the one who rises to boil water in the hearth, to mix the concoction of honey and thistle. I am the one who rubs his back and sings him back from the panic that fills his eyes when he struggles for breath. My cousin Paolo means well, but what can he do, with his lame leg and his weakness? How will he take my place?

My father tried to assure me that they would get on fine without me.

"Maria," he said, grasping my shoulders, "I see now that I have been selfish in keeping you here for longer than I should have. When you return to us I will have secured a proper betrothal for you."

I feel my heart sink now, just as it did when he spoke those words.

"Go," he had said. "Learn all you can about the colored pigments, my daughter, for ultimately if our trade is to have any future it is in *your* hands, not mine."

Mercifully, I begin to drift into sleep, but an image of a man with oozing black boils all over his legs suddenly appears in my mind. Fear grips me, and I sit up with a start, my heart racing in my chest. Antonella's snoring stops.

"*Stai bene, cara?*" she asks in a slurred voice.

"Yes, I am all right. I am sorry," I say. I press my head back on the straw-stuffed mattress. Antonella turns over, and the soft wheezing resumes. Inside my head, the pounding of my heartbeat is deafening. I feel perspiration form on the back of my neck even in the cool night air.

I know that every measure is being taken to combat the contagion, and that I am safe here in the painter's house. But no amount of reason can calm my fear.

I want to see them, to see for myself that they are all right. More than anything, I want to go home.

Chapter 3

Under a birch tree in the quiet garden behind San Giovanni Elemosinario, I find a few stolen moments of bliss.

"I have only a minute," I whisper into his ear as he presses my body to him. His strong hands are laced behind the small of my back. I turn my head toward the gate. "The painter's servant woman. I left her at the fruit seller's table. I invented an excuse but she will be looking for me soon enough." My lips sting from his ardent kiss, a kiss that has brought me back to life from the brink of despair.

"All that matters is that you are here," Cristiano says, and I press my flushed face into his chest, inhaling his scent as if to imbibe him to the core of my soul, as if the very smell of him might sustain me for seven days. I fill my nose with musk, leather, and dust from my father's workshop.

"My father..." I say, raising my eyes to meet his. "And Paolo?"

"They are well," Cristiano says.

I search his face to see if he is telling the truth. "You are not just trying to console me?"

He pauses, then sets his eyes on me. "Your father... He had one of those breathing fits," he says.

I feel my throat clench.

"I made a tea of honey and garlic," he says. "He recovered quickly."

"How did you know to do that?"

"You think I have not been watching your every move for months now?" He laughs.

I feel my face flush. I do not admit that I have also been studying him more closely than I have ever studied anything in my life.

"Anyway, it worked. Maria, they are fine," he says again. "I swear it." His teeth flash, and I feel myself exhale for the first time in days.

"I brought something for you," he says. I feel him pull away and reach into the pocket of the leather apron he always wears. He pulls out a small hammered gold ingot strung onto a black velvet cord, and presses it into my palm. "I made it," he says.

I turn the golden rock over in my hand, watching it glow in the evening light. "Beautiful," I say. He takes it from me and runs his hands along either side of my neck. I watch his jet-black eyes flicker before he presses his lips behind my ear and fixes the clasp.

"I will never take it off." I press the golden ingot down into my dress where no one will see it, then kiss him again, a long, lingering, tender exchange that I wish would never end. "I want to stay here with you forever," I say, running my palm along his forearm. "My only consolation is that I will see you in two days' time. We will have to pretend as usual around my father's table, but it will do for now."

Cristiano pulls me to a crumbling stone bench under the tree. He kneels to the ground and takes my hands in his. A shadow passes his face. "Maria. I did not know how to tell you. It was nearly impossible for me to get here, and I do not know if I will be able to come again," he says.

My heart drops like a stone, to the depths of the canal beside us. "What?"

"The contagion… It is spreading. I don't want you to worry, but they are taking precautions. I will try my best to come again next Friday but we have seen the *signori di notte* patrolling the square." He fixes me with a soft smile. Comforting, apologetic. I feel his fingers at the nape of my neck. "People are saying that they will close the streets."

"*Ragazza*! Where have you gone?"

Antonella. Her raspy voice echoes from the other side of the monastery wall. She is looking for me.

A hundred questions race through my head, but my breath feels caught in my chest and I cannot seem to say anything at all.

Chapter 4

The shrill clang of bells in the tower of San Giovanni Battista in Bragora gives me a start. Sunday. Midday.

I should be clearing dishes from my father's table, rinsing pots in the canal behind our house while the men speak of gold and the storm clouds over Murano. Instead, I am practicing trees with a small horsehair brush in the painter's studio, trying not to think of my father, my cousin, and my Cristiano huddled around the table without me on the Lord's Day.

The news of the street closings has spread beyond Cannaregio. Better that I not see the barricades myself, the painter's wife has said, and perhaps she is right.

The painter says nothing, and instead expresses his sympathy by painting by my side. For several hours, we work in companionable silence. While he works, I steal a closer look at Trevisan. His long, elegant hands might be those of a nobleman except for the small smudges of color staining the nails. He is toward the end of his fourth decade, I think, nearly twice my age. He is a handsome man, with thick chestnut hair swept away from his brow, and a neatly cropped beard as is the fashion. His lashes and eyebrows are lush, and his curved lips might be those of a woman. His body is lean yet solid, cloaked under a dingy canvas smock.

The painter is focused on his work to the point where he seems to inhabit a different world. His breeches are streaked with pigment but he does not seem to notice. He is a quiet man of few words, a more contemplative soul to complement his wife's nervous temperament. She is loud and unable to keep her opinions to herself, he hardly inclined to let us know what he is thinking at all.

Before him on the table lies a small panel of Our Lady. For days I have watched him layer the shadowed contours of her serene face, the deep blue drapery folds of her cloak, the downward cast of her eyes. He sits for hours, for days with endless patience, working on small details as if an act of quiet devotion. I wonder if I will ever be able to accomplish such a feat. I dare not disturb him.

But then, he looks up at me as if he can feel my eyes on him. I blush and turn my face to the window, but I feel I must say something to account for my looking.

"Master Trevisan," I say, "that box on your mantelpiece. I have never seen one like it."

He suspends his brush in the air and raises his eyebrows, then glances at the gilded box on the hearth. "It came here to me along with my wife," he says, and I see the corner of his mouth rise. "You may know that the signora is, like you, the daughter of a gilder."

"I did not know," I say.

"Master Gardesano."

"Gardesano. I have heard my father speak of him," I say.

"Signora Trevisan had five older brothers, and so, unlike you, she did not receive the benefit of her father's attention or training in the gilding arts."

I nod, and for a moment I hesitate to say what is in my heart, but I have never been good at keeping such things to myself. "I may have received the benefit of my father's tutelage, but perhaps it was all for nothing," I say.

"Why do you say that?" The painter's eyebrows rise again.

"Because my father says that no one wants the gold anymore."

FOR AS LONG as I can remember, our craft has been dying. "Soon enough the gold will disappear," my father told me when I was still too small for my feet to reach the floor at our worktable. My father set his brown eyes on me through the leather-framed spectacles that helped him see the details of our punchwork. "The trade of the *indoradòr* is nearly finished," he told me. "Our patrons... They want the work of Master Titian, the Bellini brothers, Master Giorgione. They are no longer asking for our old colleagues."

He gestured toward the window and my eyes followed. Our guildsmen talked of these painters as if they held some magic in their hands; I came to imagine them instead as our enemies. I expected that one day I would see Master Giorgione or the Bellini brothers standing outside in the alley, looking at us through the window with menacing eyes.

Still, my world has been gilded since the day I was born, and my father continued to teach me everything he knew. He let me select the punches to use, and praised me when I pressed neat, orderly patterns in the wood.

"What comes next, Maria?" my father would ask, and I basked in his silent approval—the tight-lipped nod, the sparkle in his eyes—when I answered correctly.

My cousin followed close behind, pressing the gold sheets into the grooves I had made. "It is too late for me," my father would say to us. "If our workshop is to continue, then when you grow up you must learn the transparent colors of the paint." I never knew if he meant Paolo or me, but I accepted what he said as fact, just as all children believe what their parents tell them. And even though I did not see any other women among our guildsmen, I never doubted that one day my father's workshop would be mine. Did my father plant this idea in my head when I was small? If he said the words I do not remember, but I never doubted that it was true.

Along one wall of our studio was a collection of metal punches, passed down from my grandfather and his grandfather before him.

As far back as anyone could count, my father told us, our family's role was applying gold leaf to the great wooden panels that, by our own hands, were transformed into sacred images. The churches of Our Most Serene Republic were covered in gilded surfaces, and our family collaborated with some of the best painters in our city, my father said.

For generations we carried out our trade in relative prosperity. Then, my father said, a few of our Republic's painters traveled to the northern kingdoms and returned home with new ideas. First the Bellini brothers turned away from the gold, he said, then Giorgione, and then other painters from outside of our Republic came to work here. After they had seen the work of those men, my father said, our noble people and our church patrons no longer wanted the gold pictures, which suddenly seemed old-fashioned.

By the time I was born, my parents had already seen our coffers dwindle, each year fewer and fewer coins in the box. Instead of buying new things, they mended or repaired the old. Instead of patronizing the Rialto market, my mother grew beans and onions in the small plot of earth along the canal-side behind our house.

When my mother died, my father told me, the neighbors said that he should send me to a convent or to another family who would be in a better position to care for a small girl from a family of meager means. Instead, my father did something unconventional: he kept me at home and taught me his trade. He also pulled his sister's young son out of the convent of Santa Maria delle Vergini. Together, the three of us cobbled together a living, a life.

The truth is that he needed us. My father was never well, and many days he took to his bed, lying on the worn mattress that I had mended so many times. At night I would hear the barking coughs begin, then he would gasp for air. Underneath my blankets I would freeze, terrified that in one of those long silences between the ragged gasps, he would stop breathing altogether. From the same neighbor woman who had taught me to sew, I learned to concoct a salve of honey and herbs that would still my father's coughing.

My cousin, weak of body and spirit, came to us hobbling. Even though he worked well with the gold, he was not able to help with much else, so I did the washing, the cooking, and tended the garden. We carried on like that for years.

And then one day the *battiloro* came to us. Cristiano. After that, nothing was the same.

"YOUR FATHER IS correct. Things are not as they once were for your guildsmen of our grandparents' generation." Master Trevisan's voice brings me back to the painter's studio. "But the gold lives on in other ways besides our great panels." The painter puts down his brush and walks to the hearth, then places his palms on either side of the box. "My mother's brother, for example, is a master of *pastiglia* boxes," he says. The painter removes the box from the mantel and places it on the worktable. I lean in for a closer look. It is of a size where you might hide a large cat or a small dog, I think.

"He sent us this one upon my marriage to Donata. My uncle and cousin make them in their shop in Padua. They once made their living gilding panels, but one day they began making these boxes using molds that they could reuse to make different compositions in relief across the surface." I dare to run my fingertips across the gilded punchwork, then across the surface of the molded figures made in white paste that resembles ivory. "These boxes... They caught the eye of the ladies at the courts of Ferrara and Mantua. My cousin has done well. Now they no longer make panels at all."

Trevisan walks over to a large wooden desk and produces a key from the drawer. He fits it into the metal hole in the box, and it opens seamlessly.

Inside, the box is lined with padded purple satin. I imagine that it might be designed to hold a precious trove of jewelry, or a collection of medals or gems.

Instead, it contains more gold leaf than I have ever seen in my life.

I gasp, gauging the value of the pile of paper books. It is enough to gild a dozen altarpieces.

Trevisan smiles, gratified by my reaction. "Much as your father offered you to my workshop along with gold leaf, Donata's father offered her to me in marriage with the same. We have only had to reach into this stash a few times for our projects."

"The signora's dowry," I whisper.

The painter smiles and nods, then closes the lid. There is no more to say. He locks the box, returns it to the mantel, and slides the key back in the drawer.

Then the painter returns to his silent work, and I to mine.

THREE FRIDAY EVENINGS. Then four. Then five.

Antonella and I huddle close together, pressing our way through the crowd that funnels into the bustle of the Rialto market. The *marangona* bell in San Marco tolls its brassy sound, calling the *arsenolloti*, those men who toil as day laborers in the state shipyard, home from their work. Wives with bags over their shoulders and under their arms make their final purchases from the sellers of salted fish, cured vegetables, and other meager selections of the winter market.

"I hope there is something left for us at the bakery," Antonella says, pressing her elbow forward to make a path for us between two plump women heading in the opposite direction.

"Hmm," I answer, for bread is the last thing on my mind. I finger the golden ingot that falls between my breasts, hidden under my layers of linen and wool. From a distance, the tower of San

Giovanni Elemosinario comes into view. I feel my heart race along with a deep trepidation.

The narrow alley opens into the expanse of the Rialto market. The fishmonger, a scrawny man with rope-like veins protruding from his arms, sweeps the stones around his wooden table with a broom made of twigs. The vegetable seller covers his nearly empty table with a canvas cover. Against the wall of the church, several hat makers have assembled rickety sales counters of discarded wood. A woman specializing in garlands for ladies' hair has begun to make small pomanders that noble ladies might wear around their necks or wrists, containing dried herbs. I stop to finger a satin ribbon attached to a pouch of herbs festooned with smaller ribbons and leaves.

"For the pestilence, signorina," the garland-seller says, laying several of the pomanders out for me to examine.

"I am going to see if there are any yeast rolls left for us," Antonella says, shuffling off toward the bakery.

"I will meet you there," I say. As soon as Antonella turns her back I leave the garland-seller and her pomanders behind, and hurry to the garden gate alongside the monastery church.

Silence.

The garden lies still, empty, and my heart drops. I pace the winding stone path that leads to the dusty church door, but it appears that no one has opened the door in years. Layers of dust fill its crevices. I wander past the crumbling stone bench where Cristiano knelt before me just weeks ago.

The sun has disappeared from the sky, and the monastery garden falls into shadow. I cover my head with the hood from my cloak, close the latch of the garden gate behind me, and set off for the bakery to find Antonella, who is no doubt waiting to fill my ears with chatter of the baker's latest gossip. Another Friday, and I will return to the painter's house with a basket of bread and an empty heart.

MASTER TREVISAN HAS tasked me with painting trees on a scrap page of parchment. A good way for me to learn how to handle the various shades of verdigris and malachite, he has told me.

I dab the tip of my fox-hair brush in a pot of dark green pigment left over from a painting of Saint John the Baptist that the painter has completed. Tentatively, I press the dark green glob on the page. It feels strange and unpracticed. I doubt that I will ever be able to do it like Trevisan's journeyman, like Trevisan himself, much less like any of the men who have made the beautiful pictures hanging on the wall.

Carmine. Zaffera. Orpiment. Indigo. Realgar. Azzurrite. Vermilione. The names of the powdered pigments roll through my head. I grasp them like one might grasp a foreign tongue—inferred and partially interpreted, but not truly understood. Each color handles differently on the brush, catches light from different angles, looks different each time it is laid on a page or a panel alongside another color.

Of course I know these colors by sight and from the names scrawled on the jars at the pigment seller's shop, but I have never used them myself. I pick up another brush from the box, admiring the veins in the wooden handle, and feeling the soft hairs of an animal, perhaps a weasel, that have been made into the head of the brush. I swirl the fibers around in my palm and then replace it.

The painter does not seem to notice me poking around his shelves. He has so many beautiful things; his studio is a tactile feast. I look at the jars of pigments, each labeled with a swirl of neat script describing what is inside. Umber, white gypsum, lapis, all in small cakes to be ground to a fine powder. Stacks of used palettes are gathered neatly at the edge of the table. I pick one up and admire the dark smudges of green and midnight blue, the result of many pictures. The layers of paint are caked onto the board, creating a bumpy texture under my fingertips.

My father says he recognized my drawing talent early on in life. He used to give me pieces of coal and I would trace lines on paper or parchment, or draw with the edge of a pointed stick in the sand of the *campo* near our house. But now, seeing Master Trevisan's beautiful and delicate sketches, the result of a lifetime of talent and practice, I feel I will never get it.

The door to the studio opens, and I see the face of the painter's wife. She holds her little boy's hand, and in her other arm she holds the baby.

The painter's eyes light up. "Gianluca! Off to your lessons?" The image of his family has broken his trance. The boy runs to his father, wrapping his arms around his knees.

"I don't want to go, *papà*," he pleads with desperate blue eyes.

The painter grasps his son's head between his paint-stained palms. "Oh, but you are learning to be a smart boy so that one day you can take over my workshop, just as I took over from your grandpa. You know that already. You must learn numbers and Latin before you learn the paints."

The baby girl makes a gurgling noise, and the painter's wife shifts her in her arms. I have stopped what I am doing to watch the beautiful boy with his perfect blue eyes and flushed cheeks. The boy presses his face into his father's breeches again and the painter picks up his son, smudging a bit of brown from his thumb onto the boy's white tunic. Trevisan walks his son around the studio, talking to him softly about what is on each table. "And then one day you will do this all by yourself." The painter hands the boy a paintbrush, and he grasps it in his fist, waving it in the air proudly as his father laughs.

The painter's wife laughs, too, meeting my gaze from across the studio. I feel embarrassed for being caught staring at her husband and child. Quickly I turn my attention back to my incompetent series of trees on the page.

In the shadows, I see the boatman and Antonella push open the door. Antonella strides into the studio, but the boatman seems loath to enter, as if the threshold of the door constitutes an invisible barrier. The boatman is dark and haggard, wearing a once-elegant ensemble that fits him poorly, as if it has been handed down to him from a more fortunate boatman long ago. A V-shaped scar mars the fleshy part of the boatman's cheek, just below his right eye. The scar is dark and deeply creased, a distinguishing mark of his face even from far across the room.

The boy shoots the boatman a distrustful glance, then presses his face into the rough fabric of his father's smock. The painter tousles his son's golden curls.

"Come, *figliolo*. Your father needs to work on his picture now, and your tutor is waiting for you. Boatman will take you and your mother there in the beautiful new gondola." Trevisan sets the boy back on the ground.

"*Vieni, amore*," the painter's wife says. "Your tutor is waiting for you." She reaches out her hand but the boy grasps his father's leg again.

Finally, Trevisan relents and takes the boy's hand himself. "Come, Gianluca. Let me show you the bronze horse on the gondola," he says. Trevisan walks into the kitchen, and his wife and the boatman follow.

"That man is so proud of his new gondola." Antonella shakes her head, then reaches into the pocket of her apron and produces a sealed parchment envelope. "I almost forgot," she tells me. "Earlier this morning a messenger delivered a letter for you."

My dear Maria,

Your father has asked me to write to you again. I do not know if our last letter has reached you or if this one will. We have not been able to leave the quarter and no one is willing to come here. You may know that the pestilence has spread across several streets in Cannaregio. They have erected barriers and so we cannot leave, at least not for now.

But I do not want to frighten you.

In truth, all is as well as can be expected under the circumstances. We have had new commissions from the Menegi and the Polani. You will be glad to know that our commission for Signor Rizo's series of panels is finally complete. Signora Rambaldo's baby was born this week, a little boy. Apart from that we are well but restricted in our movements outside the studio. Maria, I know you found your father's judgment harsh, but between you and me, it has been strange without you here in the workshop. It is also silent without your singing.

Bene. *Your father will never say it out loud, but without you, he feels a great void. We send you our regards and hope that you are learning new things in the painter's workshop that will help us when you return.*

Your cousin Paolo
Indoradòr in Cannaregio
On the feast of the Baptism of Our Lord

Chapter 5

Antonella has brought a small basket of quail eggs from the hennery behind the house. Their brown speckled shells are still warm from where they lay underneath the tiny birds. They seem an extravagance, for I am accustomed to the stale crunch of yesterday's bread. My cousin and I used to spoon honey out of an earthenware bowl in the middle of the table and drizzle it over the brown crust to soften it. But in the painter's house, breakfast is as much a production as the midday meal.

Antonella busies herself with a pot of boiling water hanging from an iron chain over the fire. She has peeled an onion on the wooden block in the center of the kitchen and chopped it into small chunks with a sharp blade. She carries the wooden chopping board and scrapes the translucent chunks into the pot.

The painter's wife leans forward in her chair across from me, nursing the baby, a white rag thrown over her shoulder to cover her breast. The painter's wife is beautiful, or perhaps was not so long ago, before the demands of a house and children fixed fine lines across her brow and drew her mouth tight. Her features are delicate and fragile-looking, her wrists and ankles narrow, her skin fair and clear. "Santa Fusilla, it is so cold." She seems to feel my gaze. "You must be sure to cover yourself properly."

"And it will feel even colder out there in the gondola," adds Antonella, gesturing toward the canal-side window with her knife before returning to chopping a fistful of shriveled carrots at the worktable.

I follow Antonella's gaze toward the window and feel a wave of excitement. The painter has said that we will go to the church today to see the site where our altarpiece will be installed. I am eager to get started on the commission in the church of Santa Maria delle Vergini. Up until now, I have had little reason to use the gold leaf I brought with me from my father's studio and I feel restless to work the gold again.

"Please forgive me," the painter told me the Sunday before. "I have made you toil too much during Christmas and Epiphany, even on Sundays." He walked over to where I was sitting and plucked the rag from my hand with his elegant, paint-stained fingers. "You have worked enough for the week, signorina. I fear I have set a poor example, working alongside you and even encouraging you on the Lord's Day."

"It is a privilege to be working and learning here with you, Master Trevisan," I said. "I do not wish to be anywhere else."

I saw the corner of his mouth turn up under his beard. "It is kind of you to say, but my wife is correct. I should be more careful not take advantage of your being here. Please. I insist that you take some time for your own needs, for rest."

I paused, wondering what I would do. I only looked down and shrugged. "I can hardly visit my family."

He scraped a stool across the floor, then sat before me with his fingers drumming on his knees. "No," he said. "The pestilence has seen to that, has it not?" He paused and scratched his head. "Do you have other family in the city?" he asked, setting his clear eyes on me.

I hesitated for a few moments, thinking about the many family members we have lost over my lifetime. My mother's extended family is gone, as is my father's. I never had any cousins other than Paolo.

"Only my father's sister cloistered at the convent of Santa Maria delle Vergini," I say. "It has been a long time since I have seen her."

The painter stood and wiped his hands on a soiled rag. "Consider it done. When we go to the Vergini you must remain and visit your aunt. I will instruct my boatman to bring my journeyman and myself back here to the studio, then he will return to wait for you at Santa Maria delle Vergini in my gondola. You must feel free to spend as much time as you like."

"Is that your warmest cloak, *cara*?" I look up from my small plate of quail eggs to see the painter's wife looking skeptically from across the table at my threadbare woolen shawl. Self-consciously, I pull it across my shoulders. The painter's wife shifts the baby to the other breast, expertly adjusting the top of her dress so that one breast is covered and the other is exposed. I watch the baby girl's bare head settle gently against her mother's body.

"My *tabarro* is in our room upstairs," I say, starting for the back staircase to retrieve my felted woolen cloak hanging from a wooden peg in our bedchamber.

"Wait," the painter's wife gestures to me with her free hand. "Antonella, would you please fetch it for her?"

Antonella hesitates, then sets down her knife. "Of course, signora," she says, heading tentatively for the stairs. Antonella is beautiful, too, I think, but in a different way than the painter's wife. She is her opposite, in fact: strapping, sturdy, and olive-skinned, with thick, dark hair twisted into braids, black flashing eyes and strong forearms like those of the Sicilian women who come to work in the city. She looks as if she could pull an oxcart or throw a punch.

The painter's wife cranes her neck to make sure that Antonella is out of range, then lowers her voice to a whisper. "Before you leave," she says to me, "I want you to know that you must be wary of our boatman."

She pauses, and I meet her eyes but struggle for a response. So far, I have only seen the boatman in passing. He appears each morning to fetch the painter's young son and ferry the boy to his tutor while we are working in the painter's studio. Otherwise the boatman stays inside the *cavàna*, the great private boat slip under the house, or whittles wood on the landing at the canal-side door. I have little reason to talk with him.

"What do you mean?" I say finally, when the painter's wife does not immediately continue.

She considers her words before speaking, which I feel is unusual for her. "He has just come back to us after..." She shakes her head. "It is a complicated story. It was not my choice to have him come back here, but my husband insisted on renewing his agreement even though I advised against it." She pauses again, reaching for words. "We have had some troubles with him in the past. Let us leave it at that. I implore you to keep your distance. You do not want to get yourself involved with him."

I nod as the painter pushes the hinged door from the workshop into the kitchen. He has traded his painter's apron for a handsome woolen cape, his cap for a brimmed, felted hat with a feather. He nods at his wife and then raises his eyebrows at me. "Ready?"

"I was just advising Maria to steer clear of your boatman," the painter's wife says in a loud whisper.

The painter's face darkens. "You are not spreading rumors about him to poor Maria, are you?" It is the only time I have heard the painter speak sharply to his wife or to anyone.

His wife looks down at the infant at her breast. "I thought she needed to be forewarned," she says.

The painter sighs and rubs his beard. "Donata. The poor girl has only just arrived. I have told you that I will deal with the boatman myself, *tesoro*. Do not speak with him if it makes you feel any better. In any case, I feel certain that he will find himself more loyal this time around."

She meets her husband's gaze, her eyes wide and her face still. "And why would he, Benvoglio?"

The painter shrugs. "It is as I have already told you. I have renewed the contract, but this time I have taken some precautions with his salary."

I feel immersed in something private, something that has nothing to do with me, something I do not think I want to know about between the painter and his wife. I busy myself by inspecting a spider bundling something imperceptible into a fuzzy ball on the windowsill.

The painter turns toward me and extends his open palm. "You see, our boatman…" The painter lowers his voice. "He is the third one I have had in as many years," he says. "You may know, reliable boatmen are difficult to find and difficult to keep. It can be challenging to locate servants who are both competent as well as trustworthy."

I nod but do not say anything. I have no knowledge of such matters.

Antonella's footsteps clap on the back staircase. The painter falls silent, but his wife quickly whispers, "It is best to ignore the boatman altogether. You have been warned." Her husband shoots his wife a glance filled with words unspoken.

The painter's journeyman jogs down the stairs into the kitchen, fluffing his unruly hair. "I hope I have not kept you waiting, Master Trevisan." The journeyman is nearly a man but still a boy inside and out, I think, with his wide eyes and light stubble across his chin. He presses a worn woolen hat—the kind the old men who play *bracciale* in the square wear—over large ears that protrude like jug handles. He blinks hard and I stifle a smile.

Antonella appears behind him with my felted cloak folded over her arm. I feel its familiar heft and warmth as I pull it across my shoulders. It was a gift from my father, paid for with months of commissions. Feeling its familiar softness under my palm, I feel more secure than I did the moment before.

An ancient stone staircase leads from the kitchen down into the watery boat slip under the painter's house. Light filters into the dank *cavàna* through a pointed arch covered by an iron grille that leads out into the canal. The space is cavernous, and our footsteps echo off the stones as I press my palm into the damp wall. My breath puffs into small clouds of vapor before my eyes as I descend the stairs.

On the platform alongside the gondola I see the boatman seated on a wobbly wooden stool. He is chewing on something—a piece of straw?—and eyeing me carefully as I make my way down the stairs.

"*Signori.*"

He stands. Dark locks fall over the boatman's brow as he turns his lined face toward me. I do my best not to stare at his ragged scar, its outline deeply grooved into the flesh below his eye. The boatman places one foot on the rear deck of the gondola to steady it. The painter and the journeyman step into the craft, which bucks against the wooden bumpers that prevent its surface from scratching the stone boat ramp. The boatman extends his broad hand to help me into the boat. I take the boatman's hand, and watch the corners of his mouth turn up, but it is not exactly a smile. I meet his beady eyes then look away, the words of the painter's wife ringing in my ears.

THE PAINTER, HIS journeyman, and I settle in the dark opulence of the passenger compartment. In the dimness, I make out heavy drapes and the whites of the painter's eyes. I feel the boatman push off and make the sharp turn into the canal. As we emerge from the boathouse, the diffuse winter light casts dancing, watery patterns onto the heavy drapes of midnight blue.

The boat displays all the trappings of a private *gondola di casada*. The inside of the passenger compartment has been outfitted for the cold months with velvet drapes and benches upholstered in damask and brocade. Several woolen blankets are stacked in the corner for passengers to help ward off the chill. The oarlocks and the prow have been recently coated with oil and shined to a high gloss and the boat's black surface gleams.

"The boat is lovely," I say.

The painter's eyes light up. "I am pleased that you approve. The Vianello family boatyard made it for me. It is in Cannaregio. Do you know of it?"

"Only by reputation," I say. "My father and I have done some wood gilding for gondolas made in the Rosmarin boatyard."

"The Squero Vianello is one of Our Most Serene Republic's most esteemed makers of passenger craft," the painter continues. "Everything has been made to my specifications. The brocade on the upholstery is made by one of their people. He is mute but a master at what he does."

My palm slides over the soft texture of the swirls. I have little need to ride in a gondola, and have never been inside one as elegant as this. My eye is drawn to the intricately carved walnut panels on the inside of the passenger compartment. I imagine the many layers of varnish used to coat the keel to make it waterproof. I know from working with wood how difficult it is to keep it from wearing and rotting in our humid climate.

The painter has traded his usual paint-smudged smock for a fine ensemble of woolen breeches and breast coat. He runs his fingertips along the edge of the gondola's cap rail, then raises his finger to display a layer of grey dust. Across from the painter, the journeyman makes a disgusted face. The painter pushes himself up from the cushion.

"Boatman," he calls through the parted curtain. He displays his dusty fingertips to the boatman. "This is not what I have paid for. It is your job to keep this boat clean. It has hardly come out of the boatyard."

Standing on the rowing deck at the aft of the boat, the stocky boatman possesses none of the elegance of the fine vessel. Through an opening in the curtains, I watch him press the oar into the oar-lock and steer us out of the narrow passage and into a broader canal. He is dressed in a woolen jacket and breeches, once fine but now worn, as if cast off from the painter or a highborn man.

"The city is dirty, Master Trevisan," the boatman shrugs. "Especially at this time of year." He shrugs again. "Rains. Fog. *Carnevale*."

"I expect a higher standard."

"*Certo*, Master Trevisan," the boatman says, and I watch his lips press tightly together as the painter retakes his seat.

The painter pushes himself back into the cushions and address-es me. "You already know Santa Maria delle Vergini?"

"I used to go with my father and my cousin to see my father's sister in the convent visiting room, but it has been a long time since I have last seen her."

The painter opens the leather sketchbook on his lap and thumbs through his drawings. "The sisters have an old altarpiece above the shrine of their patron saint. It is at least a hundred years old now, I suspect made by the Crivelli workshop. Your own great-grandfather may have had a hand in it," the painter gestures toward me. "I have made a few sketches of it in preparation for our project." The painter turns his sketchbook around to show me a delicate sketch made with silverpoint and brown ink, with highlights of white chalk. I recognize the arched form of a great central panel, a Crucifixion, with other panels and figures clustered across the bottom, sketched in a cursory yet expert manner. "The da Molin family is paying for the altarpiece," the painter says. "It is their donation to the convent… along with their young daughter."

"Da Molin. Deep pockets," the journeyman says. "But the convent already receives a lot of support because they take in the *abbandonati*."

"Orphans," I say. "Yes, my aunt has spoken of them. She cooks sweets in the convent kitchen. I think she must be popular among them."

"Of that I am certain." The painter smiles, and his beard spreads from ear to ear. "As I explained to your father, da Molin's donation means a major commission for us. The nuns want to make another altarpiece that matches it for the other side of the church. It will not look exactly the same as the old altarpiece, of course, but they want to make it a pendant for the other, which is why there is so much gold specified in the contract," says the painter.

"A very large altarpiece," says the journeyman.

"Seven panels' worth," the painter says.

"My father says that the gold is dying," I say, taking up the thread of our conversation in the painter's studio. "I have heard it all my life. Our patrons no longer want the gilded altarpieces like they did in the past. They want something new, something different. They want bright colors, saturated pigments. They only want the edges or frames gilded now, and small objects that unfortunately do not provide us as much income. My father says that I need to learn the pigments, for the gold is starting to disappear."

The painter shrugs. "We still use gold often, but it is true that it is less used than it was in the past. We follow the fashions. It is not as it was in my father's day. I think it is the right way to move our trade forward. But I am sorry for your father and the other gilders."

"How is your father?" asks the painter's journeyman, tapping his finger on his narrow chin.

Silence descends on us. "I… Only one letter has reached me," I say, fidgeting with the trim of my sleeve.

I turn my gaze to the horizon, where the sails of a dozen merchant galleys anchored in the lagoon have come into view. The brave captains, I am told, travel across the world, bringing silks, spices, and other treasures back to Our Most Excellent Republic.

In the silence, the painter comes to my aid. "Because of the pestilence that has come to Cannaregio, Maria cannot visit them. And her father is one of the best gilders in the city. I am sure he is very busy with his commissions."

"Of course," the journeyman says, leaning over and pressing his hands to his face. "I am an idiot," he says. "Forgive me. Surely it will pass. Who is helping your father while you are away?"

"My cousin Paolo." I hesitate. "And some months ago we brought a *battiloro* into the studio." I feel a flush of heat streak across my face. If it has turned as red as it feels, the two men do not seem to notice.

"Sensible," the painter says. "Actually a brilliant idea. But I would expect nothing less from your father." He smiles.

"Tell me about this *battiloro*," says the journeyman, leaning forward with his elbows on his skinny knees. I feel my heart skip. "I have never heard of a gold-beater housed inside a gilder's workshop," he says. "Is that a normal practice?"

"The *battiloro*..." Though he is in my mind from dawn until dusk, I struggle to know where to begin. Although they form a separate guild from our alliance of painters and gilders and also govern their own workshops, goldbeaters are critical to our work. They hammer the soft ingots into sheets, thinner than leaves, that we use in our pictures. Never before have we had a *battiloro* inside our studio. Under the circumstances, I imagine that my father will never have one again.

"It is not the usual practice, no," I say. "It was his own master's dying wish that he work alongside us. And so my father brought Cristiano into the workshop even though we might not have had the means to do so otherwise."

"I have heard of him," the painter says. "A black man known for his goldbeating skills."

The journeyman raises his eyebrows. "A Saracen?"

"Well," I hesitate again. "Cristiano's people came from across the sea but he was born here in our city."

"He is unbaptized?" asks the journeyman.

I realize only now that I do not know the answer to this question.

"He is as much Venetian as you or I and very good at his trade. He is strong."

"As Moors often are," says the painter, waving his hand dismissively. "His skill is widely known in our Guild of Saint Luke."

"It is?" I am astonished.

"Yes," he says. "Our own *gastaldo* has praised your goldbeater in our guild meetings. Before the pestilence began to spread we freely got gold leaf from Master Zuan, the goldbeater where your *battiloro* was once apprenticed."

"I have heard," says the journeyman, tapping his chin again, "that Moors can survive the pestilence when no one else can."

I feel my heart stop.

"It is true," he continues. "They are stronger than we are. Widely known but not admitted, to be sure." He chuckles to himself as if satisfied with this observation.

I nod, but I know of no such thing, and suddenly I feel seasick. I open the louvered wooden slats along the side of the compartment and feel the briny air of the canal brush across my cheeks.

"Are you all right, Signorina Maria?" the journeyman asks me. He sets his innocent wide eyes on me.

The painter stops mid-sentence and looks at me. "You have just turned a light shade of green," he says.

I feel red instead. "I am sorry," I say. "Really, I am fine. I just need some air," I say. I take a deep breath of the cold, fishy air and fan my face with a piece of parchment from the leather binder I have brought with me.

"The poor girl," the journeyman says, clicking his tongue. "I am sorry. It is understandable for you to be worried about your family."

"*Bene*," the painter says. "The pestilence shall pass; it always does. I trust that they will all remain unscathed."

From the corner of my eye I see the painter's journeyman cross himself, then all of us fall silent.

Chapter 6

The Convent of Santa Maria delle Vergini is a grand accumulation of buildings masked behind walls. A series of narrow alleys skirt around the edges of the hulking brick and plaster surfaces that define the perimeter of the convent and give this neighborhood its name. Only the large dome of the convent church is visible above the high enclosure. My aunt, my father's sister, was cloistered behind these walls long before I was born. Now, she and her fellow Augustinian canonesses take in orphans. They feed and clothe the children, teach them to read and write, and eventually push them back outside the walls to become servants to the patricians, clergy, shopkeepers, and apprentices in the Arsenale state shipyard that stands behind the abbey.

The journeyman and I follow the painter down a raucous street to the east of the church façade that faces the Arsenale. Though Carnival is still weeks away, the streets are beginning to fill with color. People on the upper floors above the street-level shops have begun to hang colored paper banners, festooned with beads and feathers, from their windows. For a few moments I am distracted by a lady shopkeeper who is talking lovingly to a parakeet perched inside an ornate cage. The cage is just one of two dozen similar contraptions, each with different colored birds inside.

Trevisan pulls a chain outside a modest wooden door in the wall and the three of us—the painter, the journeyman, and I—collect around the door to wait for a response. Behind us, the boatman lashes a rope to a wooden post at the convent's canal-side mooring.

My gaze lands on an image of the Madonna and Child carved into white marble and inset into the convent's brick wall. Below the image is an opening large enough to place a foundling, and below that a narrow slot in the marble where a desperate mother or a charitable passerby may drop donations for the care and feeding of those abandoned there. The white marble has worn down and turned nearly black from the many hands that have rubbed against it over the years, depositing money to support poor babes who have been surrendered to the care of the nuns. I run my fingers over the worn inscription carved under the window and think of a thousand reasons why a woman might want to leave her baby here.

The door opens and a stooped nun pulls us into the dimness of the compound. They are expecting us. We follow her limping, draped form down an echoing corridor punctuated by dozens of closed doors. The door latches behind us, and the clamor of the street falls away. I have seen the façade of the church from the canal a thousand times in my life, but have only been inside the convent visitors' parlor to see my aunt. I have never seen the inside of the church.

The nun opens one of the doors and gestures for us to follow. I step through, and suddenly I am cast from the dark corridor into a vast, airy space filled with heavenly light from windows at the base of the dome. Inside the church the world has fallen silent. In the presence of this magical, echoing space, the malaise I felt in the gondola has melted away and I feel calm wash over me. The boatman's gaze, the bustle of the streets outside, with the calls of the fruit sellers and fish vendors, the barge captains, and clogs clomping on the stones... Everything outside the walls has fallen away.

"Here we are," says the painter, his voice echoing into the cavernous space.

I follow the nun, Master Trevisan, and his journeyman down a dim side aisle. We hear only the shuffle of our own leather soles on the stone floor and the flutter of wings from a bird exploring the vaults high above us. I follow the picture maker past the side chapels whose walls are darkened with age and soot from thousands of candles and hundreds of years. I see large panels covered in gold and darkened paint. In the dimness, their glittering surfaces call to me.

Our pictures have always been made in this way.

Enormous panels of raw alder and poplar pieced together with oak battens and armatures. Wooden surfaces prepared with many layers of gesso made from the hides of beasts raised on terra firma. Surfaces built up with *pastiglia* to render buttons, rivets, gems and jewelry, horse tack. Layers of gold leaf beaten into thin wafers by our own *battiloro* and generations before him. Designs punched into the surface with the punches that have hung above my father's workbench for many generations. Colored tempera pigments for the faces, hands, drapery, and details.

My earliest memories in my father's studio are of being surrounded by the serene faces of super-humans, saints who performed miracles and selfless deeds. With a single brush of their hand they healed disease. Calmed a storm. Parted the seas. Brought the dead back to life from the grave itself. Every time I left the dullness of our house I was surrounded by gold. Even our modest parish church is paved with mosaic that sparkles with gilded flecks used in their making. My father says that his own grandfather and great-grandfather made the flecks of gilding that went into the pavements.

And altarpieces. We have made so many altarpieces that I could not begin to count them. These pictures have put food on our table for generations. We collaborate with the painters in our guild, of course, colorists and picture makers who paint beautiful colored figures that seem conjured from a dream. We paint around their heads and bodies, or rather it is more accurate to say that the picture makers paint within our gold. For we put the gold down first. We punch the saints' halos, patterns of stars, circles, and feathers. We punch patterns in their drapery folds, in their arm and cloaks, in their shoe buckles. When the candles are lit in the churches across our city, the light reflects the gold and makes the pictures come alive with the sacred stories of the Holy Book. It is what we do, what we are known for, the pride of our family.

In my grandfather's time, the gold often covered the entire panel. I remember a panel of Saint Chrysogonous that my grandfather and a painter made for a wealthy patron who had just returned from Crete. My grandfather used actual metal nails for the horse's armor, gilding the breastplates and spurs of the saint's armor. He built up parts of the panel with layers of gesso and rice paste and gilded them using real metal studs. As a child I remember running my small hand over the parts of the panels my grandfather had worked on. My fingers traced the texture of the saint's boots and spurs. At that time the gold was perhaps the most important part of the panel. Our patrons specified in our contracts how much gold and from where. Instead, today they specify the colors they want—lapis, vermillion, indigo—and that they want themselves immortalized above all else.

We are sometimes asked to restore an old panel that is well-loved and worn with time. I have laid my hands on so many altarpieces, centuries old already, filled with pests that have bored small holes into the wood. They come scampering out of the gilded surfaces, bringing small trails of dust with them.

"Here it is," says Master Trevisan, leading us to a space alongside the main altar of Santa Maria. Before us a gilded altarpiece stands twice as tall as a man, showing the Passion of Our Lord. We all look up to an adjacent blank space where, once it is finished, our painted and gilded altarpiece will hang. "The place where the altarpiece will go once it's finished," he explains. I look at the space and imagine seven large panels. It is the work where I will use up all the packets of gold leaf that I have brought with me, that have been wrought by the *battiloro*'s own hands.

Then, at the bottom of one of the old panels, she draws my eye. Mary Magdalene. She is always there, the sinewy woman with the fiery hair flowing over her shoulders, just like mine. My father says that I was born with hair the color of spring strawberries. It made me smile until just a few years later an old lady told me I conjured the devil himself. My friends laughed so hard that I went home and put a grain sack over my head until my father removed it and replaced it with a kiss.

"I suppose some would say that the picture is old-fashioned," the painter's journeyman says, and I see that he still feels guilty about what he said to me in the gondola, "but this is the way we have always done it in Our Most Serene City. It is still magical," he says.

I nod. "And it is helpful to see the old work so that we have the space in mind while we are working on the new."

My eye falls on one of the old panels depicting a choir of angels singing, their mouths open in song, their brows creased, their eyes closed. Two of the singing angels have been rendered with auburn hair. Even looking at the picture I can hear their voices lifted up to heaven. I feel a sense of peace wash over me, a feeling that all will be well.

"*MADONNA MIA*, YOU are a grown woman."

My aunt Agnese's pale, delicate fingers reach through the wrought iron grille. I grasp her hand, an awkward exercise through the grate that divides the convent visitors' parlor from the sisters.

Already I feel ashamed that it has taken me so long to come. Could it be that several years have passed since I last visited my father's sister? Her raised eyebrows reveal how much I have transformed since the last time she saw me. I recognize her delicate face, untouched by the sun and framed by the white linen that covers her hair. Aunt Agnese sets her clear green eyes on me, eyes like my father's. My father has said that my wavy auburn hair came from her, though I have only seen the fine stubs of her shorn hair that escape from under the cover of her thick wimple. Now I see coarse strands of grey around her temples.

"I have been praying that you would come," she says. "I have heard that a great painter is starting work on an altarpiece to be placed in our sanctuary. And that you might be with him."

I nod. "Yes. Master Trevisan. Our *gastaldo* helped arrange it with my father."

Through the wrought iron swirls she squeezes my fingers again. "*Grazie a Dio.*"

"I have been lodged with Master Trevisan since before Epiphany," I say. "Mostly we work inside his studio. This is the first time I have been here; the first time I have seen your beautiful church."

My father's sister has been cloistered behind the walls of Santa Maria delle Vergini for my entire life. "What other choice did she have?" my father asked me when I was very young, as if I had an answer. Much later, my father told me that one day, soon after his sister's fifteenth year, he saw her midsection swell strangely. On another day a baby appeared, but the father did not. My grandfather loaded Agnese and her baby into a gondola bound for the Vergini along with a meager donation. My cousin Paolo spent his early years behind the convent walls under the care of the sisters, learning how to read and work hard.

Paolo was born with a lame leg and rarely spoke, a result of the sinful circumstances of his birth, a neighbor woman once whispered in my ear. He walked with a loping gait, floundering yet surprisingly fast. His strange, scuttling movements and few words gave no indication of his intelligence. His handwriting was a thing of great beauty, the result of years of careful copying and strict discipline in the convent.

When he came of age at ten, my father called for his nephew. Paolo emerged from the convent and moved into our gilding studio as an apprentice. I was only four years old then, so Paolo became the closest thing to a sibling I ever had. At first, I adored him and tagged along behind like a hungry dog; later, I defended him when the boys in the alley played wicked tricks on him. After that, they kept a respectable distance from me.

As obedient and intelligent as he was, Paolo knew nothing of the gold. As a four-year-old, I knew more about how to lay the red bole and punch the feathered patterns in the glittering surfaces. Now he is a strapping twenty-five-year-old man in spite of his lame leg. His mother remains in prayer behind these walls.

"You miss your father," Agnese says, as if she has read my mind.

"Yes," I say. "And Paolo too." I realize now that it is the first time I have visited my aunt on my own. Each time my father has brought me along to visit his sister. Seeing my aunt's face is a bit like looking at my own father. I feel his absence now, deep in my heart.

"I have hungered for news of my brother, and of course my son. Do you know anything? Have you seen them?"

I feel even more ashamed now, realizing that she has had no direct news from us for a long time. "I have had a letter from Paolo from the feast of the Baptism of Our Lord."

From a pouch in my felted shawl, I retrieve my cousin's letter. I must have read it forty times or more, as if scouring it again might bring me some small shred of information that I failed to see before. Paolo's letter brought me both a fleeting sense of elation as well as a gaping void. There is no mention of the *battiloro*. I have written several letters back, placing the folded pieces of parchment in the messenger's hand, but I have no way of knowing if my letters have reached home.

I press the letter through the grate. "I do not have much other information to share. They were well when I left for Master Trevisan's studio. I only received the news of the pestilence after my arrival, but as far as I know, they are safe. I suppose you have heard that the pestilence has appeared in Cannaregio," I say.

She nods, a grim expression on her face. "I did not know if you had heard."

"The streets are closed."

My aunt nods. "So they have told us. Have faith, *cara*. A few of the monks from our brother institution have gone with our confessor to help the sick. Our confessor tells us that two citizens have been assigned per *sestier*. They are paid four ducats from the Salt Office to circulate through the neighborhoods and report on the spread of the pestilence."

"Who has been assigned to Cannaregio?"

"I cannot say," she says, "but I will try to find out for you. I do not know anything except that it is their job to convince people to go to the pesthouses if they fall ill."

What is strange, I think, is that the most reliable and valuable information about what is happening in my city may come from a woman cloistered behind bars, who is not free to roam the city and see for herself.

"Oh my dear, you must be so worried about them." She grasps the rosary that hangs from her waist and begins to turn the black glass beads over between her pale fingers.

"Yes." I meet her eyes. "If you want to know the truth, I am scared to death. You know that my father is not well. I have written to them but I do not know if the letters arrived." I heave a large sigh. "My biggest fear is that they need me and I cannot get to them."

"I suppose it is thanks to God's grace that you went to the painter's studio. You will be safe there." I fall silent, and she ponders the expression on my face, then grasps the bars of the grille with both hands. "Did something happen?"

I take a deep breath. "Well, my father says that it was for my own good, for the good of our workshop. We—my father, Paolo, and I—have been working with the painters for a long time on pictures and objects that require collaboration between our trades. Father says that he fears no one wants gilded paintings anymore. They want the colored pigments instead, pictures like those of the Bellini brothers and Master Giorgione, God rest his soul. But then Master Trevisan got a large commission for an altarpiece here at this very convent, where the donor's contract specified gilding throughout the panel. I brought books full of gold leaf with me to his studio. I am to stay there for a year and a half. In exchange for my working on the altarpiece, Master Trevisan is to teach me how to use the colored pigments. This he will do in lieu of an apprentice's salary. That is the agreement that my father made with him and that was approved by our guild."

My aunt stares at me for a long time and we fall silent. I feel the weight of words unspoken.

I take a deep breath. "If you want to know the truth, it was because of a man."

I had not planned to tell her, but somehow the words spill out of my mouth, unable to stay locked inside for a moment longer. I imagine that my aunt can see the freckles on my face turn red.

My aunt emits a small gasp and then her face falls with realization. She presses her back against the chair. "Ah."

It just came out, but immediately I feel immense relief at having lifted this burden from my shoulders, realizing now that it has been pinned painfully inside for the weeks I have been in Master Trevisan's studio.

My aunt looks pained. "Your father has turned you out," she says, her voice barely above a whisper. I struggle to respond. If the words spilled out of my mouth before, now they will not come. I feel my heart race, then my aunt reaches through the grille and places her hand on top of mine. "He is only doing what our own father did. *Dio.*" She brings her palms together, then wags them in prayer and sighs. "Of all people I understand, *cara.*"

"I suppose you know of these things," I say, looking at my fidgeting hands in my lap. I think of my cousin Paolo, so smart and handsome, yet hobbling around our workshop with difficulty.

She nods and sighs. "You don't think I know about the pleasures of the flesh? How do you think it is that I ended up here?" she asks, gesturing to the austere space around her.

If my aunt feels the weight of this burden, she does not show it. Instead, she manages a quick laugh that lights up her face. "Well. When my own father turned me out I was sure that I was doomed to an eternity of tedium, but it is not so bad here," she says. "I have everything I need. My meals are prepared, my needs cared for. I have my work," she says. "My pastries are known all over Our Most Serene City, and of that I am very proud. Everything else I do is for the glory of God, but I did not raise my child. That I will never get back." Her voice wavers. "And, I would not admit this to just anyone, but I always have enjoyed the company of men, and truth be told, I miss a man's touch." Her cheeks turn red against the white trim of her wimple. I flush, too.

She clucks. "*O Santa Cecilia,* my poor dear," she says, shaking her head. "Well. None of this would have happened if your father had married you off when I told him it was time." She wags her finger at me. "He waited too long. It was bound to happen. Look at you. You have been a woman for some time already."

I shrug, still trying desperately to push down the lump that has risen into my throat. I push back the flashing images of Cristiano's broad smile, his hands on my hips.

"I have said too much," my aunt says. "Forgive me."

Finally, the lump in my throat subsides. "No," I say. "It is I who have spoken too freely of such things."

Chapter 7

Through the narrow window I spy a sliver of pink. It resembles the light wash of *vermilione* that the painter uses to bring flesh tones to his delicate drawings. The dark swath of night sky lightens with each passing minute, silhouetting the tall chimney pipes of the houses on the opposite side of the canal. I wait for the orange light of dawn to appear before I dare to move a muscle.

It is clear now that I will not be going home, at least not for now. I must focus on my work in Master Trevisan's studio or I feel I will burst.

I have lain still and awake in the darkness for what must be hours, reviewing in my head the steps that the painter has demonstrated for rendering drapery in paint. I have tested the method on at least two dozen pieces of scrap panel, thick with paint from countless past lessons. I feel stupid and fumbling, like a girl who tries diligently to copy her mother's embroidery stitches and ends up instead with a tangled mess of thread.

We await the Baldi, one of Our Most Serene Republic's well-respected families of carpenters, to deliver the large panels and battens that will be used for our new altarpiece.

In the meantime, I practice what will be my new trade. My eye is drawn naturally to the powdered *orpiment*, which, when mixed with egg yolk, imparts a glistening golden-yellow tone that resembles our familiar gilding. I have learned to swirl together bits of lead white with *orpiment* on my wooden palette to create a light golden orange—the color of the dawn sky outside our narrow window. But the reds are the most important, Master Trevisan has told me, for they are what our patrons want from us, even if they do not know it themselves. And so the painter has said I must master every shade from raspberry to ruby, from soft flesh to deep crimson.

The house is quiet save for the rhythmic breathing of Antonella beside me. I listen to her deep inhale and slow exhale. She is not an unpleasant bedmate. The regular rhythm of her snoring lulls me back into a calm state between wakefulness and sleep.

My arm begins to tingle, and I realize that I have been still for so long that it has begun to fall asleep. I flip myself over, and suddenly, on the back of my hand, I feel something wet. I push myself up and through the pale light beginning to illuminate the room, I see a dark patch of blood below where Antonella is sleeping. I gasp and push myself up from the bed with a start.

The sound of my gasp wakes her and she turns her sleepy gaze to where I am looking. She sits up with a start. "Oh," she says. Both of us stand up from the bed simultaneously, and I see that blood has stained the back of her nightdress too. "*Dio!*" she says, flustered, then begins jerking at the bedclothes to remove them from the bed.

I stand and wipe the back of my hand on the bed sheet.

"I am sorry," she says to me, fully awake. "I had not realized that it was time for my menses to return." Heat rises visibly to her cheeks. "I will get these sheets boiled today."

"*Figurati,*" I say, trying not to sound flustered, "it is normal." I begin helping her roll the bedding into a ball. "Let me help you."

"No. I can take care of it." Antonella drags the bedding to the floor, then approaches the table with the water basin and begins wiping a damp rag between her legs.

I turn my back to allow her some privacy, then lean over the trunk where my meager clothing is stored. I open the planks of the lid and find my worn linen work dress and smock where I left them neatly folded last night. Underneath that layer is a nicer linen dress that I allowed myself the luxury of purchasing after my father and I got a commission to gild a set of small sculptures destined for the high altar of a convent church. I pull the linen work dress over my head and feel the gold ingot threaded onto its silk cord fall and settle near my heart. I loosen my braid, then reweave my hair into a neat package at the nape of my neck with the leather lash and small metal pins I have collected on the windowsill.

When I turn around, Antonella has removed her soiled night-dress and is buttoning the grey linen shift that she wears to clean the house.

"*Santa Margherita*, I must have given you a scare," Antonella says, chuckling. "All that blood."

I muster a smile. "Surprised, yes, but only for a moment until I understood."

"I should have known it was coming. We women in the house are on the same schedule, the painter's wife and myself, at least when she has not been with child." She pauses. "But you..." An uncomfortable laugh makes her mouth twist. "You must be either barren or with child yourself."

Antonella goes quiet and looks away, seemingly embarrassed to have aired her curiosity out loud. I want to say something to deny it, but the words will not come, for as soon as she has spoken, I feel the knot in my stomach tighten. Ever since I arrived in Master Trevisan's house, I have been calculating the days. The last time my menses came, the leaves on the linden tree behind my father's workshop had not yet turned yellow.

I have never missed my menses before, but with each passing week I have pushed the nagging suspicion away. Now, with Antonella's words, there is no more denying the truth.

And now, it is no longer a secret.

Chapter 8

"We should replenish our supplies while we are waiting for our panels to arrive, Master Trevisan." The journeyman examines the level of indigo powder in the bottom of a glass jar.

"A worthy observation," says the painter. "The carpenters..." The painter raises his pen from the paper and scratches his head. "They are good, but they are slow. I waited months for the last set of panels we made for the *scuola*. You are right to think about preparing everything in advance so that we are ready to begin when they bring our panels."

Alongside the hearth, the journeyman is putting the final touches on a boulder in the landscape of a small picture showing a miracle of San Rocco. Master Trevisan says that he has received three requests for pictures of the plague saint just this week. "Have you seen if we have enough of the red bole for the project?" Trevisan's journeyman asks. "Maria?" It takes a moment for me to realize he is speaking to me. "Maria."

"Forgive me," I say, feeling my cheeks warm. "No. Yes. Yes, I did examine the containers," I fumble.

For days I feel that I have been living inside of a dream, disconnected from my actions. I work on my drawings, practice mixing the paints, work on my trees and my drapery, but my heart and mind are not in it.

My mind is all focused on my body now. Surely my menses will begin. I must have retired to the latrines or the bedchamber to lift my skirts and check one hundred times today. But each time, there is no sign.

"I would estimate that there is enough for one or two panels," I say, gesturing to the series of lidded ceramic jars on the shelf, "but not for the size that we need."

Master Trevisan opens the lid of one of the jars on the shelf. "Hardly any left in this one," he says, then addresses me. "Over the coming days you might visit the *vendecolore* for some new red bole. I am certain that you will know what to select better than I."

"For years my father has patronized a *vendecolore* on the Zattere. Master da Segna," I say.

Trevisan nods in approval. "Boatman can bring you there and help you carry the supplies back to us."

"Of course." I nod in agreement and turn back to my work, but my mind is far distant from the painter's studio.

CRISTIANO.

The *battiloro*.

He is all that I can think of now.

The *battiloro* came into my father's workshop as most people do, through the ties that bind us to our own guildsmen and those of our related trades.

Two narrow alleys away from our own lived an old goldbeater, Master Zuan. The Zuan name was already well-regarded in my great-grandfather's time for the family's fine sheets of beaten gold, free of all impurities and thinner than the most delicate autumn leaf. The bonds between the Zuan and our own workshop went back generations, my father had told me when I was a small girl. Master Zuan's own father supplied my *nonno* with the gold leaf, and on before that as far back as anyone could remember.

Some Sunday afternoons, Master Zuan's stooped figure would appear in our doorway. He would remove his felted wool cap and grasp my small shoulder in greeting with a wiry hand. I poured Master Zuan and my father small glasses of watery brew while the old goldbeater regaled my father with stories through his toothless grin. My cousin and I sat quietly at the men's feet or under the worktable, rolling a roughly carved wooden ball back and forth while the men passed the hours in amiable companionship before the fire. Paolo and I shared secret smiles as we heard the goldbeater repeat the same stories over and over, and listened to my father respond as if he were hearing them for the first time.

Master Zuan had no sons of his own. His elder daughter was given in marriage to a maker of gold rings. The younger had died of a fever before she became a woman; sickness took the goldbeater's wife soon after. Even as a small girl I suffered the old man's loneliness as if it were my own, and felt his satisfaction in capturing the ear of a patient friend.

On one of these Sabbath visits the old *battiloro* told us that he had taken in an assistant to learn his trade. A half-Saracen, he told us, still a boy. The boy came to him by way of a wealthy patron who had just passed to the World Hereafter, Zuan said. The patron held a deep respect for the goldbeating trade and a longtime affection for the goldbeater himself, whom he had tasked with making gilded objects over several decades. According to one of the provisions in the man's last testament, his house-slave was made a freedwoman, and her own son was apprenticed to Master Zuan as a token of the dying man's appreciation. Old Master Zuan was teaching the boy to hammer the ingots into nearly weightless leaves, cut and package them between vellum sheaves, then compile them into small books. He showed promise already, Master Zuan told us. His name was Cristiano.

Years would pass before I laid eyes on Cristiano myself. By the time my father brought him into our own workshop, he was a man, as respected among our guildsmen as old Master Zuan himself.

From the day he appeared under my father's roof, things would never be the same.

"I HAVE A solution to your... circumstance."

Antonella wipes down the wooden table in the center of the kitchen with a damp rag. Across from me, Trevisan's little boy is licking a batter of eggs, milk, honey, and rice flour from a wooden spoon. The mixture makes splattered patterns across the table, the remnants of Antonella's baking in preparation for Carnival. The aroma of the fritters we call *chiacchiere* lingers in the air. Normally I relish tasting the dough myself, but today I feel as though I will vomit. I know that I will need some energy, as the painter has asked me to visit the color-seller to select the gesso and bole for our panels. I select a pear from a bowl on the table, no doubt set aside in syrup in a glass jar before the winter. I taste its tangy sweetness as I push back another wave of nausea.

"*Vale*," Antonella lifts the little boy under his arms and sets him on the tile floor. "Your mother is waiting for you upstairs." Young Trevisan sets down the spoon, then races to the staircase. He clambers up the worn wooden treads on his hands and feet.

Above our heads, I hear a door slam. In my mind's eye I see the half-dozen doorways on the main floor. They must lead to the private chambers of the painter and his family, but I have not seen these rooms, for the doors always remain closed, casting the stairwell into darkness.

"*Mamma!*" I hear the boy's shrill voice fill the dark stairwell above our heads. Then there is the screech of metal hinges.

"*Vieni, amore.*" The muffled voice of the painter's wife. Another door slams, then the clamor upstairs falls silent.

"Now." Antonella puts the hand with the rag in it on her hip, then scrapes a chair across the floor and sits next to me. She lowers her voice. "My cousin Bartolomea," she says. "She lives in Dorsoduro." Antonella points to the back wall in the direction of the neighborhood on the other side of town. "She came before me from Sicilia with her parents. Now she is grown and works alongside the midwife to deliver babies, but she is also good with herbal remedies. She knows how to cure headaches, back pains, even make poisons. But she also knows how to make other... concoctions."

I return her whisper. "Concoctions?"

Antonella rubs a sticky spot on the table with her rag. "Well. She has taken on cases of gravidness that were... inconvenient."

I stare at Antonella silently for a few moments.

She shrugs. "*Cavolo*, you think you are the only one in Our Most Serene City carrying a child by accident?" She wags her hands at me.

"I never said that I am..." I feel my shoulders drop, realizing that it is futile to lie about such matters to a woman with whom I share a bed, who is aware of the monthly cycles of all the women in the house. "I never said it was an accident."

Antonella snorts loudly into the air. "*Pallini.* You are not a wife, not even promised. You cannot convince me that you came into the painter's house knowing that you were with child. I was not born yesterday. *Fidati di me.* I have seen it before. Young girls... old girls. There are certain circumstances when it is inconvenient. Undesirable. Dangerous." She stops to consider my face but I say nothing.

"I even know of a woman who was impregnated by a Moor," she continues, lowering her voice even further and leaning closer.

"Do you not think she was the first in line for my cousin's concoction? Ha!"

I feel my mouth open, but no words come out. I scrape my fingernail across a piece of dough stuck to the wooden tabletop.

"I do not know about you, but the last thing I would want to bring forth into this world is a baby like that. The poor child would have no chance. Better to end things and go forward with your own life," she says.

I can no longer remain seated, and I begin to pace aimlessly around the kitchen. "You do not know anything about my situation," I say, hoping that she cannot see the heat rising to my face or hear my heartbeat, which surely must be so loud that it is audible.

"I only know that you did not come into this house with an idea that there was... something... forming in there." Antonella waves her rag toward my stomach, then crosses her arms. "Either you became pregnant before you came here," she pauses and sets her black eyes on me, "or shortly after you arrived."

"You are crazy," I say in a loud whisper, my heart beating uncontrollably in my chest as I stare daggers into her black eyes. I cannot process what she is suggesting, and I feel I must leave the room or I will strike her. I make my way toward the door to the painter's studio. "I am going on an errand for the painter. Perhaps he has already let the boatman know." I begin to push the door with my palm, but Antonella grasps my sleeve and I stop.

"I do not mean to push you," she whispers, her sour breath puffing on my neck. "But just... think about it."

I press the door open with my palm and let it swing closed behind me.

Chapter 9

Already there is blood.

As the painter's boatman turns the gondola into a narrow canal, I see a stocky man—surely too old for such foolery—standing at the crest of a rickety wooden bridge with red streaming from a gash in his forehead. Strangely, he is smiling. The man stumbles backward, and the crowd that has gathered to cheer on the bloodshed heaves to catch him as he reels.

The Carnival brawling has begun.

They are not allowed, of course, not since the Council of Ten outlawed such bridge fights only a few years ago. But the decree has only made the skirmishes more anticipated and more exciting to watch, at least so my cousin Paolo says. Now, more crowds than ever before gather to cheer on grown men who bloody themselves for sport.

On the left side of the bridge, I recognize the colors of the *castellani*, the men of the ship-building quarters of Castello, San Marco, and Dorsoduro. A few lanky boys lead the charge, coursing over the crest of the bridge and pushing back the *nicolotti*—their adversaries from the remaining quarters—including my own.

But I do not cheer on my own team of fishermen cast against the ship-builders. I find the fights distasteful, well-respected men acting like belligerents. The painter's boatman seems to think differently. As we pass under the crooked wooden slats of the bridge, he lets out an ear-splitting roar that echoes across the water. I lean forward on my knees and cover my ears. I hear his loud cackle muffled in my head.

At last, we push through the boat traffic surrounding the bridge and leave the dispersing crowd behind us. Ahead, in the San Marco quarter, the aroma of fried dough is overwhelming. The air seems thicker than I can ever recall with the sticky-sweet smell of *chiacchiere*, the tiny twists of pastry made only at Carnival time. My mouth waters as I can almost taste the warm bread drizzled with honey melting on my tongue.

Even the sky has turned a happy shade of pink. The Carnival season is always like this, lifting the long shadows of winter that have cast their grey mantle over the façades along the canal. But I do not feel its brightness, its usual sense of hope and excitement. Not this time.

I run my palm over the green upholstery of the wooden chair set in the painter's gondola, trying to derive some sense of comfort from the smell of dough and the plush texture of the velvet. For days I have felt on the verge of panic, trying to calm my frantic heart while at the same time trying to summon my menses through force of sheer will.

For years I had no idea about such things, for I have never had a mother or any other female in my house to tell me about them. When I was small, a mean older girl down the alley told me that the devil came to visit every girl once a month, and I was terrified. When blood appeared in my undergarments in my twelfth year, I thought I was dying or had surely been possessed. My father tried to explain it to me but did not have the words. A neighbor woman took pity on me and did her best to inform me about the way that babies came into the world. Only years later, in the deep envelop of Cristiano's embrace, did any of it begin to make sense.

I try to distract myself by counting the variety of boats trafficking the Grand Canal: a modest water-seller's boat; a flat-bottomed skiff to ferry passengers from one side of the wide canal to the other; a fine gondola with gilded ornamentation on the prow. Behind me, the boatman presses the oar into the oarlock. I steal a glance at him, his woolen scarf pulled tight around his neck, his dark locks brushing against the crooked scar beneath his eye.

The oar makes swirling patterns in the water, stirring shards of colored Carnival confetti. The multicolored scraps of paper are the detritus of parties that people insist on hosting even though the authorities of Our Most Serene Republic have warned us that congregating in large groups might spread contagion. I watch the shards of paper float and spin on the surface of the dark canal waters until their colors begin to blur through stifled tears.

On the quayside, butchers, fishmongers, and fruit-sellers have set up makeshift tables in a neighborhood morning market along the bank of the rio San Lorenzo. A pair of men wearing masks runs past, grabbing handfuls of apples as the fruit seller yells at them. I contemplate a slimy trickle of yellow yolk on a pink façade, the result of naughty boys who throw spoiled eggs at one another and at well-dressed but unlucky ladies who walk under their windows at an ill-timed moment.

Though Carnival season has begun to overtake Our Most Excellent Republic, I feel as though I am watching it unfold from far away, through the veil of a dream. Everything around me appears normal, but I am not really present. I feel as though I am floating above myself, watching myself go through daily activities. I cannot begin to grasp that there may be a living being developing inside my body, that I may be a vessel for human life.

I feel the boatman's eyes on me, and the back of my neck prickles. I am accustomed to people staring at me, of course. It is my hair. In the sunlight, the strands of red glint and sparkle like golden threads, at least so I have been told. I attempt to look the boatman in the eye. Usually this makes people look away, ashamed for having been caught staring at my reddish locks. But his eyes meet mine, and he does not waver. I do my best not to let it show, but I am unnerved.

"You are not engaged to be married?" he blurts, cocking his head to one side. From under a new-looking rust-colored cap, his eyes stay steady, studying my face. Strands of greasy black hair hang across the boatman's cheeks. I imagine that Trevisan has supplied the velvet hat and the brocade waistcoat to make his boatman look elegant, but no amount of dressing can change his unnerving presence.

I do not answer but instead turn my gaze from the boatman's face to the horizon. I do not like that I am the first to turn my face away. Surely I do not owe him an explanation?

I implore you to keep your distance. You do not want to get yourself involved with him.

The words of the painter's wife ring in my head.

"Your father has betrothed you to someone?" he tries again.

"No," I say, perhaps too quickly, but I ponder his query.

In truth, the question of my marriage was delayed for longer than even my father might have imagined. I have lost count of the requests that my father's colleagues in the guild have made of me. These men were intelligent enough to realize that the daughter of the *indoradòr* would be an asset in their own painting workshops. But as much as my father understood the potential for an advantageous barter, I believe he viewed keeping me in his own workshop as even more desirable. If I married, it meant that I no longer belonged to my father. It meant moving to another man's house. My father would be left with Paolo to rely upon, and our workshop would suffer. All of us knew it, but it went unspoken for all these years.

The truth is that they needed me. The truth is that they need me now. I feel the sting of my father's rejection as if it were fresh.

My stomach clenches into a knot again, and I feel that I might vomit.

"Surely there is someone you want?" The boatman prods again, screwing up one side of his mouth in an exaggerated smirk.

"I cannot see how that is any of your concern," I manage to say, pulling my shawl tightly around my shoulders and turning away from his gaze. I feel his eyes on me, but he does not respond. I do not want to share any of this information with the boatman. I do not want to fall under his gaze any more at all. I duck into the passenger compartment, and the chaos of *Carnevale* falls away.

As soon as I sink into the upholstered cushions, I feel the weight of the irony that my father has sent me to Trevisan's house. After all the years of keeping me sheltered from a potential husband, love came to find me at home. And then I was the one who was pushed out of the house.

"I have been negligent; please forgive me," my father said. "Now I see that is past time for you to be married, Maria," he told me as he helped heave my trunk to the canal-side mooring behind our workshop, his eyes heavy but his jaw set. "When you come back from your apprenticeship with your newfound painting skills, I will have found a husband for you." It was supposed to make me feel better about leaving.

As my father and I watched our neighborhood glide by from our seats in the painter's fine gondola, I thought that surely any moment, my father would change his mind, tell me it was all a mistake. Instead, the façade of the painter's house came into view, with its soft brick and lovely archways. Surely any minute Father would tell me that it was a cruel joke, that we would turn the boat around and go back home. Instead, my trunk was lifted onto the wooden dock outside Master Trevisan's studio. Instead, a hand appeared to help me up out of the boat and onto the wooden planks. Instead, my father planted a dry kiss on my forehead and let me go.

Perhaps I was naive to expect to stay in my father's house forever. I do not try to imagine what my father would say to me now, or what the future will be like. I cannot imagine myself with a baby. More than that, I cannot imagine my life without Cristiano. I do not want a husband that my father cobbles together for me from amongst the men of our guild. I want *him*. Cristiano. Our *battiloro*.

When I return, what will the man my father has chosen for me think of his disgraced fiancée? Women have been sent to the Doge's prisons or banished to convents for lesser offenses. And what will my father think of me? I cannot begin to propose an answer to any of these questions.

Inside the shadows of the gondola's passenger compartment, I sink down into the damask cushions piled onto the bench. I close my eyes and push my face into one of the pillows, and wonder if I am capable of taking my own life.

I imagine lowering myself over the edge of the gondola, feeling the cold water envelop me. The world would turn blue and green, the moss-covered pilings around me disintegrating into shimmering blurs. I imagine my hair floating out above my head, its tangled strands catching wet shards of Carnival confetti as I sink into the muted depths. The water fills my ears and quiets the noise of the outside world. I cross my arms over my chest and imagine sinking all the way down to the bottom of the lagoon.

Chapter 10

The color-seller's shop lies near the tanneries along the Zattere, with a view to the Giudecca beyond the canal. The stench along the canalside is overwhelming, the result of the carcasses of beasts sacrificed for the skin trade. Piles of hides are stacked beside a stone warehouse slung low along the waterside. Here, there is no sign of Carnival revel or misbehavior; only backbreaking work that continues without ceasing.

Even though it takes everything in me to stand and clamber out of the boat without vomiting at the stench, it is a relief to wriggle from beneath the oppression of the boatman's stare. I press my palm over my nose and mouth, hurrying past the skins stretched across the wooden racks where they are scraped of their hair and cured in the sun. I rush past the tanneries toward the shop where my father has always sought the best gesso and red bole.

My father has purchased raw materials from this particular *vendecolore* for as long as I can remember. He says he would not buy from anyone else, that the byproducts of these buffalo skins are the city's best, that Signor da Segna's materials impart a quality that accounts for the glistening of our gold that sets our work apart.

In the alley alongside the *vendecolore's* shop I pass the giant wooden vats where a poor young assistant has been tasked with boiling the tissue from the animal hides being stretched between the wooden slats of the racks in the tanneries further down the quayside. The skinny young boy stirs a stick slowly in a large metal cauldron over a fire, his wiry hair sticking up and his face smudged with dirt as if he has been living in the woods.

When I cross the threshold, the baggy-eyed color-seller searches my face for recognition.

"I am Maria," I explain, "daughter of Bartolini the gilder in Cannaregio."

"Of course! *Vieni, vieni!*" he says, bustling his hefty frame around the counter to greet me. The buttons on his doublet seem as though they might burst, and his jowls hang in folds around his reddened nose.

Signor da Segna's shop is deceivingly modest. Little more than a cave in an alley littered with shops and workspaces, its dark interior is overwhelmed by shelves stacked high with glass and ceramic jars with various concoctions, a cluttered apothecary of pigments. Other guildsmen have told my father that Signor da Segna's pigments are known as far away as London and Constantinople. They say that painters from far across the sea seek out his concoctions, especially those made of lead, which is not allowed to be traded outside the control of Our Most Serene Republic.

"I was only surprised to see you here by yourself," he says. "Normally you come with your father or his assistant."

"My cousin."

Signor da Segna clasps my hand in both of his. "Yes!" I feel the rough skin of his pudgy hand and see the coarse white whiskers on his jowl move with his smile. "But I hope this means that everyone is well?" he says, a concerned look in his bright blue eyes.

"Truthfully, *missier*, I do not know." I slide my hand from his grip and place my woven sack on the rough wooden counter. The empty containers from the painter's studio rattle on the knotted wood. "My father, my cousin, and our *battiloro* are still in our family studio, but unfortunately the pestilence has come to the quarter and they cannot leave. Nor can anyone else enter."

The color-seller's face falls, and he wipes his hand on his dirty breeches. "Yes," he says hardly above a whisper. "I have heard of it, the ferries lined up to take people to the *lazzaretti*. God help them. But you are not there with them?" he asks, puzzled.

"My father has placed me—temporarily—in the workshop of Master Trevisan the painter. I am tasked with the gilding for a church commission at the Vergini and the painter is also teaching me to use the pigments."

"Master Trevisan." His eyebrows rise and he wags a finger at me. "Ah, you are fortunate indeed. One of our city's best painters, if you ask me. I hear that he has done wonders with the paintings for the confraternity of the Misericordia," he says.

"I would not know," I say. "I am only beginning to understand. Truthfully I am doubtful that I will ever learn the colors. Anyway, I have come for some gesso as we are beginning a new altar for the sisters at the Vergini in preparation for gilding. I convinced the painter that your buffalo skin gesso is the best."

Signor da Segna lets out a burst of laughter. "Your father has taught you well!" he declares. Signor da Segna puts a glass ring to his eye and pores over the rows of glass jars on the shelves. He pulls out a heavy jar and places it on the counter. With a wooden spatula, he spoons some gesso into my empty container. I watch the white material jiggle inside the jar.

"I must ask you," I say. "I have seen a most beautiful gilded box in the painter's studio. It has white figures on it, molded from tin molds. I do not know what they use."

"Musk paste!" he exclaims without hesitation.

"*Pasta di muschio*?"

"It can only be," he says, and runs his fingers along the shelves again until he selects another ceramic jar from the bottom shelf. "I have seen such boxes on terra firma. It is lead mixed with rice flour paste. We also add musk or civet to scent the boxes; the ladies like that." He opens several sachets and puts them to my nose. "This one was developed to protect against the pestilence," he says. "I can hardly keep up with the demand for it."

I bring the sachet to my nose and inhale its pungent mixture of sharp scents that seem to make the hairs of my nostrils stand on end. For a moment, I had forgotten my unsteady stomach. The musk paste begins it rocking again, and I place it back on the counter.

"I have an arrangement with one of the spice merchants who brings things from the east on the merchant galleys," he tells me, gesturing to the canal in view of his shop. "This one is a particular type of *muschio*," he says. "It is concocted to help disinfect the air and to protect its owner from the pestilence. Some of my artisans are beginning to mix it with their materials."

I crinkle my nose. "It smells like animal urine."

Signor da Segna laughs as I fish out the coins that Master Trevisan has given me for the purchase.

"You are alone?" he asks.

"Master Trevisan's boatman has brought me," I say, glancing toward the door and dreading going back into the boat.

"Here," he says, placing three sachets in my bag. "I will give you some. At a minimum you can hold it to your nose as you ride around the city," he says. "At all costs we must ensure that you ward off the pestilence."

I turn toward the door.

"Wait," he says. "I have something else for you. I have just received this." The *vendecolore* brings out a small book of golden-colored sheaves set between slivers of vellum. "It is sold in sheets much like the ones your *battiloro* prepares for you. It is not gold, but it is made of a certain alloy that is much less expensive." I hold up the small book and consider the brassy-colored sheaves. It is clear to my eye that it is not pure gold, but would one untrained in the gilding arts be able to tell the difference?

"It looks like gold, but it is not," I say.

The *vendecolore* points at me. "Intelligent as well as lovely." He looks over the top of his glasses at me. "I am certain that you can see the advantages."

ON THE WAY back to Master Trevisan's house, I gather my courage to ask the boatman for a favor.

"Would you pass by the rio della Sensa?"

The boatman slows the movement of the oar. "A detour?" His eyes narrow into dark slits.

"My quarter," I say. "Cannaregio. I have not been home in some weeks."

"Ah," he nods and raises his eyebrows. "I see. Well. Normally, signorina, there is a... surcharge... for such deviations."

I do not respond, but instead cross my arms to see if an uncomfortable silence might prompt him to yield to my request.

"But," he says, "it is not so often that I have a woman such as yourself in my boat. I will consider that payment enough—at least for today." He makes an exaggerated bow and then his black eyes settle on mine. A shudder makes its way up the bones of my back, tingling and tickling beneath my linen undergarments.

The boatman realigns the oar into the lower notch on the oarlock, and turns the boat into one of the narrow cut-throughs that lead from the banks of the Zattere toward the Grand Canal. I turn my face to the wind.

For a while, I lose myself in the rushing sound of the craft creasing the still water. Billowing clouds and palace façades reflect in the canal waters, shimmering, wavering mirror images of life above the waterline.

Near the turn into the Grand Canal, a mask maker's young son stands at a table on the quayside, stacking newly made black *baute* and more elaborate faceplates decorated with color. A group of a half-dozen young noblemen wearing the patterned stockings designating their neighborhood association stop to banter with the mask maker. Shards of their conversation float through the air—a joke about a woman, the price of the masks, a stick fight that is being organized on a bridge in San Polo.

The boatman makes another sharp turn northward toward my neighborhood. At the corner of the narrow waterway, a black gondolier is tying off a fine gondola to a mooring post. He smiles in recognition as we pass, and Trevisan's boatman reaches out to clasp the other man's hand in a brief greeting.

This short, wordless interaction seems an unspoken doorway from one world to the next. As we make our way down the narrow rivulet, the bustle of the Grand Canal and its Carnival preparations fall behind us. Ahead, there are no market-goers, no shopkeepers, no stocking-wearing young men. The boats along the quayside lie covered and still. The quieter the canal becomes, the more wildly my heart seems to beat in my chest.

When we finally turn into the confines of Cannaregio, I feel a deep pang—a mixture of anticipation, excitement, and trepidation—well up in my breast. Before I know it I am standing in the boat, planting my feet firmly to steady myself as I scan the familiar façades as they unfold along the canal-side. The canal should be full of barge captains selling vegetables and linens from the decks of their boats. Women should be rushing toward the Rialto markets for the ingredients of their midday meals. Instead, a vast silence hangs heavy in the still air. The stone quayside is devoid of life.

At last, we turn into the rio della Sensa and the first wooden barrier comes into view. The boatman stills his oar, seemingly struck as silent as the stone quaysides. We drift alongside the entrance to one of the alleys that snakes back into the tangle of streets surrounding my father's house. What they have said is true. Men have erected a solid wooden barrier across the opening to the quarter, and a large black cross has been painted over it. A banner hanging above the cross announces the ban handed down by Our Most Excellent Prince.

Trapped. They are trapped behind the barrier. That is the only thing that fills my mind.

My father. My cousin. My Cristiano. If I worried before that I might not find a way to reach them, there is no longer any doubt.

Chapter 11

"I have something for you."

Antonella peers through the doorway between the kitchen and the painter's studio, and gestures for me to follow.

I find myself alone in the painter's studio again, as Master Trevisan and his journeyman have left the studio to meet with a patron who is paying for a portrait of his wife. On the table before me, I have opened a large, leather-bound book of engravings. I spent the morning trying to copy several figures using the silver-point pen as Master Trevisan has instructed me. Dust puffs into the still air as I close the book and leave it on the table. I follow Antonella reluctantly into the warmth of the kitchen.

Antonella has stoked the fire in the hearth and a pot of water roils in the heat. On the table in the center of the kitchen, she has been chopping beets, the blood-red juice trickling down the veins of the wood.

"Yesterday during my trip to the Rialto market I went to see my cousin," she says. "She gave me the concoction I told you about."

In absorbing myself in Master Trevisan's book of engravings, I had momentarily pushed the image of the wooden barriers of Cannaregio and my missed menses back into the far reaches of my mind. Now I feel a strong twist in my gut.

Antonella produces a small woven bag from her apron pocket. She pulls opens the drawstring with her beet-stained fingers. "I will mix it for you," she says in her thick, Sicilian-accented tongue. "It will make the kitchen stink; best to do it while the family is out." She makes a fanning gesture with her hand as if she is already trying to get rid of the smell even before she has boiled the dried ingredients.

"I... I have not decided," I say.

Her black eyes widen into large circles. "*Madonna mia*. Surely you are not considering the alternative? If I walked in your shoes I would have taken care of it weeks ago, *cara*, as soon as I learned I was encumbered. The last thing you need right now is a babe. It will ruin you." She pauses, and I see a shadow pass over her face. "Trust me."

When I do not respond right away, Antonella sighs and heaves herself down on a stool. "I shall tell you what happened," she says, waving her hands and strong forearms in my direction even though I have not asked her to tell me anything. "Five years ago I found myself a young man apprenticed to a silk merchant in Santa Croce. Not so beautiful to look at," she says, wagging her hand from side to side as if to weigh the man's beauty, "but passing. He had a future. Since that time he has become one of the most important men in the trade." She shakes her head. "But I run ahead of myself. I managed to turn his head."

"You did?" I say.

"Why do you look so surprised?" she asks, placing her hand on her hip. "He was smitten, I swear it. Of course, my father was thrilled. What dealer of secondhand goods would not want to see his daughter married to a silk merchant? It was perfect."

"You did not marry him?"

She shakes her head. "I was stupid. I threw it all away. Too full of myself for my own good. I fooled around with one of the fruit-sellers in the market, and well, I found myself encumbered."

My jaw drops.

She nods. "As you might imagine, once my budding silk merchant discovered that I was with child, the marriage plans evaporated. *Ecco*! Just like that." She swipes her hands together as if dusting flour from them. "Then my parents locked me away in their house for the remaining months. I am lucky my father did not murder me with his own hands."

"And where is the baby now?"

She shrugs. "As soon as I gave birth in the house my parents whisked it off to the steps of the foundling hospital."

"It?"

"I never knew if it was a boy or girl. They refused to tell me. After that, I left," she snorts. "Never spoke to them again."

For the first time I register vulnerability on Antonella's face. She rubs her eyes vigorously with the heels of her hands.

I turn my gaze away from the intensity of her emotion, as I feel that I too might crumble under the weight of the circumstances.

Antonella shakes her head vigorously as if shuddering off the pain, then huffs a loud sigh. "So. Here I am." She gestures grandiosely around the kitchen. "Servant to the painter and his runny-nosed children. Not married to a silk merchant, not even married at all. No husband or children of my own. And I spend my day wiping the fat *culàte* of those children anyway. I could have had a house of my own, servants of my own. Instead, I am stuck in this life, working for others. A reversal of fortune. And all because of a *gravidanza* that I did not want."

"I am sorry." I struggle for better words to say.

She shrugs. "I have never told anyone before," she says. "I share it with you only so you know what can happen. Unless you have some fine gentleman to pick you up in a boat and whisk you away to a better life, I promise you will thank me later." For a brief moment I allow myself to imagine Cristiano arriving outside the

painter's house in a fine gondola, before the weight of such prepos-
terousness falls upon me.

No. Pestilence or not, there is no hope for us. Ever. I feel my
shoulders fall, as if the weight of this truth might press me to the
wooden planks of Master Trevisan's kitchen floor.

Antonella upends the small cloth bag and a series of tiny paper
packets falls out onto the table. One by one, she unfolds the packets, each one revealing a different-looking dried herb. One has flat,
purple leaves. Another, spiky green sprigs.

"What is it?"

Antonella has regained her composure. "A mixture of several things. The most important one is birthwort; here is what it
looks like." She grasps the edge of the paper between her finger
and thumb and shows me a small cluster of leaves. "It's what gets
the contractions going. Then there's pennyroyal; we use that for
bleeding. The rest is a mixture of pine resin, white wax, and myrrh.
Some people add bdellio and glabano and mix everything with
olive oil. You can make a paste out of it and spread it around your...
down there," she says, gesturing to my groin, "and over the belly,
but it's more effective if you make a tea out of it and drink it."

"How do you know all of this?"

"I studied the plants a bit myself," she says. "My aunt—my
cousin's mother—she is the master. I did not want to do it as my
profession. Back home I have seen too many healer women accused
of things they did not do. They take the blame for too many mis-
haps that arise for other reasons."

I nod and sit on a wooden stool at the knotted table in the
center of the painter's kitchen, watching Antonella walk to the
shelf and grasp a ceramic cup. She plunks it down before me.

"Ready?" She looks me in the eye.

I hesitate for a moment, revisiting the fantasy of Cristiano
rescuing me in a gondola. I force myself to push the image from
my head.

"All right. Yes. I'll do it." I place my palms flat on the knotted wood and stand.

She smirks, a side of her mouth rising. For a fleeting moment, her black eyes flash. Antonella walks to the pot over the flame and dumps the packets of herbs into the water. After a few moments, the vapors rise into the air, and an acrid odor fills the room.

"It smells terrible." I put my palm over my nose.

"But it works," she says. "A small price to pay and much better than the alternative." Antonella stirs the concoction with a wooden spoon. She dips a ladle into the pot and fills my cup, then places it in front of me. The vapors rise up into my nose and sting my nostrils. It is steaming hot; I wait. I peer down into the dark liquid. Small flecks of herb float and spin on the surface.

"Drink up," says Antonella.

I pinch my nostrils closed and sip the sharp liquid from my cup. "*Santa Maria!*" I gag and press the inside of my elbow over my mouth. I take a deep breath and down the rest of the hot liquid, then fold over with a sputtering cough that wracks my body.

Antonella, unfazed, refills my cup and moves on to another topic.

"Now. My next task for today is to replicate your aunt's pastry recipe. She would not give it to you, eh?"

I shake my head and regain my voice. "She said it was a convent secret. They cannot afford to have it spread to the other institutions. People come from all over the city to buy the pastries, and their donations help fund the convent and their charities," I say.

Antonella huffs. "Stingy rather than charitable if you ask me," she says. "Filling their own coffers instead."

I do not respond. In a great ceramic bowl under the window, Antonella has made a large ball of dough. She pinches a bit and puts it on her tongue. She shakes her head. "You must press her for details about the ingredients. Perhaps I must add more nutmeg," she says, wagging a finger at me. "I have not given up hope."

The pungent steam of the mixture has filled the kitchen with a foul chemistry. I inhale the vapors from my cup again and make a sour face.

"Hurry up and drink it," she says. "We must get the smell out of this kitchen before that painter returns." Antonella walks over to the window and pushes open the leaded pane. A whoosh of February air rushes into the kitchen from the canal, fresh and briny. Then she walks over to the great hearth and stokes the fire. The wood crackles, and the smell of smoke fills the room. She takes the pot of water and opens the door to the boat slip. I hear her footsteps on the stone stairs, then I hear her pitch the saturated herbs into canal and rinse the pot with the salty water.

"*Cin cin*!" she says, reentering the kitchen. "Bottoms up!"

I pinch my nose again and down the rest of the cup.

"Good girl." She claps her hands together and flashes a wide grin. "You will thank me later."

I take a big gulp of air. "So now what happens?" I ask.

"*Bene*. You should start to feel different, maybe cramping. And then you will bleed. Your body will take care of the rest."

I nod. I realize only then that I have not thought beyond drinking the foul concoction.

"My cousin says that it worked for a lady that she served, a noble lady who made a poor choice for a lover. She says the lady only bled for ten days. After that she could get out of bed and resume her normal routine."

"Ten days?!" I feel my eyes widen.

Antonella shrugs. "What is important is that it worked." She begins to chop the beets on the table again. I watch the red juice slide through the cracks.

"But I cannot afford to be in bed for ten days!" I stand up. "The painter... I... We have work to do."

Antonella wipes the remaining leaves of the herbs off the wooden table and into her palm. "Maybe for you it will not take that long."

"Has your cousin ever had anything go wrong? Like a woman who went on to deliver a baby anyway?" I realize now that I should have asked a lot of questions before trusting Antonella and her concoction.

"I would not know. She does not deliver babies."

"What?!" I feel my chin drop. "You told me that she delivered babies. I thought you said she was a midwife. She is not a midwife?"

"Well, sometimes she works along with the midwife. During the day she is in domestic service as I am. She works for a noble lady in San Polo."

"*O Dio*, I have made a giant mistake." My words barely come out as a whisper. My palms fly to my mouth.

"Nothing to fear," says Antonella, raising her palm to me. "As I told you, she has special knowledge of herbs. Her mother, my aunt, had an herb garden and was known as a healer. She learned from her as well as her grandmother. Trust me. You will see the result."

As soon as the words come out of her mouth I feel my heart-beat begin to race, then the contents of my bowels liquefy. A wave of nausea overtakes me, and I feel I will vomit or empty my bowels right there in the kitchen. I gather up my skirts and stumble toward the back stairway that leads to the latrines. I fling open the door and run toward the two holes cut into a plank of wood behind the painter's house. While my bowels are voided uncontrollably, I press my palm over my mouth to prevent myself from vomiting at the same time. I feel foul-tasting saliva emerge from my cheeks and finally, I cannot hold it back anymore. The vomit spills onto the ground over and over, my body wracked by convulsions.

I have been told that I am an intelligent girl. So how could I have been so stupid? I do not even know the woman who made this concoction. And now I know she may not even be a midwife, only a house servant. I should know better than to trust Antonella, and I swear to myself that I will never trust her again.

For the better part of a half-hour I am in utter agony. During that time a thousand thoughts race through my head. What will happen to me? Will I die? Will my father send me to the convent where I will sit behind the iron grille with his sister? Will my baby—if he or she comes into the world after this horrible torture—be born with no limbs or a deformed head like the poor souls we see begging on the streets? Or be given up on the steps of the Hospital of the Innocents? My baby wrapped in a package, drawn into the walls of the convent of Santa Maria delle Vergini on the great turning wheel?

When I emerge from the latrine I feel as though I have been through a battle. My hair falls loose and frizzy, with strands stuck to the sweat on my neck. My skin feels pasty and damp. My eyes must be sunken and dark.

As far as I know, I am not bleeding.

When I appear at the top of the stairs, back into the kitchen where Antonella is rolling out the dough, her eyes widen in alarm.

"You should go lie in bed now," she says tentatively. I make a move toward the back stairway. When I pass Antonella I see her flinch, and it takes all my strength not to strike her.

Chapter 12

I wake at dawn to the sound of the cock crowing from the courtyard that adjoins the painter's house, a scratchy, vexing sound that works its way under my skin. The poor creature is trapped with a scattering of hens in the hennery where we gather our eggs to mix as a binder for the tempera pigments. The sky remains dark, but a rim of pink begins to outline the tall, narrow brick chimney pots of the house across the canal, framed by the narrow rectangle of the window.

I turn over in the bed gingerly, listening to Antonella's deep, regular breathing.

As far as I can tell, the concoction I drank four days ago has had no effect except to make me feel as though I have been flattened by a donkey cart full of mounded earth. All the energy has drained from my body. In the small hand mirror in our bedchamber, my reflection looks sallow, my eyes sunken, my lips parched and cracked. I look like death.

There has been no blood. My breasts are swollen and sore, my stomach constantly upside down with nausea. To be fair, little has happened. At times I have felt my abdomen heave and contract, but I have seen no red streaks in the undergarments that I have lined with layers of linen just in case. I have resumed my work in the studio as best as I can. If the painter, the journeyman, or the painter's wife has noticed my sunken eyes or my greenish complexion, they have said nothing.

As for Antonella, she looks worried. Each time I have passed through the kitchen, Antonella has pleaded with me in loud whispers to go see her cousin in Dorsoduro so that she can check me. I ignore her poisonous whispers in my ear.

I wonder what will happen next. The images and scenarios run through my brain like horses running in a hundred different directions.

I have heard about women who become pregnant in inconvenient circumstances. Some disappear for months, some forever. If the mother, or the child's father, is married to someone else, they may even be sent to the hell of the Doge's prisons. It happened to Carlo Crivelli, one of Our Most Serene Republic's most gifted gilders. I cannot imagine what my own future holds.

The cock in the courtyard has fallen silent, his awkward screeching replaced by the gentle chirping of what must be dozens of birds. I know I am supposed to get up and go to the church with the painter today. I wonder if I will be able to sit up without feeling like I will vomit. Slowly, I press my palm against the straw-stuffed mattress and push myself into a sitting position on the edge of the bed. Antonella stirs and runs her palms over her face as if to force herself to waking.

I remove my work dress and smock from the wooden chest that lies under the window. Turning my back to the bed, I remove my linen nightdress. I pull my work dress over my head, then push the black cord with the gold nugget into the front of my dress.

All I can think is that I must hide the reality of my situation. It is bad enough that Antonella knows of my predicament. I must not let anyone else know about it.

"What is that thing you wear around your neck?" Antonella leans up on her elbow in bed and attempts again to open a conversation.

"Nothing," I say, addressing her for the first time in three days. There are no words I could use to describe what it means.

She nods. "A gift from your man?"

I turn and shoot her a searing glance but say nothing.

Antonella sits on the edge of the bed and reaches her arm around my shoulder. I feel my body freeze under her touch, and I shrug her hand away. "You have not seen any blood yet? You are supposed to bleed at some point."

I cannot stay silent after all, and I turn to face her. "Maybe because it is not working!" I spit out the words in a loud whisper so that no one else in the house will hear. "Have you considered the possibility that your cousin is not what she claims?" All the anger that has been bottled up inside of me for days feels ready to burst from my body. I stand and yank the smock over my head and twist it around my body, fiddling with the ties behind my waist.

She stands and crosses her arms over her chest. Her hair is wild like a bird's nest, her linen nightshift a pile of wrinkles. "My cousin has helped many women; that is the God-given truth. They line up at her door to pay for her concoctions." She gestures emphatically, as if she is putting coins in someone's hand.

"Your cousin did not help me at all," I say. "All she managed to do was make me feel as if the pestilence itself had struck. And now the painter is wondering why I have been spending so much time in bed over the past days instead of working downstairs like I'm supposed to be."

"*Bene.*" She shrugs. "We told him you were not feeling well." I do not think that is so out of the ordinary. People get sick all the time," she says. She hesitates. "You did not tell him, did you?"

I look at her incredulously. "What? Why on earth would I do that?" I feel like I am screaming even though I am trying my best not to raise my voice above a whisper. I move close to her and point my finger right under her nose. "If you tell anyone about this, I swear..."

Antonella's eyes close to near slits, and she glares at my wrinkled brow, then she cuts her eyes to the side.

"Oh no," I say, feeling my shoulders sink. "You have already told someone..."

She raises her chin and shakes her head slowly. "Not to worry, *cara*. Your secret is safe. Trust me."

For a few moments, all we hear is the urgent cheeping of the birds as dawn breaks and light filters through the window. "You are the last person I trust," I say.

"*Vedi*," she says. "You are the one who chose to drink the potion. I did not force you."

I sigh and say nothing, realizing that she is right on that count.

She lowers her voice. "In case you are interested, I do know a *medico* who specializes in this type of thing. We can go to him and he can take more," she pauses, seeming to search for the right word, "drastic measures."

I look at her incredulously. "Oh no," I say. "I do not want you... influencing me... for one more second. Nor some kind of doctor who may not even be a real *medico*. Do not talk to me about it ever again. *Hai capito?*"

Her lips purse.

One floor below, I hear the painter's baby send up a hurling cry, and then the painter's son cries. "Mamma! Make her stop!" I hear rustling from the bedchamber below and the shushing sound of the painter's wife.

I give Antonella an admonishing look, then I open the door and walk with great conviction toward the stairway, hoping that no one can hear my heart thundering in my chest over the spine-tingling cry of the infant downstairs.

THE SECONDS SEEM to pass like hours as I wait outside the convent door where I have rung the brass bell. I cast my gaze away from the opening in the wall where women lay their swaddled packages, turn the wheel, then cover their faces and walk away. I cannot bear to think of it, much less lay my eyes on the opening under the benevolent gaze of the Madonna and child carved into the marble. Instead, I clutch my leather-bound sketchbook to my breast, study the cobblestones, and pray for one of the sisters to open the door.

At my back, the market street unfurls with fruit mongers, butchers, cobblers, and clothing merchants calling out to passersby, their voices trapped between the high walls lining the narrow alley. Two men press their way past me, their long black robes trailing fox or weasel fur to ward off the damp. Their women clomp behind them in the high-heeled clogs that look stylish while allowing them to avoid soiling their feet in the filth of the street. I glance down sheepishly at my own scuffed leather mules, one of two pairs I have owned since I have become fully grown.

"Ladies, look at these ripe figs!" A brawny fruit-seller bellows to the two finely dressed women as they pass. "*Mamma mia!* I challenge you to find anything fresher in Our Most Serene Republic!"

From across the alley, an old seller of straw brushes, his cheeks as gnarled as the trunk of an olive tree, roars back. "Fresher than your wife?" The ladies giggle, and one presses a lace-trimmed linen to her mouth as if to prevent anyone from seeing her smile. Then they follow their husbands, casting smiling eyes back at the bantering men.

Mercifully, at that moment a nun appears at the door. She pulls me into the dark warmth of the convent corridor, and I hear the iron lock latch behind us. Suddenly, I am transported to another world. The bustling streets and dirty canals fall away as I follow the nun's flapping habit down the dim corridor. Trevisan's boatman, whittling wood as he waits for me in the gondola just the other side of the high convent wall, suddenly seems far, far away.

From the corridor, I hear them singing.

I do not know how many women are assembled in the choir high above the main altar, but their voices lure me toward the sanctuary. The nun summons me with a hand gesture and a warm smile. I follow her into the otherwise empty church and seat myself on a wooden chair alongside a great pillar.

Above my head in the nuns' choir, the harmony of voices begins to fill me from my feet to the top of my head. I close my eyes, listening to their individual sounds become one, lifted up for the glory of God. I press the back of my head against the stone pillar, and for a few precious moments I feel my own burden begin to lift.

After a while, I open my eyes and look across the church at the blank space where our new altarpiece will go. I thumb through the drawings in the small leather-bound book in my lap. My own ill-drawn sketches do not begin to convey what I think Master Trevisan will paint, but when I imagine the panel's gilded surfaces sparkling in the candlelight, I feel peace. I send up a prayer for my father, my cousin, and my Cristiano, and I beg for them to be spared from the pestilence that has come to Cannaregio.

I know I must see my aunt for, though cloistered behind these walls, she may hold more information about my father, my cousin, and Cristiano than anyone else. I need to know of their welfare and so I come to see her, praying that she will not see me so changed.

But the truth is that I have delayed seeing her, for I feel that the moment she lays eyes on me she will know my situation. Surely a woman who has walked in my shoes, who has delivered a baby that she did not plan, will know immediately that I am with child. I do not know what to say. I do not know how I can begin to carry on a conversation without telling her my secret. My stomach has not yet begun to swell, but perhaps a woman like her could read it on my face?

The song ends, and I listen to the quiet shuffle of the nuns retreating from the choir. I close the leather binding of my sketchbook and make my way across the cavernous and now deafening silence of the church to the visitors' parlor.

"*DOLCEZZA*! FINALLY. I expected you long before now." I cross the threshold to see my aunt's face behind the swirls of iron.

"I am sorry, *zia*. The painter has kept me occupied with his commissions. It is only today that I could get away to draw some figures in the sanctuary. Master Trevisan has said it was important for me to sketch here so that I would feel the space." I gesture to my sketchbook. "Plus, I have been ill," I say, "but thankfully it has passed."

"*Grazie a Dio*." She crosses herself and wags her clasped hands in my direction. "I have news." My aunt produces a folded piece of parchment from the pocket of her habit. "Our confessor tells us that several houses on the via San Marco have been marked with crosses," she says. "We have heard that two ferries have lined up at the *traghetto* near Madonna dell'Orto to carry those from the quarter who are sick to the Lazzaretto Vecchio. Any family members without lesions are in quarantine at the Lazzaretto Nuovo. Father Pietro has written their names for me," she says, holding the parchment sheet in her hand at arm's distance and narrowing her eyes. "Bonito, Ozaki, Zen." She refolds the parchment and meets my eyes. "That is all I know."

I feel my heart drop and a tingle run up my spine. "Zen. I know the family. Their daughter and I played together as girls. God save them." Years ago, I crouched under the brick bridge near the bakery in the Campo Sant'Alvise with Daria Zen. Wide-eyed, she relayed the wondrous information she had learned from her older sister about what happens between a woman and a man. "It feels strange to be cut off from them completely when we are in the same city. I want so desperately to go and see them."

"I do not recommend it, *cara*," my aunt says, shaking her head. "The last thing you want to do is expose yourself. Besides, the *guardia* will not allow you to pass through the barricade."

"You are right, of course. It's just that... I cannot abide that they are there suffering and I cannot help them. My father has always been sickly. Poor Paolo, God bless him. But I am the one who cares for them, *zia*. How can they endure this horror without any help? Without *me* there to help them? Who else will do it?"

My aunt nods. "We have been ordered to pray ceaselessly until the mantle of the pestilence has lifted. Our abbess tells us that the Health Office is doing everything it can to stop the spread of the contagion, and that vigils have been organized within the convents and monasteries across Our Most Serene City for continual prayer. We can only hope that that is true. We are divided into groups and we take turns going into the church so that we may pray without ending. I have just finished my turn in the nun's choir. Of course I have put your father and all of you at the center of our prayers."

For a few long moments we sit together in silence on either side of the grille. I watch her finger the black glass rosary beads suspended from her waist.

She stares at me for a long moment. "No doubt you feel the loss of your man," she says.

The words hit me like a kick below my ribs. I swallow to push back the knot that has suddenly formed inside my throat, but it is too late. A tear spills over onto my cheek. Panicked, I wipe it away firmly with my sleeve and resolve not to let another one fall.

"*O cara mia,*" I hear my aunt say. "I am sorry."

I shake my head and take a deep breath, trying to rid myself of the image of his face, the smell of his neck that has just been conjured in my head. "I do not understand why Paolo fails to say anything about his welfare in his letters," I say.

"Paolo knows about this man?" My aunt pushes herself forward on the chair, and her brow wrinkles.

I nod. "Yes. He is our *battiloro*. My father took him into our house in the spring."

"This man lives in your own household?"

I nod again.

My aunt pushes her back against the chair and sighs. "I see. Well. I can see how you... became involved." She falls silent.

I lean forward and lace my fingers through the swirls of iron that separate us. "I do not remember my life before him, *zia*," I say. "I know it sounds absurd, for we have only known one another for a few months. But he is part of me."

"And your father surely knew all of this?" I see her brow wrinkle again below her veil.

I shake my head and try to steady my voice, which sounds like a squeak. "He only recently discovered it."

"Let me understand," she says. "Your father found this man fit enough to bring into his house and work alongside you. And then he discovered that you loved him, a man from your own trade, in your own household already. But he did not find this man fit enough for you to marry? To me it sounds like that might have been a logical solution for everyone, Maria."

I take a deep breath and sigh. "I know. But is more complicated than that, *zia*." I meet her green eyes. "Cristiano is a Saracen. Well, half-Saracen."

I see my aunt's mouth fall open, but no words come out.

"You can see then," I say. "It is not what my father would have planned for me," I continue, when my aunt says nothing. "Besides, I do not even know if he is still in my father's house. Perhaps he has sent him away, too."

"Well." My aunt wrings her hands and tugs at the rosary in her lap. "This is indeed complicated. My dear, I do not doubt that your love for this man is sincere. But surely you do not hold out hope that you... I mean, you do not believe that your father will agree to your marriage with this Cristiano?"

I feel the hot tears come again. As soon as she has spoken these words I know they are true. My father will never see it fit. I cannot begin to respond.

"Does the painter know?"

"*Santo Cielo*, no," I say, wringing my handkerchief. "The painter and his wife... they have no idea. The story is that I have been sent to learn the pigments. And Master Trevisan needed a gilder for his new altarpiece. Our *gastaldo* helped my father organize everything."

"But otherwise all is well in the painter's house?" My aunt changes her tone to one of happiness.

"Yes," I say, looking at my lap. "The painter and his wife are treating me well. I am beginning to learn the pigments, though truthfully, I am much more at home with the gold." Suddenly I remember the painter's gondola—and his boatman—waiting for me at the quayside. "I must get back to Trevisan's studio."

"Wait," she says. "I want to send you back with some of my *chiacchieri*. You must convey my appreciation to the painter and his wife for taking care of you during this... difficult time."

I watch my aunt's small frame disappear into the dim hallway. In the silence I feel the weight of the small life forming inside my body. I cannot bring myself to tell my aunt. It is more than I can admit and I have already told her more than I ever intended. But I can no longer lie to myself. As much as I may have spent weeks in disbelief, I can no longer deny the reality of it. I am with child, and there is no turning back.

Chapter 13

"Maria Magdalena."

The boatman opens his wide, calloused palm and offers it to me as I lift the hem of my skirts to step into the gondola.

"That is not my name," I say, catching my balance and eschewing the boatman's hand. I sit on the elaborately carved and lacquered wooden chair perched on the back side of the passenger compartment as the gondola sways gently. "Just Maria."

The boatman takes his place on the aft deck and presses the oar into the stone quayside, pushing the boat away from it. Then he presses the oar against the dark water and moves out from the narrow canal. The convent wall and the gaping opening of its foundling window fall from view as we move into the flat, open water of the canal.

The boatman projects a wad of spittle into the water and tries again. "But people call you Maria Magdalena all the time. No? How could they not?"

He is right, of course, but I do not concede that all my life people have likened me to that great sinner of the Bible, making the comparison either aloud or in their own heads. It is my fate that my hair falls down my back in waves the same way that Mary Magdalene is shown in thousands of altarpieces and painted miniatures. I keep it braided and neatly tucked into my cap as much as possible.

We turn into the Grand Canal, and the vast shimmer of the Venetian lagoon comes into view, with its infinite variety of boats. From the quayside near the Doge's palace, a consul is being escorted into a gilded gondola bedecked with golden birds and scarlet curtains. Beyond, several dozen cargo boats, private gondolas, and public ferries traffic the great basin that extends between the Piazza San Marco and the island of San Giorgio Maggiore. In the distance, a cadre of men is rowing a large ferry between Murano and San Marco.

"Maria Magdalena, just like her," the boatman tries to provoke me again. "No wonder you are the painter's new favorite." Above my head the boatman's paunch bulges over his leather belt, and he is chewing on something with gray, square teeth that make me think of the mules lined up near the docks where people travel to terra firma.

"The painter is seeing to my education," I say. I turn back to the vista in the canal, feeling the cool, damp air whip fine strands of hair across my mouth. I have been taught to distrust boatmen. Who has not heard their foul language echoing down the canals, seen them clapped in the stocks for smuggling goods or extorting passengers?

"Well," says the boatman, spitting again, "I would advise you to be cautious of that painter."

In spite of my better judgment, I ask, "Why do you say that?"

"I should know," he says, poking his thumb into his chest. "I have worked for the man for a long time. I tried to pry myself away from him for a while. Would not have come back at all if I had had any other choice."

"You left for another position?"

The boatman puffs air loudly. "I am a guildsman, and therefore I am bound to work for others, am I not? I know how to steer a boat, not much else. I am good at it, too, by the way."

"You have worked in the Arsenale?" I ask, gesturing toward the part of the city where our Doge's great shipyard lies. The Arsenale employs most of our men in the boatbuilding and related trades.

The boatman shrugs. "It is not so easy as people think to convince them to hire you," he says. I watch his fingertips brush the deeply burned scar in the flesh below his eye, a fleeting gesture of which I am not sure the boatman is aware. "Then there was no work at the ferry stations, and anyway, that painter would not agree to bear witness on my account, so..." He trails off.

"So you took your old position back," I say.

"You could say that," he says, "but mostly I came back because the painter owes me money. If I wanted any chance of getting back what he is bound to me, I had no choice but to return. Heh! *Casso!*" the boatman bursts suddenly, making a rude gesture with a meaty hand. I turn to see a cargo boat blocking the narrow canal where we are trying to pass. A skinny boatman is unloading crates from the grimy skiff onto a wooden dock on the back side of a shop. The boatman utters a stream of obscenities under his breath. The skinny boy turns around slowly to meet the boatman's gaze.

"You cannot dock there, *Sior*," the boatman yells, mocking a noble way of speaking by emphasizing *Sior* in Venetian with a sarcastic lilt. He spits into the canal through his square teeth. "What are people thinking?" he growls to me under his breath. I watch the skinny boy raise his hand in supplication, then back the skiff awkwardly out into the wide part of the canal. We resume our path.

"How does the painter owe you money?" I venture, not certain if I want to engage him further, but I am curious.

The boatman wends his way around the skiff and resumes rowing. "Normally I am paid my salary every fifteen days, but when I left he was already in debt to me by nearly three months.

We had already agreed on the contract. By my calculations he owes me for nearly a half year's worth of work."

"Why did he not pay you on time?"

"That is what I am trying to tell you, Maria Magdalena. "These people," he says, gesturing to the tall houses lining the canal, "they cannot be trusted. He was trying to retain me, to make me indebted to him."

"And surely you are."

He shrugs again, and one side of his mouth turns up. "At least he must trust me, for he has sent me out with a lady alone in a boat. Now that *is* a delicate proposition."

When I do not respond to his implication, the boatman falls mercifully silent. I want to wriggle out from under his scrutiny.

I feel a deep wake rock the gondola from side to side, and then a dark form on the canal catches the corner my eye. I turn to see a large ferry making slow progress in the direction of the outlying islands. The back of the boat is so laden with passengers and cargo that it seems as if the ferry might take on water.

"*Caxìn*," I hear the boatman's curse, barely above a whisper. He squeezes the oar under his arm and quickly crosses himself.

Even though I have never seen one, I recognize the boat immediately. It is one of the ferries that the Sanità is using to transport people to and from the pesthouse islands. The boat is sluggish and low, heavy with plague victims and their earthly belongings. As the boat draws nearer, I can see some of their sunken, beaten faces peering out of the boat. As the boat passes, a young boy turns his ashen face toward me.

I feel as though my insides have been turned out. A wave of nausea overtakes me, and all I can think is that I do not want to vomit on the painter's beautiful brocaded cushions. I stumble across the hull of the gondola and fall to my knees. I grip the varnished rim of the boat and hang my head over the green water, feeling the wave overtake me. The aroma of cabbage and rot fills my nostrils.

A long string of spittle hangs from my lips and drips bubbly into the canal. Then it passes. I push myself from the edge of the boat and slump down into the floor. I feel the wooden curve of the keel against my back.

I feel the boatman's eyes on me again, as if his gaze could sear a pattern on the skin along the back of my neck just as a mark has been etched into his face with a hot iron. I pull my shawl around me and cover my chest. I put my face in my hands, not wishing to encourage conversation.

Another wave of nausea overtakes me, and this time I am unable to stop it. Just in time, I grip the side of the gondola and vomit into the canal. I slump down against the side rail of the boat and wipe my mouth with the back of my hand. The boatman is wrinkling his nose. "*Che cazzo*?!" the boatman yells to me from his place at the stern the boat.

"The wake has gotten to me," I say.

I hear the boatman make a chortle deep in his throat. I look up at him, holding up my hand to ward off the winter angle of the sun that casts him in silhouette against the sky, his stocky frame and the oar framed in the haze.

"You are not seasick, Maria Magdalena," I hear the shadow say. I do not see his face in the glare but I imagine its sly look.

"You are with child."

MERCIFULLY, THE GONDOLA glides into the darkness of the painter's cave-like boat slip. I cannot get away from the boatman fast enough, but he has placed his body in front of the stepping stool that I must use to climb out of the boat.

"Perhaps the painter and his wife should know of your situation." The boatman's gravelly voice echoes off the walls of the *cavana.* In the shadows, I study the stubble along his chin and try not to rest my gaze on his scar.

"You would not dare."

His square teeth come into view. "I might... That is, unless I were offered something that would make it worth my while not to reveal the information."

I stop to consider his words. "You are extorting me."

The boatman makes a clucking noise. "*Estorsione.* A harsh word."

"I do not know what else to call it."

We stand in silence for a few moments, and I regard his brown eyes reflecting the wavering waters of the boat slip. The only sound is the lapping of the small waves against the stones.

"How much?" I say finally.

"*Bene.*" The boatman rubs his thick palms together. "I could be satisfied—for now—with one hundred silver *soldi*."

I stand in the rocking boat. "One hundred *soldi*! Who has access to such sums?"

"You may not have money, Maria Magdalena, but I hear that you are a gilder's daughter, no? *L'oro.* Now that is worth something."

My mind races. "You want me to give you gold leaf so that you can sell it. And in exchange, you will say nothing about me to the painter and his wife."

He nods, a smug smile on his face.

"And if I refuse?"

The boatman shrugs. "It is a simple transaction, signorina *doratrice*. You pay my fee. I seal my lips." He brings his fingers to his lips and gestures as if he is turning a key, then his mouth spreads into a wide grin.

Chapter 14

I make my way down the narrow stairs to the painter's studio, my body heavy and sluggish as though filled with rocks. For days it has taken all my strength to drag myself from bed when the cock crows. I have recovered from the utter horridness of Antonella's concoction, but exhaustion envelops me.

I have avoided the boatman at all costs and have spoken little to Antonella. I have tried to devise a way to keep them quiet that does not involve handing over the precious gold leaf I have brought with me from my father's studio, gold leaf forged with Cristiano's own hands. How could I not have seen that Antonella and that hateful boatman were in alliance? Why did I trust her? Clearly she has told him about my situation. What can I do to keep them from telling the neighbors, their friends—God forbid, the painter and his wife? I fail to imagine what will happen to me then.

I feel a pang in the middle of my ribs, a twist in my gut. I am resigned that this encumbrance is out of my control, that I have no more persuasion over it than I do to direct the dark hand of pestilence that has laid itself on my quarter of the city. I am resigned, but I do not know what my future holds.

Some mornings when I wake, for a moment I forget that I am with child. When the truth comes pressing in, I must catch my breath. It is difficult to believe the reality of the situation. I am only relieved that my aunt did not seem to read it on my face. I cannot imagine how I would form the words to tell the painter, his wife, my father, Cristiano. But I can no longer deny the truth to myself.

And if I go home with a swollen belly or a swaddled baby, will my father accept me? Will the *battiloro* still love me? Will he claim his child? Will I be thrust out into the street? I have seen the convent of the foundlings and I wonder if that is the fate that awaits me.

I want to go back to my life the way it was before—without the plague, without the pregnancy. For a moment, I permit myself to relive the delicious, heart-wrenching, bittersweet memory of Cristiano's broad hands on my hips. Without thinking, I bring my fingers to the hard outline of the gold ingot that I wear around my neck. I pull it out and twist the warm gold between my finger and thumb.

I think about what Antonella has told me, that she can take me to a *medico*, but I will not do it for anything. I will never again trust Antonella, the only one in the house who might have been my friend.

For now, there is only one person who might be in a position to help me, and that is the painter's wife.

"*BONDÌ*, SIGNORINA MARIA." Master Trevisan's journeyman offers an innocent smile as I enter the workshop. His skinny frame crouches before a large panel as he makes delicate strokes along the bottom of a cloak with a fine paintbrush, an imitation of embroidery trim on a rich textile pattern.

I grasp a leather apron from a hook on the wall and tie it behind my back. "Where is Master Trevisan?"

"He has gone to see a patron about a new commission for San Giacomo dell'Orio," he says. "They have asked for a large panel of one of their patron saints. I do not imagine that you will be working on that one. They have not asked for gold."

I nod, knowing that Father was right. I must learn the colored pigments if there is any future in our workshop. If I am ever to return.

I pull back my braids and tie them off with a small leather strap. I go to my worktable and resolve to work on drawing rocks and trees using the method that Master Trevisan has demonstrated for me. The worktable where I have laid out my meager gilding tools is cluttered with supplies from some previous apprentice: a stack of sketches on parchment and paper, several paint-splattered ceramic containers, a haphazard collection of pens and brushes caked with pigment. I fish through the jars with pens and the small glass containers of brown and red inks used for making washes. It feels as though the old apprentice has left suddenly on an errand and might be back any minute. I have not found it my place to clear the table.

Master Trevisan has shown me how to practice shading with the silverpoint pen and has laid out a number of his own sketches on the table so that I can use them as a model. I carefully observe the cross-hatching that he has used to render depth to a surface of a craggy rock. I do my best to follow the example laid before me.

The two of us work in silence, the journeyman at his painting and I at my sketching, but the air feels heavy and uncomfortable, full of words unspoken. It is the first time, I realize, that Trevisan's journeyman and I have been in the workshop alone together. We have hardly had a conversation without the painter in between.

He is the first to break the silence.

"I suppose you must miss your own workshop, your family," he says. He does not lift his brush or move his eyes from the panel, but his words hang heavy and ripe in the air.

"It is only my father and my cousin," I say. "And our *battiloro*."

"Ah yes, I remember," he says. "And your mother?"

"She died before my second year," I say. "Took my baby brother with her to the World to Come." With a small metal scraper, I scrub the ugly hatch marks I have made on the paper, trying to remove them from the page so that I can start again. "I have no memory of her." My answer must appear callous, I think, but my mother has been gone so long, the victim of a difficult labor and a stillborn child. Though I have tried my entire life, I cannot imagine her face and she is no more than a shadowy, fleeting figure in my mind. "For as long as I can remember, it has been only my father and my cousin Paolo," I say.

"My condolences," the journeyman says, pausing to look at me, his brush suspended in the air.

I shrug. "My father raised me. I have known nothing other than the gold." I muster a smile.

"But," he hesitates, "your father did not see fit to have you married? I mean..." He trails off, and I register the irrepressible curiosity on his face in spite of the discomfort of his asking. He tries again. "I mean that it is unusual for a girl such as yourself to be apprenticed rather than betrothed."

"Yes." I hesitate. Surely it is clear that I am well past the age at which many girls in the trades are married. Most of the guildsmen in my quarter had selected husbands for their daughters long before they became capable of bearing children; many of the girls I ran through the alleys with as children have already celebrated marriage masses. A few have begun to tote one or more babies on their hips.

For me, things were different.

I do not know how to begin to say any of this to the painter's journeyman, so I simply shake my head.

"You will return to your father then, when you are finished with Master Trevisan's commission?" he asks. I perceive a fleeting sense of worry in his voice. It has not occurred to me before now that the journeyman might feel threatened by my presence in his master's workshop.

My father's words ring inside my head. *When you return, Maria, we will have found a husband for you. We must not deceive ourselves any longer. It is past time.*

"Yes," I say to the journeyman. "Yes, I will return home without a doubt."

I retie the strings of my work apron behind my back and turn over a nub of charcoal, which immediately blackens my fingertips. "My father's agreement with the painter lasts for a term of eighteen months, but the contract may be extended if they both agree," I say. "And of course it depends on what happens with the pestilence."

The conversation has veered into uncomfortable territory and I am eager to change the subject, so I turn to another difficult question.

"The painter's wife and the children..." I say. "They have gone with Master Trevisan to see the commission?"

The journeyman snorts out a curt laugh. "*Santo Cielo, no.* The signora does not get involved in the master's work. Once every two weeks she takes the children to visit her parents. I have heard that, years ago, the signora showed interest in the master's work, at least enough of it to marry well. Marriage to a renowned painter like Master Trevisan; well, I am certain that you can see the advantages for a gilder's daughter. But now..." The journeyman has abandoned his painting and presses his thumb to his chin. "Between you and me, I believe that she would rather not get involved in the studio. And I am certain that she wants nothing to do with the people that Master Trevisan chooses to bring into the house, especially after what happened with that boatman and our old apprentice."

"The old apprentice," I hesitate. "What happened to him?"

The journeyman's eyes scan the clutter at my worktable. "Well." He sets down his brush, takes a deep breath, and turns his bright face toward me. "He was the son of one of the pupils of Master Bellini the Elder. A quiet boy with a talent for drawing figures," he says. "At least we thought he was quiet. It turned out he was just hiding something."

"Hiding?"

"Yes. On the surface he appeared conscientious. But later we discovered that he had been using his salary from Master Trevisan to entangle himself with a smuggling ring. They were bringing raw silk thread from terra firma, partially working it, then selling it for high profits." I hear thinly veiled excitement in the journeyman's voice. "They were going around the established trade channels for silk. They made a small fortune."

I feel my eyes widen. "How did they do that?"

The journeyman shrugs. "There were a group of them. They were smuggling in heaps of illegal raw thread; we learned of it only in retrospect. They were bringing it in on boats, hidden in sacks of grain or in coffers under layers of clothes."

The journeyman stands and, abandoning his picture, he begins to pace the room. "There's more," he says. "Our boatman was involved." He lowers his voice and gestures with his thumb toward the boat slip. "He knew about it. He was even carrying the thread in Trevisan's old gondola. He was skimming the profits."

I feel my jaw drop. "What happened?"

"They were caught," the journeyman says. "Boatman claimed he knew nothing about it, but I doubt that." He chuckles. "I mean, would *you* trust anything a boatman says? The authorities seized Master Trevisan's boat."

That explains why Master Trevisan has a new gondola, I think. "Is that how he got the scar…" I gesture toward my own cheek.

"No," the journeyman says. "I believe that boatman was marked with fire long before he came here. I suppose Master

Trevisan should have heeded the sign. But the apprentice," he continues, gesturing to my worktable. "He was supposed to pay his price with a sentence on the slave galleys, but then we heard that he fled the city with all that money, all his share anyway. I have no idea where he is now, but he got away with a lot of money. That's all I know." The journeyman shrugs and returns to his seat before the painting.

I realize that the former apprentice will not be back in Master Trevisan's studio. The space is mine for as long as I last here. The journeyman and I return to our silent work.

I walk over to the table where Trevisan keeps his charcoal, silverpoint pens, inks, and paper for sketching. I recognize the small collection of folios that Trevisan had brought along when we were in the boat on the way to the church. I open the cover and thumb through the sketches: a few images of Madonnas, a whole page of hand studies, some architectural details, the prow fork of his own gondola.

I pick up a pen and attempt to copy one of the hands that Master Trevisan has drawn. Under my breath I begin to hum, a kind of compromise for not being able to sing aloud like I used to in my father's workshop. I turn to see if the journeyman is watching me, but he is deeply engrossed in replicating embroidery trim.

I turn another page of Master Trevisan's sketchbook, then freeze.

There is a girl, a girl with long wavy hair, sitting in a boat. I turn another page and see another girl—or perhaps the same girl—this time sketched from behind. It could be any girl, I tell myself, but then I recognize a pleated detail from the bodice of my work dress appearing from beneath her smock. In a couple of the drawings the painter has even washed them with a rust-colored ink wash, remarkably the same auburn hue of my own hair.

My heart begins to race and I turn page after page after page. Dozens of sketches, all of them girls, all of them the same girl.

All of them are pictures of me.

Chapter 15

With a two-pronged fork, I pluck what I believe to be kidneys from a rock hen and place them on the rim of the earthenware plate before me. As much as there is something brash and raw about Antonella's character, she takes great care with dishes she prepares in Master Trevisan's kitchen. She has done her utmost to make the bird look appetizing, dressing it with soft sage leaves and a sliver of citrus, and spooning warm farro paste alongside it in an artful arrangement. The aroma of roasted onions and poultry fills the first floor of the painter's house. We do not eat like this in my father's house and normally I would approach such a meal with delight, but tonight I have little appetite. As much care as Antonella has taken, the sight of the creature's innards exposed, its limbs akimbo, the bumps where its feathers have been plucked, make me squeamish.

There is a visitor.

Master Trevisan has introduced the man to me as Pascal Grissoni, a fellow painter, and has led him to sit across from me at the table. The man is pulling apart the limbs of the rock hen with enthusiasm, so I steal a closer look. He is around Trevisan's age, I judge, with hair in dark waves brushed back from his temples. Beyond the door I hear Antonella's voice and the low rumble of the boatman's response; they are eating their own meal at the rickety table in the kitchen. I hear soft conversation broken by the occasional crackle of laughter.

"Grissoni is a pupil of Master Titian," Trevisan addresses me from the head of the table.

"But I have my own studio," the visiting painter says, puffing out his chest.

"Of course," says Trevisan. "Forgive me for giving the wrong impression. Master Grissoni is an accomplished painter of mythological subjects, not to mention portraits. He has a long list of patrician patrons. He has decided to give up the panels in favor of the new canvas."

"Canvas!" the painter's wife exclaims. "There is no more wood?"

The visiting painter laughs. "There is plenty of wood, signora. Master Titian has enough panels to last a lifetime and I can get one any time I want. He owns a lumberyard and a piece of forest in Cadore. But I have traveled with a contingent of painters from our guild to the Low Countries." Grissoni sets down his fork and leans into the table. "You must go there to fully understand it, signora. The guildsmen there are painting on canvases stretched over wooden frames. Truth be told, they are using canvas almost exclusively. Have no doubt, signora. Our patrons are beginning to ask us for canvas and I feel that the wooden panels shall fall from favor." Grissoni picks up his fork again and digs into his plate.

"We must see this, Master Trevisan," the journeyman says. He has already polished off nearly everything on his plate, pushing the last bits of onion and bird onto his fork with his fingers and shoveling them into his mouth.

Pascal Grissoni nods. "You should. In the Low Countries they have recognized the advantages of canvas over the wooden panels. It is lighter, and of course it does not warp. And the painters there are beginning to use oil-based paints over egg tempera. I am convinced that it is a better conduit for the pigments."

"But canvas…" I say, and suddenly everyone's eyes are on me. "It is too flimsy to support gold ground."

"Indeed," the visiting painter says. From the corner of my eye I see Master Trevisan study his meal. Everyone at the table falls silent.

The painter's wife breaks the awkward quiet. "Signor Grissoni, Maria's father is a well-respected master gilder."

Pascal Grissoni nods. "So our *gastaldo* has told me," he says, meeting my eyes briefly and smiling across the table. I feel my heart begin to pound, as the realization hits that this meal was planned with me in mind.

I do not touch my food.

Instead, I focus my gaze on the beautiful baby girl across the table from me. The painter's wife cuts the meat into tiny cubes and places them in front of her daughter, who chews and looks at her mother with eager, bright eyes. She works to grasp a small piece of poultry between her pudgy thumb and forefinger as her mother wipes her mouth. Beside her, Trevisan's young son pushes the bird around idly with his fork.

"We have news to share." The painter wipes his bushy mustache with a piece of linen, then looks at his wife as if to ask for permission to speak again. Her face flushes momentarily, then she gives a firm grin and nods.

"My Donata is carrying a baby," he says, beaming and grasping his wife's hand in his. She smiles and blushes in full now.

I hope that in the flickering candlelight they cannot see the look on my face.

"*Auguri*, Master Trevisan," says Pascal Grissoni, and raises his glass.

The journeyman beams. "Fantastic news!" he says, then looks at me, his eyes large and innocent, looking for agreement. "Isn't that wonderful, Maria?"

I feel at a loss for words, but they are all looking at me again and I feel I must say something. "*Che meraviglia*," I manage to say. I pick up my brass goblet and put it carefully to my lips, hoping they will not see my hand shake.

"That is the right word for it," the painter's wife says, nodding at me from across the table. "A miracle for certain. Truth be told, since little Besina was born I have not been successful in bringing a live child into the world. We have lost two pregnancies in quick succession. But maybe this time it will take hold."

"Yes, hopefully a boy this time, a boy to inherit my studio," the painter says.

"You already have one," the painter's wife says, ruffling little Gianluca's hair. "And anyway, girls are capable of working along-side their fathers," she reminds him. "Am I right, Maria?" She looks at me and nods.

"Of course," the painter says. "I did not mean to offend you," he says to me. "It is just that... Well, from the point of view of inheriting a studio..."

"My father's studio is my own," I say, interrupting him. "Of that I am certain."

"Of course it is. Up until you marry," says Trevisan's wife, her eyes skirting over to Pascal Grissoni and then to her children, as if she does not know where to settle her gaze.

Strained silence falls over the table again. "Well," says the jour-neyman, "that may be true since your father does not have a son. But he already has two men working with him, does he not?"

"Yes," I say, "my cousin and the *battiloro*, but I am the blood child. "Surely that carries more weight." It is the first time I have put forth this long-held opinion, and also the first time I doubt it.

"For certain trades perhaps you are right," Pascal Grissoni says. "But it is the dream of everyone to have a son to pass the studio onto—and the name."

I am not hearing them now. I am only thinking about the life forming inside my own body.

"To bring a son into the world," says Trevisan, "is a feeling that cannot be described. It must only be experienced firsthand."

"Maria, you have hardly eaten a bite," the painter's wife says. "Are you feeling ill again?"

I shake my head and blush, trying to find the words.

"Oh dear!" she scolds her husband, shooing him with a linen napkin. "You have caused her to be upset with all this talk about girls not being able to inherit their father's studios."

"*Si figuri*, signora," I say, mustering a smile. "The meal is delicious as always. I am afraid I am still not feeling very well."

In truth, I feel horrible. I dream of climbing under the warm blankets on the bed and pulling them over my head, closing my eyes, and never waking up. As dinner mercifully ends, I excuse myself, and watch the look of disappointment pass over the visiting painter's face as I nod my farewells and push the door into the kitchen.

I place my plate on the wooden block near the hearth. At the cramped table near the door to the boat slip, Antonella and the boatman sit across from one another, their heads together. When I enter they immediately break apart. Antonella rises and reaches for my plate.

"It was delicious—thank you," I say, heading toward the stairs.

"One would hardly know; you barely touched it. Master Trevisan spends enough on food. Seems a waste to feed it to the cats in the alley."

I ignore her comment and climb the stairs. She shrugs and takes a piece of meat from my plate, stuffing it in her mouth.

As much as my desire for the mercy of sleep, it is hard work moving my legs up the steep back staircase to the servant's quarters in the painter's house. I grip the rickety handrail for support and stop every once in a while as I feel that I will vomit.

When I reach the room, I quickly remove my dress and pull the linen shift over my head. I push myself under the woolen blankets and the nausea abates. I am already asleep by the time my head settles on the mattress.

HOURS LATER, AFTER Antonella has finished with her chores and enters the room, I awaken feeling disoriented. For a moment I perceive that I am in my own bed in my father's studio until a new wave of nausea overtakes me, and I sit up on the edge of the bed. As soon as I am vertical it wells up, and I am lucky enough to slide the copper chamber pot from under the bed before I vomit into it. I stand and open the window, dumping the contents into the canal four stories below. I feel heat spread across my cheeks as Antonella watches me cross the room to rinse the pot with the water from the pitcher.

"I am sorry," I say, sliding the metal pot back under the bed. I feel the cold air swirl around my ankles and I push myself back under the pile of woolen blankets. "If I could stop myself from vomiting I promise I would."

"You are sick. It is normal for women in your condition. I have been cleaning a mess from the painter's bedchamber for weeks now. You and the painter's wife must have conceived around the same time."

"You are not very good at keeping secrets about other women's bodies," I say.

"What does that mean?"

I turn to face her in the bed. "You told him!"

"I do not know what you are talking about," she says.

"That boatman. He knows. You are the only one other than myself who is aware of... things."

"It may have slipped out," she admits.

"Why would you do that?" My voice rises to a loud whisper.

"I imagine that it will not be hidden much longer, *cara mia*. Hard to keep a secret such as that."

Antonella and I lie in silence for a long time, pretending to sleep but both painfully awake and staring at the ceiling. I watch the reflection of moonlight on the canal make wavering patterns on the ceiling, and I think about the irony of the painter's wife having a baby in the painter's studio, and myself outcast from my own, my family and my man unaware of my situation.

"Who is the father?"

Antonella's whispered question sounds loud and important in the dark silence of the bedchamber.

I shake my head even though she cannot see me in the dark. Then I turn my back to her and close my eyes, feeling them sting against the heels of my hands.

Chapter 16

Signora Trevisan is mending her daughter's dress by the light of an oil lamp, the children having been put to bed. I hesitate on the landing of the stair and watch her silhouette through the half-open door to the painter's private chambers.

For the first time, one of the doorways of the *piano nobile* stands partly ajar. I dare not take another step in case the wooden planks should creak under my foot. I crane my neck to peer inside. The painter's wife is framed by an arched opening behind her. I perceive a richly patterned textile on the wall, a stone parapet overlooking the canal, and flecks of dust hanging in the evening light.

"Stefano? Is that you?" The painter's wife seems to sense my presence.

"It is I, signora." I take two steps forward. "Maria."

Signora Trevisan lays her mending on the side table and stands awkwardly, pressing her stomach forward as if it is already heavy with child even though she shows no sign yet. When she reaches the door she pulls it nearly closed behind her, her hand resting on the knob. The narrow glimpse of the Trevisans' private bedchamber disappears again behind the heavy door.

"Is something the matter?"

"Excuse me for disturbing you, signora. I..." I hear my voice echo in the stairwell and I am rendered nearly mute. "I want to apologize for having spent so much time in bed of late. I have not been feeling well."

Signora Trevisan makes a clucking noise with her tongue, then brings her thumb to my chin. She raises my face to the waning light that remains in the corridor and I dare to take in her blue eyes, her creamy, fair skin. For a long moment, she peers into my eyes. "You seem quite recovered now," she says, lowering her hand.

"Yes," I say, hesitating again. "Thanks be to God. It's just... I feel remorse on your husband's account. It was not my intention to miss days of work in the studio. I fear that I have not lived up to Master Trevisan's expectations. I did not have a choice, you see... The malaise..." I gesture to my stomach. I hear shuffling in the stairwell above me, and I pause.

I watch the signora's mouth pull into a thin line and she seems to bristle uncharacteristically. "I cannot speak to the affairs of the workshop. Those arrangements are entirely between Master Trevisan and your father." She blanches. "And our *gastaldo*," she adds. "I cannot... I am busy managing my children and my household."

"Of course, signora," I say.

"When you have your own husband and children, you shall see."

I feel my face flush and I muster a laugh that comes out almost as a cough. "That may not be for some time. I..."

The thin lips turn into a smile that is almost a grimace. "Then I would advise you to do your best to rouse yourself and take advantage of the opportunity that the men have arranged for you. It is more than my father ever did on my account," she adds under her breath. It has not occurred to me that the painter's wife might trade fortunes with me if she could. "Your father must care very much for your welfare."

"Yes. You are right, of course, signora. I am most grateful for it."

The painter's wife nods. "Well. I am pleased that you are improved." She leans on the doorknob, and with this small gesture, I feel that I have been dismissed. I turn for the stairs.

"Maria."

I pause.

"In the future, if you are taken to your bed, Antonella can recommend a *medico* amongst her kinsmen. We have had him tend to our servants before."

I feel the skin on the back of my neck prickle. "Thank you," I manage to say.

"You may rely upon her support. I trust her with my own children." Signora Trevisan gives me a final nod, then presses the door and latches it behind her.

The stairwell is cast into darkness and although my eyes are wide open, I see nothing but black.

I HAVE WAITED until there is no more sound from the upper floors to pull out my books of gold leaf. One by one, I count the thin packs of gold leaf stored beneath my worktable in the painter's studio. The gold feels reassuring and familiar in my hands, the nearly weightless sheaves that flash and reflect in the candlelight as I turn over the vellum dividers with my thumb.

The last thing I want to do is bribe the painter's servants, but I feel that I have no choice. How else to keep that boatman's mouth closed until I can divine my path? When the painter and his wife discover my situation, surely they will expel me from the house, but where am I to go? I cannot return home with the streets closed for contagion. I do not want word getting back to my father and my house before I can reach them; certainly not before I can get to the *battiloro* myself.

I need time to reach them, time to figure out a solution. Until then, those servants must remain silent.

In my mind's eye, I see Cristiano on the day he first arrived in my father's workshop, the old goldbeater's assistant now grown into a man. His face was agitated. He told my father that old Master Zuan had fallen ill, barely clinging to life. Of all the people in the world the old man had called my father to his bedside. My father dropped the brushes he was using to gild a small panel of Saint George, and followed the young man down the path to the old goldbeater's studio.

My father was gone for a full day while my cousin and I continued our work. He returned late that night after the flames of the lanterns in the *campo* had been extinguished. I called out to my father from my bed. He lit a candle and whispered that the old man had passed to the World to Come. I pushed myself under my woolen blanket and crossed myself, saying a prayer for the old goldbeater's soul.

The next morning I awoke to find the goldbeater's assistant in our house. His broad shoulders filled our doorframe, and his head nearly reached the rough beams over our table. My father engaged two young guild apprentices from our neighbor's larger workshop to help transport the wooden stump, hammers, and other supplies from the goldbeating studio. Paolo, not being able to lift heavy loads, scuttled back and forth excitedly as the men transformed the courtyard behind our house into a goldbeating studio over the course of a day.

The *battiloro* set up his supplies on the wooden table in the small courtyard garden. I washed out copper pots in the canal behind the house more slowly than I had ever done before, curious to watch the Saracen goldbeater organize his tools. He gave me a wide smile when I asked if he needed anything, and when I expressed my sorrow over the loss of old Master Zuan.

My father mounted the ladder leading to the old wooden loft above our hearth, cleaning out years of clutter. I was tasked with dusting the cobwebs and creating space for the rough-hewn wooden bed and straw-stuffed mattress dragged from the old gold-beater's studio. By nightfall, we had a new member of our household. By the next day, we also had a new way of working that changed everything.

From the far reaches of the shelf under my worktable in the painter's studio, I gather the sheaves of gold leaf and calculate how many I will need for Master Trevisan's altarpiece commission. How many can I spare to pay the boatman? I pry a few sheets from one of the books and place them inside a small bag with a drawstring. How many could I afford to pry away before it becomes clear that something is missing?

"Still awake?"

I stifle a scream. Antonella. I thought she had already retired to our bedchamber, but she is standing at the door, leaning on a mop handle, a small metal bucket in the other hand. My heart races in my chest.

"You startled me." I whisk the rest of the gold leaf books to the shelf under the table, but not before she has seen me counting them, I think.

"Accounting for your work?"

"It... it is for our panels," I say. "I brought some things from my father's workshop."

Antonella nods, then smirks. "Well. While you are here just make sure you get paid yourself." She has understood that it is gold leaf.

"What do you mean?"

"Let us say that the painter has not always been reliable. Boatman," she says, lowering her voice to a whisper and gesturing toward the door that leads to the stairs of the boat slip, "has only returned to the house recently. He left because he was so poorly treated. That painter... They had a row. Boatman was even put into the stocks for a few days because of him."

"Is that how he got the...?" I touch my cheek just below my eye.

"No," she says. "That happened long before he came here. A hateful old woman accused him of stealing and it was her word against his. He was too young for the branding iron but there was no one to defend him. An injustice," she says, shaking her head. "Anyway, boatman does not trust that painter. Now he has agreed to come back, but Master Trevisan has yet to pay him what he's owed. He is holding back some of the money to try to keep him here." She puts her hand on her hip and places her dark eyes on me. "That's why you must be careful."

"I am being paid with instruction, not with money," I say, immediately regretting sharing this information. In fact, I wish I could close my ears and not hear this woman's poisonous words. I have said too much. Servants have a reputation for inciting trouble but I have little experience knowing how to navigate their schemes. We never had servants of our own.

"Count yourself lucky," Antonella says. "Those of us who are paid with money must chase it."

"I am sure that is not for me to know," I say, closing the drape over the shelves under the table and starting for the door.

Antonella's face comes close to mine as she leans on her mop handle for support. Her voice lowers. "I am telling you because you must use caution and be smart with him," she says, gesturing toward the door where the painter has disappeared to the upper floors. "And do not get me started on the wife," she says, rolling her eyes. "She can hardly stop herself from talking, but watch your back. She only cares about herself and her status with her husband's patrons, trying to push her husband up in the guild ranks. He would not have the courage to do it himself."

She twists the mop over a metal bucket, releasing dirty grey water into it, then drags the damp rags over the uneven surface of the tiles. The not-unpleasant aroma of vinegar fills the room.

"She has been kind to me," I say, wondering if Antonella has overheard my strained conversation with the painter's wife in the stairwell.

Antonella pauses her mopping. "She is full of sweet talk with you right now," she whispers, "but be careful. She would have had boatman sent to the Doge's prisons in the batting of a cat's eye." She makes a flicking gesture with her hand. "But the painter has a kinder heart. Plus, he is weak."

We hear footsteps on the ceiling above us. Antonella's voice lowers to a barely audible whisper.

"I am telling you this as your friend. Trust me. Watch yourself with those two," she says. "Especially the wife." She picks up her bucket. I watch her press her palm to her lower back and hobble out of the room.

EVEN THOUGH I no longer expect to find my Cristiano in the monks' garden behind San Giovanni Elemosinario, I still go there every Friday evening, just to be sure.

For a while, I sit on the stone bench and look up into barren branches of the birch tree that once sheltered our stolen kisses. I cast messages to him into the vast grey sky, hoping that somehow my words may travel over the narrow *calli* and canals, that somehow he can hear my silent pleas to keep the pestilence at bay, the cry that together, we have created life, a fact that wants to burst from me with a force beyond my reckoning.

In the markets, all has gone to grey. Normally, the end of Carnival heralds the beginning of spring. But this year, the last burst of Carnival festivities ended with a stammer, and now everything seems returned to winter, to silence, to grey.

I have also written a letter. My Cristiano does not read, not having had the benefit of the education my father and my cousin thought fit to indulge me in as a child. I finger the parchment pages that I have folded into the pocket of my felted cape. I have written down everything I can think to say to my father and my cousin— details of our work in the painter's studio, descriptions of my visits to my aunt and her convent, news of the painter's pregnant wife. What I want to say most is what is missing, what is still held only inside my heart.

Chapter 17

"Signor Grissoni's father is a well-respected guildsman."

The painter's wife bounces her baby girl on her lap. In recent days Donata has been spending more time inside the painter's workshop, pacing the room with the baby in her arms, flitting about with a feather duster, or making small adjustments to the arrangement of paintbrushes on the table. "And his mother," she says, "came from a highborn family in San Polo."

"Mostly he is talented with the pigments," says the painter, looking up at his wife from one of the sketchbooks where he has collected pages of drawings of my hair, my face, my hands, long before I realized he was doing so. The painter has turned to a fresh page and is working through the arrangement of figures composing a Lamentation. My eye goes immediately to the figure of Mary Magdalene, which he has begun to sketch over and over in his book.

"I am sure that is true, though I have never seen his work," his wife says. "But owing to his family pedigree anyone would be fortunate to be allied with him."

I say nothing, not knowing how to respond. It is clear now that the appearance of Pascal Grissoni at our dinner table had little to do with painting, and mostly to do with the seeming need for me to wed, with arrangements that are being made for me outside of my own view. A marriage with Pascal Grissoni or any other painter is the last thing on my mind. I cannot begin to imagine what any husband would say about my condition.

I turn my focus to the small scrap panel where I have been practicing painting drapery folds with various tones of red. Master Trevisan follows my gaze, then comes to stand so that he can look over my shoulder. In the beating silence, he watches my hand move slowly and awkwardly with the brush.

"Hmm," he says, pressing his fist to his mouth as if to prevent himself from blurting a comment. "Allow me." I hand him the paintbrush. He picks up a small bead of amber-colored pigment, then traces a fine line along the edge of one of the drapery folds I have begun to form. "Do you see how this highlights the edge of the umber?"

The truth is, I do not see. I simply nod. "Yes," I say. "*Grazie.*"

He puts the brush back in my hand. I try to replicate what he has just shown me. The painter nods, then presses his hand over my own in order to direct my brushstroke. I feel his warm breath at my neck, and smell a hint of perspiration over the egg-like scent of the pigment binder.

"You will master it, I assure you," the painter tells me. "We have at least a year to get it right." He raises his eyebrows at me and grins. "Fortunate for us. Am I right, Donata?"

"Yes," the painter's wife says, and her lips spread out to a thin-lipped smile that looks pained. "*Fortunata.*"

"Bring me the red ink wash," says the painter to his journey-man before returning to his sketchbook.

Stefano rises from where he is seated in the corner, stabbing green on some trees in the background of a picture of the Madonna and Child that they are preparing for the confraternity of drapers. As he passes the canal-side door, the brass bell outside of it jingles.

"Signor Baldi," the journeyman says, opening the door. In the frame of the doorway I recognize a familiar face and feel my heart lighten.

"Baldi!" the painter smiles. "You are a welcome sight."

Signor Baldi, a carpenter from my old quarter in Cannaregio, steps into the painter's studio, followed by three of his sons. The carpenter is a shaggy-looking stray dog of a man with a gaggle of children too large to count. Since his wife died in childbirth last year, he has employed all of his children, even his twin toddlers, in his dilapidated yet bustling carpentry studio several streets away from my father's. I never thought I would be so happy to see anyone.

"I have brought your panels, painter. And your new lantern." He gestures to a small skiff docked at the painter's wooden mooring. Cold, damp air rushes in from the canal and I peer through the open door to see the dingy boat filled with a stack of poplar panels of the kind we use to paint and gild for altarpieces and other works.

"At last. Excellent. Please... bring them in."

Signor Baldi gestures to his sons to bring in the panels. The carpenter's sons, all three handsome boys in the flush of youth, bring in the panels one by one. The journeyman follows to help them, then shows the boys where to stack the hulking wooden panels along the wall.

"Maria." Baldi removes his hat and approaches my table. "There you are. We have heard that you were here working with Master Trevisan." He fidgets with his hat, running his grubby fingertips along the brim of the green felted wool. His face is prematurely lined, and he brushes his thinning, wheat-colored hair away from his forehead as if he is suddenly worried about his appearance.

"Yes," I say. "Since Epiphany I have been here."

"I saw your father," he says. "Some time ago. I brought him some of the small alder wood panels he likes, you know the ones."

He gestures as if to convey the idea of a small square. "He told me that you were coming here."

"You have seen my family?" I interrupt. "You have been in the workshop?"

The carpenter's face darkens and a grim expression passes over his face. "It was more than two months ago now, I suppose," he turns to me. "Before they began to block the streets."

"You saw my cousin? And Cristiano—our *battiloro*?"

"*Sì*," he says. "They were all well when I saw them." I feel all the breath flow out of me.

"It was good timing for Maria to come join us here," the painter's wife says, "given the spread of the plague in Cannaregio."

"Fortunate indeed, Signora Trevisan," says the carpenter. "Yesterday I heard that they have docked two passenger ferries at the *traghetto* in Santa Croce, and two more at Rialto. They are beginning to ferry people to the plague islands."

"*Madre de Dio!*" the painter's wife exclaims.

The eldest son, a lean boy of about twelve, sets an ornately carved wooden lantern on the worktable. His father says, "We will be back with the battens to fasten together the panels after you have prepared them, Master Trevisan. In the meantime, we have finally finished the lantern for your new gondola. Please forgive our delay."

The painter pats Baldi on the shoulder and brings the lantern to my worktable. "A work of remarkable beauty. Maria, this one is for you to gild." I examine the ornate wooden contraption, a four-sided, lidded container for an oil lamp that may be hung from an iron hook on the aft deck of the gondola so that the craft may be seen at night. I run my hands over the finely carved swirls and leaf patterns that the carpenters have crafted along the sides and the lid. I can already imagine the lantern gilded, swinging suspended above the boat where it glitters in the night.

"The loveliest thing!" exclaims the painter's wife.

"Exactly as I wanted," says the painter.

"I know how proud you are of that new boat," the carpenter says. "I would not have done my job if I had not tried to match the craftsmanship of the gondola."

Trevisan smiles. "You have succeeded, and that is no simple task. You may know that the gondola came from the Squero Vianello, perhaps the best boatyard in Our Most Serene City."

I step out from behind the table, eager to turn the conversation back to my family. "What does that mean, that the boats are lining up at the *traghetto?*"

Signor Baldi returns to my table and presses his knuckles on it. The creases in his face deepen as he chooses his words. "It means that the officials from the Health Office are taking the sick out of the neighborhood and to the old *lazzaretto* before the pestilence spreads any further," he says. I feel my heart begin to pound. "The sick are being coerced to board at the ferry stations. They and the contents of their houses."

"And they are burning people's stuff!" The carpenter's youngest son has been distracted by the tools on Trevisan's worktable and has stopped helping his older brothers. He runs his dirt-stained fingers over the metal scrapers as he sets his wide brown eyes on me. I sense wonder, if not fear, in them.

His father steps in. "The belongings from the houses where the pestilence has struck are being sent to the Campo Sant'Alvise to be burned on the pyre." My heart begins to pound as I imagine the small public square nearest my father's house. "It is a normal measure to stop the spread. There is some rumbling that Our Most Excellent Prince will soon declare a *quarantena*. If he does, then the war galleys and merchant ships must anchor in the lagoon for forty days before mooring. That way they ensure that no one is sick before disembarking."

"*Santo Cielo*, a quarantine! It is getting worse!" The painter's wife rushes to her husband's side and grasps the widest part of his arm for support.

"I do not know that it is worse than in past outbreaks, signora, but ever since Our Most Beloved Prince was struck down the *Sanità* seems to be taking it seriously." I have heard people speak of Our Most Excellent Prince Giovanni Mocenigo, who fell to the pestilence just a few years before my birth. Signor Baldi continues. "The Lords of the Council seem to be taking measures to ensure that it does not spread like it did the last time."

"I hope they are successful this time," says the painter. "We cannot afford to have our population decimated as has happened in the past."

Baldi shakes his head. "An unpleasant job; I do not envy them. My cousin told me that the men assigned to Cannaregio—the ones who are being paid to record the names of the sick and manage the ferry transportation to the pesthouses—are having a difficult time convincing people to leave."

"Who would want to leave their home and go to one of those God-forsaken *lazzaretti*?" The painter's wife's voice has lifted to a high-pitched plea. She clutches her baby tightly against her body.

"They are going to have to start paying people to leave," says the carpenter's oldest son. "That is what the baker told me."

"The doctor does not come and visit them when they get sick?" I ask. Everyone looks at me with wide eyes.

"Doctor?" says Trevisan's journeyman, shaking his head. "What can a *medico* do? What can anyone do?" He shrugs his skinny shoulders toward his ears. "In the end it is futile to fight the pestilence. Once such a scourge gains a foothold there is no stopping it."

ANTONELLA IS ALREADY in bed when I step into the dark room. I quietly remove my dress in the cold, then pull my linen shift over my head and slide under the woolen blankets. I feel Antonella stir beside me.

She clears her throat and speaks softly in the darkness. "The wife is spending more time in the studio than usual."

The moon casts just enough glow for me to see half of Antonella's face, a smooth arc of light in the darkness. "I have noticed. I do not know why," I say.

Antonella turns toward me, propping her body on her elbow so that the light illuminates all of her face. She makes a soft snorting sound under her breath, almost a laugh. "Is it not obvious? You have turned the painter's head."

I puff air in disbelief and meet her gaze. "What are you talking about?" I say. "That cannot be true."

"Why would he not be smitten?" she says, her large black eyes shiny and flashing in the moonlight. "A beautiful young woman like yourself in a tradesman's workshop. Talented with your hands as well as beautiful. And that hair!" Antonella reaches out and grasps a few strands of my hair that have escaped my braid, turning them between her thumb and forefinger. She picks up my braid to catch the shine in the moonlight, then lets it fall back across my shoulder. I turn onto my back so that my braid presses into the mattress, out of her grasp.

"I can assure you that I have done nothing to lure him," I say. I sink my back into the mattress and press my forearm over my closed eyelids. Suddenly my mind is flooded with the sketches I discovered in Trevisan's notebook, dozens of small renderings of my hair, my hands, my face.

"Well. Whether he is lured or not, the important thing is that the painter's wife thinks her husband is being tempted. She has told me that much herself."

"What?" I sit up in bed and turn to look at her incredulously. "When?"

Antonella shrugs. "We spend a lot of time together, the painter's wife and I. And, as you have seen, she is not very good at keeping things to herself." Antonella reaches out to finger a strand of my hair again. "She has asked me to keep an eye on you."

Chapter 18

Over the San Pietro canal, the heavens hang low and heavy like a great blanket of grey. Winter's chill has disappeared, replaced by an atmosphere both still and stifling. The ominous swath of sky seems to press down from above, as if the heavens themselves have announced the end of *Carnevale* and the ushering in of the Lenten season. It is the type of calm that spreads out languorously just before the rending of the clouds, the silence before the storm.

In the eerie stillness, all of us—the boatman, the painter, the journeyman, and myself—remain silent, too, as the gondola slices the still waters toward the Church of San Vidal, where Trevisan wants us to see the work of his father. His father, he has told us, painted this same subject of the Lamentation years ago. We must make a pilgrimage to the church, Trevisan has said, in hopes that it might spark inspiration. I watch the striped façades clip by as if for the first time, reflected upside down in the mirror-like canal as slick as glass, wavering and shimmering in the wake.

Inside the passenger compartment the painter and his journeyman speak in whispered tones. Through the curtain I see Trevisan's leather sketchbooks propped on the seat beside him. I have positioned myself outside the passenger compartment, choosing to perch on the wooden seat near the aft deck. Above my head, the new lantern, gilded with my own hands, swings gently with each push of the oar. Trevisan was thrilled with the result, he told me. It made the gondola seem complete, thanks to my contribution of this finishing touch.

The boatman presses his feet into footrests so that he can better counteract his weight against the oar. Here, on the wooden chair outside the passenger compartment, I feel that I can breathe. Over the past week my undergarments have begun to tighten across my midsection. I have stretched some of the stitching, while at the same time I have bound the swaths of linen more tightly around my middle. I feel that if I move behind the curtains of the passenger compartment, pressed with the stifling air, my nervous energy will overflow.

There is no putting it off any longer.

From deep inside the pocket of my felted wrap I pull out a small woven drawstring bag, one that carried the last of the coins my father gave me, and I have now emptied to make room for the sheaves of gold leaf I have packaged neatly in a cloth. I feel the rough weave of the bag in my palm, nearly weightless in contrast to the value inside.

I set my gaze on the boatman's stubbled face, but it takes a few moments for him to realize that I am trying to catch his eye. When he finally looks down from the horizon to my direction, I wave my fingers slightly and cut my eyes to the bag in my fingers. He nods, a silent acknowledgment. The painter and his journeyman, who I can see from the corner of my eye, remain placid inside the passenger compartment, ignorant of the impending transaction.

I reach up and place the bag in the open tracework of the gilded lantern. It remains there for only a second. With one swift motion, the boatman snatches it from the lantern. With one foot, he slides back a board on the aft deck to reveal a small under-deck compartment. He drops the package in, then closes the compartment.

It is done.

I turn my back to the boatman and cross my arms over my chest. I return my attention to the reflections of the façades in the water. In this wordless exchange I feel as dirty as the canal waters. I wish to leave the boat and return home to wash myself.

As we turn into the wide basin of the lagoon, a soft breeze emerges from the stillness and stirs my hair. Through the haze at the horizon, the outline of the old plague island comes into view. I recognize the hazy, cragged outline of the walls on the small island they call the Lazzaretto Vecchio. The pesthouse stands on what appears from this distance to be nothing but a shifting piece of land in a vast basin of water. Narrow funnels of smoke swirl upward from the tall chimneys, dissipating and collecting with the expanse of grey sky.

In the distance, a handful of merchant ships and galleys are moored in the lagoon. It is as the carpenter has said. Our Most Excellent Prince, Doge Leonardo Loredan, has already declared a *quarantena*. The poor souls on those boats must remain in the lagoon, within sight of our city's rooftops, for forty days before they are allowed to disembark. If anyone on one of the ships breaks out in black boils or evinces fever, they are transported to the *lazzaretti* and may never set foot in the city they can see from the decks of their ship.

I thank God that I have a place on our waterlogged land and not on a crowded merchant galley. I watch the line of sails, still against the murky sky, and I cannot imagine what it must be like to be confined to a galley for forty days, in sight of land but not able to feel it under my feet.

I feel my heart begin to pound as malaise rises up within my core. Beyond the silhouette of the islands on the horizon, I cannot turn my gaze away from the quarantine lineup of grey sails and ship hulls, a great and horrifying armada of death.

"SHE IS A quiet girl. Guarded, you might say."

The painter's voice. I stop in my tracks, my hand on the door to the studio. I press my ear to the wood and the voice continues.

"It is difficult to know whether she is content to be here with us. However, she has been diligent in practicing everything I have shown her. She shows promise."

"I assure you, Master Trevisan, that Maria possesses intelligence and a high level of skill with the gold. Her father, as you know, is one of our guild's most esteemed gilders." I suck in my breath. I recognize the second man's voice, too. It is our *gastaldo*, the head of our guild, a lifelong friend of my father's. "I am certain that her skill with the pigments will only be a natural outcome of her training."

The painter's voice again. "She is young and I believe you are right in attesting that she will be an asset wherever she settles after my contract with her father is finished."

"She has met Pascal Grissoni." The *gastaldo*'s voice again.

"Yes," Trevisan says. "We invited him for dinner. They did not spend much time together. She was feeling ill that night." I feel my heart begin to race.

"Good. Grissoni is one of our guild's most promising members. He learned well under our Master Titian and has established his own workshop."

"*Perdona?*" I open the door with a tentative push. The two men turn toward the door.

"There she is! Maria." The *gastaldo*'s eyes light up. Aureo dalla Stava is an old man, perhaps in his fifth decade, with a swath of grey hair that frames his fleshy face. At a younger age he was no doubt strong, and he remains sturdy and broad across the shoulders. He is a kind soul who has been reelected several times because he has proven himself to do what is fair for the members of our guild. All of the painters and gilders respect him. He is diplomatic and knows all of us who work in the related trades of gilding and pigments.

"*Gastaldo*," I say. "I thought I heard a familiar voice."

He grasps my hands. "I have come on your father's behalf."

"You have seen him?" My heart surges.

"No," he says. "The streets between the Misericordia Canal and Madonna dell'Orto remain blocked, I am sorry to report. But I have spoken with the neighborhood representatives. I asked specifically about your father and your cousin."

"And Cristiano?" I ask. The *gastaldo* looks momentarily confused. "Our *battiloro*? Did they see him?"

The gastaldo scratches his head. "I did not think to ask. But if we have not heard otherwise, Maria, then there is nothing to fear. I am in regular contact with the officials assigned to our quarter by the Sanità. Of course it is difficult for them to transact business under the circumstances, but the important thing is that they are well. Some of the convents, bakers, and market vendors are donating food."

"But… how are they getting food into the quarter? There are barriers."

The *gastaldo* nods. "Once a day the *guardia* allows a small barge into the rio della Sensa. They are paying a Saracen boatman from the ferry station near Rialto to deliver the supplies. They will not go hungry, I assure you."

If the *gastaldo* can hear my heart leaping in my chest, he shows no sign of it. Instead, he sets his sincere blue eyes on me and grasps my hand again. "I pray your father, your cousin—and your *battiloro*—will keep in health until you may see them again. In the interim, I am gratified to see that you are in good hands here with Master Trevisan. It sounds as though you have a promising future ahead."

Chapter 19

Friday evening. The vendors of the meager Lenten rations at the Rialto markets are covering their tables and turning the locks on their wooden battens. With Carnival behind us, Our Most Serene Republic has returned to grey, its façades dull in the waning light.

This time, I have not ventured into the quiet garden behind San Giovanni Elemosinario for I know that Cristiano is not there.

Instead, at the ferry station, I place a nearly weightless sheaf of gold leaf into a Saracen boatman's hand.

Yet another sheaf of gold from the stash I have brought from my father's house. I am loath to part with it, but if this boatman from the ferry station is successful in reaching Cristiano, then it will have been a small price to pay.

Yes, the black boatman tells me. He is the one who is being paid to bring food behind the barriers into Cannaregio. Yes, he will do his best to relay my message to the *battiloro* whose workbench borders the narrow canal behind my father's house, which I describe to him in detail.

The boatman stretches out his palm to me, and I observe his muscled forearm the color of amber. An image of my Cristiano flashes in my head. I entrust my message to him and press the sheaf of gold into his palm.

The first thing I noticed about Cristiano, I think, was his forearms. At his workbench behind my father's house, he rolled up his sleeves to reveal skin the color of oiled olive wood. Cord-like veins and muscles rippled under the surface of the flesh, like those of a cat, the result of a lifetime of hammering metal into fine sheets.

"Can I try?"

The corner of his mouth turned up then, and he said nothing, but met my gaze and placed the iron mallet in my hand. Goldbeating, I soon discovered, seemed simple until you tried to do it yourself.

Watching him work was much more satisfying. Cristiano stood at the large wooden table behind our house and turned the small ingots into flat, uniform sheets with hammering and cutting tools. From the tanneries, the *battiloro* told me, he procured hundreds of sheets of vellum made from ox intestines. These, too, would be cut into small sheets to place in between each square of gold leaf so thin that it could blow away in a breeze.

The more I watched, the more I asked questions, the more I realized that as different as we looked on the outside, we shared a common passion for working the gold. For Cristiano, as for me, the gold was not only the work of his hands but also the work of his heart. It needed not be expressed in words, for I understood it somewhere deep inside.

With the *battiloro* in our workshop, my father could turn out gilding commissions faster and could also sell sheets to his colleagues: those making jewelry, mosaics, and gilded threads for the ornamentation of ladies' clothing and hair.

Cristiano said little at first. He was quiet, perhaps reticent and doubtful of how we might treat him. Perhaps shy. I thought he was beautiful.

Slowly, over days in the workshop and evenings around the table, we learned more about him.

"Who brought you here?" I dared to ask one evening.

He turned his dark eyes on me. "I was born here, just like you," he said, and I felt remorse for assuming anything else. But then his face softened toward me and the words began to flow. "It was my mother who was put on a ship. I suppose that it is thanks to God that she has little memory of it. When she arrived she was first placed in the service of a family in Santa Croce, but then she went to live with old man Piasentin the banker in San Marco. His wife asked for a tiny girl as black as they could find, my mother told me." He turned his face toward the fading light of the window. "He was my father."

It takes me a moment for me to process the information. "Your mother's master?" I feel my mouth form a large circle.

He nods. "It is the first time you have heard of such a thing?" he says, flashing his teeth in a fleeting smile. Again, I feel embarrassed to have asked. Of course it is the fate of most of the mixed people in Venice, those who traverse our streets with skin in every shade of boiled sugar cane.

"What happened to him?" my cousin asked.

"The old man?" Cristiano shook his head. "I never knew him. He died before I was born. In his testament he gave my mother her freedom. She always told me that she would have found a way to get out from under the old man's wife anyway. My mother did not want me raised there, dressed up like some kind of pet and paraded around on the end of a chain for the benefit of that ugly woman's friends."

I feel a shiver run down my spine. "It is a blessing that the two of you were able to find your way to a new life."

He shrugs. "A blessing and a curse, at least for my mother. It was her home for fifteen years, the only place she knew. She was free and yet we had nowhere to go. I did not realize it at the time of course, but now, looking back, I see that we had nothing."

On subsequent evenings around the dinner table, we heard more of Cristiano's story. We learned that he was apprenticed to the old Master Zuan the gilder when he was very small, and that he had been brought up having only seen others of his race in the trades where they were most valued, as gondoliers or house servants. At least they were not like the Jews, he said, and that he went to bed grateful that he and his mother were not locked up at night. He said he had never seen anyone else of his race placed as a *battiloro*. Nor had we.

Over a plate of steaming rice and peas, I learned that the *battiloro* may already be spoken for. The old Master Zuan had his eye on a girl for marriage, he told us, a young half-Saracen who worked as a servant to a well-known jeweler in San Marco, a girl who might even be the jeweler's own daughter, Master Zuan suspected. The girl was still young and had not begun her menses yet, Cristiano told us, so old Master Zuan had not put the arrangement in writing before he died. My father, I am certain, would not be in a rush to arrange such a marriage, as it might mean losing the *battiloro* or bringing a young girl into our house, when we barely had enough to feed ourselves.

Still, even though I hardly knew the *battiloro* in those days, my heart already sank a little to think of him with someone else.

SIGNOR BALDI THE carpenter has delivered a raw alder wood box to Master Trevisan's studio. It is almost exactly the same size and shape as the unusual box on Master Trevisan's mantelpiece. "No charge, signorina," the carpenter said, tipping his hat to me with a grin.

Running my hand over the smooth wood of the box, I consider the feast of San Giuseppe, when the whole city stops to march in celebration of fathers. Every year I make something for my own father, which is why I have asked Signor Baldi to make this box for me. I have sanded and coated the box with several layers of gesso, and am determined to make it as beautiful as the one that glints and reflects the fire in the hearth across the room. I am certain that Father has never seen one like it. With the fashioning of this gift, I feel the presence of my father begin to draw near. I imagine his lively brown eyes and kind smile when I finally have the chance to place the box in his hands.

Mostly, I am excited to share my newfound knowledge with my father and Paolo when I go back home. I will try to apply the alloys that the *vendecolore* has given me, the ones that imitate gold leaf. I smile, thinking about what my father and cousin will say about these new materials. I thrill to think that they might find delight in it, that they might praise my skill.

I feel the skin on the back of my neck tingle and I look up to find the painter staring at me in an odd way. My face warms, and I look down to make sure he does not see my flushed cheeks. From the corner of my eye, I see the painter fidget with his hands.

"You are making a box," he says.

"It is for my father," I say. "The *vendecolore* has given me some metal alloy sheets that imitate gold leaf."

His eyebrows raise. "Ah!" he says. "Much like the blue *smalto* pigments we grind to imitate the more expensive lapis lazuli." I nod, thinking of the deep blue pigments that the *vendecolore* showed me, made from luminous ground glass. "That is our job—is it not—to deceive the eye?" the painter says.

"My father has always said so, yes."

The painter stands back and regards me intently, his finger poised across his lips. "Signorina Maria," he begins. "May I ask you something?"

I nod. I hope my face has returned to its normal color.

"Your hair... It is the most remarkable shade, almost the same as your gold." He walks over to the table where I am working. Self-consciously I run my palm over my braid and twist it around my hand like a rope. "It is not the first time someone has made that observation," I say.

"This may seem strange," the painter says, "but would you consider letting me paint you?"

My mouth opens but all that comes out is a guffaw. "Me?" I manage to say.

"As you know," the painter says, gesturing with his charcoal, "our commission for the altarpiece for Santa Maria delle Vergini calls for an image of Mary Magdalene among the Holy Women. I was struggling with how to compose her in the image until I realized that I have the perfect idea right here in front of me. Now I realize that you might be just the inspiration I need. Come. Let me show you."

"*Maria Magdalena*." The boatman's mocking voice rings inside my head.

I follow the painter to the leaded window. "*Per favore*," he says, gesturing for me to stand so that I imagine the light making a halo effect around my head and shoulders. Trevisan pulls up a wooden stool and observes me for a moment, pressing his sketchpad against his thigh. I feel his eyes running over me. "Would you mind letting your hair down, signorina?"

I pause for a moment, then release the leather tie that binds the end of my braid. Slowly I unravel the braid and the leather ribbon woven through it. I shake my head and pull the waves forward across my shoulders. Immediately, I see the painter's eyes light up, creases forming on either side of his brown eyes. "*Ecco*," he whispers, then begins making careful lines on the page with his charcoal.

In the heavy silence, I feel the canal air slide across my shoulders from the window. I have never sat for anyone to draw or paint; it seems awkward and strange. I watch the painter's tentative hand move across the parchment, and I feel his brown eyes on me. A shiver runs up my spine, and my eyes study the patterns of grout lines on the tile floor.

I hear the door latch scrape against the wood. The painter's wife and their young son appear from the kitchen. Little Gianluca holds his mother's hand, half hiding himself behind her skirts. For a moment she looks disoriented, as if the room she has entered was not the one she was expecting. She blinks at me, then cocks her head toward her husband. "What is this?" she asks, gesturing toward me.

Shame washes over me even though I have done nothing wrong. The painter comes to my rescue. "Maria is posing so that I can work out a composition for the Magdalene," he says, scraping his stool across the tiles and moving back to the worktable.

I gather my hair into my hands and twist it into a long rope. Then I pick up my leather braid ribbon from the table and stand. The painter's wife looks at me with a frown. "Benvoglio! You are making her nervous," she says to her husband.

I feel a rush of heat to my face. "I do not mind, signora," I say, returning to my workstation and busying myself with examining the sanded edges of the alder wood box that the carpenter has brought. The atmosphere in the studio is thick and full. "It is true that I... I am not accustomed to being on the other side of the picture." I laugh but the sound of it falls flat.

"I thought you were going to the market," the painter says to his wife. I see him fidget with his fingers, busying himself by lining up the nubs of charcoal on his table from smallest to largest.

"I want a *biscotto, mamma*," says Gianluca, turning his wide eyes up to his mother.

"Yes, *cavolino*. We are going to do that," she says to the boy, then turns to her husband, "only that boatman of yours is nowhere to be seen." She clucks in exasperation. "I told you it was a bad idea to allow him to come back to us after that disaster."

"*Tesoro*," the painter raises his palm toward his wife, "I am certain that the last thing Maria wants is to hear about our troubles with our household staff."

IN A CROWDED alley, I press my back against a cool brick wall and wait for the procession to begin.

Brightly colored guild banners careen above the heads of the disorganized crowd. A group of youths dressed in matching, multicolored tights sprints past me, their laughter and adolescent screeches echoing off the stone walls. They weave through the crowd, stumbling into the chaotic swirl of costumed guildsmen that has assembled in a small *campo*, the starting point of the parade. Men's whistles and two random bursts of the bugle make me clap my palms over my ears.

For as long as I can remember, I have gathered with the other families of our painter's guild to watch the procession of the feast of San Giuseppe, the patron saint of fathers and my own father's namesake. This is the first time I have celebrated San Giuseppe without my own father by my side.

The Lenten season is upon us and the annual ban on mask-wearing has been handed down until next winter. Yet even the pestilence has done nothing to dampen the spirits of the parade-goers. Many have decided to watch the procession while holding oiled and scented cloths over their noses and mouths; a few noble ladies wear balls of herbs strung on ribbons around their necks.

The painter has taken his young son by the hand and led him to where the men of our guild are gathering to march. Among the men I recognize a few familiar faces, fellow guildsmen I know by appearance if not by name. I search for someone who might give me news of my father or through whom I might pass a message.

But this year, the number of men from the Guild of Saint Luke is meager, composed only of those lucky enough not to be sequestered behind the wooden barriers of our quarter. No one in the raucous crowd seems to acknowledge our small cluster of painters and gilders. Am I the only one who feels the void of our missing guildsmen? The main face missing is that of my own father. He loves this feast and reserves his best set of clothing to march with his fellow gilders. What was once familiar now feels empty and strange.

Several wives of our fellow guildsmen stop to greet Signora Trevisan. She and Antonella have worn their best and taken care to arrange their hair. The wife has dressed the baby girl in a pale green gown with embroidered cuffs. I have made a fumbling attempt to style my hair like Signora Trevisan's, winding it in small piles and pinning it around my brow line. Will our guild families see me as part of Master Trevisan's household now?

While we wait for the procession to begin we watch several day laborers directed by the drapers' guild to set up a pyre in the square for a great bonfire after the procession. Other women and children line the wall to watch. The bakeries have opened their doors to the square. The smell of *zeppole* fills the streets, so overwhelming that I can almost feel the stickiness of the fried dough and its weightless pastry cream on the roof of my mouth.

The procession begins with the loud cry of the horn, and it only takes a few minutes for the main attraction to arrive. Each March a young boy about ten years old is chosen to portray Joseph, the father of Christ. This year's youth is a handsome boy with a fair, round face, bright eyes, and hair as dark as coal. With pudgy fingers, the boy tugs on the gold thread of his blue robe and looks nervously at the crowd. The gilded leaves encircling his head shimmer in the morning light. Behind him, a man leads a donkey with Mary, a slight girl dwarfed inside an enormous white and blue dress, also trimmed in gold. A red-cheeked toddler is dressed as the Christ child, balancing an enormous gold halo on his soft head. The child's father grasps his small leg so that he does not fall from the donkey's back as they amble down the alley in their mock flight into Egypt. Men with wooden flutes come next, puffing out a plaintive song that fills me with emotion.

Our own guild of Saint Luke, the painters' guild, follows the musicians. Immediately I recognize Master Trevisan toward the front of the crowd; he has lifted his son to his shoulder so that he can see over the tops of the men's heads in front of him. His journeyman marches behind, a bored expression on his face. The painter's wife sees her husband and waves frantically, holding up the baby girl to see her father.

Trevisan's young son has made something for his father, a small drawing carefully scrawled on a scrap of parchment recovered from his father's studio. It's the new gondola, the boy proudly told his father at breakfast, and I watched the painter's eyes light up when he traced his son's crude outline of the boat with his finger.

"*E bellissima, amore,*" the painter said to his son, his eyes creasing as he ruffled the boy's hair with an elegant hand. I think about the gilded box I am working on for my own father, and I wonder how long it will be before I can present it to him.

As the jugglers at the end of the procession pass, Antonella and I follow closely behind the painter's wife. We funnel into a tight crowd heading toward the Piazza San Marco. Near the square, the merchants try their best to hawk their wares to the crowds pressing their way into the space.

The procession spills into the Piazza San Marco and disperses into a confusing mass of tradesmen. I stick closely beside the painter's wife as we wend into the familiar square anchored by the façade of our Basilica of San Marco. The piazza is the stage where Our Most Serene Republic proclaims its wealth and power to an audience of its own citizens as well as the traders, diplomats, nobles, clergy, and foreign visitors who ferry themselves here to our damp cluster of islands in unceasing numbers. I have witnessed every manner of public spectacle here, both official and otherwise: religious processions, masked balls, musical performances, humiliations, executions.

My eyes scan the crowd, for I am looking for someone—anyone—from our guild who might have news of my father and Cristiano, and more importantly, who might be able to get word to them. On three sides of the piazza, long arcaded passageways house sellers of glass and lace. On the east side, the façade of the basilica of San Marco dominates the square. I have heard stories about how Venetians wrenched Christian treasures—precious chalices, altarpieces, jewel-encrusted statues, holy relics—from the hands of the infidel, and brought them to Our Great City, where they are housed in the basilica's treasury. The greatest trophy of all, the four bronze horses atop the church, the *quadriga*, has been brought from Constantinople itself. Ever since I was a girl I have wondered how those horses were made, their golden surfaces gleaming in the sunlight.

To the south of the church the Doge's palace sparkles in the sunlight. A fire nearly destroyed the ducal palace when I was just a child, and the place has teemed with stonemasons, carpenters, painters, and other tradesmen for as long as I can remember. Our own Master Bellini has even painted a picture of Our Most Excellent Prince himself, I have heard.

"Signorina Maria." I turn to see Pascal Grissoni making his way toward me, pushing through a group of women pressing their noses with cloths infused with scented oils. Instinctively I suck in my stomach. I constantly worry that someone will take note of my burgeoning shape. The painter's wife greets Grissoni with a smile.

"I have just spoken with Master Trevisan," he says, bowing to the painter's wife and me. "I wanted to invite all of you to come and visit my family's studio. I want you to see a cycle of paintings that my father and I are doing for the church of Santo Spirito. I am having a small reception with some of the other members of our guild so that everyone can see the pictures up close before they are installed in the church."

"A lovely invitation," the painter's wife says.

"Perhaps after the festivities are over in a few days," he says.

He reaches out to touch my sleeve. He turns and sets his brown eyes on me. "Signorina Maria, it would please me if you would come."

Chapter 20

Antonella has given me a miniature set of sewing scissors which I have used to prick the small stitches of the *camicia* that I wear beneath my dress. I have little appetite, but my middle has begun to bulge, a small rounded ball. I layer my dress and a leather apron over it, tying it only loosely in hopes that no one will take note of my changing form.

It is only in my work that I forget.

Now that the carpenters have delivered our panels for the Vergini altarpiece, I can turn my attention to my traditional gilding work, the only part of the process where I feel in control. The large, symmetrically cut pieces have been stacked along the wall on one side of the studio where they take up the entirety of one wall. After we have gilded and painted images on them, the carpenters will help us assemble them inside the church. They will fasten large battens of wood to create an armature in a final configuration that will stand taller than three men. Trevisan's journeyman and I have almost finished sanding the panels and the painter has sent Stefano out for more horsehair cloth.

Trevisan and his journeyman have placed one of the sanded panels atop the worktable in the center of the room for me. I run my hand over the surface, feeling for imperfections. Poplar is vulnerable to warping, and I stoop to examine the surface in the raking light. Overnight I have soaked large swaths of fine linen in three buckets filled with the gesso purchased from the *vendecolore*. Piece by piece, I lay torn pieces of linen over the surface of the panel to conceal any flaws. With my brush, I soak and press the linen pieces down to the surface, just as my father showed me to do when I was barely tall enough to see over the top of the table.

I dip my brush into the pot of gesso, watching the white, gelatinous mixture jiggle as I load it onto my brush. Slowly, I begin to coat the surface of the wood with the animal skin glue. The gesso is the foundation, the support and adherent for the egg tempera colors and especially the gold leaf.

The best gesso is made from the boiled skins of the water buffalo. That is what my father has always said. Over generations in our workshop, we have tried making the priming material using the hides of mountain goats, minks, and other beasts great and small. Now, the buffalo-skin gesso is the only one we use. When we add powdered gypsum and water it imparts a dull white color to the jellylike mix that transforms even the oldest panel into the perfect surface for gold leaf and tempera pigments.

Over generations my family workshop has become known for our perfectly prepared panels. We work with several carpenters to select the pieces of poplar and maple, shipped on great rafts from the mountains of Cadore and seasoned in store rooms and along quaysides of the canals. Still, I must carefully layer the ground in order to do justice to the reputation of my father's workshop, and to the quality that Master Trevisan expects of me.

Egg tempera paints impart beautiful and translucent color to our panels, but only when the panels are well prepared for paint. Using brushes of mink, fox, and horsehair, we brush many light layers of sizing on the surface of the wood, covering each layer with powdered charcoal, then scraping down each layer with a flat metal blade to make the smoothest surface possible. Once the surfaces are perfected, I will add red bole, then the gold, then decorative punchwork. But weeks will pass before it is done.

After I have applied the linen to the entire surface, I arch my back and stretch, replacing my brush in one of the now-empty pails. The sizing must dry before I begin to apply another thin layer. This small act of running my brush along the surface of the wood washes my soul in peace. I have no power over where the hand of the plague decides to fall. I have no sway over the small life growing quietly but insistently inside of me. It is only with the brush or the palette knife in my hand that I feel I have any influence over anything at all.

Ever since the painter's wife found Master Trevisan drawing me from life, she spends more and more time in the workshop. While Antonella sees to the children, the painter's wife tidies books on the shelves, dusts motes from the windowsills, stokes the fire, comments on the trees that the young journeyman is dotting in the background of a small portrait. If the painter is flustered by his wife's incessant chatter and flittering about, he does not show it. Still, we all seem to breathe a collective sigh of relief when she finally settles herself by the window with her embroidery ring.

Now it is clear to me that Signora Trevisan senses that there is something more going on inside her husband's workshop than meets the eye. Perhaps it is the heightened state of carrying a child that brings forth a sixth sense. I can now attest that I see and smell things I did not before.

At the central worktable, Master Trevisan mulls over his preparatory drawings for the altarpiece. He has turned the pages hundreds of times, studying, scratching his beard, making small notes in the corners of the parchment sheets, scraping others and making adjustments to his drawings. With a nub of charcoal, he makes careful marks on the side of a parchment sheet on the table at his side. For several days he has worked on this single figure, wiping lines clean with a rag, then reusing the charcoal to make a new line.

The journeyman has drawn a grid over the page so that it can be easily transferred over to the final painting.

As strange as it seems, I have become accustomed to feeling the painter's eyes on me. After several awkward tries we have abandoned my more formal modeling sessions, some with his wife watching from her embroidery, and instead the painter now contents himself with simply drawing me while I go about my work. I feel his gaze follow me as I move across the studio. He is not obtrusive or leering; he simply follows me with his eyes, drawing quietly in his sketchbook, the only sound the canal water lapping against the side of the stone building. I prefer it this way, for I am filled with nervous energy and cannot fathom how I would go about sitting still.

THAT EVENING, IN the kitchen, I find Signora Trevisan sitting at the table with her infant daughter at her breast. The dirty dishes from the midday and evening meals are stacked on the wooden table before her. Her face looks lined, her eyes ringed with shadows. If her husband had not announced it, you would not know that she was with child.

Women carry secrets, I think. It is what we learn to do from childhood.

"Are you feeling all right, signora?" I say.

"Exhausted beyond words, if you want to know the truth." She huffs a little burst of laughter. "Nothing beyond what every mother endures."

"I would not know," I say. "My mother was gone before I had a chance to learn such things." For a moment the air feels heavy and silent, and I wonder if I have it in me to share my own secret.

"You have work of your own sort. But you will know such exhaustion soon enough. When you marry."

"Signora…" I begin. My mouth opens, but I pause, not knowing how to begin such a conversation. "I…"

At that moment the painter's young son runs into the room crying, having cut his finger on something sharp in the painter's studio. Signora Trevisan leans down to see, cradling her baby on her lap. Then Antonella bursts into the room to check her boiling pot.

Amidst the clamor, my moment is gone.

IN THE ARTIST'S studio there is a book with engraved pictures illustrating the strange story of ill-fated lovers.

When I opened the book the first time, it fell open to a page with an image of a woman and man speaking to one another through a crack in a wall. Their bodies pressed against either side of the wall, and I felt I could almost hear their words whispered through the crack. I turned the pages, watching a seeming courtship bloom around a garden fountain. On the final page, I recoiled to find the couple falling on their swords.

"Pyramus and Thisbe," the painter's journeyman tells me, looking over my shoulder. He knows of such things, for his own father was a painter of ancient stories, and he says that he learned them from an early age.

"Who are they?" I ask, running my fingers over the old vellum, the pores of the animal that was sacrificed in the name of the book trade still visible on the page.

"Their parents were neighbors—and sworn enemies—but the two declared their love for one another through a crack in the wall that separated their houses. They began to sneak out to meet near a stream outside the city walls." I turn the page and follow the journeyman's tale. "One day Thisbe was waiting for her love to arrive when a lioness arrived, with bloodied jaws from a fresh kill. Later, when Pyramus arrived, Thisbe was gone, but the lioness remained.

He had the mistaken idea that the lioness had killed his love, so he threw himself on his sword. When Thisbe discovered his body, she too took her own life."

"That must be the saddest story I have ever heard," I say, closing the cover of the book.

The journeyman shrugs. "All of those books are filled with sad stories," he says, gesturing to the many books on the painter's shelves.

"How does Master Trevisan have so many books?" I ask, and the journeyman purses his lips as if he is calculating an answer.

"He says that he inherited many of them, but I often see him receive books as gifts." I run my fingers across the gilded stamping on the bindings. "There are works of antiquity, accounts of the Trojan War," he says. "Master uses the pictures as inspiration for his pictures. I have never seen him read the words."

The journeyman pulls a large religious book from the shelf and places it on the worktable. "There are many like this one," he says, opening the binding to reveal an elaborate hand-painted frontispiece with lettering decorated with ivy leaves. "Breviaries, prayer books, an enormous psalter that the Irish ambassador gave him, monastic manuscripts with marbleized end papers and gilded stamped words on their leather bindings. Would have been the pride of any monastic library," he says. "But it is the ancient love stories that people want now." He laughs. "Even—I might say especially—the ones that end badly."

I DESCEND THE stairs into the dark boat slip, but as I approach the gondola, I hear whispering and giggling.

The boatman is not alone.

Through the wooden slats of the passenger compartment, I see figures moving and hear scuffling. The boat rocks against the wooden bumpers that have been placed to prevent the gondola from scraping the stones of the boat slip.

Having heard my footfall on the stone stairs, the boatman emerges from the compartment, his hair disheveled and his doublet turned sideways. I hold my palm up to the side of my face and turn my head away.

"Signorina?" he says breathlessly.

"I... Please excuse me. I just wanted to see if you would take me to Rialto."

At that moment, Antonella emerges from the passenger compartment, her face flushed. She is fidgeting with hooks on the front of her dress. She sets her black eyes on me, and fixes her mouth in an expression I am not certain is shame or mockery.

"Give me a few moments and meet me at the mooring," the boatman says.

"No," I say quickly, returning to the stairs. "Never mind. I will walk there myself."

Chapter 21

At the ferry dock near Rialto, I scan the quayside for the Saracen boatman. Has he been successful in relaying my message?

The *traghetto* is quiet, with two boatmen sitting idly in their gondolas, waiting for passengers to exchange a *bagattino* for a ride to the other side of the Grand Canal, or more for a specific destination. One of the boatmen has stretched his feet up onto the aft deck of a grubby gondola, his head pitched forward, napping. In the shadows, before a rickety wooden hut, the scrawny station master whittles a piece of knotted wood with a small knife.

I have walked all the way from the painter's house, trying to banish the image of the boatman and Antonella from my head. I wish I had never seen them. Perhaps I have been naïve not to realize that the two of them were more than collegial house servants. Now I see how she shared my secret, and I understand that nothing I do or say is protected under Master Trevisan's roof.

"You need to go somewhere, signorina?" The station master stands and ambles down toward the edge of the canal. I reach my hand into the pocket of my cape and finger the parchment sheets folded tightly together, along with a long missive that I have written to my father and my cousin.

"No," I say. "I am looking for someone. A man, a Saracen boatman who brings food from the market into the rio della Sensa in Cannaregio. I want to deliver a message."

"Alfredo," the man says.

I shrug, realizing that I do not know his name.

"The only Moor I have."

"Where could I find him?"

The station master coughs and projects a wad of spittle onto the stones. "You cannot." He turns his pale green eyes and grubby face toward me.

"What do you mean?"

He shakes his head. "Gone," he says. "To the *lazzaretto*." He gestures out in the direction of the far islands of the lagoon. "Alfredo... I told him he was crazy for going in there... beyond the barriers," he says. "But he was lured by the *soldi*." He presses his fingertips together as if rubbing together coins.

"He is sick?"

"Came down with a fever two days ago," he says. "Loaded onto a ferry yesterday."

A long silence falls between us under the weight of this revelation.

"Is someone else bringing food into Cannaregio?" I ask finally.

"Not from this *traghetto*," he says. "Not anymore. I cannot risk another one of my men."

THE *GASTALDO*'S WORKSHOP lies on the outer edge of Cannaregio. It is large and light, much nicer than my father's. The studio sits on a well-trodden thoroughfare overlooking a small square with a carved wellhead in the center of the cobblestones. It is the abode of the man our guild has elected as its leader no less than three times. If there is one person from our guild who might be in a position to help me, it is Aureo dalla Stava.

I have never asked anything of our *gastaldo*, but with the barriers closed and the Saracen boatman from the ferry station gone to the pesthouse, what other choice do I have to reach my family and my *battiloro*? Surely Pyramus and Thisbe risked more than this for love.

Through the shop window I see the *gastaldo* sitting with his legs spread wide, his hands on his knees. On the workbench before him stand several tools in disarray and a litter of gold shavings. His spectacle, secured with a leather strap, sits oddly at a skewed angle atop his head.

After a moment, I see the *gastaldo* sigh and stand, pressing himself behind one of his tall sons at a back worktable. All three of the man's strapping boys work with their father, crowding into the space. Each of his sons is an attractive man, well made, two light like their father, one dark-eyed and olive-skinned like their mother, who died years ago as a fever overtook the quarter. They have been taught well under their father's tutelage. All of them are quiet and respectful men, all married well to the daughters of our city's best painters and gilders.

I open the creaking door.

"Maria!" the *gastaldo* exclaims. "*Che sorpresa!* You are the last person I expected to see here."

"I know," I say. "I realize I am not supposed to be here but I am dying for news, *gastaldo*. I feel helpless and I have so little information about my family."

He grasps my hands. "I am in daily contact with the men the Sanità has assigned to the quarter. They report to me at the end of each day if anyone has fallen ill or has been removed from the neighborhood."

"My cousin? The *battiloro*?"

He shakes his head. "I have no news of any of them, Maria, which means they are well, as I have already told you. You must trust in that and be thankful for it."

"I am going to try to get in. Will you come with me?"

He huffs, then shakes his head vigorously. "I am afraid that visiting them is out of the question, my dear. The street is blocked and the Sanità has stationed at least three *signori di notte* to guard the barricades. If it brings you any solace, I have not been able to see them myself. They will not let us enter, I promise you. Only the priests and health officials are going in."

I feel my shoulders drop. I sigh audibly and nod. "I smell smoke," I say.

The *gastaldo* gestures in the direction of a nearby square. "They have established a burning place in the Campo Sant'Alvise," he tells me. When someone with lesions is removed from their home, the belongings are brought out of the house and put on the pyre. It has been burning like that for weeks now." I feel a shudder run through my body and am not able to rid my nose of the smoke, which seems to infiltrate my entire body.

I feel the *gastaldo*'s light eyes settle on me for a few moments. "I see for myself that you are fit. All is well in the painter's workshop?"

I nod. "Truth be told, I am not sure I will ever master the pigments but I do my best. Master Trevisan is experimenting with painting on canvas. He says it is the way of the future."

"Canvas?" The older son scoffs from the back of the workshop. "That's only for festival banners, stage props. If the painters of this city are painting religious pictures on canvas rather than on wooden panels, then we are finished," he says.

The *gastaldo* shakes his head. "Absurd," he calls to his son. "It will never happen. We have been gilding wood for many centuries and you all will continue doing so long after I have gone to the World to Come, I can assure you of that. But now, *cara*, you must get back to San Marco. It is not a good idea to be out on the street alone once the sun begins to sink." He sets his eyes on me. "Maria. If there is any news of your family at all, I promise I will come deliver it to you myself. Now, let me walk you back at least as far as the baker's bridge."

"No, thank you, *gastaldo*. I do not want to take any more of your time. I prefer to walk alone."

From the *gastaldo*'s workshop, I take a familiar shortcut under a low passage and over a narrow wooden bridge. I cross just as a gondola slips silently through the water beneath me. Its black bow parts the water like an arrow, then a hulking figure appears. A young gondolier emerges on the other side of the bridge. A thick leather belt cinches tightly around his strong frame, and breeches with vertical stripes hug his muscular thighs. A feather springs from his close-fitting cap. He turns and nods at me. The man's body sways rhythmically as he rows away, a natural movement that makes him seem as if he were part of his craft.

As the boat slides around the corner and out of view, I am racked with guilt about the poor Saracen boatman, Alfredo, whom I tempted into exposure to the pestilence. I am sorry for him, but I think of all the thousands of boatmen in Our Most Serene Republic, and a selfish, desperate part of me wonders if there is another one out there who would be willing to take such a risk.

Along a street on the other side of the bridge, I slip into a small door in the façade of our parish church. The familiar dank smell of the building fills me, taking the place of the smoky aroma from the bonfires in the *campo* that still lingers in my hair. I sink into the solitude of the space, its quiet familiarity filling me, and I make my way to a small chapel along one of the side aisles.

I settle myself before a large gilded altarpiece that I have known my entire life. My father says that my great-grandfather and several other painters collaborated on it many years ago. It is an image of the Virgin and Child surrounded by saints. Saint Luke, the protector of painters, gazes out passively from the center panel, his halo punched and decorated with tools we probably still use in my father's studio. I can picture each tool they used to punch the gold, and admire the particular indigo pigments sourced from the east and no longer available to us today.

The panel is still beautiful, though old and warped from years of enduring cycles of dryness and moisture. I see a new crack in the surface near the top of the picture, and I wonder if anyone else who sits in this spot has noticed it. I wish that I could scrape the dulled paint, sand and fill the cracks, and bring it back to its original luster. I wonder if there are small insects already eating the panel from the inside.

Before the gilded altarpiece, more candles have been lit than I have ever seen. I take a fresh taper from the box and light it with flame from a nearby candle, then press it onto one of the metal stakes fashioned for that purpose. Then, I lower myself until I feel my knees press on the hard, cold wood. In the candlelight the gold glows brightly, and I feel the slight warmth of the flames in the drafty cold of the old church.

I look at the image of the Virgin and Child, their passive faces and halos glimmering in the candlelight. I send a prayer up to her, to her son, to Saint Luke, to the other saints painted on the panel. In my heart I send up a silent plea for my Cristiano and for the child growing inside my body, and I wonder if anyone is listening.

BACK ON THE canal, in the waning daylight, I see that the main street that leads into my family's block has been barricaded. There is a formidable enclosure and a notice painted on a wooden panel over a doorway, a warning of contagion. I cut through an alley to the quayside along a narrow canal where I can make out the misty silhouettes of several moored gondolas, their boatmen absent. The shutters of all the houses bordering the canal-side have been battened closed.

When I turn the corner into the alley leading to the bridge where our workshop lies, I see that another wooden barricade has been erected across the entrance to the street. One of the *signori di notte*, sleek in a dark blue waistcoat, leans against the wall, checking his fingernails. On the other side, an older official stands by, dislodging something from the crack of a cobblestone with the toe of his shoe. Ignoring the men, I put down my head and hike my leg over a jumbled part of the wooden barricade where a board has already been loosened by someone else trying to cross.

"Signorina!" the younger man springs to life, his low voice echoing across the square. "You cannot enter. This section of the quarter is under a ban."

"I live here," I say. "My house is just there." Through the cracks in the wooden barricade I point in the direction of my father's house.

"Which house is it?"

"My father is the *indoradòr* Bartolini... beyond the bridge," I say. "We make gilded panels. It is my father, my cousin, and myself, plus a *battiloro*."

The younger man looks to the older guard for a response, and the older man shakes his head. He walks over.

"Signorina. You left home? How did you get out of the quarter?"

"My father brought me out. I am apprenticed to a painter in San Marco. Please, I must see my family. My father is ill."

"How long ago did you leave home?"

"It was before Epiphany."

"And you have not been home since?"

I shake my head.

"Signorina, you must understand that this barricade has been placed here for good reason. You cannot simply travel in and out of the quarter. It is under ban. I suggest that you return to San

Marco. You will not be allowed back into the quarter until the ban is lifted." The younger man squeezes my arm firmly and presses me back away from the barrier.

Reluctantly, I walk back to the painter's house.

HEAVY, WET SNOWFLAKES have begun to fall, a rare March event. The dusting of white casts the covered boats in the canal into silhouette. Snow fills the crevices of the leaded panes with small drifts and piles. Dusk has come earlier than usual and the oil lamps in the painter's studio flicker and dance. I watch a small brown bird land on the windowsill and ruffle his feathers against the chill. I stoke the flames in the hearth, feeling the heat warm the front of my dress. For a fleeting moment, I allow myself to place my palm across my swelling midsection and feel the hardness there.

New life.

I send another silent message to my *battiloro*, willing it to travel across the snow-dusted alleys to Cannaregio, and I wonder if he has any inkling of it.

I feel the hairs on the back of my neck prickle, but it is not the cold. I turn to find the painter standing behind me, watching me with an intense gaze. When I meet his eyes he turns back to the table and appears to scrutinize his wooden palette. He clears his throat.

"Now that we have the panels for the Vergini commission prepared we can turn our attention to them in earnest."

I nod, feeling grateful and excited that it means I will be able to turn back to the gold.

"We must get moving on this commission or it will end up here on my wall," he says, gesturing to the pictures hanging from floor to ceiling.

"You have many," I say. The painter's studio is filled with pictures. Some of them are old and gilded. I run my hands over one gilded panel that my grandfather or great-grandfather might have made. Alongside it there is another picture that has captured my attention, that of a young woman reclining, with her head lolling on her arm. "Who is she?" I ask.

I hear the painter chortle. "Yes," he says. "That one has a story." He comes to stand beside me, enlacing his fingers behind his back. "A failed commission."

"I did not imagine you would have such a thing," I say.

He waves his hand in a gesture of dismissal. "It happens to all of us."

"And so all of these pictures..." I begin, and the painter nods.

"Many of these are commissions that have failed for some reason—either for me, my father, or his father before him." He shrugs. "The patron abandons them, changes his mind, or turns out not to have the money to pay. Sometimes patrons die before I finish their commission. More rarely," he says, running his finger along the top of the frame to remove a layer of dust, "as in this case, the love affair runs its course before the portrait is finished." He smiles, then turns back to the picture.

"The patron lost interest."

The painter nods. "Alegreza Antelini," he says, gesturing to the painting. "This one falls into the category of a love affair that ended badly before I could finish the portrait."

"You did not have a contract?" I ask.

"I did, as always," he says. "More importantly than that, I had a verbal promise from one of the most upstanding men in Our Serene Republic. A member of the Ten."

"And he never paid you?" my eyes widen.

The painter shakes his head. "I was still very young, naïve enough to think that the *signor* would come to claim the picture, or at least compensate me for the many hours I had spent observing the woman's face and body, and replicating it in paint."

I imagine the woman in the painter's studio, shuddering against the cold. I blush, but thankfully the painter does not seem to notice. Somehow the picture does not fit in the great space of the painter's studio. It is a private painting, a cabinet picture meant to be savored, consumed. Consumed by one pair of eyes.

"And so," the painter continues, "eventually I became resigned that this picture would end up hanging on the walls of my own house. In retrospect, I should have finished the picture before things went sour. I should have seen it coming."

"What do you mean?"

"The young woman was… encumbered," he says. I feel my stomach turn. "I saw it as soon as she disrobed to sit for the picture. I should have finished it that day and whisked it to the patron and asked to be paid before he discovered it." He chuckles. "He was not the father."

"What happened to her?"

The artist scratches his beard and shrugs. "You can imagine her father was not pleased. They did what parents in this situation do. They decided that their daughter was best suited for a life devoted to God. I heard from a reliable source that she took the veil and her vows. She was escorted to a cell at the convent of San Giovanni Evangelista on Torcello. The parents made a respectable donation of jewelry and religious paintings, which of course could be resold to offset the cost of housing their daughter for the rest of her days."

Trevisan runs his fingers lightly over the textured surface of the paint, tracing the hourglass outline of the woman's narrow waist and full hips. "Alegreza Antelini," he says again. "She was one of our city's great beauties, the envy of countless women, object of desire of countless men." I try to imagine the curves of her body now obscured under the black habit of the Benedictines.

Trevisan stands back and observes his work. "This is a good one, if you do not mind my saying," he says, tapping the panel with the back of his hand. "Too bad no one will see it." He turns and smiles at me, the creases of his eyes wrinkling.

Chapter 22

I know that the painter is finally happy with his sketch for the altarpiece, as he has opened a small glass jar of black ink and selected a fine brush for applying it. Carefully, he traces his charcoal lines, laying down the final design on the great panels I have prepared with gesso. The under-drawing may show under the paint, I know, and it is those lines I have to pay attention to when the panel is ready for my gilding.

I see that the painter has intended some of the under-drawing to show, in order to provide for more modeling of the drapery and the shadows of the arms and faces. Along the edges of the under-drawing I run my sharpened metal stylus so that it will provide a border for my gold leaf.

I swirl the tip of my brush into a small pot of bole, watching the ruddy liquid coat the soft brown horsehairs. The smell is at the same time repugnant and comforting, the peculiar odor of the glue made from animal fat mixed with red clay from the mainland which has filled my nostrils since the day I was born. I press my brush against the side of the pot, letting the excess drip back into the dark liquid, then I begin to apply it to the prepared wood. At first, it goes on as bright, blood-red liquid, but it dries to a dull ruddy hue.

The poplar panels that the carpenters have made for us have already been prepared. Now the panels are stacked vertically around Trevisan's studio, five large pieces that will be fastened together in the church. Trevisan, his journeyman, and I work in companionable silence, each doing his or her task as the fire in the hearth crackles and spits. I watch the reddish bole coat the white gesso underlayment, moving my brush slowly to avoid lines between the layers.

"Most people believe that the gold is completely opaque, but that is incorrect," my father told me countless times, wagging a finger under my chin before dipping his own brush into the bole. I nodded, though I had heard this proclamation many times. I was not one to question this assertion, for he knew his trade.

I knew that it was important to go slowly in applying the bole because gold leaf highlights any nicks, rough spots, or imperfections in the wood beneath. Any of those can show through the layers, and the gold leaf will magnify them all the more. It is important to take the time to prepare the surface as perfectly as possible so that nothing shows through.

"What is underneath the gold has everything to do with the final appearance," my father continued as if telling me for the first time. "The red bole brings warmth to the coloration of the panel, and it works in harmony with the reds, browns, and other such pigments of the painting."

"And since it shows through the layers of gold leaf you must layer on the bole as perfectly as possible. All the more reason to take your time."

My father stopped in mid-sentence and smiled. "*Brava.*" He pressed his brush down on the worktable emphatically as if he were done for the day. "Do you see?" he said, turning to my cousin and the *battiloro*, who were occupying themselves quietly on the other side of our workshop. "I have taught my daughter well."

Cristiano caught my eye then and I saw the wrinkles alongside his eyes as he flashed a private smile that made the color rise to my face.

The pleasant image of the *battiloro* in my head is rudely interrupted as the painter's wife charges into the room. "He is the son of a ferryman, so what does that tell you? Humph! It is no wonder that he cannot pretend to have elegant manners." The painter's wife blows a puff of air as if that explains it all. She shifts her sleeping baby to the other arm.

The painter shrugs, as if resigned that the subject of the boatman is destined to continue. "I have expended my own time and effort to instill the manners of a private boatman, to teach him all that is required of a good servant. Not to mention that he has the chance to row one of the most magnificent new gondolas in our city. I challenge anyone to find one any more beautiful." The painter turns his attention back to his paintbrush.

I do my best to stay focused on the red bole on the tip of my brush. The painter's wife moves toward her husband. "But don't you see? He has been anything but faithful, Benvoglio. He has been nothing if not ungrateful. We provide him with a fine roof over his head, food to eat, even cured him of that nasty infection when we signed the contract and he came into our service."

The painter scratches his head nervously, then smooths his wavy hair away from his face. He shoots a glance at me then looks quickly at the floor. I do my best to focus on my brushwork.

His wife continues. "And do not forget that we have bought him a collection of clothing at a not insignificant sum."

I try to push the vile image of the boatman and Antonella from my head.

"Please excuse us, Maria," the painter says, looking at me sheepishly, "for airing these matters with our servants."

"I would not know," I manage to say. "We had no servants. My cousin and I did everything that needed doing in my father's house."

The painter's wife puts her hand to her mouth. "I am sorry, Maria. As usual I have said too much." But she continues, tugging at her husband's sleeve. "We had better be careful about paying him in case he decides to disappear again."

All I can hope is that that hateful boatman does not have the instinct to chatter on like the painter's wife.

"Donata!" the painter barks sharply to his wife.

She puts a hand on her hip. "I am sorry, husband, but why do you think that this time is going to be any different from the last?"

"Because I have a plan," says the painter, finally exasperated.

"What is that?"

"I plan to withhold his salary." The painter casts a fleeting glance at the gilded box on the mantel. I am not sure that he is even aware that he has done it. "Instead of giving him payments up front I will pay in arrears instead."

The painter's wife raises her eyebrows. "That is unusual," she says, "but I suppose if it keeps him in place."

"The boatman is here now, signora." I hear Antonella's voice, then I see her head appear through the barely opened kitchen door. I wonder how long she has been standing there and if she has been listening to the conversation. She smiles tight-lipped at Trevisan's wife. "He is waiting with the gondola in the boat slip, signora."

I think of the golden sheaves I have paid the boatman over the past weeks. What would the painter and his wife say if they knew that I had bought the boatman's silence? And what is that slimy boatman doing with gold leaf anyway? Surely he must be pawning it for *zecchini* somewhere else in the city. I imagine him trading gold leaf for the gold coins in his pocket.

Despite my efforts, I realize that I am now embroiled in the painter's matter with the servants, and I cannot share my secret. Once again, desperation begins to fill my heart.

Chapter 23

The aroma of freshly baked pastry wafts from the small, beautifully wrapped package that I carry back from my aunt in the convent. I anticipate the taste of the soft leaves made with milk and fresh butter from the convent's goats cloistered behind the building. We always have these pastries at Easter time, served along with roasted piglet, radicchio, and tender pea shoots. My aunt is exceptionally talented with them, and in my pregnant state I crave sweets, more than I have ever wanted to eat.

"Your aunt is a genius with the spatula and the fire," the sister says to me as she escorts me from the visitors' room to the main entrance of the convent. I would not call her elderly, and I suspect that she appears older than she is. Even though I cannot see her legs under her long habit, I imagine that one leg is significantly longer than the other because she hobbles, carrying her weight on one side.

"I am certain that her skills are well known here, *sorella.*"

"She is famous!" the nun flashes a few greyed, crooked teeth. She herself is carrying another bag with pastries inside. I know that Antonella will be waiting for me back at the painter's house, wanting to study my aunt's confections with great interest, spending many hours trying to recreate the recipe.

I have been avoiding my aunt but she has written to me several times. At Master Trevisan's canal-side door I have received small folds of paper with her delicate, looping handwriting, entreating me to visit.

Even though she is the one locked behind the iron grille, she seems one of the only ones who can give me the information that I so desperately desire. And so I come to see her, and pray that she will not see me so changed.

Suddenly, a small door swings open and a small boy spills into the convent corridor. "*Dolci*! I smell *dolci*!" His high-pitched voice booms in the brick-vaulted corridor, and he rushes toward the nun.

"Get back inside—*cattivo*!" The nun yells in a stern voice. She swats the boy with her hand, then grasps his shoulders and presses him against her girth, as if she might squeeze the breath out of him. "These are not for you!" she says. He wriggles free, laughing, and escapes through another door open to the corridor. "*Cattivo*!" the nun yells again, then flashes a smirk at me to show that she is joking.

My eyes follow the running boy into the room. I see flames in a great hearth. Around the room are several steaming cauldrons and piles of linens. Children of all ages with their heads wrapped in rags are beating out the linens over the heat. From the small sliver of an opening in the door I see that the convent laundry is vast. I watch a young girl, her sleeves rolled up to reveal muscled forearms, rubbing a cloth over a washboard.

"I did not know there were so many children here," I say.

"What in heavens do you think we are here for?" the nun shrugs. "This is what we do. They work, yes. We give them jobs in the laundry, the kitchen, the boathouse, cleaning the dining hall, the latrines. But we also teach them their letters. Many of them go on to do great things in the city and on terra firma, I am proud to say." She gestures vaguely in the direction of the mainland.

"All of them are orphans?"

She nods. "Well, nearly all. They come to us every day. Right here in fact."

We approach the side door to the convent, the one I have seen from the quayside, the one with the opening where people leave small bundles in the middle of the night and press money through the opening in the marble to pay for their care. On the interior side of the door I see that there is more than an opening. There is a giant wooden wheel like a grindstone, set horizontally to turn around a vertical column. Part of it projects outside the convent wall to form a ledge beneath the window. When people place their unwanted babies on it, they turn the wheel and the baby is ushered seamlessly inside the convent walls to the care of the sisters. A small wooden trap pricks a string that operates a small brass bell.

"When the bell rings we drop what we are doing to come see what God has brought us," the nun tells me.

I stare at the wheel and ponder the many reasons why someone might to want to hand over a baby.

As if reading my mind, the nun says, "Sometimes there is a letter that comes with the baby. "More often not."

"A letter?"

She nods. "So many unfortunate stories," she clucks. "Most often those born outside the sanctity of marriage. Or the privilege of money. It costs to raise a child," she says, rubbing her fingers together as if she were fingering a coin. Then she shrugs. "But then others with charitable intentions place money in the box, so the Lord provides for these poor babes."

I reach my hand out to touch the wooden wheel, feeling it budge and creak on its metal track beneath my hand. Just then, I feel a small kick in my side.

Chapter 24

If the orphan wheel, that creaking wooden *scaffetta* that draws the infants behind the convent walls, has haunted me, then the tiny kick in my side has unnerved me to the core. As I hear the convent door latch closed behind me and I melt back into the bustle of the city, I feel lightheaded, as if I might faint. I press my palm to the rough brick convent wall for a few moments, judging how many steps I must take from here to the painter's gondola.

The painter's boatman is waiting for me.

He is seated next to Trevisan's gondola with his legs hanging over the stone lip of the quayside. Beside him, a tall, slim boatman with a red velvet hat is sharing a husk of bread.

"They stuff themselves with sausages and sweetbreads, while we only have a ration of bread and wine, and hardly enough wood to keep the bedchamber warm," I hear him say to the other boatman.

They have not seen me. I think of the dank room off the kitchen where the boatman sleeps. Part of me feels pity for him.

"Count yourself fortunate," I hear the other boatman say. "I am sleeping in a corner of the chicken yard."

I step carefully to the waterside and lower myself into the gondola. The other boatman gestures in my direction and Trevisan's boatman notices me for the first time. He scrambles to his feet and jumps into the boat, grasping the oar from where it is tucked along the side of the keel.

I have no desire to engage the boatman in conversation. I press myself into the passenger compartment and close the curtain behind me. I place the package with my aunt's pastries on the seat beside me, their aroma still wafting from the linen wrapping. I close my eyes. I feel the boat rock as the boatman takes his position on the aft deck. I hear him place the oar into the carved oarlock. Then I feel the gondola begin to ply the water. Mercifully, he does not speak during our journey to the painter's workshop.

After a while I feel the gondola make a turn into the cool darkness of the painter's *cavana*. I stand and gather my package of pastries, knowing that Antonella will be waiting in the kitchen to see what I have brought. But when I try to climb out of the boat, the boatman is blocking my path. I try to go around him, but he moves to stand in front of me. I hesitate for a moment, then meet his gaze.

"*Perdoname*," I say, squaring my shoulders to his. But he does not budge. His eyes form large, expectant orbs.

"Surely you cannot expect a boat ride without paying the fare, signorina." The corner of his mouth rises into a smirk.

"You have already been paid," I whisper, meeting his gaze.

"And I have sealed my lips," he says. "So far."

The cold canal water laps against the stones and makes wavering patterns of light against the dark, cavernous space of the painter's boathouse.

"I cannot continue to siphon off gold leaf," I say. "Soon I will have exhausted the supply I brought with me from my father's workshop. I cannot go back home to get more. I will also not have any more to work on our commission, and the painter will know that it is missing," I say.

The boatman shrugs. "But you misunderstand, signorina. I am a reasonable man and payment may come in many forms. Surely you have access to more of value than gold leaf." His pupils look wild and shiny in the darkness of the boat slip.

"What are you suggesting?" My whisper echoes off the cavernous, damp walls.

"I am suggesting that I am only getting what is rightfully owed to me. There are many things of value inside the painter's house," he says.

I remain silent.

"The painter's wife has a jeweled necklace," he continues. "Her husband gave it to her, but she never wears it. It now sits in the back of a cabinet; at least that is what I have heard. They will never know that it is gone. But for me it will bring a pretty penny with the secondhand brokers."

I feel sick, as if I might vomit right there in the boat.

"You cannot expect me to steal from Master Trevisan and his wife," I whisper loudly. "That is out of the question."

"Unfortunate," says the boatman. "Well. Perhaps I might be satisfied with something slightly more meager."

"Like what?" I say, hoping that dread has not crept into my voice.

His eyes flicker again in the darkness. "I understand that you have a necklace of your own. You might part with that one instead."

Antonella. That wretched woman has described my golden ingot to the scheming boatman.

I try to stop myself, try to deny the truth of its existence, but it is too late. My fingers have already crept up to protect the *battiloro*'s gold ingot, where it is hidden beneath my linen undergarments.

Chapter 25

Gold is a beautiful and reflective metal, one of the most precious materials known to man. But in spite of its sparkle, gold can be deceiving. For what lies underneath is often dull, dingy, mean. Gold makes even the most common object seem something it is not. It can melt in a heartbeat. When beaten out into a leaf, it is as thin as a hairbreadth and can blow away with the slightest breeze. Gold leaf is a foil. It lies.

Our city is full of shimmering materials: mosaic shards, glass vessels, metals precious and shining. But just as you might introduce your finger to the surface of a shimmering lagoon, one touch and everything shatters.

Things are not as they appear.

When I was a child my father showed me how to lay the gold leaf around the corners of a panel so that the wood beneath was invisible. "*Bene*, Maria," he began. "What kind of wood is underneath this altar?" Although his voice was stern and serious I saw the skin around his eyes begin to crinkle. It was another one of my father's endless questions.

A game. A challenge.

Now I see that it was his way of teaching me, of showing me the way with the gold. Of course it was impossible to know what kind of wood was there as long as we had done our job well.

I turn the wooden box over in my hands now, considering how I will attach the molded figures just like the box above Master Trevisan's hearth. The rest of the house is asleep. Everything is dark. I pick up my brush and swirl it into the pot I have prepared with the glistening medium. I add a little egg from Trevisan's hens to thin the paint. It jiggles and reflects the flickering candlelight.

In the silence, I feel my heart beating through every fiber of my body. The fact of my pregnancy is irrefutable, and Antonella is right; it cannot remain a secret forever. The *battiloro*. He must know about it first, before anyone else. I must know if he will claim his child, and if he will claim me. I must reach him before the painter, the *gastaldo*, my father, or anyone else discovers it.

For now, I must keep Antonella and that boatman quiet.

But I am not a thief.

It is not within me to take something that belongs to someone else. I know that now. As much as we have had our uncomfortable moments, the painter and his wife have been kind to me, and I cannot steal from them.

But that boatman has gone out of his way to extort me, and I must respond.

The last thing I want to do is hand over the most precious object I own, the golden ingot strung around my neck by the *battiloro*'s own hands.

But if that boatman is to ask something precious of me to keep his silence, then I think that I must ask for something from him in return. He has named his price and now I must name my own.

Chapter 26

Green shoots have begun to push their way through the cracks of the cobblestones. Among them, a few brave, pale blooms open their delicate faces to the new angle of the sun that heralds the Easter season. The light has lured children into the *campo*, and their voices echo against the walls as they play at *pallina*. At Rialto, boatmen unload purple heads of radicchio and white asparagus spears into the market carts from cargo barges shipped down the rivers from terra firma.

Trevisan's boatman has removed the wooden *felso* of the gondola's passenger compartment, with its slatted windows and curtains of heavy brocade. I have seen the awkward contraption placed for storage on trestles in the shadows of the boat slip. He has replaced it with a lighter, more open wooden frame with silk curtains the color of the spring sky.

I watch the light curtains unfurl in the breeze as we float toward the studio of Pascal Grissoni. Master Trevisan has insisted that all of us come with him—his wife, his journeyman, and myself. Antonella has stayed behind to tend to the children. Trevisan and his journeyman have ceded the passenger compartment to us women. They sit on the wooden chairs toward the stern of the boat and the boatman silently rows toward San Marco.

I steal a glance at the painter's wife, seated on the cushioned bench across from me. She has expended great effort getting ready for today, her hair coiffed with two points at the forehead in the current fashion, with pearls intertwined in her fine curls and looped around her neck. The beads disappear into the neckline of a gold and green satin dress cinched tightly under her breasts. She seems not to know what to do with her hands, devoid of her infant daughter. She twists the lace of her sleeve in the fingers of her opposite hand and, through the opening in the blue drapery, she watches a water-seller's skiff pass within a hand's breadth in the narrow canal.

A small bulge emerges below the beaded trim of her gown, and as if reading my mind, she runs her palm over the front of her dress and rests it on the side of her rounded form. Her full breasts break the surface of her neckline. She has already given birth to two children, and her body knows what to do. She has taken to wearing dresses cinched up under her breasts so that the drapery falls across the perfectly rounded form of her abdomen, showing her blossoming shape to full advantage.

While the painter's wife has done everything she can to highlight her pleasant, burgeoning form, I have done everything in my power to conceal my own. My breasts are swollen and sore, and I have taken to binding my midsection with a roll of firmly woven linen before putting on my shapeless shift. In the studio I leave my apron untied, and wear an extra layer of underskirts, which make the bottom of my dress flair and look fuller, drawing attention—I hope—away from my midsection.

The painter's wife turns her gaze to me. "Your dress flatters you," she says.

"It is kind of you to say," I look down at the floor of the gondola. "I did not have anything suitable for this occasion, so I altered an old dress from my trunk."

Not owning an elegant gown appropriate for today's visit, I have reconceived the only dress in my trunk that is not reserved for working. It is old; I have only worn it to funerary masses, marriages, the procession of our guild's feast of Saint Luke. Over several days, working in my room by candlelight, I have let out the stitches at the back of the dress and added two swatches on either side of the waist that Antonella has retrieved from her own mending box.

Before leaving the painter's house I considered my reflection in a faded mirror in the corridor. I felt satisfied with my handiwork and felt that the swatches coordinated closely enough, not a bad solution under the circumstances. Now, sitting across from the richly appointed painter's wife, I see that the edges of my neckline are frayed, the once-rich deep blue turned grey from many washings. My hair is twisted into my usual braids and tucked under a worn cap. Compared to the colorful finery of the artist and his wife, I look like a dull, grey moth.

"Pascal Grissoni lives in a fine house with a large studio, one of the most beautiful of all the guild," the painter's wife tells me. "His grandfather did well with commissions for the Council of Ten." She pauses. "You would do well to marry someone of his kind," she says. "Any girl would."

If I suspected that Pascal Grissoni was being offered for my consideration, or rather I for his, there is no longer any doubt. I am being offered up by our guild's *gastaldo*, and probably my own father.

"I am sure I would have nothing to offer in return," I say. "Our *gastaldo* means well, but he must know that my father has no way to amass a dowry on my behalf."

The painter's wife lowers her voice to a whisper and casts her eyes outside the passenger compartment to ensure that the men are not listening. "A beautiful woman is always in demand," she says. "Besides, women may be of use to their husbands in ways other than beauty, possessions, or wealth." The painter's wife sets her clear blue eyes on me. "You may not have a dowry, Maria, but you have beauty *and* skill with the gold. If I possessed the skills you do I might have been of greater use to my husband."

"You underestimate yourself, signora."

She shakes her head. "My father was a gilder, like yours, but he saw worthy only to pass on the trade to my brothers, not to me. I wish that I possessed the knowledge that you do. It serves you well. You must accept it—and use it to your advantage."

The painter's wife's words echo inside my head as we turn our attention to a group of children skittering across a sagging wooden bridge with no railings. I squint into the bands of sunlight that streak down the water beneath it. Through the glare, two dark-skinned merchants elbow forward over the bridge, rugs and colorful silks draped from their outstretched arms. They move toward a cluster of ladies at the corner, muttering prices with one of the thick accents we hear from Slavia, Ifriqya, Arabia, Albania, and other faraway places. I hear the languages but do not know how to tell them apart. We move into San Marco, a bustling, prosperous part of the city with fine façades reflecting their pale colors like a rainbow in the canal. Along the quayside, a group of women chat loudly as they negotiate a barter of glass beads at a small table.

The boatman slides his oar into the bottom rung of the oarlock and turns it to slow the gondola. We approach the mooring poles outside a house with large, coursed stones.

"Benvoglio Trevisan!" A man on the quayside waves his hand in the air. There is a cluster of fellow painters, plus a few wives, waiting at the doorway of Pascal Grissoni's house. Trevisan looks embarrassed; he is not one to make a grand entrance. The boatman leaps onto the stone stairway to offer his hand to each of us as we alight from the boat.

As soon as the painter and his wife exit the boat they are swarmed by fellow guildsmen. A man grasps Trevisan's cheeks between his hands and kisses him. A woman engages the painter's wife in conversation. She beams and chats, as if she has finally found an appreciative audience. The painter's journeyman skulks behind his master like a stray dog.

For a moment the boatman and I are left behind, standing awkwardly. I see my opportunity.

"I might give you your next... payment," I say to the boatman under my breath.

His eyes widen.

"But in exchange, you must help me," I say.

"And what does that entail, signorina?" His voice lowers, tinged with anticipation.

"I am trying to reach a man in Cannaregio. You may be in a position to help me."

"What kind of a man?"

"In my father's workshop near the Campo Sant'Alvise, we have a *battiloro* who beats the sheets of gold into the thin leaves you know so well." My eyes stay straight ahead, but from my peripheral vision I can see that he is closely tracking each word. He says nothing. "He is a tall man with skin the color of walnut."

"A dark-skinned man in your father's workshop. A Saracen?"

I nod.

I hear the boatman snort. "You must be mad to suggest that I go there. The streets in that section of Cannaregio are blocked, signorina," he says. "None of us can get through."

"It will be worth your while," I say.

He hesitates. "You might pay a boatman from one of the *traghetti* to deliver a message. I am not your man."

"No," I say. "I am not looking to send a message."

"What then?" He shrugs.

"You must bring him to me."

The boatman's eyes widen into great orbs, then he huffs. "Signorina, surely he will not be allowed to leave. The entire quarter is under a ban. They have stationed guards at each one of the barricades."

I know he is right, but I push again.

"Our Most Serene City is best navigated by water, not by alleys, you know that. Surely you can find a way. You must tell him that I have sent you, that it is critical that I see him."

The boatman says nothing, but his face has turned contemplative. For a few long moments, he seems to wrestle with the offer I have presented. I feel dirty, and I do not want him to know any information about my personal life. But I am so desperate to see Cristiano, to decide the future of the life growing inside of me, that I am risking my sense of decency and privacy.

"None of the boatmen want to go into the quarter," says the boatman finally. "They are all afraid of being infected. And I am not going there. You can forget about it."

"I see. Well, that is unfortunate." I bunch up my skirts and begin to climb out of the boat.

"Wait." He grasps my sleeve. "You want him to know of your condition."

I feel his eyes burning my skin. My mouth moves but no words emerge.

His eyes flash. "And if I am successful in bringing this man to you, or at least conveying this… information?"

Ahead, the small group of painters is filing into the door of Pascal Grissoni's studio. Trevisan's journeyman looks back and gestures for me to follow. I see the artist and the other guests filing into the doors of the house.

I hesitate, but only for a second. I have come this far and so I continue. I lower my voice. "In exchange, you will have my necklace. An ingot of pure gold. You might imagine that I know its value. Bring me my man, and I promise it will be worth your while."

Ignoring the boatman's outstretched hand, I climb out of the boat and follow Master Trevisan without looking back.

Chapter 27

"Do you see, Maria?" Master Trevisan says, reaching out as if to grasp my arm. He hesitates just before his fingers brush the ragged trim of my sleeve. "See how the paint has been built up in thin layers? The oil captures and reflects light in ways tempera cannot." His hand leaves my side and his finger traces a drapery fold on an elaborate red cloak of Saint Jerome.

"Mmm." I try to concentrate on the picture, but I am distracted. Pascal Grissoni's workshop is overwhelming, a feast for the eyes. There is a pinkish, blown-glass chandelier suspended from an iron hook in the coffered ceiling. An arched loggia overlooking the wide canal. Light streaming from leaded windows on three sides, making bright streaks along the marble floor. Smiling angels swooping from a lofty ceiling painted to resemble the sky. Crackled mirrors along one wall. Velvet-upholstered chairs and impressive-looking swords and halberds mounted on the walls. Pascal Grissoni's home could be that of a nobleman rather than a humble painter.

Yet there are paintings. Dozens and dozens of paintings. As in Master Trevisan's studio, pictures are hung floor to ceiling, with others stacked haphazardly along the walls or propped on wooden easels. I recognize some old panels, but there are also new canvases stretched and nailed across wooden frames.

Grissoni's father, a strapping man with a broad chest and a generous beard, guides us to an elegant room filled with men. In addition to the four of us who have traveled to Pascal Grissoni's studio, there are a handful of others who have come to see the pictures before they are sent to a monastery where no one other than the brothers will see them.

Master Trevisan and his journeyman join the group of guildsmen, but I hesitate, unsure where I should stand, or where I belong in the makeup of this esteemed group. I hang back with the painter's wife, close enough to hear the conversation but not in a position to join it. Alongside us, a portrait of a woman with a small dog stands on an easel. I pretend to examine it with great concentration, and in truth, I am captivated with the rich colors on the canvas surface.

"Exactly right." I hear the voice of Master Bellini, the most well-regarded painter in our guild. I know him only by reputation and by his pictures, but have never seen the man himself. All of us turn our attention to him. "The oil pigments are slow to dry, which means that they can be blended better than egg tempera. They also account for the translucency and light reflection that I'm sure all of you can see."

Master Bellini is now, unbelievably I think, standing alongside me, after I've spent a lifetime imagining him as our enemy. What would my father say? Bellini is one of the men my father faulted for the demise of our trade, his name spit out with a strange mixture of disdain and admiration. He is one that I, as a girl, imagined seeing outside my window, the one who would take our gold away. Now I see that he is nothing more than a stooped old man.

"That is what I learned in the Low Countries," Pascal Grissoni says, and I see his father nod with pride.

"Our Master Giorgione would approve," says Master Bellini, "God rest his soul." Several of the people in the group cross themselves, and we all stand quietly for a few moments of respect for the painter who showed such promise before the most recent outbreak of pestilence took him from our guild.

"Look, Maria." The painter's wife whispers at my ear. She cuts her eyes to the side to prompt me to follow her gaze. At the far end of the painting studio, the door to the kitchen has opened. Before a roaring fire in the hearth, several servants work at the table, stacking serving dishes and wiping goblets clean. Beyond, a back stairway leads to the main floor of the house. I gaze into the darkness above the stair and work to imagine climbing the treads to the bedchambers on the upper floors.

For a moment I feel a tingle pass through my legs and up my spine. What would it be like to be mistress of this house? I never could have imagined such a fate for myself, the daughter of a humble gilder. Yet my father, my *gastaldo*, and perhaps even the painter's wife, are conspiring on my behalf.

I imagine the private chambers upstairs, surely as fine as the rooms on the lower floors. Would it be possible to work myself into Pascal Grissoni's marriage bed, then bring the baby into this world as his own child?

"You like it, Maria?"

Pascal Grissoni has broken away from the circle of men surrounding him. He comes to stand alongside me before his easel. I feel the heat rise to my cheeks and I hope that he will not see them flush. Could he read my mind, filled with images of the two of us entwined in his bed sheets?

I lean forward and feign intense interest in the portrait. After a few long moments, I feel his soft brown eyes on me, and I feel I must respond.

"If I must be honest, *missier*, I am uncertain about the oil on canvas," I begin tentatively. "Those of us in the gilding trade... Well, it is not how we have done it for so long. My father and I."

Pascal Grissoni laughs. "Then I see that we shall have a lot to talk about."

Fearing that I have offended him, I add quickly, "But your pictures are beautiful."

Grissoni bows slightly toward me. "Then my efforts have been rewarded. Your observations have made me more gratified than anything the others have said."

I RUN MY hands across the surface of the small alder wood box that the carpenters have delivered to Master Trevisan's workshop.

When I asked the carpenter for a small box the size of the one on Trevisan's mantelpiece, he brought it to me within a day, the wood still infused with the aroma of the forest. "You know what to do, Maria," Master Baldi told me, his eyes droopy and soft. He set the box on my worktable and I felt his pity. For a fleeting moment, I saw what he saw: a gilder still working in the old ways—one of the *Crivelleschi*—pulled away from the influence of her father.

Crivelleschi. That is what they call us.

It is the name given to those of us—painters and gilders—who follow the style of Carlo Crivelli, those of us who continue to make elaborately gilded panels even as our patrons' taste has led us elsewhere. When I was young my father told me how his own father had befriended Crivelli when their master brought them under his roof as apprentices. The rest of us only knew Master Crivelli by reputation, as much for his masterful use of gold as for what put him in the Doge's prisons. My grandfather claimed that Master Crivelli signed his pictures as a proud Venetian, *Carolus Crivellus Venetos*, even long after he had fled Our Most Serene City.

He had been exiled already before my father was born, but Master Crivelli set the path for our own workshop's gilding practices. It was Master Crivelli who inspired my grandfather to build up the gesso to make the saint's halos, the details of cuffs and hems seem to protrude from the panel, Crivelli who showed our forebears the possibilities of creating raised surfaces under the gold. When I was a small girl my father picked me up and set me on his shoulder so that I could see Master Crivelli's altarpiece in the church of San Trovaso, where he had built up the glistening metal armor and horse's harness with layers of gesso and gold. "That is gilding," my father had said, and it was all I could do to stop myself from running my small fingers across the raised surfaces of the spurs of Saint Michael's pointed-toe boots.

I have covered the raw wood of the small box that the carpenters made for me with several thin layers of ox gall. I fished through Master Trevisan's limited collection of gilding punches, rummaging through two drawers of neglected tools. One with a small wooden handle and a metal wheel that makes stippled patterns when you roll it across the surface of the soft wood caught my eye. I have improvised by alternating patterns of diamond shapes and palmettes. Next, I have applied more layers of red bole over the surface, overlaying the stipple work to prepare it to take the gold leaf. This part I could do in my sleep.

The busy work helps distract me for a time, for otherwise my mind turns to that boatman. Has he made his way beyond the barriers in Cannaregio? Has he found my father's house? Has he reached my Cristiano? All I can do is wait, so I return to my work.

The part that remains in question are the raised surfaces that I must fashion if this box is to resemble the one on Trevisan's mantelpiece, the one made in his cousin's workshop in Padua. The raised surfaces will take more than a simple building-up of gesso. They must be molded instead.

On the worktable before me, I lay out the tin molds that Trevisan has shown me. There is a mold to make a palm tree, several male and female figures in different poses, a cat that may be a panther or a lioness, an archway, and several small molds for making repeating decorative patterns. I imagine that the elements could be arranged in different compositions across the surface of the box, so I shift the tin molds around to try out various combinations.

Next, I take the book of engravings from the shelf and open the binding so that the book lies flat on the table. I turn the parchment sheaths until I reach the now-familiar image of the ill-fated lovers, Pyramus and Thisbe. Following this model, I arrange the molds of the male and female figures on either side of the tree. On one side, I place the mold with the cat.

The color-seller has sent me home with a box of supplies to try, and I finger through its contents to consider how I will proceed. At first, the *vendecolore* seemed intrigued when I told him I wanted to make a box for my father, that I wanted to emulate the one in the painter's studio. The more I described the box in Trevisan's studio, the more excited the *vendecolore* became.

"*Bianco di Venezia*," he said, waving a small glass jar filled with white powder in front of me. "Lead paste. You will need to mix it." I already know how to expose the flaky white mixture to vinegar vapor in a sealed jar. Mixed with egg white, it takes on a particularly pungent scent and becomes pliable for molding into various shapes.

"I am not sure I can pay for so much, Master da Segna," I said. "I am sorry. The painter is paying me with instruction, not with *scudi*."

"Understood." He nodded, scratching his head. "The lead is expensive because of the levies the Republic puts on them," he said. "Our Most Serene Republic holds the exclusive right to manufacture and sell lead white in our territories. The guild inspectors monitor the quantities I sell and the prices I charge. I am not at liberty to give it to you at no charge; otherwise I would do so gladly. But," he said, wagging a finger at me, "I have heard of people achieving the effect of lead paste by binding a little rabbit glue with rice flour. "You might try it," he said, as I considered asking Antonella for a sack of rice flour to try mixing the concoction on my own.

"And one other thing!" The *vendecolore* dragged a wooden stool to his shelf and produced two small glass vials filled with amber-colored oil. "You could also try mixing the scent of musk or civet to the paste you put in the molds," he suggested, his eyes bright. He poured a single drop of civet onto a wooden stick then waved it before my face. I wrinkled my nose, unsure if the animal-infused scent would be considered pleasant or not. The color-seller shrugged. "They say it wards off the pestilence."

Inside the box I brought home from the *vendecolore* there is also a container of rabbit-skin glue, which he assured me would have the greatest adhesive properties to attach the molded pieces to the box. Finally, there is a pack of sheets of the alloys that resemble pure gold. These he provided to me at no charge. I run my fingers over the small sheets, which seem stiff and dark compared to the brilliant leaves beaten by my own *battiloro*. They do not resemble pure gold at all to me, but others might be easily fooled. In the dark silence of Trevisan's studio, I fan my face with the small leaves fake gold, and I wonder what Carlo Crivelli would think.

When I was a girl I overheard the neighbor women whispering about our own Master Crivelli, and I felt they must possess knowledge of him that no one else did. As I grew older, I realized that everyone knew the story. Crivelli had become smitten with the wife of a sailor. Crivelli managed to spirit his lover away from her brother's house, where she stayed while her husband was at sea. He kept her hidden away for several months in the attic of his own house. Once his adultery was discovered, Crivelli paid a large fine to the Council of Forty and spent several months in the Doge's prison. Upon his release, he fled the city and never returned, leaving behind churches full of gilded panels that inspired the generations to come.

As I arrange and rearrange the tin molds on the worktable, I think about Master Crivelli and his hidden lover in the attic. I think about Pyramus and Thisbe, the doomed couple whispering to one another through the cracks in the wall of their parents' house. And I think of my own *battiloro* and myself, hiding away in the root cellar below my father's workshop. I feel my throat begin to constrict and with the back of my hand, I press back the hot tears that threaten to spill. With concentration, I force myself to imagine laying the gold alloys across the surface of the molded images on my box. It will be simple, I think.

In the end, the gold is easy. It is love that is complicated.

ON A BRIGHT autumn day, I found myself alone in the house with the *battiloro* for the first time. One of our fellow painters had called my father to visit a convent refectory where we were to collaborate on a set of panels illustrating the life of Santa Lucia. My cousin was supposed to be working with me to burnish the bole on a new panel we were preparing, but a friend, the grubby son of another gilder down the street, appeared at our doorway and called him out to visit the market.

"There are girls there. And food," the boy said.

My cousin rarely received such an invitation, and with my father away, Paolo did not hesitate to set down his brush and hobble down the alley after his friend. He did not give me a second thought. Not once did it cross his mind that he should stay to watch out for me. That I might need watching. It would not have crossed my mind either.

It happened in an instant, with no premeditation. We fell into each other's arms, found each other's skin under layers of clothing. I never would have believed it before that day, but I was the one who started it. I reached out to touch his arm, then my hands moved up to follow his broad shoulders and press into his cheeks.

After that, all of our moments were stolen, chipped away from pieces of the day when my father was out of the workshop, or my cousin had been sent on an errand or momentarily turned his head.

At that time I did not think about what it meant, what would happen, how we would possibly continue. All I knew was that I went through my day as if floating on air, as if I might burst with joy, whether anyone saw it or not.

FROM MY FATHER'S workshop I have brought a cloth made of horsehair. It was an afterthought, something I pressed into my trunk just before leaving home. I do not know what I would have done without it. It is slightly abrasive, with the perfect amount of roughness to bring the wood layered with bole to a high sheen. We have used horsehair cloths like this for as long as I can remember, procured from a certain brush seller who makes them from horses from the Levant and sets the cloths aside for us behind the counter in his shop.

Master Trevisan's workshop is now full of red panels. They are propped along the walls, each one coated in red bole except for the parts where Trevisan has outlined the basic composition of his figures. On those sections the white gesso beneath shows, along with the sketchy lines of charcoal and black ink that Trevisan and his journeyman will use to fill in with pigment. If you squint your eyes, you can begin to imagine the finished altarpiece.

I am glad to have something physical to do, for I am filled with nervous energy. The boatman and Trevisan's gondola are gone from the house. Is he on an errand for the painter? I wonder if he is going to get my *battiloro*, and I feel my heart beat faster. Will he be able to get past the guards, weave his way into the canals, and into the narrow stretch behind my house? Will he be able to bring him to me? Will the *battiloro* agree to come? What will the signora say if a Saracen stranger arrives at her door? I push the doubt to the back of my mind and try to refocus on the panel before me.

Trevisan has sketched an angel and a saint, both outlined with black charcoal. Around the edges the red bole is no longer shiny but has dried to a dull, ruddy color. I put the horsehair cloth in my left hand. I like to change sides from time to time so that the muscles of my right arm are not twice as large as the ones of my left. I rub the horsehair slowly but firmly across the dried bole until the dull surface begins to show a characteristic sheen.

The burnishing process cannot be rushed, for it is the careful preparation of the surface that will make all the difference when the gold is applied. My father taught me to wait until the bole begins to impart a certain gloss, a sheen that cannot be described but only observed with time and experience. The burnishing process is what imparts the rich, multicolored and layered texture of the gold surface. That is when the tide starts to turn, when you feel the excitement build, when you start to visualize the final product.

As much as I admire Pascal Grissoni's oil paintings, I cannot deny that it is only in the gilding where I feel the excitement, and I wonder what will happen if canvas takes hold of our guildsmen's imagination.

Chapter 28

The Vianello boatyard stands alongside a narrow canal near the church of San Trovaso. As it lies a short distance from my father's workshop, I have passed it either from the canal side, where its long ramp slopes into the dark canal waters, or from the land side, where its stone façade looks like any other house in the alley and you would never know that behind stands a large boatyard.

"*Càvol,*" the painter says, shaking his head as he watches the boatman struggle to lash the rope to a mooring post outside the boatyard. "He is going to scratch the varnish." The painter pushes himself from the passenger compartment. "Watch the varnish!" he wags a finger at the boatman. "This boat has hardly made its way out of the *squero*. Master Vianello will be as angry as a beast."

"Forgive me, *missier,*" says the boatman. From my position inside the passenger compartment I see him roll his eyes out of view of the painter. I pretend not to notice.

"*Bondì,* painter," I hear a boy say. Through the opening in the curtains of the passenger compartment I see a handsome youth in a soiled work shirt holding a paintbrush in his hand. Two other men are applying black varnish to the keel of another boat turned upside down on trestles. Along the ramp a dozen or so gondolas are turned on their sides, each in various stages of finishing.

"Greetings, young Master Vianello," the painter hops from the gondola and tousles the boy's hair. "Your father is here?"

"*Papà!*" After a few moments the father emerges from the low building along side the boat ramp.

He grasps the painter's hand with both of his, then presses Trevisan on the shoulder. "How is the ride?"

"I do not remember life before this boat," says the painter.

In return, the gondola maker barks out a hearty laugh. "We have your new summer upholstery. It took a long time. Our upholsterer is getting old and it takes him a while to finish. We are few but we are good."

"*Bellissimo*," says the painter. "Thank you." But I see that the gondola maker is not listening. Instead, he is staring at something on the gondola and has not heard anything that the painter has said.

"Where did that lantern come from?"

"Baldi the carpenters prepared it for us," says the painter, "and my new apprentice gilded it."

Through the slats of the passenger compartment I see the gondola maker approach. He grasps the lantern from where it hangs on the hook near the boatman's position on the stern. He turns it over in his hands, inspecting the swirls and carvings through squinted eyes. He runs his fingers across the gilded surface. "You say your apprentice has done the gilding work?"

"Yes," says the painter. "She is more than an apprentice; she is the daughter of one of our most renowned gilders."

"She?"

The painter's eyes turn toward the gondola, and he gestures. "Yes. She is here with us. Maria!"

When I emerge from the passenger compartment I see the old gondola maker's face make several expressions as if he does not know how to react.

"You are young," he says finally. I feel his eyes burning on me. "Who is your father?"

"Giuseppe Bartolini, by the baker's bridge near the rio della Sensa," I say, gesturing in the direction of my father's workshop.

"Ah," he says. "That area is closed for the pestilence. It is a miracle you were able to get through here as many of our streets are closed." If the gondola maker notices my reaction he does not show it, for his eyes are back on the lantern. "You gild lanterns?" he asks.

"I am no longer in my father's house; I am in Master Trevisan's studio for now. My father and I have not done gondola ornamentation before, sir," I say. "We work on altarpieces and other panels."

The gondola maker runs his hands across the lantern again, then returns it to its place on the hook on the gondola. "We could use your services," he says. "For years we have worked with old Master Zuan, but unfortunately he has passed to the World to Come."

I feel my stomach lurch. "Master Zuan! We knew him well," I say. I find myself staring at the stones of the boat ramp.

"Maria has come to spend a year and a half with us to learn the pigments," offers the painter.

"But it is clear to me that her skill lies in gilding, Master Trevisan. You must not use your pretty colors to lure the girl away from her true talent."

"They say that no one wants the gold anymore," I am bold to say.

"That may be true for those paintings that Master Trevisan makes for the churches," says the gondola maker, "but we have constant need for gilded ornamentation on our gondolas, more so than ever before now that our noblemen want to outdo one another with their displays. With old Master Zuan gone we can hardly keep up. Perhaps you would consider doing some gilding for us? I would be most grateful."

I do not respond but instead look to the painter. "We are busy with a commission for the orphanage," says the painter, "but perhaps Maria would like to take some work on the side if things slow."

"Yes. I would be honored to help you," I say, and I feel a flicker of happiness in my heart.

Master Vianello pulls the painter into the covered area of the *squero* to examine a boat under construction, and the journeyman follows. It is unclear whether I am expected to follow the men, so I hesitate, standing near Trevisan's gondola and watching the gondola maker's sons paint lacquer on a boat's keel. The older son carefully paints around the maple leaf emblem that forms the *catanella*—the mark of the Vianello boatyard—much as Master Trevisan's signature marks each painting his own.

"Signorina." I hear the boatman's hissing voice at my ear. I turn to see his eyes on me. "Your man," he says.

I feel my throat tighten. "You have found him?" I whisper.

He shakes his head. "Not yet," he whispers back, his brown eyes growing wide. "The *signori* would not allow me through the canal."

My heart sinks, but the side of the boatman's mouth turns up in a half smile.

"But I have found another way into the quarter," he says. "One of my colleagues at the *traghetto* has promised to help me... for a price." The boatman's eyes land on my neck. "Paid in advance."

I resist the instinct to bring my hand to my necklace. "What assurance do I have that you are telling me the truth?" I say.

The boatman shrugs, then glances over to where Master Trevisan stands deep in conversation with the gondola maker and his sons. "That painter trusts me. Why shouldn't you?" I see the grey lines of his teeth as a smile spreads wide and thin. "And in the meantime," he says, "I can offer you something in return for your... deposit."

"What is that?"

"I may not have reached your man yet," he says, "but I have found his mother."

"His mother?" It had not occurred to me that the *battiloro's* mother might still be in the city, that I might be able to find her.

My heart leaps with hope at the idea that she might have a way to reach her son.

He nods. "Your necklace," he says. "A guarantee. An assurance that we will bring your man to you. And in the meantime," he says, "I will tell you where you may find the signora."

EACH DAY BRINGS increasing numbers of flat-bottomed barges moored at the ferry stations, waiting to carry the sick to the plague islands. The ferries move slowly, silently, back and forth between the *lazzaretti*, carrying the disease-struck, the recovered, the dead, the widowed, the orphaned, along with any belongings that have not been burned in the square. It has become a spectacle, a pageant for the Triumph of Death. In the sheer horror of it we have all become immune, numb to the despair.

Many of us have chosen not to look, and have secluded ourselves inside our homes, closing the battens on our shops and shuttering our windows. I spend most of my time inside the painter's workshop, going out only on Fridays at dusk to trail the small line of vineyards that begins behind Master Trevisan's hennery and ends at Rialto, at the monastery garden gate where I dream that one night, my *battiloro* will magically appear.

Today is different. I stride with purpose, following the trailing vines from the painter's house toward Rialto, for I have an important mission. I must find the *battiloro*'s mother.

I have refused the boatman's offer to bring me in the gondola, so disgusted I feel with myself for having unlatched the black cord from my neck and handed over the golden ingot to him. Instead, I walk along the northern quayside toward the washhouse where the boatman has said the *battiloro*'s mother spends her days.

From the stone embankment, I take in the sweeping view of the marsh reeds, the lagoon, and the sea beyond. On the horizon, the masts of several galleys stand like sentinels, their sails furled. The lagoon sparkles with the shimmering reflection of the sun, casting twinkling lights across the crests of the waves. The briny air pulls wisps of hair from my braid and whips them across my cheek. The vista is beautiful, and as long as you keep your head turned in this direction you could ignore, for a moment, the looming silhouettes of the plague islands beyond.

I turn down an alley that leads into the market, where the bustling vegetable sellers hawk their wares. The normally busy square is deserted, and a chill creeps up from the small of my back. Only a small mouse lopes through the market stalls, following a path through a crack that zigzags its way between the cobblestones. As I pass, it leaps to the gutter where the walls meet the street, then disappears into a small hole in the façade of a butcher's shop with its dark wooden doors battened shut.

Beneath the great archways a few blocks away from the market, women have gathered to wash. Three rows of large copper and wooden basins stand so that some two dozen washerwomen might labor over them simultaneously. In one corner, a man with soot-stained cheeks tends a fire under a great copper cauldron, the vapors rising into the spring air. Across the vaulted space another cauldron hisses with steam rising from it. A pile of white linens sits on the stones beside it, waiting for the boil to roll across the surface.

I approach a small, hunched woman wringing out linen over a large pot of water. Her hair is stuck to her head and the side of her face, the upper part of her back crooked over in a painful-looking hump. "Signora. I am looking for a Saracen washerwoman. Can you help me?"

"*Qua*," she says, opening her mouth to reveal a single tooth on the bottom row. Her face resembles a shriveled apple, and she cocks her head to one side to indicate a direction on the opposite side of the space. I follow the direction of her head and see a tall black woman with linen swaths wrapped around her head. She leans over a drying board and rubs a piece of cloth with strong, steady strokes.

"Signora?" I approach her tentatively. "You are the mother of Cristiano the *battiloro*?"

For a moment she suspends her scrubbing on the metal. The woman turns her head and looks at me with wide-set eyes the color of coal. Then she nods cautiously. "Yes. Why do you ask?"

"I am Maria Bartolini. Your son is our *battiloro*. He works in the studio of my father, the gilder."

She wipes her hands on a rag hanging from a metal hook on the stone wall. "Yes, he told me that he was going to live with the *indoradòr*." Her brow furrows and her black eyes meet mine. "You have news of my son?" she asks.

"Actually I was hoping that you would be the one with news."

"I have not seen him in weeks," she says. "I cannot get through to the house. Where is he?"

"I can only believe that he is still there," I say. "I have also been gone from my father's studio for a long time now. I have not received word from him. The pestilence has come to the neighborhood, so I have not been able to go home."

Her eyes grow wider. "*Dio*," she says. "I hope it has not gotten worse. I have tried to reach him myself, but I cannot go farther than San Giobbe." Her soft accent rolls off her tongue like a song from a distant land.

"I have no reason to believe that they are in danger," I say, trying to sound convincing. "It's just that... I have not been able to receive any messages from them in some time because of it and, well, I am eager for news from my family."

The tall woman nods and resumes scrubbing the linen garment, rubbing it down on the board with her able hands. "Let me think," she says. "He came to tell me of his new location some time ago; I don't remember exactly when. It was just beginning to turn cold. He told me that the old man who taught him his trade had

died, and that an *indoradòr*—your father, I suppose—had taken
him in." Her eyes brighten. "He was happy with the arrangement,
it seemed to me."

"We all were, yes," I say. I cannot help but feel the smile cross
my lips. "Your son is very skilled with the gold."

She nods, then her eyes turn to slits. "You are no longer living
with your father? You have married then."

"No," I blush and look down at the wet stones under my shoes.
"I am working as an apprentice to a painter in San Marco. I am no
longer in my father's house. Unfortunately. What is your name?"

"Zenobia."

"How long have you been in Venice?" I ask.

The woman takes a large cake of lye soap from a table against
the wall and drops it into a cauldron holding water the color of the
canal. Small bubbles emerge across the surface. Even though it is a
cool day, beads of sweat dot her forehead. She wipes her brow with
the back of her forearm. "Too many years to count," she says. "I
was small."

"Cristiano says that you left the home where he was born, that
he went to work for Master Zuan when he was still very little."

She shakes the water off her hands. They are large and calloused, with stains of ash and lye. "I raised my baby in a boarding
house down the *calle* with some others like us who were brought
here on the galleys." She gestures toward the shadows of a nearby
alley. "But as soon as he was old enough to do things for himself, I
arranged for him to be apprenticed. In his sixth or seventh year, I
think. And it was the best thing for him. He deserved a better life
than the one I could give him, living in a crowded room with all
those people," she says, going back to beating the garment on the
board, then she stares out into the alley behind the laundry.

"I would like to see him more, to spend time with my boy, but
he must make a living to eat and so must I. And so we only see one
another now and again when we have food and money to share,

or to take time on a Sunday when he comes to the *pensión*." She shrugs. "Of course I want to see him. He belongs to me."

I feel a smile grow across my face. "You should feel proud, Signora Zenobia, for your son has done well," I say. "He has made a name for himself among the *indoradòri* in our guild."

"So he has told me."

"For years my father and I used the products of his work when he was working with the old *battiloro* down the street. He became known for his skills in beating the gold, both within our guild and through our circle of patrons. That is why my father brought him into our workshop as soon as the old *battiloro* died. And he became part of our household, with my father, my cousin, and myself. Above all he knows his trade." I find myself talking excitedly.

The woman stops what she is doing and stands to face me. I see the smooth skin of her neck, as black as the night sky. "Let me ask you something," she says. "Why are you trying to find Cristiano now?"

"I thought you might be able to help me. I am trying to find a way to see him or at least get a message to him from someone I trust." I think of the boatman and shudder. "Cristiano needs to know..." I hesitate, but only for a moment, then I meet her gaze. I look into the deep pools of her eyes. "...that I am carrying his child."

Chapter 29

The painter's workshop glitters. The great panels of our altarpiece are propped against the walls. Everywhere there is gold, and I feel my heart lighten.

The last panel that needs to be gilded lies on the worktable in front of me. I have torn off the last vellum pages of the last book of gold leaf from my father's workshop. One by one, I apply the leaves across the surface of the bole, overlapping them carefully up to the outlined figures where Trevisan and his journeyman will fill in with the pigments. Trevisan has reserved several sections for me to practice my new skills on the rocks and trees in the background.

When my hand tires of laying the gold leaf, I pick up a small agate stone and begin to make light strokes over the areas where I have laid the gold leaf. The brilliant gold begins to take on a rich texture and in some areas, the red-clay bole underneath begins to show.

I think about the box I have hidden on a shelf under my worktable, the one I have been making for my father. It is not as beautiful as the box on the painter's mantelpiece, I judge, but for a first attempt, it is passing. I am happy with the way the alloy has emulated the brilliance of pure gold. To the untrained eye, it looks like gold. I have hidden it away under my worktable, placing a cloth over it until I see my father. I feel a bit ashamed of it, and do not want Master Trevisan to see.

The painter and his journeyman have gone to work on their commission at the *scuola*, the one that does not require gold. The boatman has taken the painter's wife and children to visit family in Dorsoduro. Antonella and I are left alone in the painter's house.

Antonella ambles about the workshop, idly dusting the surfaces of the tables and shelves, ignoring other areas where there are layers of dust. For a half-hour, she has moved sluggishly around the room, appearing to wipe surfaces but mostly airing her complaints to me about the painter's wife. "And a woman like that, with two babies already and another one coming..." She stops and turns to me. "She needs more help, and I have told her that on more than one occasion. But she is being cheap. Do you not agree?"

I hesitate. "I cannot comment," I say, "for I do not know what it is like to have the responsibilities of Signora Trevisan." Immediately I cringe and wish I could take it back.

"You will know soon enough unless you do something about it," she says, waving a rag at my stomach.

My face feels hot. "The painter and his wife have been more than generous with me."

Antonella makes a loud huff, a sarcastic sound. "Ah, but that is the irony of it," she says. "You have the idea that you are one of them, but the signora trusts *me*," Antonella says, pressing her thumb to her chest. "I have made sure of that. It's *you* she distrusts."

"Why are you so bitter?" I ask.

"The contract I have with them," says Antonella, picking up a broom and stopping to lean on it, "was made back when Signora was pregnant with the boy. As you may imagine, my work has tripled since then. But not my salary. It remains the same."

"Have you spoken with Master Trevisan or the signora about it?" I ask.

"More than once," she says. "Signora says that my salary is the normal rate for house servants. And now with number three coming soon..." She shakes her head. "I would find another position if I could, but they are difficult to come by."

"And the boatman feels the same?" I ask, not certain that I want to broach the subject.

She runs her fingertips over the freshly gilded surface of the panel on the table. "Boatman and the painter have a... complicated arrangement," she says. "It has to do with the apprentice who was here before you."

"What happened to him?" I feel curious to see if Antonella's story aligns with the one the painter's journeyman has shared. Antonella props her broom against the wall and drags a stool over to the table where I am working. She heaves herself onto the stool.

"He was an odd sort of fellow. Quiet. Did not say much." She gestures to my worktable, where the old apprentice's things remain cluttered under the table along with the new box I have made for my father. She wags her finger as if to emphasize a point. "I knew there was something more than what appeared on the surface. It was hard to put a finger on it, but I had a feeling about him."

"Were you correct?"

She nods. "It turns out that he was smuggling. He was helping a group of men who were running boats back and forth to Chioggia. They were bringing in raw silk hidden in grain sacks, working it in one of the warehouses in Rialto. Then they were reselling it outside of the silk workers' and silk merchants' guilds. They made a small fortune." Her black eyes go wide and shiny.

"The boatman was helping him?"

She nods. "He was only being paid to do a job. He helped transport the sacks in Trevisan's old gondola."

"But the boatman knew what was inside the grain sacks? That it was not actually grain?"

"Of course," she says. "They were sharing the profits from the silk that he transported. An advantageous trade for as long as it lasted."

"And you also knew about it?"

She nods.

"But you did not tell Master Trevisan."

She shrugs. "Servants do not share half of what we know. That should be obvious. It is part of our job. Have we not kept *your* secret so far?"

So far. I think about the boatman's request for me to steal from the painter, and my heart begins to pound. I hope that Antonella cannot read panic on my face. "They were caught?" I ask.

She nods again. "One night the *signori di notte* followed them from Chioggia. They boarded the painter's gondola to search the sacks. It was not the only boat they boarded. There were others—skiffs, cargo vessels—a group of them traveling together. That is probably what tipped them off. Some of the boatmen managed to row out of reach, but not our man. They seized the painter's gondola. That is how the painter found out what his apprentice had been doing the whole time."

"Master Trevisan never got his boat back?"

"No," she says. "They burned the boat on the pyre to make an example for other smugglers. But the authorities realized that the painter had nothing to do with it. So after the burning, they compensated Master Trevisan for the loss of his boat. That is how he has a new one."

"And what happened to the apprentice?"

Antonella stands and presses her palms on the table. "He was sent to the Doge's prison for several weeks. We did not hear anything of him for a time. Then one day we heard that his case was judged and that he was sentenced as a rower on the slave galleys," she says, gesturing toward the window as if we could see the great sailing ships anchored in the lagoon. "Three years." Suddenly her eyes grow wide and flash. "But then, he escaped!"

"Escaped? From the Doge's prisons? How?"

"When they opened the prison doors to lead him to his sentence on the galleys, he broke free and ran to the docks near the Arsenale. Some of his old friends who had not been caught were waiting there for him. Somehow they had gotten messages to him in the prison. They collected all their money and before they could catch him he was already half way to Pellestrina!" Antonella's chest heaves, her eyes large and shiny orbs. "He got away with all of it. All of it! Enough to live well on terra firma for the rest of his days." I see that she is impressed with this feat, that she herself has lived vicariously through this sneaky painter's apprentice.

"And the boatman?"

"Ah, now that is more complicated," she says, heaving herself back down on the stool. "That hateful wife would have had the boatman put in the Doge's prisons, too, but the painter said that he only needed to go in the stocks for a while."

"And then they let the boatman come back? To work for them?"

She nods. "Believe me, if he could have found another position he would have, but as you might imagine, it was difficult for him to find another engagement once the news of the smuggling spread. And as he is marked by fire, well…"

"Master Trevisan had a new boat made and he needed a boatman," I say.

She nods. "But things are… delicate. If that painter and his wife treated us poorly before, you can imagine. They are even withholding his salary! Unfair. And he has not found any side jobs yet. He is working on it." She presses her lips together in a smug expression. "Anyway, the painter thinks he was successful in luring the boatman back, but the reality is that he could not stay away from me any longer." She bursts out laughing, a haughty, ragged sound. "Ha! So he came back to us. The painter renewed both of our contracts." Her lips form a tight smile. "I have told you. There is more going on in this house than meets the eye."

"You are really having... relations... with the boatman?" I feel compelled to ask. "In the gondola?"

She sets her black eyes on me. "Where else are we supposed to go? And what do you care? Surely you are not in a position to judge?"

I remain silent, knowing that she has a point.

Antonella picks up her broom and a pail, then heads toward the kitchen. "Sometimes we give our hearts to the ones who make the least sense." Before pushing the door, she takes another long look at me and shakes her head. "Am I right, *cara?*"

THAT NIGHT, I dream of Master Trevisan's gondola gliding to a stop in the narrow canal behind my father's studio. In my mind's eye, I see the boatman dressed in a fine ensemble, stepping out of the gondola. He hands my newly gilded box to the *battiloro*, who stands on the quayside.

"A treasure for you," the boatman says, bowing as the gold beater takes the box in his hands. "She made it with her own hands."

"THERE IS SOMEONE here to see you," Antonella says when I descend the stairs into the kitchen, my head still heavy with the dream of my Cristiano holding my gilded box in his hands. Antonella is wiping the baby's face with a rag. When I pass, the little girl squeals with excitement and beats the table with a wooden spoon.

I place my hand on the door leading to the artist's studio, but something makes me pause. I hear men's voices on the other side.

My palm rests against the cool wood of the door, and I strain to hear what they are saying.

"I do not know how much I should tell her." I hear the voice of Signor Baldi the carpenter. His voice is deep and gentle, and I recognize it immediately.

"Probably best to let her hear the truth," I hear the painter say. "Might lessen the shock if something happens."

I push open the heavy, swinging door. "Let me hear what?"

"Signorina Maria," says the carpenter. His eyes are ringed and dark, but he makes himself smile. "It is a pleasure to see you. You are faring well?"

"I am... well," I say, consciously avoiding the urge to touch my stomach. The painter's wife has set herself near the window with an embroidery ring, while her young son scribbles with a nub of charcoal on a piece of paper lying on the floor. The painter's wife seems to observe my face carefully.

"Has something happened?" I ask.

The carpenter hesitates. "My sons and I have brought you a few more gondola lanterns. Orders from the Squero Vianello," he says, gesturing to several ornately carved lanterns of raw wood stacked on the worktable. "Signor Vianello the gondola maker asked me to make them and deliver them for you to gild. From the looks of it you have a good side job here." I walk over and run my hands over the delicate swirls. "We have also made you a few more boxes with lids," he says. "Federico is bringing them in from the boat," he says, gesturing to the doorway, through which I can see the boy rummaging around in the small craft similar to a gondola that we call a *scipion*. The carpenter hesitates, fingering the brim of the hat in his hands.

"Is something wrong?" I try to meet the carpenter's eyes but he stares at the floor tiles and rubs his fingers more vigorously along the felted hat.

"*Bene*. Since your father is not able to visit you, nor you him, I suppose you do not have much news from the quarter. I have heard about something and I felt it my duty to share it." He casts his eyes briefly toward Master Trevisan, who gives the carpenter a barely perceptible nod.

"You have seen my father?"

"Not directly," he says, taking a few steps toward me. "I have not been to the house personally as they have blocked the street to visitors, but I trust that all is well." Behind the carpenter, I see the painter run his hand through his thick hair and finger a few paintbrushes on the table.

"But?"

"But my nephew lives on the edge of the quarter, and he has seen the latest list that the authorities have posted. I am sorry to report that Signora Granchi's name was on the list. The old lady has died."

My first reaction is one of utter relief, followed by shame for feeling such an emotion over the death of the old widow, who has lived upstairs from my father's workshop my entire life. "I am sorry," I say. The carpenter nods.

"Signora Granchi is the widow of one of our *indoradòri*. She has lived on her husband's guild pension since his death many years ago," I say to Master Trevisan.

Signora Granchi also shared her small garret with at least a dozen cats, which she lured with bits of sardines or the soft shells of the small green crabs we call *moteche*, pulled from the brackish retention pools at the edges of the lagoon. I used to watch Signora Granchi haul her stooped, frail body up and down the steps to go to the market each day, cats swirling around her ankles, mewling, fluttering their tails and rising up on their hind legs as she clucked to them through her shriveled mouth. I was always afraid that one of the cats would make her miss a step and fall, surely shattering her fragile bones. The news of her death, though sad, does not surprise me.

"There is more," says the carpenter, scratching his beard. "When they went to retrieve the signora's body, they reported signs of the pestilence." He lowers his chin and stares at the floor. "Boils."

"*Dio.*" I sit down on one of the wooden stools next to Trevisan's worktable.

"*Madonna mia!*" the painter's wife wails in a high-pitched voice.

"How is that possible?" I ask. "She rarely left the house."

"Yes, and she was by herself as you know," the carpenter says. "The *pizzicamorti* had to break through a window to get into the house."

I imagine the old woman's body brought out of the house while the cats peered down from their perches on her windowsills, and our neighbors looked on from doorways and windows, weeping and covering their noses with scented cloths. I envision the corpse-bearers, the *pizzicamorti*, those poor souls whose job it is to enter—and break in if needed—to remove the bodies of the plague victims from their infected homes. I feel an involuntary shudder run through my body.

The carpenter raises his hand. "Not to worry, signorina. It has not spread to your father's house," he says. "But, even though they show no signs the *Sanità* has confined them to home for forty days. It is not only them. Everyone on the street is confined to home in hopes that the contagion will pass."

"*O Dio!* It is getting worse!" The painter's wife raises her voice even higher.

The carpenter approaches me and attempts to grasp my hand, but I feel compelled to push it away. "I struggled with whether I should tell you," says the carpenter, glancing again at the painter. "Master Trevisan felt that you should know the truth."

"You have not seen them?"

"No, as I said the street is closed. But the inspectors said that they are well."

"Everyone? My cousin? The *battiloro*?"

"Yes, as far as we know."

I exhale audibly.

The painter's wife is fanning herself, one hand on her bulging belly. "Oh dear God, we must have a mass for the signora. What a horror!" She stands and begins pacing around the studio. "*Che Dio ci aiuti!*"

Little Gianluca begins to cry.

"You are upsetting the children," the painter says to his wife. "And you are going to upset Maria, too, *cara*. Will you please leave us in peace?"

The painter's wife ignores her husband's request. "*Madonna mia*, what if they are transported to the *lazzaretti*? What if they die? What will happen to Maria?"

The painter's wife has given words to my worst fears, and I feel that I might vomit again.

"Donata!" says the painter sharply to his wife. "*Per carità*! You must not say such things."

The carpenter scratches his lined forehead, and for a moment, I think I see his hand shaking. "Well, if, God forbid, that were to happen, then surely the guild would pay Maria's bereavement stipend according to the *mariregole* guild statutes. That is under your *gastaldo*'s jurisdiction. It would be his job to make sure that she is cared for. In our guild, where I am *gastaldo*, it is my responsibility to make sure that funds are dispersed to bury dead, dower daughters, cover stipends for widows or those who are sick."

"It will not happen," I say, standing with my fists balled next to my hips.

"Of course not, *cara*," the carpenter says, trying to grasp my hand again. This time I do not resist. "You are right," he says. "They will be fine. I am certain of it." His eyes look sunken and tired, but he pulls his mouth into a firm grin as he squeezes my hand.

From the corner of my eye, I see the painter's wife cross herself, then press her hand to her mouth as if forcing herself not to speak.

Chapter 30

It is the silence that lures me from my bed. Long before the first streaks of orange break the horizon, the hens should be making their *bruck-brucking* sounds while they scratch the straw below our window as if nervously awaiting the sun. But this morning, there is only a strange stillness.

In any case I have not slept, my mind haunted by the image of Signora Granchi's pestilent body pulled from the window above my father's house. In the dark silence, I draw my dress and cloak over my head and tiptoe down the stairs. I step out into the alley that runs behind the hennery. I shall walk to Cannaregio all the way from San Marco, for the last thing I want to do is ask the boatman for a favor.

I know I am taking a risk, but I cannot help myself. I need to see them with my own eyes.

As soon as I emerge from Master Trevisan's house it is clear why the birds have fallen into a stupor.

Caigo.

It is the kind of deep fog that only rolls into Our Most Serene City once or twice a year. I step into the street and I am enveloped in a heavy cloud of white. In the thick blanket of mist, I make my way tentatively from doorway to doorway, for it is as far as I can see. The white air hangs just inches from the cobblestones beneath my feet, and I see only the toes of my shoes. Everything beside me and in front of my face is obscured in the thick cloud that has descended.

My quarter of the city, which has felt so far away these last months, should only take a short time to reach on foot. But in the nearly opaque mist, I make my way slowly from a wooden post marking the edge of a canal to the stone doorjamb of a fine house; from a wrought-iron grille of a window to the dark silhouette of a stone well-head in the middle of a small square. Dawn should have broken, but as I step through the mud around a laundry trough, the air hangs dark and heavy with wet mist that fills my lungs. My cloak feels weighted, covered in a fine, web-like mist of small droplets.

I cross over a rickety wooden bridge with no railing, looking ahead to what was always a busy thoroughfare, now quiet. The streets are barren. As I approach Cannaregio, an acrid smell of burning wood fills the air. I feel a slight alarm and move quickly across a small *campo*. I pull my light scarf over my head and wrap it in front of my nose to ward off the smoky smell.

I no longer care that I am at risk. I must see my family. And if the *battiloro* wants me, if he loves me, if he wants his child, that is all that matters. I do not know how much time we have.

I walk ahead in a daze, turning down a familiar market street I have traversed for as long as I can remember. In the early morning hours such as this, the fruit sellers, butchers, cobblers, and clothing merchants should be calling out to us, their voices casting echoes against the stone buildings in the narrow alleys.

But the streets have fallen grey and silent, devoid of life, as if everyone has vanished. There is no market. No shoppers. No fruit sellers. No one. Only a strangely familiar street now shrouded in white as if in a dream.

I move like a ghost through the maze of alleys, picking my way along the cracked stucco walls. I pass the brick façade of Madonna dell'Orto, the parish church where Father Filippo poured water on my head when I was just eight weeks old, and where, some twelve years later, in a stifling narrow booth I had confessed to the same Father Filippo about the feelings I had for another gilder's son down the street. I pass the bakery where my father used to send me to buy bread encrusted with raisins, and where Signora Pegano was known for making the best sweet cakes at Easter. The windows are boarded and still. On the same street, Signor Fabio's tailoring shop and the elder Signor Calvi's cobbler's bench stand dark and quiet, their doors boarded and their windows tightly battened.

When I arrive at the barricade, it is barely visible in the fog. I run my hands across the wood, feeling for a plank that might be loose, or a place where loved ones might have made a hole to push through food or gifts. They have already repaired the hole where I tried to hike my leg the last time. The wood feels rough under my palm, and I feel that at any moment a splinter might find its way under my skin.

"Signorina!"

The face of the young *guardia* appears before me, hazy in the mist. "You again!" He says. "We have already told you. You cannot go through. Official orders. Toderino!" He calls out to another guard who remains invisible in the mist.

The young man reaches out to grasp my arm. "Come with me, signorina."

I feel the man's fingers brush my sleeve but I turn on my heel and run with abandon into the white wall of fog.

I CANNOT MAKE it far without stopping to catch my breath. I duck into a doorway and stop to gasp for air.

After a few minutes, my heartbeat slows. I no longer hear the footsteps of the guards.

Next to me is a building with a narrow lip of stones projecting over the edge of a canal. I remove my worn leather shoes and press them into the deep pocket of my shawl. I reach up to grasp the molding of a windowsill with the tips of my fingers. Tentatively, I step onto the narrow projection, feeling the cold stones under my toes. For a moment I hold my position, making sure that I can support myself with only my fingertips and the small pads of my toes. One misstep and I will splash into the coldness of the water below me.

Slowly, I begin to shimmy my way along the wall, not daring to look down at the green canal waters. The hardness of my stomach presses against the wall. I do not know how far I will have to shimmy like this on my tiptoes, as the other end of the building is shrouded in the fog.

After what seems an eternity, I see the other corner of the building, and I heave a sigh. I inch my bare foot around the edge until it touches the narrow quayside. Finally, I let go of the stones and rub my stinging fingertips along my dress.

I am inside the barrier.

For a moment, I stand with my palms on my knees, sobbing with relief and worry. My heart pounds again, uncontrollable in my chest. I draw my shoes from the pocket of my shawl and put them back on my aching feet.

I duck into another narrow alley, little more than a tunnel that is a well-worn shortcut to our street. Beyond, I see nothing, as the vista is shrouded in white, but the smell of smoke rises into the air from the Campo Sant'Alvise, the small square nearest our house. With my heightened sense of smell I seem to ingest the smoke, the dirty canal, into my very being. It smells of cabbage. Rotten eggs. Ghosts. Death.

In my head I hear the voice of Trevisan's journeyman. *"The Sanità? What can they do? They only handle matters after the fact. All they can do is take away the bodies and burn people's belongings after they die. There is nothing they can do to prevent the pestilence from spreading across the city."*

I press my shawl over my mouth and nose to avoid vomiting. Ahead of me, a patch of white fog swirls upward, revealing the familiar crooked roofline of my childhood home. I feel a surge of hope and break into a run, turning the corner onto our street.

Then I see it.

For a moment, time is suspended and I feel that I might fall to my knees. The sound I make wells up from somewhere deep inside, but I hear it as if it came from outside of me. It is a heart-wrenching sound that I cannot believe I have made myself.

A wooden cross has been nailed over the door.

Chapter 31

I duck under the rough-hewn wooden beams that line the ceiling of the root cellar under my father's house. The health officials have neglected to bar the cellar door, perhaps overlooking it or not caring to take the time.

Looters, however, have already found it. I feel the crunch of glass shards under the soles of my shoes, and observe the circles outlined in dust where our winter provisions were once stored. A year's worth of bounty from our garden—small glass containers of asparagus, cabbage, shallots, artichokes. All gone. Only the wobbly table in the center of the room remains.

The table. I feel a shock like a bolt of lightning run through my entire body.

The day my father discovered us here under the house, the *battiloro* and I had been sneaking away for several weeks already. In retrospect, I am not sure how we avoided notice that long. After all, we lived in close quarters all the time. We ate from the same pot, worked alongside one another, slept under the same roof.

My cousin must have realized it. But if he recognized the flush in my cheeks, the stupid grin on my face that would not disappear, my sudden distractibility, he said nothing of it.

When my father happened into the root cellar that day to discover me entangled against the wooden table with the *battiloro*, he said nothing. I dared not meet his gaze, but stood frozen, staring at his scuffed leather shoes and the bottom half of his worn breeches framed in the light of the cellar doorway. Then he turned and walked up the stone stairs.

When I returned to the house a few minutes after, flushed and staring at the floor, my father said few words but acted swiftly. As quickly as the *battiloro* had entered our workshop, I left it. It happened in a heartbeat, within a day. There was a hushed conversation between my father and our *gastaldo*, a mention of Master Trevisan's name, a contract of eighteen months, a plan for learning the pigments, a new commission, and suddenly I was whisked with my trunk onto a fine gondola bound for the painter's workshop with a promise to return home with newfound skills and a promised husband.

Cristiano and I only had one more stolen moment to exchange words. For a few precious seconds, we cleaved to one another in the courtyard next to his goldbeating bench. We consoled ourselves that we would lay eyes on one another for the Sunday midday meals. We hung our hope on the moments when we might slip away to meet in the monastery garden at Rialto on Friday evenings.

Neither of us imagined that it would end with a few hurried exchanges, a small golden token of affection now handed over to a crooked boatman in vain, and a cross on the door.

I LIFT THE wooden hatch door that leads from the root cellar to the interior of my father's house. I climb out and stand in the center of the grey, dusty workshop and take in the barrenness of the once-familiar space. I recognize the walnut beams of the low ceiling, the hearth with its single chain now devoid of a pot, empty of firewood. Only the wooden table before it remains, with its forlorn-looking chairs, one turned over on its side. All of the linens, rags, and cloth have been removed from the house, presumably burned. The sagging mattresses have disappeared, leaving the skeletons of the old oak bed frames in the bedchamber and the loft.

The house feels familiar yet strange at the same time, as if the entire world has fallen silent. I push the back door open and venture into the courtyard, where a few new green buds have appeared on the tree that shades the *battiloro's* workspace. In the canal behind the courtyard the water stands stagnant and still. The old chicken coop stands empty and in need of repair, its door hanging sideways off the hinge. The hens have disappeared, and the small garden plot where we grow onions and root vegetables is dry, untended, and full of weeds. A tattered-looking cat, perhaps one who has wandered away from Signora Granchi's upstairs rooms, lolls in the garden dirt and regards me through squinted yellow eyes.

I duck under the covered area along the canal and see the hammers still lined up on the worktable. The plunderers who rustled through our house neglected to reach the courtyard behind the house. In the drawer, I finger several gold sheets still intact in small vellum packets under the table.

It is as if the *battiloro* was here just a moment ago. I imagine that he has been sent out on an errand for my father and will return at any moment. I pick up one of the mallets, and in my mind I hear the noise of it ringing on the gold ingots. I stand at the table and place my hands on the plank of oak, full of knots.

Then I feel his presence as if he might walk into the courtyard where I stand. I feel filled up for a fleeting moment, then I feel only a void, only loss, for it is silent save for a bird rustling in the leaves of the tree branches above my head.

Chapter 32

Hearing the squeal of the metal hinges as I throw open the door, the *gastaldo* lurches forward in his seat. "Signorina Maria!" He pulls the leather strap that holds his spectacles and props it to his brow, making wisps of grey hair stick straight up on top of his head. "You gave me a scare!" His eyes light up for a fleeting moment, then the *gastaldo*'s face turns dark. "But you should not be here, *cara*. The ban... You are risking yourself by coming to the neighborhood."

I stand frozen in the doorway. For a few moments I cannot find my voice. The *gastaldo* and his sons in the back of the workshop watch me in expectant silence, but I am unable to speak, as if the floodgates are dammed.

The *gastaldo* clambers up and staggers across the space. "You must not be here," he says again, taking my hands in his. His palms feel thick, warm, and rough. "You risk catching this horrible disease. More streets have been blocked and the *guardia* has sent more men... You are breaking the law." He stops and looks into my eyes. "Maria... *Madre di Dio*, what has happened?"

"Where are they?" Finally my voice emerges, scratchy and small in my ears. "Where is my family?" His face registers confusion. "I am sorry but I could not stay away," I say. I begin to feel the hot tears run down my cheeks. I feel the *gastaldo*'s warm, rough hands as he squeezes my own. "There is a cross on the door." My voice comes out as a squeak.

"What in God's name? *Dio*." He pauses, letting the information soak in. "Why have the *signori* not come to inform me?" He lets go of my hands and rubs his palms over his face as if trying to wipe it clean.

"It is hardly the only one," the younger son says. "There are more crosses on doors in this neighborhood than there are cats. Surely they cannot be bothered to report them all." The *gastaldo* casts his son a dark look.

"I beat on the door, even tried to pry the wood off with my bare hands," I say, "but all I heard was silence. So… I found a way in through the root cellar."

"You went inside! San Rocco," the *gastaldo* says under his breath. "It can only mean one thing. They have been transported to the *Lazzaretto Vecchio*."

I feel the tears roll down my cheeks. "What? And when were you going to tell me?! Signora Granchi… It must have come through her."

"Maria, I did not know. I tried to go check on them a few days ago, but they would not let me pass through the barricade," he says. "How on earth did you get through?"

"I… It took a few tries."

The *gastaldo* sighs and pounds his fist on the worktable. "The representatives are supposed to inform me of such things, but I have not seen them in days. Perhaps Father Filippo can tell us something. His presence is required along with the health officials whenever someone is found sick."

"That old priest is probably staying at home trying not to get sick himself. Or under ban already. Who would want to read rites to the plague-ridden?" the younger son tries again.

"What is there to discover?" the older son says. "You must know that it is the procedure for those who are sick. They are transported to the old pesthouse—good as dead."

This time the *gastaldo* does not hold his tongue. "*Basta!*" he says sharply to his sons. "That is enough. The poor girl." The *gastaldo* grasps a large iron ring heavy with keys from a hook by the door. He pauses to look into my eyes. "I must go see the neighborhood representatives. I promise I will get to the bottom of it."

I feel my body shudder, and the *gastaldo* takes me in his arms. I press my face into his vest, which smells of leather and smoke.

The *gastaldo* grasps my cheeks in his hands and turns my face to his. "Maria, it is not a death sentence. Those who recover—as I am sure will be the case with your family—are eventually transported to the Lazzaretto Nuovo. That is also the place where family members who seem well and have not shown signs of the plague go."

"You are going to need to restock your house, no doubt," the older son says.

"Yes." The *gastaldo* fingers the keys in his hand. "Unfortunately, Maria, they require that all the belongings—especially the linens, be taken out of the house. Some things are burned right away in the *campo*. The more valuable objects are transported to the *lazzaretto* with their owners. There they are aired out with the hopes that they will no longer spread the contagion."

"None of it matters," I say. "We have nothing of value beyond our tools and whatever gold leaf was left unused. I am only concerned about their health."

"Of course. I am sorry." The *gastaldo* places his hands on my shoulders and looks into my eyes again. "I want you to feel certain that they will get well. Once they are better they will transport them to quarantine until they are no longer contagious. The authorities are requiring those released from the *lazzaretti* to stay there for forty days to ensure they show no more signs of the pestilence. Then they are released back home. You must hold out hope for that."

The information seeps into my being, and I feel my shoulders fall. I must accept the fact that I may not see my family for some time. "We must look for the good," the *gastaldo* says. "I am grateful that this twist of fate has brought you to the painter's house, for it means that you have been spared. It must mean that God has something else in store for you."

"If you had stayed in your house you would also be in the *lazzaretto* now," the younger son says.

The *gastaldo* nods. "On that count my son is correct. You yourself would have been there now had it not been for the fact that you were safely housed with Master Trevisan," he says. "As long as you stop sneaking back into this neighborhood you will be fine. Now please, for the love of God, go back to the painter's house before you end up in the *lazzaretto* yourself." His eyes, surrounded by wrinkles, look kind and sincere. "Come," he says. "I will walk back to San Marco with you."

I nod, wiping another hot tear from my cheek with the back of my hand. I step back out into the street, strangely quiet and still, the air filled with the overwhelming dry smell of smoke from the square. The *gastaldo* offers me his arm and I gratefully take it, for I feel that I might fall to my knees. He does not try to make small talk. He only pats my hand in the crook of his arm and leads me quickly into the street that will take us out of the quarter and toward the painter's house.

If the *gastaldo* is right and God has something else in store for me—if he is listening at all—I do not know what it is. We make our way quickly down the quayside in the direction of San Marco, where the white blanket of fog has finally lifted. The sun's rays pierce through the clouds, making sparkling patterns across the basin of the lagoon. I cannot begin to imagine my own future and the fate of this life growing inside my body, under the layers of my dress and my giant smock.

A BLANKET OF silence has fallen over the painter's house.

The painter's wife uttered a shriek of despair when the *gastaldo* shared the news of the cross over the door and my father's empty house. After that, only hushed conversations and the squeals of the children fill the house.

"Maria, you must feel free to take as much time as you need," the painter told me.

"That's very kind of you, Master Trevisan, but I prefer to work," I said.

He nodded knowingly. "Understood." Then he returned to his easel and left me to prepare the surfaces of the new gondola lanterns with my jar of gelatinous primer.

The journeyman, without words, placed his hands on my shoulders and squeezed. I gave him a thin-lipped but sincere smile, for there are no good words for such a time.

Now, I press down the leaves of gold just as my father showed me when my fingers were hardly big enough to do it. Just as he did. Just as his father and his father before him. In a contemplative state, I honor my father with the skills that he taught me. Without thinking about it, I hold my breath while I separate the gold sheaf from the vellum, for a whoosh of breath, a sneeze, a laugh could send it spinning to the floor. Better to keep my hands and my mind occupied. It is the best that I can do.

For a moment, I dare to hope that when my father returns home from the pesthouse, I will be able to give him the gilded box under the table, or a better one that I have made in the weeks while they are convalescing.

When Master Trevisan and his journeyman begin to fill in the outlined spaces on our gilded panels with the brightly colored pigments, I practice working with them, too. *Rosso, vermillione, azzurro...* They used to sound like a foreign language, feel strange loaded on the brush in my hand. But I am getting better.

At night, I lie in bed and beg for sleep that will not come. I stare at wavering patterns on the ceiling made by moonlight on the canal far below our window.

"You are not alone," Antonella says in the dark, placing a tentative hand on my shoulder. When I do not respond or turn toward her, she tries again.

"My cousin says that some of the people who perish do not suffer very long. They just break out in black boils or vomit blood, and within a day—just like that—they are gone. The suffering does not last."

She cannot see me press my eyes closed. I only wish I could close my ears, too.

Chapter 33

From a distance, the small mass of land where the Lazzaretto Vecchio stands looks like any other island in the lagoon. It stands lonely and grey in the expanse of still water that surrounds it. I ponder its soft outlines in the dull haze as the boatman rows eastward toward the Lido in Master Trevisan's gondola.

The air is still, and the lagoon reflects the light like a mirror. We are surrounded by an array of watercraft—ferries, passenger gondolas, cargo rafts. A long boat with finely dressed people glides into the lagoon, perhaps on a hunting expedition or a joy ride, silhouettes of grey in the stillness. As Our Most Serene City slips into the distance, I admire its church towers and jagged roofs, marred only by several funnels of smoke that drift skyward from the squares of Cannaregio and Dorsoduro, the pyres where people's belongings are disintegrating in the flames.

From his place on the aft deck of the gondola, the boatman looks down at me and shakes his head. "You are *pazzesca* for wanting to come here," he says.

"I am paying you to be quiet, not to comment on my situation," I say. I am filled with self-loathing at the thought of asking the boatman to bring me here, but I could think of no other solution. Besides, I have lost patience with him and no longer worry what he will think. He agreed to take me on this secret foray to the pest islands of the lagoon, but has not returned my necklace. "I paid it to my friend at the ferry station," he said, "for your man." His hands went to his pockets, and his eyes searched the floor. I felt in my heart that it was a lie, but how could I prove it and to whom would I make my appeal?

All I could think about was getting to the pesthouse; I could not imagine doing anything else. But now I wonder. Do I really want to see with my own eyes the things I have heard about—the people like rags, mere shadows of their former selves, their eyes sunken, raging boils on their legs and arms? Do I really want to hear the suffering cries of the sick and dying?

None of these images is visible before me; the horror only appears in my mind's eye. For now, all I see is a massive brick wall enclosing the island, and a plume of smoke rising from its center. We glide farther across the stretch of slick water that separates the pest islands from the city. From this distance, the *lazzaretto* resembles an ominous fortified city, a castle whose walls reach to the very edges of the island. As we draw nearer, a patch of golden light cuts through the soupy haze and the island comes into sharper focus. Several chimneys and towers loom from a great brick wall that surrounds the edges of the island. I can see the roofs of several long buildings, and the bell tower of a church. I can also see laundry airing out over the top of the brick wall. And I see smoke emerging from the chimney pots.

As we draw closer to the pesthouse, the other boats in the lagoon fall into the distance. There are no passenger ferries, no cargo boats, no one out for a leisurely ride. Eventually we are the only ones anywhere near the island. The boatman's face has assumed an expression I have not seen before. He seems to have lost all of his color, his skin the same pallid grey as the sky above us. He goes silent and slows his oar to a gentle swirl in the still water.

From one of the quaysides a small, agile passenger boat, a *scipion*, is suddenly moving in our direction. As the boat gets closer I realize that it is heading straight for us. Its boatman holds his hand in the air and gestures to us, then rows his small craft alongside our gondola. I stand. I see the man's uniform and realize that he is not a regular boatman but an officer from the *Sanità*.

"*Bondì!*" The boatman salutes the man on the *scipion*.

"What business do you have here?" the young man says, turning his oar to slow the boat and saluting with the other.

"My passenger is looking for someone," the boatman says in his gruff voice.

"I am looking for my family," I say, pressing my palms against the rim of the boat. "We believe they are here."

"You cannot moor your gondola at the island," the man says, turning his gaze back toward the pesthouse. "Only the official ferries may dock here. You must turn around and go back to the city."

"That suits me. You could not pay me enough money to dock this boat there," the boatman says, his face still devoid of color. "I am not going any further than this."

"Please, *missier*," I say, "I am looking for my father and my cousin, and another man who works in our gilding workshop."

"Signorina, we do not accept visitors to the *lazzaretto*. I am certain that you can understand."

"I am trying to find them, to see if they are all right. To learn of their condition."

"Were they brought here from their home?"

"Yes, in Cannaregio. There is a cross over the door. I saw it myself."

"All the names of the people who have been transported here are held in the Health Office in San Marco. If you are looking for someone specific you may inquire there. Now I must please ask you to turn your boat around and go back where you came from."

"With pleasure," the boatman says, smirking at me.

I sit in the new chair that the gondola makers have placed on our deck. A gentle breeze stirs the surface of the water as the boatman reverses the gondola to head back toward San Marco.

"I told you there was no way they were going to let us in there," he says. "You are fooling yourself, Maria Magdalena."

"If he asks, you must tell the painter that I have gone to visit my aunt at Santa Maria delle Vergini," I say. I do not meet his eyes.

"*Puttana*," the boatman growls under his breath, but I see the corners of his mouth turn up into a crude smile, taking pleasure in calling me such a rude name. "Full of deceits," he says. "Full of secrets. They keep growing."

I turn my back so that the boatman will not see my face. I watch the smoke of the pest island chimney pots swirl and circle into the grey sky, growing smaller as we make our return to San Marco.

"You think you can control what others believe, but you are hardly in control of your own situation, signorina," he says. "If you ask me, your future is about as bright as that *lazzaretto*. It is only a matter of time."

"You know nothing of me," I say. I duck inside the passenger compartment and let the drapes fall closed behind me.

"FAMILY NAME?"

I look down at the crown of the man's head seated behind the hulking wooden desk in the center of the room. White flakes emerge from his dark strands of hair, and a few shavings of dry skin fall onto the ledger in front of him. He does not look up at me.

"Bartolini," I say. "The gilder. Our workshop lies at the edge of the baker's bridge in Cannaregio."

"How many in the house?"

"Three. My father is Giuseppe, and there is my cousin Paolo. We also have another man who works for my father. Cristiano Bianco. A *battiloro*."

"Cannaregio," he says, making a clucking sound with his tongue. "Yes. The pestilence has been slow to spread there, but it has been particularly virulent." The man stands and hobbles awkwardly to a shelf with leather-bound books, their bindings stamped in gilded letters. "Worst in all of the city." He removes a volume from the shelf and returns to the desk.

He runs his crooked finger down a long register of names. After what seems an eternity, he pauses.

"Bartolini, here it is. Giuseppe the gilder and Paolo his nephew and apprentice. Ponte Forno in Cannaregio."

My heart sinks.

"They were removed from the house on the feast of San Pietro," he says. "Most likely they were put on one of the ferries that have been stationed at the *traghetto* in the quarter. In any case, they were destined for the Lazzaretto Vecchio." He runs his finger down the page again, squinting at the names and notes scrawled in a list ruled with thin lines of black ink. "The doctor recorded them sick. With lesions."

I feel as though someone has kicked me.

"I am sorry, signorina," he says, finally looking up to meet my gaze for the first time. "That is all I can tell you; that is all it says in the book. God help them." He stands and begins to close the register but I hold out my hand.

"Wait!" I say, slapping my hand over the open spread of parchment.

"What about Cristiano Bianco? He was also working in my father's studio."

The man runs his finger back down the page again, then shakes his head. "I do not see any mention of a Cristiano Bianco here," he says. "Was he living in your household?"

"Yes," I say.

"Strange. The doctors and notaries are required to document everyone in the house." He places his index finger on his mouth. "Was he a servant?"

"No," I say. "*Battiloro*. He came from a goldbeating workshop in the quarter to help my father."

"*Me scuxa*," he shrugs, clipping the words with a sharp Venetian dialect. "I simply have no record of him. It happens." He returns the book to the shelf, then pauses and puts his finger on his chin. "Hmmm. Bianco. By any chance, was he a Moor?"

"Yes!" I say, realizing that "White" is a common name for blacks.

"That might explain it," he says, resting the ledger in the crook of his elbow and turning to the back pages. "There is a long list of Saracens, though they mostly do not record the names." He runs his finger down the list.

"I see a few Moors listed in Cannaregio but none that match the date or location of your father's removal from the quarter."

"Do they not record everyone in the house?"

"The doctors and notaries are supposed to, yes. Sometimes they are recorded with the household, sometimes here in the back, sometimes, I am sorry to tell you, not at all."

The man cocks his head and looks at me with a strange expression. "It is your father's workshop, signorina?" he peers at me over the top of his glasses.

"Yes," I say. "My home."

The man suddenly looks alarmed. "And you were not ferried away with the others?"

"Oh. No, I did not explain that correctly. I was not there with them. You see, my father sent me away to work with Master Trevisan the painter in San Marco."

"How long ago was that?"

"Before Epiphany," I say. "That is when the pestilence began in the neighborhood."

He looks at me now with piercing, dark blue eyes.

"You have been checked for lesions by a physician?" he asks.

"No, of course not. I told you, I was not in my father's workshop. I was in the painter's house."

"Would you please come with me, signorina?" He crosses the room and opens a door to a long corridor.

"I already told you. I am not sick."

"Signorina, we are required by the laws of the Republic to examine anyone who has come in contact with a victim of the pestilence. Follow me, *per favore*." He grasps my arm with a claw-like hand.

I am speechless. I freeze, my feet glued to the tiled floor.

The old man turns back and sets his blue eyes on me. "Signorina, I am sorry. I truly am. But I am afraid that if you do not comply with the examination we will have to ferry you into quarantine at the Lazzaretto Nuovo by default until we can clear you."

Inexplicably, I find myself following the man down the corridor. The man knocks on another door and pushes his way in. He grips my forearm firmly and pulls me into the room.

"*Medico*," the man says to another seated behind a desk. "The signorina's family has been transported from Cannaregio to the Lazzarretto Vecchio," he explains. "You will want to check her." He presses me further into the room and closes the door behind me.

The man stands and greets me with a tight, wordless grin. "Signorina," he says, bowing his head of grey hair.

I have never been examined by a doctor. I feel my tongue go dry and my heartbeat quicken.

The *medico* opens the door a crack and presses his head into the hallway. "*Sorella Vittoria!*"

The doctor looks in my eyes and asks me to open my mouth. I stick out my tongue and look into his dark brown eyes. He stands so close that I can smell the sourness of his breath. My tongue still wagging, a nun in a long, black habit enters the room.

"Please remove your dress," the doctor says to me, turning his back and opening the door to a cabinet along the wall.

"What?" I say. I look to the nun for help.

"Please remove your dress. You may leave on the underskirt."

My mouth opens but no words come out.

"Do as the *medico* says, please, signorina," says the nun. "It will be all right."

Reluctantly, I remove my cloak, then untie the ties of my homemade dress and let it fall off my shoulders. The nun grasps it and lays it over the back of a chair.

The doctor grasps my left wrist and lifts my arm, looking under my armpit. Then he repeats it on the other side.

"Any fever?" he asks. I shake my head.

"Coughing?"

"No!" I say with exasperation. "I understand that you are only doing what is required of you, but it is as I have already told the inspector outside," I say. "I have not been exposed. I have been working outside of my father's shop since Epiphany. I was not living there when they got sick. No one is sick in the house where I am currently living."

"I see. Please lie down," he says.

I lie on the table, and the nurse lifts my underskirt. Instinctively I push my hands down to my groin and around my pregnant belly. The doctor presses his fingers into my inner thighs and examines them closely, then runs his hand across my stomach. I wince.

"Ah, well," says the doctor. "You may not have been exposed to the pestilence, but it seems there is more than at first meets the eye."

He walks across the room and grasps a large wooden funnel from a shelf. He returns and places it on my stomach. For a few long moments, the room is cast into silence. I wonder if the doctor or the nun can hear the loud pounding inside my head.

The doctor raises his head. "You are just a wee thing, *Maria Vergine*! But I hear a heartbeat."

"A heartbeat?" I am dumbstruck.

"Yes. You are further along than you appear."

I feel my own heart begin to race. "How much time do I have?"

The doctor shrugs. "Sixty, maybe ninety days."

I feel my stomach lurch. Surely not enough time to marry Pascal Grissoni and convince him that the baby is his.

"You are feeling well?" the doctor asks.

"Better than I was a few months ago," I say. "But I still vomit."

The doctor gives me his hand and helps pull me to sitting. "That is to be expected," he says. "*La nausea* is a sign of a healthy baby. I am sure the old ladies in your neighborhood have already told you that." I can think of nothing to say. "I hope you are eating plenty of eggs and cheese," he says.

The nun nods. "You are very thin, *cara*," she says. "You must eat even if you do not feel like it."

The doctor pulls me up to standing. "No lesions. You may get dressed, signorina. I will let the inspector know." Without another word, the doctor disappears through the door.

I fumble with the ties of my dress, then feel a cool hand on my shoulder. "I am sorry you had to be submitted to such an examination, signorina." I turn to see the nun's clear eyes on me. "You must understand that it is required of us in these dark times. Perhaps you will take comfort in knowing that not only are you not sick with the pestilence, but in spite of your thinness you look healthy and so does your baby."

I nod.

"If it is as the *medico* has said," she adds, "this baby may come sooner than you think. You will want to advise your husband."

Chapter 34

I recognize the *battiloro's* mother from across the square.

We hardly know one another, yet as soon as our eyes meet we cleave to one another with all of our strength. I feel the tautness of Zenobia's wiry frame, her muscled arms, her strong back built through years of labor. We cling to one another with everything we have, with all the despair and fear in us. I do not care what the others in the crowd think of the slight, secretly pregnant white woman with orange hair embracing the tall, black washerwoman. I have called for her and she has come. It is all that matters.

When I went looking for her at the Rialto washhouse she was not there, and for a while I feared that I had lost track of her, that she had disappeared like so many in this city who are already invisible. I feared that she had slipped through my hands like Cristiano himself, lost without a trace. But a kind laundress took me aside and promised that she would get word to Zenobia, that she would pass on my message to meet me at San Rocco for the plague mass at midnight.

"You have news of Cristiano?" I wonder if she hears the desperation in my voice.

She shakes her head. "I only know what the washerwomen from your quarter have told me. That the workshop has a cross on the door. That they have most likely been transported to the pesthouse. You?"

I shake my head. "I know nothing. I have been to the Sanità, but they have no record of him. Only my father and my cousin. It is as if he has vanished."

"The *lazzaretto* is the only place he can be, child. I have seen a few more plague outbreaks than you have. This is what they do."

"I tried to inquire there, too, but they turned me away."

"You went to the *lazzaretto*?"

I nod. "They turned me back. Of course they did. How silly of me to think I could get inside."

Zenobia takes a deep breath and looks into my eyes. "You love him."

"With all of my soul," I say.

"Come." Zenobia grasps my hand in hers, and I feel the tight, comforting grip of someone stronger, more confident than I. She pulls me through the throngs of people who have made their way to the San Polo quarter, and into the burgeoning crowd that has amassed in the square around the church of San Rocco.

There is no moon. People fill in the spaces around us, some carrying lanterns with them, lit up like fireflies in the dark. Normally such a crowd would form a raucous frenzy, but tonight, it is silent enough to hear the shuffling feet of those who have come to ask God to spare their husbands, wives, parents, children, brothers, sisters, and friends from the indiscriminate hand of the pestilence. We have all gathered for one purpose: to pray for a miracle, to return our people to health, to atone for whatever wrongdoing has brought this horror on Our Most Serene Republic.

Inside the church thousands of small flames illuminate the vaults of gilded mosaic. There is the sound of people plunking coins inside metal boxes and the sonorous din of monks intoning the prayers in the lofts above our heads.

Not long before my birth, I have been told, the bones of San Rocco were brought to Our Most Serene Republic on a great ship. It was San Rocco himself who, on a pilgrimage from the Frankish kingdoms to Rome, healed plague sufferers, and even saved himself from the pestilence. Now, the relics of San Rocco lie below the altar, and all of us direct our prayers to he who, it is believed, holds the singular power to deliver us from the scourge.

Inside the church the crowd grows louder, as small conversations, pleas, prayers, gasps, and cries echo throughout. Behind us someone has led a donkey into the aisle, and a scuffle breaks out as the beast is shooed outside. I pull a coin from my pocket and place it inside the metal box for candles. I light the wick and place my candle on the metal stake alongside many others placed there, sending up illumination that makes the mosaic tiles above our heads sparkle and shine.

I return to the long wooden bench where Zenobia is seated. She takes my hand in hers and squeezes it tight. She is steady and calm, even though her eyes evince a profound sadness. The feeling of her hand on mine brings me comfort and strength.

"Do you think it will work?" I say. "The people believe that the relics of the saint hold the power to heal." We gaze at the gilded reliquary on the high altar and the new frescoes and shiny new church around us resplendent in the candlelight.

She looks at me and shrugs. "I do not know if I believe in such things. Whatever faith I might have had sunk into the sea when I came here," she says. "But I do believe that *you* would do anything to bring him back." I inhale deeply and try to prevent the tears from spilling over. "You must know that my Cristiano is a strong man," she continues. "If he has become sick, I believe that he has the power to get well again."

I lean my head on Zenobia's shoulder and she grasps my shoulders under her arm. I allow myself to bask in the comfort of this woman, nearly a stranger. She spreads her fingers gently against the tautness of my stomach, and I feel the warmth of her palm spread across my mid-section, bulging against the linen wraps. I place my hand on top of hers, and we sit like that for a long time, her strong hand under my palm. I close my eyes and feel the cool air of the church on my face. For the first time in months, I feel a glimmer of hope. She has brought me comfort, and that is something I have not felt since leaving home.

MY GAZE TRAVELS across the studio to the gilded box on the mantelpiece.

I should have offered the boatman the box of gold leaf instead of my necklace, which now seems relatively worthless since my man is no longer in my father's house.

"There is a gilded box on the painter's mantel that is filled with enough gold leaf for you to live well for the rest of your years," I should have said. "Find my man and the box will be yours."

If I had said that instead, would the boatman have worked harder to lure away my *battiloro* from the barriers of Cannaregio? Would he have brought him to me before he was taken away to the pesthouse?

"You could make a good living with those," Master Trevisan says, gesturing to my worktable. Has he read my mind? I feel my face flush.

"Is that so?" I brush a layer of gesso on the new lidded boxes that the carpenter has brought. Now that I have one complete, I feel more confident about making another one while Master Trevisan watches.

"Indeed," he says. "My cousin in Padua does very well. The ladies love those molded boxes. As soon as he makes one it goes out the door. In Our Most Serene City there must be many more people than in Padua who would buy them."

While I work, Trevisan and his journeyman brush the colored pigments onto the panels, inside the outlines that I have made with the gilding. It is painstaking, slow work.

Within the week, a cargo barge will dock outside the artist's studio, and the carpenters will load the panels, placing sheets of canvas between them to protect the colored surfaces. From there, the boat will wend its way through the canals to Santa Maria delle Vergini, where they will be unloaded and brought into the great church where my aunt is cloistered. It will take a full day or more for the carpenters to hammer the battens across the backs of the panels that will support the great altarpiece.

Trevisan paces back and forth, scratching his beard and looking at the images of the saints surrounded by the great swaths of gold that I have laid down with my own hands. Trevisan takes account of the saints beginning to take shape on the panels. Saint Peter. Christopher. Barbara. He stops before the panel with the figure of Mary Magdalene and gestures to the picture with his long, elegant finger.

"Maria Magdalena," he says, smiling at me. The likeness is uncanny; it is true. Once the picture is hanging in the church, no one will ever know that the model for the picture was a gilder's daughter, a wretch who found herself hiding a secret inside the studio of the painter that made this very altarpiece. They will only see the great sinner with the flowing hair.

"What do you think?" Trevisan asks. "Too heavy on the vermillion?"

"It is difficult for me to judge," I say. "I never could have painted that."

"You do not give yourself enough credit," the painter says. "You have grown in the months since you have been here. Come." I approach the worktable where I have been practicing painting hands. Trevisan picks up a small panel I have used to practice, and holds it alongside a panel painted mostly by Trevisan's journeyman. He stands close to me, and I smell the musk of his breath, sending a strange tingle down my spine.

"See?" he says, and I must admit that my hand is not so much worse than his.

"Signor Zanchi has invited us to his home after the installation of the altarpiece next week. You may recall that he is the one who has made this donation to the convent. He is hosting a large celebration and inviting his associates. I typically decline such invitations. I do not enjoy crowded parties, but I do not feel I can say no this time. He has been exceptionally generous, and there may be other potential new patrons there for us. Under the circumstances," he says, "my wife will not go." I imagine Signora Trevisan napping upstairs, her enlarged stomach heaving up and down with each breath. More and more often, she has taken to her bed.

"But Stefano will be there," he says, "and I would like for you to come too. It would be a shame for you not to receive the credit you are due."

"MARIA."

My aunt presses forward, urging me to look at her. My eyes stay in my lap, fingering the black glass beads of the rosary that she has pushed through the iron swirls of the grate. I watch their dull reflections flash as I turn them over in my hands.

At this very moment inside the abbey church, Master Trevisan and his journeyman are meeting with the carpenters, discussing how to fasten together the prepared panels, to secure the battens on the back of the panels that will prevent them from warping in our damp environment. I know the men are there taking their time, scratching their heads, gesturing with their hands before the vast empty space of the altar, strategizing a way to move and mount the panels in a way to take advantage of the light.

"You must have faith," my aunt urges with as much sincerity as she can muster. "Our congregation—and many others across the city—are praying well beyond the holy offices for the healing of those in the *lazzaretti*. You must believe that they will come home."

I nod, but her words fall hollow on my heart. In the core of my being, I fear the worst. The image that pollutes my head now is that of the officials dragging our goods, our bed linens, and God forbid—the tools of our trade—through the crooked door of my father's house and stacking them on the ox carts to be burned in the square.

"You must count yourself fortunate that you are lodged with the painter," she continues. "God has spared you the suffering. There is a reason for it. He has placed that artist in your life for a reason. He has also brought you here to this house of God, Maria."

She speaks my name again, softly but insistently, as if she is trying to coax me back from a dream far distant. She reaches her hand and wrist through the grate and squeezes my fingers around the rosary in my hand. "I have spoken with our *badessa* about you." She falls silent for a few long moments until I meet her clear, green eyes. "I want you to consider coming here to be with us at Santa Maria delle Vergini."

I feel my heart skip a beat and my mouth form a large circle. I feel awakened now, and meet her eyes. "What do you mean? Me? In this convent?" The idea seems so ludicrous that I stifle a laugh.

"Yes," she says, and I think I see the sides of her mouth turn up into a grin. "Think about it. You are already a natural-born singer, from what your father has told me. Your vocal talents would be greatly appreciated here."

I hear myself gush, then the laugh comes out, but when I look at my aunt's face, I see nothing but seriousness. She has been thinking about this for a long time. "*Zia*, I hardly know what to say." I try to imagine myself sitting in the choir stalls singing for the rest of my days, looking at the altar panels that I have made partly with my own hands.

"Say yes," she says, flashing her teeth. "It would be a joy to me to have you here. Besides, convent life is not so bad. Everything here is taken care of. Our cooks are some of the best in Venice. You have already tasted our pastries, have you not? You must try some of the other dishes."

"I know you all eat well, but..."

"Listen to me," she says. "I know your father wanted to arrange for your marriage, but now that things are as they are, under the circumstances..." She hesitates, and I see the lines crinkle around her eyes. "Well. Things are tenuous for you. A woman artisan on her own... Yes, it is done under certain circumstances but you must admit to yourself that it is the difficult path."

I do not respond, but only twist the ragged edge of my sleeve around my hand.

My aunt continues. "You must consider joining us here in the convent, as soon as it can be arranged. Your father may not have scraped together enough money to dower you, but surely it is enough to make a donation suitable to place you in a house of God where you will be able to ply your skills for His glory. You must follow the path that is laid out for you by God," my aunt says. "If you search your heart you must know that it is what is meant for you. Come to us, Maria."

In the silence, I try to search my heart to see if there is an inkling of truth there. Is this what God has willed me to do? And why is she pushing me to this path of life?

"Why are you trying to help me?" The words come out of my mouth before I can stop them.

My aunt suddenly seems out of patience. Her face turns serious now, the smile gone, the face grave and sincere.

"Because, my dear girl, you of all people need help. Will you be the last to admit it?" She leans in close to the grate and grasps the wrought iron with both hands. For a moment she looks in the direction of the dark corridor to see if anyone is there. Then she looks at me in the eyes and lowers her voice to an insistent whisper. "You may be trying to hide it, but it is clear as day to me that you are with child."

Chapter 35

The painter's wife has taken to her bed, overwhelmed with spasms in her abdomen that come and go over the days. She spends more and more of her day there as her body burgeons, and Antonella is more occupied with the children and chores.

From her bedchamber, the painter's wife has dispatched Antonella with a frock for me to try. Antonella has carried the beautiful billowy dress, deep green with lace trim, destined for the party we are going to attend after the unveiling of the altar panels. I try it on in despair, watching in the mirror as the dress hangs on my frame, my thin arms poking out of the puff. Antonella comes to my rescue, producing a darning needle and tucking pleats under my breasts so that the silk falls and hides my middle that presses against the bindings made with long swaths of linen.

"The painter's wife is working hard to make sure that Pascal Grissoni cannot bear to take his eyes off of you at this party." Antonella sets her dark eyes on me, full of thinly veiled envy.

The shoes that the painter's wife has sent are too large, so I have done my best to shine my own. In the end, I hope that my scuffed leather mules will simply be hidden beneath the copious drape of the green silk.

"I rather think that instead she is trying to get me out of this house sooner rather than later."

Antonella bursts into a laugh that ends in a cough. "Who could blame her for wishing you married as soon as possible?" she says. "You have upset the balance. Be still." She fumbles with a knot in the thread.

"I have done nothing," I say, keeping my fingers busy by running them through my hair to untangle a snag, then redoing the braids. I think about everything I *have* done.

The truth is that I feel that I might burst, that maybe I should just tell Master Trevisan or his wife the truth. That I was only sent here as a way of separating me from my lover, that I am with child, that the boatman is trying to steal from them, that I do not want to marry Pascal Grissoni, that in spite of everyone's expectations of what I should do, I love someone else. That I have siphoned off the gold leaf I brought from my father's workshop, that the man who made the gold is my secret lover from whom my father tried to separate me by bringing me here to Master Trevisan's workshop. It all seems impossible to unravel, and all I can do is hold everything inside.

I do not know how the painter and his wife have not realized my condition. The painter, after all, has been watching me for months, replicating my hair, my face, in his sketchbooks and on the panel. But I realize that his vision is tempered by what he wishes to see, to the point where he does not see reality. That is what he does best. And the painter's wife is focused on herself, on her own body, the distractions of her own family, and the delicate balance of running her household.

"That may be true," Antonella says, "but I have overheard the painter and his wife arguing about you."

"About me?"

She nods. "You are correct that the wife would like for your betrothal to be secured as quickly as possible." She tugs at the thread at my side. "But the painter... He wants you to stay. He says that he must honor his contract with your father, but I rather think that he likes having you in his workshop." She flashes her black eyes up at me again.

I feel heat rise to my face. My aunt's words ring inside my head. *It is clear as day to me that you are with child.* All I want to do is hide. I wish I could run home to my father and my cousin.

My cousin. He was raised in the convent. And now my aunt is trying to convince me to go there, to raise my child up the way her own son was raised. By the time he came to us as a seven-year-old, he had learned to write and read. In the convent my cousin was well fed. He learned how to work. Perhaps it is not so bad, if not for me, for the child inside of me.

"There," Antonella says, breaking the thread with her teeth. "No one would ever guess what's beneath all this silk." She runs her hand along the fabric. I look down at the dress and must admit to myself that it is lovely. Her teeth glow white in the evening shadows, and her voice comes out like a hiss.

"*Bellissima.*"

"HAVE YOU BROUGHT your fare?" the boatman says as I step into the gondola in Master Trevisan's boat slip. He offers his hand, but I ignore it, lifting my skirts with one hand and grasping the iron lantern pole with the other. When I do not respond, he tries again.

"It only costs a few sheets of gold leaf for a gondola ride, signorina."

I meet his wide grin with a steely gaze.

"I have already paid you," I say, steadying my balance in the rocking boat. "All of the gold leaf that I brought with me from my father's workshop has been used up in the making of the altarpiece.

And you already have my necklace. There is nothing left. Besides, you have not lived up to your side of the bargain. You have not brought me my *battiloro*."

"Ha," he says. "Your *battiloro*. I think it is time that you tell the truth about him."

"What do you mean?"

His dark eyes narrow into slits. "I mean the trip to the *lazzaretti*, all that talk about the Saracen man. It is all smoke," he says, spreading his fingers before my face. "I am beginning to think that your *battiloro* does not exist."

My mouth falls open.

"Tell us the truth, signorina *indoradòr*. You have been hiding it from us all along."

"He is a real person," I insist. "He lives... lived in my own house. Ask anyone in our guild!"

The boatman's mouth forms a smirk. "I believe that you have been sending me down a false path, signorina. This *battiloro* may exist, but I think you are trying to distract all of us from the truth. *Dai*, admit it," he says, gesturing toward my midsection. "The painter is the father of your child."

"You are... *pazzesco*!" The word comes out like a sputter, a whisper that should be a scream if I dared to raise my voice in the painter's house.

The boatman's mouth twitches a few times as if he might burst into laughter, but instead he lowers his voice. "But it is a reasonable conjecture," he says. "The wife is already suspicious, eh? Wives... They have a way of sensing the truth even when no one else can see it."

"That is a lie!" Another quiet scream.

"But it is you who is lying, signorina." The boatman's eyes seem to turn black. "There is more gold leaf in the painter's house," he says. "A lot of it, from what I understand." I am left to wonder how much Antonella has told him.

"A *cassetina*," the boatman continues, hissing the word under his breath. "A golden box."

My heart begins to pound. The signora's dowry box. Would he really take it from Master Trevisan's hearth?

"If you bring it to me," he says, "then I might change my mind about telling the painter's wife what I know about you and her husband." Now I begin to see the outline of a plan to extort Master Trevisan and leave the house behind. What I did not realize until now is that the boatman plans to implicate me, too.

At that moment, Master Trevisan and his journeyman appear at the doorway to the boat slip, and step down the stone staircase. The kitchen door clatters shut behind them.

I lower my voice until it is barely audible. "You are evil—and just wrong. And if you want that box, you will have to get it yourself."

I duck into the passenger compartment and heave myself onto the upholstered bench. Out of view of the boatman, I press my face in my palms and try to calm my wildly beating heart before the men step into the boat.

I think of Carlo Crivelli, the gilder-painter who was so accomplished in his trade and yet paid the price for his adulterous secret with months in prison and exile from Our Most Serene Republic.

I refuse to pay the boatman one more thing. My mind searches wildly for another way for my situation to remain a secret in the painter's house. But perhaps I am fooling myself. Surely it will not be long before it becomes obvious and there will no longer be any hiding it from anyone.

Chapter 36

I have never been inside such a house. I have only admired the grand palaces of our city's wealthy people from the outside, their tall, colorful façades reflected in the canal waters. I follow Master Trevisan and his journeyman across the threshold into an entrance hall paved with giant white stones. The room holds a single piece of furniture, a narrow, uncomfortable-looking bench against the canal-side wall. A small window affords light through thick, clear leaded panes. Before me stands a curved marble staircase that disappears into the second story. From an iron chain above my head hangs a gigantic chandelier crafted from the antlers of what I guess amount to four or five doomed mountain creatures. The interlocking horns support a dozen white candles whose wax has dripped into haphazard molten shapes. Above our heads I hear the loud din of conversation and laughter.

"Master Trevisan!" A small, dark-haired man with a receding hairline approaches the painter. What the man lacks in stature he makes up for in his grandiose manner. "The man of the evening!" He grasps both cheeks and kisses them. "Your altarpiece is truly a wonder!" Trevisan looks sheepish and caught by surprise by the lavish attention.

Master Trevisan deflects the man's exuberance and turns his eyes to us. "This is my journeyman, Stefano, and my apprentice, Maria. They worked on the panels, too."

On either side of the entrance hall a set of doors stands partially open, and I glimpse what I judge to be a tremendous kitchen. The smell of stewed meat and freshly chopped onions wafts into the waiting room, and I salivate.

We follow a manservant up the marble staircase and are immediately enveloped into a large crowd. A table in the middle of the room is stacked high with braided breads and silver platters spilling over with crustaceans. Stewards carry pewter carafes of wine, refilling the goblets in the hands of each guest with liquid the color of gold. The women are dressed in incredible finery, with golden threads woven into their hair and pearls at their bosoms. There is laughter and tinkling of glasses. Immediately I realize how out of place I am. The dress that the painter's wife has lent me has saved me from looking like one of the servants, but I am still so far underdressed compared to everyone else.

"Maria." I turn to see Pascal Grissoni, and I feel relief to find a familiar face. "I hoped that I might find you here," he says. I let him take my hand in greeting. "I have the news of your family. It has grieved my father and me greatly. We pray for their survival."

"Thank you," I nod and set my eyes on a loggia overlooking the basin of the Grand Canal and the twinkling lights from the lanterns of the gondolas moored there.

"This is the man who has done the impossible, who carries the creation of God in his hands!" A man appears out of nowhere, his arm around Master Trevisan.

"We have heard of your beautiful work in the Vergini," another man says.

"Thank you, but the credit goes to my journeyman, Stefano, and to Maria, daughter of Bartolini the gilder," says Master Trevisan, gesturing to me and deflecting the attention from himself again. "Maria has done all the gold work on the altarpiece." The journeyman pushes me forward and the men in the group all bow in my direction.

"Her father is a well-known gilder in Cannaregio," says the journeyman.

"That is true," says Master Trevisan, "but it does not diminish the talent she has in her hands." The men around him chuckle and an old man in the group raises his silver goblet in my direction.

"Talented *and* lovely," says another. I catch Trevisan watching me, a proud expression on his face.

"Thank you," I say, then push my way back into the crowd.

Other men begin to crowd around Master Trevisan. He looks surprised and somewhat awkward, doing his best to shake everyone's hand, though I feel that he would rather turn around and go home. A man pats him on the back, and the host pulls him by the hand and begins to introduce him to others in the crowd. The journeyman straggles along on the heels of his master, but I find myself left behind.

Given a moment to breathe, I feel the weight of being at such a party when my own father and cousin languish in the pesthouse. It is impossible for me to see people drinking and celebrating when in other parts of the city, monks are flagellating themselves, mothers and wives are lighting candles inside San Rocco, and others are trapped behind doors with crosses nailed over them. It does not seem right. The unreality of it nearly takes my breath away.

In the gaiety of the party I begin to feel my own despair more sharply. I do not belong here. I step out onto the terrace overlooking the canal to get some air.

Before me, several dozen private gondolas are moored in the water before the façade of the palace. Each of the boats has a lantern lit, and, bobbing in the water, they flicker as if candles before the altar of San Rocco. The gilding on the gondolas catches the firelight and flashes, glittering across the small waves.

From here, I see the painter's eyes flicker around the room, and he is no longer paying attention to the men bustling around him. Who or what is he looking for? A way to bow out of the crowd like I have? Beyond, I spy Pascal Grissoni pressing his way through the throng. His eyes are also searching, seeking. Are both of them looking for me?

As the two painters approach the terrace where I am standing, I react without thinking. I scamper down a stone staircase that leads from the terrace into a courtyard on the ground level. I push through a small wooden door that leads out into the street, and break into a run.

The street opens to a small *campo* with a dark church façade looming over the deserted square. I press the door of the church and it heaves open. The space is dark, empty, and overwhelmingly silent. The bustle of the party now behind me, I drink in the silence of the church.

I make my way to a small side chapel where a single candle flickers before a large gilded panel. I lift the candle and touch the flame to the wicks of several others, watching the flames dance in the darkness. Immediately, the gilded panel above the altar sparkles to life.

For a moment I stand and catch my breath. As soon as peace washes over me, I begin to feel guilty instead. Why would I leave such a tremendous party? What was I thinking? The invitation was exceptionally generous. Master Trevisan and Pascal Grissoni, at least, are looking for me. Surely they will wonder what has happened.

"Maria."

Startled, I turn to find Master Trevisan standing behind me. "I saw you rush out. I followed right after you. Are you all right?"

I feel my face flush. "I am sorry, Master Trevisan," I say. "Truly. I apologize. I... I needed some air. I am not accustomed to such celebrations."

"It is I who am sorry," he says, bringing his hands to either side of his head and shaking it vigorously. "I should have thought better of bringing you here. This must seem very strange to you," he says. I nod but cannot find the words to respond. "I mean, to see people reveling when there is so much despair in the city and your own family is... well. Clearly it was not appropriate for me to expect you to celebrate. I should have thought more of it. I am filled with shame. It was wrong of me to require you to come tonight. Forgive me." In the candlelight, his eyes are shiny, his pupils dilated.

"Please do not berate yourself," I say. "You were generous to invite me to such a wonderful party, for your wife to arrange for this dress." I run my palms over the green silk. "It is more than I could have ever dreamed. I have never worn anything so beautiful. Thank you." I cannot find it within me to turn toward him. He talks to my back while I turn to the picture. The atmosphere suddenly feels heavy and charged.

"Well." Trevisan says. "I felt that you should get the credit you deserve for the work that you have done on the altarpiece. I am sorry if I made you feel uncomfortable."

"It's all right," I say, feeling my heart begin to pound. Something has changed. It is as if the space between us has filled with a crackling energy, like the lightning that blankets the sky over the lagoon on a hot, humid night. "It is just... I am not accustomed to being the center of attention."

"You and I are alike," the painter says. "I am not comfortable being in large gatherings such as that. I know it defies reason. But you have every right to be proud of yourself for your accomplishment on the altarpiece. No less than my journeyman and myself." Trevisan follows my gaze, and the two of us look at the gilded painting in silence for a few moments. "Mesmerizing, is it not?" he says, as if reading my mind. "I think there will always be people who want gold. There is nothing else like it," his voice turns to a whisper.

The artist stands directly behind me. I feel him push my hair to the side and his breath on my neck, just behind my ear. "It is the truth," he says, barely above a whisper. "Maria." I feel my body freeze, then the warmth of his body press me from behind. "You are a most remarkable woman." His face brushes the side of my neck, sending a tingle down my arm to my fingertips. "I am sorry, but I cannot help myself," he says. "Surely you must feel it, too."

I turn to face the painter. He brings his palms to my cheeks. I turn my face to the side and step back out of his grasp just as his lips search for mine. I press my hands on his chest.

"Forgive me," I say. "Things are not... as they seem."

I lift the hem of the dress and run toward the door. The great iron clasp clatters shut behind me and I plunge again into the darkness of the square. I keep running this time, clambering, wending my way through a tight alley and into the shadows. Behind me, in the house of the banker Signor Zanchi, there is only fading laughter and the tinkling of glass.

Chapter 37

The next morning I lie awake wondering how I will meet Master Trevisan's eyes, what I will say, how we will go on working together side by side now that he has crossed the chasm that turned out to be merely a hair's breadth.

I have stared at the ceiling all night, thinking of what I have done to invite him, to lure him to follow me into the church. His breath at my neck.

Surely you must feel it, too.

It was just a small thing, really, but it has upset the balance, fundamentally changed it all. He realized his mistake immediately, pulling away and letting me run from him without following. I wonder now if he pulled me close enough to have felt the hardness of the bulge around my middle, or if he suspected. My aunt, after all, said it was plain as day.

It takes every bit of courage I can muster to make my way down the stairs and into the painter's workshop. I know I am late; the birds have long fallen silent after their dawn concert. I will need to account for my tardiness.

But when I arrive in the workshop, Master Trevisan is not there.

Instead, the journeyman is pacing the studio, running his hand through his hair. "*Bondì*," I say, but he only salutes me with a weak wave and continues his pacing. The air is thick and still. The journeyman walks nervously back and forth, as if searching for something but doing nothing productive.

"Master Trevisan is gone," the journeyman says finally.

It takes me a moment to register what he has said. "Gone?"

He nods.

"What do you mean—gone?"

The journeyman shrugs. "It is odd. When I came down early this morning I found him packing his tools. Pulling individual brushes out of the jars and wrapping them in a satchel. He seemed in a great rush. He said that he was going away from the studio for a while."

"Away? Where?"

"Mmm," he nods, running his fingers through his hair. "Terra firma." His cheeks look flushed. "He said that it has been nearly two years since he visited his family's ancestral farms near Padua. Our work for the convent is now done and, well, someone there has promised him a new commission. He needs to go there to see it."

"But his wife," I say, gesturing toward the stairs. "She is about to be delivered of a child."

He nods. "Yes. That. Well, Master Trevisan said that she birthed the other two without his assistance, and that she will be capable with this one, too. Antonella will help her, and once the labor has started it is in the midwife's hands." He throws up his hands as if to demonstrate. "That there is not much that men can do in these circumstances. I suppose he has a point. Anyway, it was strange. It felt kind of rushed. He has never left so quickly like that before."

I feel my heart sink, knowing that the real reason he has left is because he cannot face me. I know nothing of his heart, but I have observed Master Trevisan enough to know that he is a shy, decent man and that for him to make himself vulnerable to me must have taken every bit of courage or a complete loss of self-control. His wife was already suspicious. Now I see that she has had every right to be.

"His trunk was already loaded in the gondola when I came downstairs. Boatman is ferrying him to Pellestrina right now. From there, he said, he will hire a coach to take him inland."

"And what are we to do?" I ask.

"A fair question," the journeyman says. "Master Trevisan placed the commissions in my hands for now, for he does not know how long he will be away. He asked me to tell you to keep practicing your trees. Perhaps you will work on your boxes."

At that moment there is a knock on the canal-side door, and the journeyman stops his pacing to open it.

There in the doorway I see the portly silhouette of our *gastaldo*. He holds his hat in his hands and looks at me with a dire expression. Behind him, there is another man uniformed in the manner of those assigned by the Sanità to report the plague-affected in our neighborhood. The men say nothing, but stand there as dark sentinels in the morning light.

As soon as I see the look on the *gastaldo*'s face, my hands fly to my mouth. The *gastaldo* approaches me and looks at me with drooping eyes like those of a dog. Then he runs his palm over the top of his head and opens his mouth, pausing, as if trying to find the words. I feel my hands start to shake and everything before my eyes goes blurry. Before the *gastaldo* utters a word I have already fallen to my knees before him on the stone floor.

Chapter 38

The *gastaldo* places his hat on the artist's worktable and bends down to take both of my wrists between his broad, warm hands. He pulls me to my feet.

At that moment the painter's wife appears in her husband's studio. "What has happened?" she says.

"Maria," the *gastaldo* begins, ignoring Signora Trevisan and pulling me to him in a tight embrace. I press my face to his shoulder, filling my nostrils with the musk of his leather doublet. I feel his warm breath on my cheek as he strokes my hair as if I were a small child.

"*O Madonna!*" the painter's wife rushes to my back and grasps my shoulders with both hands as if to hold me upright. "You poor girl!"

"Signorina Maria," the *gastaldo* tries again. I cast my gaze to the floor and cannot bring myself to look at their faces. "I am deeply sorry. The Sanità posted the names for Cannaregio this morning. I saw them on the list and I came right away."

Behind the *gastaldo*, I see the buffed leather shoes of the health official from the Sanità, shifting from one foot to the other. He is scribbling something in a leather-bound book with a long feather pen. "Signorina," he says. "It is my burden to notify family members in the *zestier* of Cannaregio. Your *gastaldo* insisted on coming with me to tell you. It is our duty, charged by Our Most Serene Republic, to inform you of the deaths of Giuseppe Bartolini the gilder and his assistant Paolo in the Lazzaretto Vecchio."

The *gastaldo* embraces me again. "They were administered their last rites in the pesthouse," he says softly. "They have already done the burial there. That is how they do things with the infected. They bury them as soon as possible. You must realize that there is no other way, Maria."

"I wish I could assure you that they did not suffer in their final days," says the man from the Sanità.

I hear the painter's wife gasp. "And are you charged by the Provveditori alla Sanità to be so tactful?" For a few long moments the studio falls silent, and all we hear is the sound of raindrops plunking into the canal outside the open door. "It is the worst that we have feared," the painter's wife speaks for me to the *gastaldo* and the health official.

"Please accept my deepest condolences," says the official. "The priest in your parish has been notified and will contact you with services to be done on their behalf. The parish church in Cannaregio is still open so we will be able to arrange funerary masses for them."

"I'm very sorry, Maria," the *gastaldo* says again, then turns to the painter's wife. "I might have a word with Master Trevisan."

"He is not here," she says. "He left just hours ago to see to his family's lands on terra firma."

"I see," says the *gastaldo*. "I wanted to assure him that, even under the current circumstances, nothing will change with our arrangement. I will personally ensure that Maria's father's wishes are honored."

"Of course," says the painter's wife, pulling me close to her shoulder. "Thank you for bringing the news. Of course Maria is safe here under our care. *Povera*." She clucks with her tongue. The *gastaldo* lets go of my hand and turns to pick up his hat from the table.

"*Gastaldo*, wait." I finally find my voice. He turns and looks at me, his eyebrows raised.

"What about the *battiloro*?" I manage to say.

"*Battiloro*?" The health official turns and looks at me with a confused expression.

The *gastaldo* responds. "Maria's father and cousin had another man working with them, a Saracen specialized in beating gold. He was living and working with them there in the same workshop."

The man looks confused for a moment and shuffles through the last few pages his leather-bound book.

"I am sorry, signorina, but I cannot say," says the man, looking at the paper in his hand then looking me in the eye. "According to the official record there were only two people from that house recorded with lesions and transported to the *lazzaretto*."

"I know for a fact that he was working in the studio," the *gastaldo* says. "Saw him there myself before the disease began to spread. Surely he was put on the boat if the other men had lesions."

"I need to know what happened to him," I say, trying to keep my voice in check but I have lurched forward to take the *gastaldo*'s arm for support.

"We cannot get into the house yet," the man says. "The street is still under a ban as they have not finished clearing out. There is still danger that people will fall ill. I am sorry, signorina, but I cannot allow you to go back home to investigate."

I move forward. "Surely you must be able to find out what happened to the *battiloro*."

"Can you work with the Health Office or ask the neighbors?" the *gastaldo* asks.

"We have no other record of him, signorina. I can assure you, though, that if he was in that house he has gone to the *lazzaretti*. There is no other conclusion."

THE LAST TIME I walked into our parish church my father and my cousin were by my side. This time, I am alone.

In the vestry, I find the *gastaldo* is waiting for me. His brow is already covered in beads of sweat. His leather belt has been cinched up tight across his full abdomen. I take note that he has tried to dress himself up for the occasion.

"*Cara*," he takes my hands and squeezes them tight. "What a difficult day for you. For all of us. And for our guild."

"*Grazie*." I nod, meeting his sincere blue eyes.

"You must not feel slighted if few of our guild attend the funerary mass. This disease is keeping many of us at home." He pats my hand. "My boys are coming," he says, as if it is a consolation.

I know this is not the only funeral mass being celebrated across Our Most Serene Republic for bodies that are not actually there. These dark celebrations are happening all over the city right now, many in this very church. As the bodies pile up in the pesthouse cemeteries, the churches around the city are lifting up prayers to heaven for the souls of the dead.

"You came by yourself?" the *gastaldo* asks.

"Master Trevisan is still away. He does not know. His wife and the journeyman accompanied me here. I was fine coming by myself, but they insisted. I suppose it is only right. They want to do something."

"I am glad for you that they came. Do not forget, the painter and your father are bonded by our guild after all."

"Yes, I know," I say. "I am still in the midst of the arrangement." I muster a dark grin.

Through the open doorway from the vestry I see people begin to straggle in. I see the painter's wife and the journeyman, the back of their heads visible in the crowd. I recognize a few other familiar faces, including the carpenter Baldi and his sons.

"Father Filippo?"

"He is coming," the *gastaldo* says.

I think about the grim tasks that our parish priest must carry out among the sick and dying of our quarter. Just then, he steps out of the shadows behind me, a slight man in dingy robes who looks as if he has not slept in days. "Maria," the parish priest says. Father Filippo's face looks dark and drawn, with great circles under his eyes. His thin hair barely covers his nearly bald head and dark shadows draw his mouth into a permanent frown. He seems to have aged a decade since the last time I saw him, just a few months ago.

"My dear, my deepest condolences," he says in his gravelly voice, and the sourness of his breath fills the air. "I am very sorry, signorina. You must feel at peace that they have had a Christian burial. Normally there would be many people here in the church for these services, as you know. Everyone respected your father. But these are dark times and this scourge is keeping many people away. So many of the families are affected and they are staying home, either by choice or by force."

I nod. "I understand. Father Filippo, can you tell me what happened to the *battiloro*?" The old priest is my last ray of hope.

"The *battiloro* in your father's workshop? I do not have any news. I only know about your father and young Paolo. The Sanità has required my presence at all the places where people were sick. Because your father had boils the Sanità put me under a ban as well. The doctor too. Thanks to God neither of us got sick. I have only come out of the ban this week."

"You did not sign for him when my father and cousin were sent to the ferries?"

"Yes," he says, "I signed for your *battiloro*, too."

I feel my heart drop to my stomach. "He was sick?"

The priest shrugs. "On the day I went with the *medico* to examine your father and cousin their lesions were large and pustulent. You must understand that things were dire for them. And as your *battiloro* was present in the house with them, well… In a case like that it is automatic that anyone in the house should board the plague ferry."

I feel that I can hear the blood coursing through my veins, filling my ears with pounding. I do not want to imagine the scene in my father's house, but I have no choice.

The priest looks at me with a serious expression. "Now. Signorina Maria, before we begin the service for your father and your cousin there is one other matter to discuss." I watch the *gastaldo* fidget with his hand and look nervously at the priest. He seems to be intensely interested in a crack in one of the giant scuffed stones that make up the floor.

"What is it?" I say. I study his eyes.

"Your father... Before he was taken to the *lazzaretto*... Well." He clears his throat and struggles to find the words. "Your father left something with us before he boarded the ferry for the Lazzaretto Vecchio. I have been holding it for you." From his vestment pocket, the priest produces a piece of parchment rolled up and tied with a green silk ribbon. "I suppose we could describe it to you at some length, but you are capable of reading your father's words yourself," the priest says.

I unfurl the small piece of parchment, searching their eyes for clues to what lies inside. Immediately I recognize my cousin's neat handwriting.

I, Giuseppe Bartolini, suffering from the pestilence, do hereby entrust my soul to God and to the Holy Spirit. Should I not survive the grip of the Hand of Death, I leave my gilding workshop and all of its contents to my nephew Paolo, who is as able and capable as any son to run it as I and my father and his father before him have done. I entrust my daughter Maria in marriage to Pascal Grissoni, the son of Grissoni the Elder in San Marco, whom she will join in holy union and who has already agreed that in lieu of a dowry, to have her work alongside him in his workshop as any able partner, my daughter now having become skilled with colored pigments. My nephew has already witnessed and agreed to this arrangement and it has been approved by the master of our guild. If my nephew does not survive the pestilence, then my gilding workshop shall be sold and the proceeds used as a dowry for my daughter Maria.

Recorded by Paolo Bartolini on the Feast of Saint Anthony
And witnessed by Father Filippo of Madonna dell'Orto and Aureo dalla Stava, gastaldo of the painter's guild

"Pascal Grissoni." My hands falter and the paper drifts like a leaf and lands with a swoosh on the stone floor. I feel my hands press together as if trying to wring the life out of them.

The bells ring in the church tower, a sound I've heard all my life that now somehow sounds sad and distant.

"Father." The deacon appears in the doorway and looks expectantly at the priest, the *gastaldo*, and myself. Behind him the acolytes press together in the doorway, nothing more than innocent faces and white robes with open sleeves. The deacon gestures for us to follow him through the door and into the church.

"It is time."

Chapter 39

The boatman seems to have lost the ability to speak, and for that I am grateful. He swirls the water with his oar and looks out onto the horizon, the breeze lifting fine strands of greasy hair. I feel his eyes on me but I ignore him. Since the funerary mass I feel numb, and he seems to sense it.

I manage to stay composed until I see my aunt in the convent visitors' parlor. Then I fall apart.

Between the iron bars of the convent grille, my aunt grips my fingers. A beautiful, intricate rosary with tiny beads of red glass hangs from her thumb and forefinger. I lace my fingers through the iron bars and grasp her delicate fingers in mine.

For a while neither of us says a word. Then, she lifts her head and makes the sign of the cross.

"I am sorry for you, *zia*," I say. "I cannot imagine what it must feel like to lose a child. It is not the natural order of things."

She nods. "And my brother, your father."

"And the *battiloro*." It comes out as barely a whisper.

She pauses. "Your man?"

I nod. "He was put on the ferry with the others. I was not sure, but Father Filippo confirmed it."

"Oh my dear." Her fingers squeeze my hand and I feel the hard little beads of glass against my palm.

She lifts her head and attempts to brighten. "Your father was very proud of you," she says. "God rest his soul."

I shrug.

"He would not have worked so hard to keep you in his studio, to make a plan for you to stay there, if he was not," she says. She wipes her eyes and looks at me in the face.

"The funeral mass was a comfort," I tell her. "I wish you could have been there."

"We have had services for them here; you might imagine," she says. "Maria, our confessor tells me that the Sanità has come to your father's house. Everything that was left has been pulled out of the house and put on the pyre: the furniture, the curtains, the bedding, everything in your mother's trousseau. I am sorry. It could not be helped."

I nod, and clench my throat to try to stop the tears from coming. I have already seen my father's house bereft of its contents. The trousseau is the least of my worries. I have hardly had time to sew anything in past years. I have only been focused on working the gold.

"There is nowhere I can go to see the bodies, where I can pay tribute."

My aunt's head falls, and she, too, wipes her eyes.

"We will continue to have masses for them here," she says. "Their souls will be lifted up in song and prayer for all eternity, as it will be written in our book," she says.

We sit in silence for a while, contemplating the gravity of it all.

"In his testament, my father betrothed me to Pascal Grissoni." My voice hardly rises above a whisper.

She sits back and looks at me, her eyebrows raised in surprise. "Oh my. And this is a good thing?"

I can only shrug, for I have no words.

"Oh my dear. I am sorry," she says, and sighs. "Even when a father loves his daughter as your father did, sometimes there is no accounting for a father's choice."

"It is not that he is not a suitable husband," I say. "He is more than I might have hoped for, more than anyone might hope for. It is just..." The words fail me again. "Pascal Grissoni is coming with his father to visit me any day now," I say. "The painter's wife has told me to prepare myself. Without my father it will be up to me and our *gastaldo* to set the arrangements."

She pauses. "But does Pascal Grissoni know about your... situation?" She looks down at my stomach.

I shake my head again. "That is the problem, *zia*."

"Nor Master Trevisan and his wife?"

I shake my head again more vigorously, hoping that she cannot see my cheeks go aflame.

"Thanks be to God," she says, pushing back against the chair. My aunt grips the bars with both hands. "Listen to me. There is more than one solution to this problem. I have already told you. You must come here and join us. If God has spared you, then there must be a reason for it. Before this man comes to take your hand, you must announce your intention to take your vows. You tell no one about your situation, do you hear me? We will take care of you and your baby better than anyone outside of these walls. Think about it, Maria. It is the solution to everything. Now, more than ever before, you must know it is the right thing to do."

"*BENE*," SAYS ANTONELLA, glancing over her shoulder at me, "I hear that that overblown painter is coming for you after all."

She stirs a pot of rice over the fire. In a small wooden cradle tucked under the kitchen window, the painter's baby daughter sleeps fitfully.

I do not answer right away, not wanting to engage Antonella on this topic. I take a bite of a small piece of bread and chew silently, but she persists.

"I suppose he was lured by youth and beauty if not by dowry," she says, her voice tinged with thinly veiled envy.

I shrug as if brushing her hand from my shoulder. "It is not decided."

"Boatman says that he got word the painter will arrive with his father tomorrow in their fine boat," she says. "They are coming for you."

My heart begins to leap in my chest. "I do not put much trust in what comes out of the boatman's mouth," I say. "I am afraid that he is inclined to indict me." The words come out even though I don't mean for them to.

"I would not worry about the boatman," Antonella says. "I do not expect he will be here much longer." She pauses. "Nor I."

I stop chewing. "You are leaving?"

"Shhh." Antonella glances quickly at the baby's cradle, and then at the back stairway. "I do not think it is a secret that the painter owes both of us," she says, wiping her hands on a rag and coming to stand next to me. She lowers her voice. "We are working on a way to make sure we get what is due to us before we leave. Once we do, we will not be here one day longer." She presses her index finger on the tabletop. "Boatman believes he has found a way. But don't tell anyone. I know your secret," she says, swiping her rag toward my stomach, "and now you know mine."

For a few moments we remain in the silence. I am left to consider the gilded box on Trevisan's mantel.

Antonella returns to her boiling pot and inserts the long wooden spoon. Then I hear her speak again but she does not turn to face me this time.

"And what shall you say to that painter when he comes?"

WHEN PASCAL GRISSONI comes, I must tell him the truth. I will never tell Antonella this, of course, but I know in my heart it is what I must do.

There is not much time left. I can feel it. Marrying Pascal Grissoni and passing off the child as his is no longer a possibility. It is too late for that. The *medico* at the Health Office said it himself. I am near my time.

I watch the carpenter and his sons lift the heavy gilded and painted panels, now wrapped in swaths of canvas and paper, and carry them gingerly to the cargo skiff waiting at the painter's boat landing. The finished pieces are finally leaving the painter's workshop and will soon make their way to the great altar of Santa Maria delle Vergini.

Perhaps there is a way to explain it all, I think, watching the carpenter's young son careen under the weight of a great wooden panel. Pascal Grissoni seems a man who can see reason. Would he find it within himself to take pity on me or at least understand my circumstance? Would he still want me for a wife in spite of it all?

If I am realistic, I know that he is likely to reject me outright, but the truth is that I want more than anything to work with my hands. Going with Pascal Grissoni seems a more viable way to do that than committing myself to the convent. And if he says no, then perhaps I will have found a way back to my father's workshop on my own, which, if I am honest with myself, is what I want more than anything else.

And so, when Pascal Grissoni and his father come to ask for my hand, I will say yes.

And then, when I can find a moment alone with him, I must tell him the truth, for better or for worse.

In the meantime, I must make sure that the servants remain silent long enough for me to do what is necessary. Long enough for me to hide the gilded box containing Donata's dowry from the boatman's reach. And long enough for me to find the right words to say to Pascal Grissoni that will secure a future for myself and my baby.

AT NIGHTFALL, I wait for the house to grow silent before extinguishing the lanterns in the painter's studio. Antonella has already retired to the upper floor. I no longer hear the pattering feet of the painter's young son on the ceiling above my head. The baby's warble and her mother's soothing voice have long fallen silent.

I grasp the handle of the single lantern with its wick still aflame, and set it down on the mantelpiece above the hearth. The gilded box with its raised figures comes to life, glistening in the candlelight. With both hands, I remove it from the mantel and set it on one of Master Trevisan's worktables. I fish the key from the drawer where I have seen the painter store it. I turn the key in the lock and open the velvet-lined lid. Inside, Donata Trevisan's dowry is all there, more gold leaf than I would ever need in a lifetime. I run my hands over the nearly weightless sheaves stacked in small, neat books of vellum inside the box. Then I close and lock it again.

I return the key to the drawer, but instead of returning the box to the mantel, I carry it to my own worktable. I push back the drape that covers my table, and set the box on the lower shelf, pushing it back into the dark clutter among the jumble of painting and gilding supplies. In the shadows, I reach for the box I have made with my own hands, my feeble first attempt at copying the box on the mantel.

Would anyone know the difference?

Chapter 40

Something is wrong.

Before I am fully awake, I know it. I cannot put my finger on it, but my body feels strange. Different. I run my hand across my midsection, which binds into a ball for a moment, then falls still. I turn on my side and feel my muscles relax, but the sense of foreboding remains.

I reach my arm out in the bed. The sheets are still warm but Antonella is gone.

Gone.

Did she flee in the night with that boatman?

Bright sunlight filters through the narrow window of the bedchamber, and the silhouette of the brick chimney pots across the narrow canal come into view.

Pascal Grissoni and his father. They are coming. The painter's wife has told me to be prepared. "Of course, my husband would like to honor the contract he made with your father. But under the circumstances, if you receive an offer of marriage, you must not feel beholden to us," she told me. "You must honor your father's wishes for you, not for us." I know that the painter's wife wants me out of the house as quickly as possible, but she is trying to be polite.

"Besides," she says, "any girl might count herself so fortunate to make such a match. Especially the daughter of a gilder."

Reluctantly, I rise and take the dress that the painter's wife lent me for the party from a hook on the wall. What else am I to wear for such an occasion, I think? I bind my midsection with the roll of linen, then awkwardly step into the painter's wife's dress.

As I fasten the last silk-covered button at my waist, from somewhere downstairs, a sudden howl, a blood-curdling scream, breaks the silence.

The painter's wife. My heart stops.

I imagine Donata standing before the empty mantelpiece in the painter's studio, and I struggle for what I might say to her.

ON THE STAIRS, the journeyman presses his lanky frame past me, jogging down the crooked treads, still in his nightclothes. I grip the handrail to avoid pitching forward into the darkness of the stairwell.

"I am sorry, Maria," he says as he passes. "Signora!" he calls out. "What is it? What has happened?"

I stop on one of the treads, doubling over with a gripping pain in my abdomen. My breath comes in ragged huffs for a few moments, then the grip subsides.

Another shriek echoes up the stairwell. The sound that comes from her mouth is hard to describe, but it makes the hairs on the back of my neck stand on end. The baby begins to wail in unison with her mother.

When I finally arrive at the bottom of the stairs, I realize that the shrieks of despair are not coming from the painter's studio as I had judged. Instead, the painter's wife stands in the kitchen, peering down into the boat slip from the doorway at the top of the stairs.

"Boatman!" she yells, a crazed tone in her voice that echoes into the dank space. "Where is he?!"

"Signora," I say. "What is it?"

Her answer comes out as a wail, and the journeyman and I crowd into the doorway alongside Signora Trevisan so that we can see into the boat slip.

Where the silhouette of the gondola should appear, I only see the prow forks barely visible above the surface of the water.

The gondola is sinking.

"BOATMAN!" THE PAINTER'S wife yells again.

"I will go look for him, signora," the journeyman says, jogging back up the stairs.

"I knew it!" the painter's wife howls in my direction. "I knew it!" She tears at her hair. "Rotten. Rotten! I told Benvoglio a hundred times that we should not have trusted that boatman, that it would all come back to us in a way that we could scarcely imagine. And look what has happened! Santa Lucia!"

To quiet her squalling infant, the painter's wife has jerked down the top of her dress and pulled out a skinny breast without taking time to cover herself. She presses the baby to her, tugging the small blanket around the baby's body. Her young son appears at the bottom of the stairs now, his eyes still sagging with sleep, two fingers in his mouth. He presses his face into his mother's skirts. "I need to go to the latrines, *mamma*," he says.

"Antonella!" the painter's wife yells. Silence.

"Boatman is not here, madam," says the journeyman, reappearing in the kitchen. "His things are gone from his bedchamber." Now I know that Antonella is gone, too. Both of them, with a worthless box they believe to be filled with gold leaf.

The journeyman lopes down the stairs of the *cavana* with agility, and is already at the edge of the boat slip when the painter's wife, with the baby attached to her breast and her son tugging on her skirts, begins to make her way down. I follow them tentatively, trying to ignore the new gripping feeling across my midsection.

"He had the keys to the gate!" the painter's wife says, gesturing to the great wrought iron door that normally keeps the boat slip closed to the vagaries of the canal. "That is the only explanation. That blasted boatman! He is the only one who could have done this!"

"Look, signora!" the journeyman says. "That is the reason it is sinking." We see that the boat has a great gash in the hull, a ragged gap just visible above the water line. Below the water line we can see the wavering reflection of a pile of giant rocks loaded into the boat to make it sink.

"Antonella!" the painter's wife yells again.

"Signora, she was not in our bed," I say quietly.

The little boy begins to cry, tugging on his mother's skirts as she presses the wall to balance her unwieldy body. The baby, hearing her brother's sob, detaches from her mother's breast and joins him in a wail that reverberates around the cavernous structure of the boathouse.

The journeyman grasps a rope from the detritus in the back of the boathouse, and loops it around one of the metal cleats driven into the stone. He makes several flailing attempts to capture one of the prow forks with a loop on the other end of the rope.

"We must send a message to Benvoglio," says the painter's wife. "And report this to the authorities!"

"The oarlocks are gone, signora," says the journeyman. He has succeeded in looping the fore prow fork with the rope, and pulling the boat out of the water far enough that I can see the brocade upholstery, turned dark and soggy.

"Benvoglio is going to be furious!" the painter's wife says. The little boy screeches again and stamps his feet.

The journeyman pulls the keel slightly up out of the water, but his lanky frame is not strong enough to hold it, and the boat splashes back into the water. "It is too heavy, signora," he says. "I cannot hold it."

"We need help," she says. "Quickly, run to the neighbors' house. Tell them to send as many men who can help us. Give me the rope."

The journeyman hesitates. "Signora, in your condition…"

"Give me the rope!" she insists. "Now quickly. Run!"

The journeyman hesitates for another second, then scrambles up the stone stairs and disappears into the house to make a run for the landside door.

"Maria," she turns to me. "We must do what we can to keep it from sinking. Do you think you can hold the other end of the rope?" I can hardly hear her over the wails of the children, which echo and fill the chamber with horror.

Not knowing what to say, I bend over and grasp the other end of the tether.

The painter's wife pulls one side, and I pull the other. She strains to pull on the rope, her large belly protruding.

I pull on the rope and immediately my back begins to ache. Suddenly, I feel something that is more than pain. It is as if my entire midsection has pulled up into a ball.

"Oh," I say, holding the rope with one hand and putting the other on my back. The boat falls down a few inches and the painter's wife attempts to grab her side harder. The boat makes a loud splash in the water and falls on its side. It starts to sink lower.

The painter's wife screams, and the children wail even more loudly. I stumble forward and squat down to prevent my body from pitching forward into the water on top of the sinking gondola.

At that moment, Pascal Grissoni and his father come to claim my hand in marriage.

THE TWO MEN appear at the canal-side opening of the boat-house, dressed in their finest clothes. I can see the prow of their own gondola, which is docked at the entrance to the painter's workshop. Pascal Grissoni, wearing a brown velvet ensemble, looks as if he has gone to great lengths to groom himself. His father, no less elegant, stands behind him. For a few moments, they stand at the entrance to the boathouse as if frozen.

"*Signore!*" the older man cries suddenly, and he ambles as quickly as his ample body will move to the painter's wife. He pulls the rope from her hands. She presses her hands to her stomach and stumbles backward to lean against the stone wall, the two children attached to her. With all his strength, the old man pulls one side of the boat almost completely above the surface.

At that moment, several men from neighboring houses rush into the boat slip, along with several wives and children whose curious faces appear around the opening.

"Maria, hang on!" Pascal Grissoni yells to me across the boat slip, and he leaps over piles of rags, stacks of wood, and other clutter to get to me. I hear his voice at my ear. "Thank goodness I came when I did. When my boatman dropped us at the dock we heard the commotion in the boathouse and came right over. Who did this?"

I cannot answer. The contraction comes again in a wave, as if taking over my body. I fall to my knees and pause on my hands and knees like a frightened cat, my head hanging, the rope pressed under my palm.

"Maria!" Pascal Grissoni's voice again at my ear. "Are you all right?" His voice echoes across the stone. Suddenly he is crouching over me, his hand on my back.

"Maria!" the painter's wife yells from across the boat slip. "What happened? Are you injured? What is it?"

"No, not injured," I say. I lift my head. Before me, the faces of at least a dozen people are turned in my direction: the painter's wife, the children, Pascal Grissoni and his father, the curious neighbors. I feel that my eyes must look wild, crazed, and I wonder if they can see that I feel the air itself is going to crush me. "It's just that..." A huge wave of contraction overtakes me and I cannot help but emit a grimace of a type I have never made before. I let go of the rope and the boat heaves into the water on its side with a great splash. It takes several more deep breaths before I find my voice again.

"It's just that... I think I am having a baby."

Chapter 41

For months, I have carried a secret child in my womb. And now, as my contractions come in waves, I am surrounded by an unlikely audience. In addition to the painter's wife and children, and the man my father intended for me to marry and his own father, there is also the journeyman and a half-dozen neighbor men who have answered the call for help. While a few of the men work together to hoist the boat and tie it off to a mooring, another man runs for more help to pull the boat from the water. The men try to avert their gaze, but they cannot tear their eyes away from me, the painter's apprentice making her childbed in the corner of the boathouse.

"Antonella!" the painter's wife screech echoes through the boat-house. "Where is that woman when you need her?"

But of course, Antonella is nowhere to be seen.

"Send for the midwife!" the painter's wife says to a neighbor woman whose husband has called out to her from across the canal.

"No!" I say. "I have already caused you too much trouble, si-gnora. Please. I must go to the convent of the Vergini."

"Maria," says the painter's wife. "Come inside and lie down. We will have the midwife attend to you."

Another wave of contractions wracks my body. I lean over and press my hands to the stone wall. From the corner of my eye, I see the pained look on Pascal Grissoni's face, and I cannot begin to imagine what is going through his mind.

"Antonella!" the painter's wife screeches again.

"She is not here, signora. Please, I beg you," I say more loudly, "take me to Santa Maria delle Vergini. My aunt will help me."

"Master Grissoni," says the painter's wife. "Call for a gondola from the *traghetto*." The painter's wife shoos him out of the boat slip with her hand. The neighbor men have succeeded in tying off the boat to an iron ring in the wall.

"Signora," says Pascal Grissoni's father. "You may take our gondola. Our own boatman will be of service." He gestures to his son to fetch the gondola, and Pascal Grissoni scrambles out of the boathouse. I imagine that he is relieved for an excuse to leave this strange scene.

The crisis averted with the boat, the painter's wife now turns her attention to me. The poor journeyman paces back and forth, bewildered about what to do or how to help.

"Sit, Maria," the painter's wife drags a small wooden stool over and gestures for me, but my back aches and I feel like standing and leaning with my palms against the wall. I watch droplets of water drip down the stones. The painter's wife pats the small of my back where it hurts the most.

"Let us get her to the boat," the elder Grissoni says.

"Oh!" A contraction comes, and I cannot hold back my sobs this time. I slump down onto the floor as it wracks my body. The painter's wife does her best to kneel down on the floor beside me.

"Do you think she will make it all the way to the convent?" the painter's journeyman chews his nails, his brow wrinkled. "What if the baby comes in the boat?"

"The boat is ready, signora," one of the neighbors calls.

"Help her up, please!" the painter's wife calls. The journeyman springs into action, grasping my forearm with both of his hands.

"She is young and it is her first child," says the painter's wife, putting her arm behind my back and offering her other hand to help me stand. "It will take some time."

"No, signora, please," says the journeyman. "Do not strain yourself. Allow me."

Pascal Grissoni has reappeared, and he and his elegant, grey-haired father stand on either side of me. They lift my arms.

"I expect it will be many hours before the child is born," says the neighbor woman. "Better that she is there among the women in the convent than here with you. They will know better what to do and can take care of them better than we can."

"What's wrong with the lady, *mamma*?" little Gianluca asks.

"She is in child labor, *caro*," the painter's wife says, and I hear the fear in her voice.

"She is going to have a baby?" he looks up at his mother with huge, innocent eyes.

"It appears so."

I feel Pascal Grissoni's arm under my own, but I dare not meet his eyes. I cannot imagine how the pain could possibly get worse than it is now, or that I will endure many hours like this. I focus on putting one foot in front of the other. The two men propel me carefully forward, step by step. I make it halfway across the boat slip when a contraction possesses my body as if a demon has taken it over. I bend over, gripping the painter's wife's hand and grimacing as they support my arms.

The painter's baby starts to sob again.

"*Cristo santo*," whispers the painter's wife.

"Don't worry, signora," says the journeyman. "I took care of my younger brothers and sisters. I will take care of the children while you take Signorina... Signora Maria to the convent," he says.

"No," says the painter's wife. "Come with us. We will all go."

"That's it," she says to me as the men help me hobble to the Grissoni's fine gondola docked outside the painter's house. "One foot in front of the other," she says assuredly, but when she looks at me I see that she has gone white as a sheet. "Let us get her to that boat."

I hardly feel that I can walk, but the two men propel me toward the canal-side door. I grip the doorjamb and look out to see the polished black prow and the gilded lanterns and dolphins decorating the front of the gondola. There are two boatmen, one at the fore deck and one at the aft. The young man at the foredeck wrinkles his brow when he catches sight of me hunched over, supported by the two men. He leaps onto the landing and quickly ties off the boat, then approaches me to offer his hand.

The painter's journeyman takes Trevisan's little son by the hand, and the two perch themselves on the foredeck near the boatman. I slowly lower myself into the gondola, hands all around me, and Trevisan's wife helps me duck inside the dark passenger compartment, her hands at my back. I seat myself on a plush, silk-covered cushion and breathe a sigh of relief. The painter's wife props her baby on her bulging abdomen. With her other hand, she fans my face with a piece of parchment that another passenger has discarded in the bottom of the boat. The contraction has passed, and I allow myself to exhale loudly.

"Maria, why on earth did you not tell us?" the painter's wife says.

My mouth opens, but it takes a few moments. "I guess I could not find the words."

"Who is the father?" Her voice is low, and she looks at me with trepidation.

"It is not your husband, if that's what you were wondering."

"I..." Her face goes blood-red and she turns away from me.

"I came to your house encumbered with child," I say. "I just did not know it. It became clear when I did not have my menses. You could ask Antonella," I say. "Well, could have..."

The painter's wife looks momentarily relieved. She stares out into space, for a moment speechless. "Your father knew about this?" she asks finally.

I shake my head. "Of course not. He would have killed me with his own hands. I did not know it myself until I had been in your house for a while."

I hesitate, then realize that at this point I have nothing to lose in telling her the story.

"We had a *battiloro* working in our workshop. He... We... Well. The story is complicated. Of course my father wanted me to work with your husband and learn from him; that was sincere. But if you want to know the truth, signora, the main reason I came to Master Trevisan's workshop is because my father was trying to separate me from the man I loved until he could make a plan for me to be married to someone else."

Then her mouth makes a large circle, and for once, the painter's wife is rendered speechless. She exhales audibly, and all I hear is the baby's suckling noise. The little boy has appeared in the passenger compartment now. He presses his cheek to his mother's side and sets his big eyes on me.

I wipe the sweat from my brow. I lie down and close my eyes. For a moment I almost drift into sleep, lulled by the rocking boat and the soothing sound of the canal water swirling alongside. I do not allow myself to think about what lies ahead.

When I open my eyes I look at the painter's wife and say, "*Grazie*. I am very appreciative for everything you are doing for me."

"*Senz'altro*, do not be silly," she says, fanning my face. I feel strands of hair stuck to my cheeks. The baby detaches herself from her mother's breast and turns her face to look at me and smile. "At this point everything is upside down," the painter's wife sighs. "I will be in your shoes very shortly. We are almost there now. Not much longer."

"Signora, your box," I say, pushing my palms against the bench and raising myself to a sitting position. "The box with your dowry."

The painter's wife presses her face in her hands. She utters a deep sob, then turns the fan on her own face and waves it wildly in an attempt to pull herself together. "It was my entire fortune," she says quietly. "That boatman..." She wags her head. "I told Benvoglio! I knew something like this was going to happen."

"Signora, Antonella is the one who took your box," I say.

Her mouth falls agape. "What?"

"Well, Antonella *and* the boatman. They planned it. They left together."

"*Dio.*" The word comes out as a breathy exhale as I see realization dawn across her face.

Another contraction begins to grip my abdomen, and I double over in pain.

"God, just let us get there without the baby being born in this fine boat," I hear Trevisan's journeyman say from the foredeck.

"That's enough!" yells the painter's wife from the passenger compartment.

I feel the gondola bump against the side of the quay where the convent lies, and at that moment, I feel another contraction grip my body. "Oh!" I cry out and feel a tear run down my cheek. "But your box, signora," I say through gritted teeth.

"Please," the painter's wife says. "My box is my problem. You have other things to concern yourself with now."

"But... It is not gone, signora. Your box is still in the studio. Look under my worktable. You will find it there." I must pause to huff out several deep breaths. "The box the servants took..." Another huff. "It was a replica that I made with my own hands. It is empty. Not even gold. Practically worthless."

I push another guttural sound through my teeth. The journeyman opens the curtains to the passenger compartment. He and the painter's wife reach for me, hoisting me up under each arm. I struggle to push myself to a sitting and then to a standing position. Over the bow of the gondola, I see the massive stucco wall of the convent appear.

"Thanks be to God," I say in a huff of air.

"Indeed." The journeyman presses his narrow body behind me and leads me to the step stool at the side of the boat.

I reach for the rope tie on the quayside as a contraction grips my body. I hoist one leg up to the quay and pull myself up as my water breaks and splashes slimy and clear into the canal.

Chapter 42

After reaching for my aunt for months through the iron grille of the convent visitors' parlor, it is I who am now cloistered from the outside world, locked behind the great walls.

There is no moon. In the darkness, I can make out the outlines of the great infirmary hall, the arched ceiling that makes the muffled sounds of the room echo and reverberate. A few twinkles of starlight are visible through the high, barred window.

In the shadows I listen to the quiet, rhythmic suckling of my baby in my arms.

My son.

I can hardly fathom that he is real, but for six days, he has not left my embrace. My eyes follow the curve of his face, the light from the candle at my bedside splayed around his head like a gilded halo. I feel his small chest rising slowly up and down, and inhale his particular sugary scent. I marvel at his small, dark hands that clasp around my pale, freckled finger. His lids are nearly transparent, his hair a fine mesh of black tinged with red.

I am in love with him, a love as fierce as anything I have ever known. I can hardly imagine life before him.

From my bed, the rotten-cabbage aroma of the canal wafts up into the infirmary from a window along the water, but I do not mind for the slight breeze cuts through the stifling air. The sisters have wedged a cot for me at the far end of the infirmary and they have hung a sheath of linen to shield me from the others in the great space who might carry contagion. For six days, I have not dared to peek around the drape, but have heard the moans of the sick, the shrieks of another young woman in childbirth, and I imagine there are others too ill to make noise. A few times, I hear the dull intoning of a priest uttering last rites.

As for myself, I am sore but starting to feel stronger. In any other circumstance I might feel anxious to leave this hall of sundry maladies and unfortunate events, but resting here behind the curtain with my child in my arms, all I want to do is make it last.

At dawn I hear the echo of footsteps and a rustle of gowns through the convent. The sisters who have kept the plague vigil overnight have sung their matins prayers and are retiring to their cells to rest. In the hallways, another wave of sisters shuffles into the church to pray lauds as the sun rises. As light begins to bathe the infirmary hall in soft shades of pink and gold, their distant voices rise in unison. I close my eyes and allow myself to be transported. The melody travels through my body, and I open my mouth to let out the words, quietly but insistently. My son opens his wide eyes and peers at me, watching my mouth moving in unison with the nuns we hear in the distance. The chant, ephemeral yet eternal, seems to swirl around us, all silver and light, before fading and rising again. For a while, I let myself fly high above the convent walls, forgetting my circumstances and what my future might hold. I pull my son tightly to my chest, and let the music fill up all the empty spaces inside.

WHEN THE PINK-FACED novice brings me a tray of warm bread and fig jam at dawn, she smiles widely at my son then avoids my eyes, and I remember that they are trying to convince me to join them. It is in my best interest, Sister Agata the head convent nurse tells me, though I doubt if they will accept a great sinner like me.

Maria Magdalena. The boatman's voice floats in my head, and I push it away.

It is also in the best interest of my child, they insist, for what else is the poor boy to do? He can hardly be expected to belong anywhere else. Who would take him? He could not grow up to expect to find gainful employment. Surely he will be relegated to the lowliest forms of work, they tell me.

"We can raise him here," Sister Agata tells me. "We will send him to one of our wet nurses here in the convent nursery; later, when he is ready he may be sent to the Pietà for his education. In the meantime, you can finish your novitiate. For what else is there for you out there, *cara*?" she implores.

I hear the words but have no response. Not yet, for all I want to do is lie here and clasp my son to my body behind the drape.

The nun gazes into the baby's round, brown eyes, and takes in his dark skin and freckled cheeks. She runs the back of her finger along his cheek and then meets my eyes. "A child like this will not have much of a chance, you must know that, *cara*. He is better off being raised in the cloister. Here, he will learn to read and write. Perhaps he will find his vocation behind the walls of one of our ecclesiastical institutions and will not need to face the ridicule he will surely face out there." The nun gestures with her hand to the barred window, where a bright blue sky lies beyond.

Others have been less kind. "He looks like one of those little monkeys that you see on the street on a leash," one of the nuns said, giggling and rustling his hair, "or one of those servant boys they dress up in lace from Burano." I pulled him more tightly to me. "Poor little thing," she said, and mercifully walked away before I could no longer hold my tongue.

Cristiano. I close my eyes. *You have a son.* In my mind I tell him how beautiful his child is, how desperate I am to hold him, how much I want things to go back to the way they were before.

The baby peers up at me with his quizzical eyes, and in spite of myself, I feel a few tears escape the corners of my eyes, along with a strange mixture of happiness, sadness, and relief. I wipe my eyes with the back of my hand and then cup my palm around his beautiful, round head and kiss him.

Then for a moment, I see my father's face in his, a fleeting reflection. There is the baby's father, that is certain, but there is something else there, some vestige of my own father. It makes me smile. The baby closes his eyes and presses his face to me.

Giuseppe. My father's name. It will be his.

Hours later, when I open my eyes, my aunt's face appears before me. She is seated on the edge of the bed, letting the baby grasp her thumb with his little fist. I stir and she smiles at me.

"I have brought you something to eat," she says, gesturing to the table next to the bed. I turn my head and see a pair of small pastries with a copper goblet of milk.

"*Grazie,*" I say. "I am starving."

"The sisters have made a place for you in the novice's dormitory," she says. "As soon as you are ready we can move you there."

"I have not decided," I say.

"Maria, what is there to decide?" I hear her trying to temper the exasperation in her voice. "What would you do, a woman on your own? How will you take care of yourself? Surely you cannot be thinking of returning to your father's workshop," she says. "That life will be nothing but hardship for you. Think of it. How will you make a living? And this precious child..." She rubs her palm over his dark hair. "Truly, how would the two of you manage?"

In spite of myself, I feel a tear escape the corner of my eye. As much as I want to take my son and run out the door into the alley, I know she is right.

My aunt presses. "You could hardly take care of yourself, and people will not accept him. Both of you are better off here with us. He will learn here. He will read and write. He will find a meaningful vocation."

I stare at the pink sky beyond the high, barred window.

When I do not respond, my aunt says, "Your *gastaldo* has paid a visit."

"*Gastaldo*?" I imagine his portly figure at the grate in the visitors' parlor, his hat in his hand.

She nods. "He got word of what happened at the painter's house."

Of course he has. I press my palm over my face, not wanting to revisit the images of the sinking gondola, the convulsing of my stomach, the horrified look on Pascal Grissoni's face, the crowd of neighbors in the boathouse, the hysteria of the painter's wife. I am certain that the *gastaldo* has heard about every detail. A wave of shame washes over me.

"He sends his best regards to you." My aunt takes a deep breath, as if steeling herself for the words to come. "He has suggested that your father's house may be sold to cover your donation to the convent." She pauses, searching my face. When I say nothing, she continues. "A suitable arrangement, it seems to me. He says that another gilder in the quarter has already expressed some interest in buying it."

My aunt draws a piece of folded parchment from her pocket and places it on the table beside my bed. "And he brought you a letter," she says quietly, then squeezes my hand and stands. "When you are ready. It is a lot to think about. I shall leave you in peace."

I adjust the baby's position in my arms without waking him. Then I slide my finger under the wax seal and pry it apart from the parchment.

On behalf of Pascal Grissoni.

Item. With reference to the contract agreed to between Pascal Grissoni, painter, and Giuseppe Bartolini, gilder, both guildsmen in good standing, previous to the untimely death by pestilence of the afore-mentioned Bartolini the gilder.

Item. Given the present knowledge of previously unknown circumstances of the state of the gilder's daughter Maria, given that she has given birth to another man's child out of the bonds of matrimony, this contract will no longer be considered valid, and from this point forward is recorded as null and void.

Recorded in San Marco
On the feast of Saint Anthony of Padua
By Giorgio Gamba, Notary

Chapter 43

Behind my ear, the scissors make a sluicing sound. From the corner of my eye, I watch a long swath of my own hair fall to the ruddy tiles. Moment by moment, the pieces of octagonal terra-cotta are obscured by fine locks of reddish-gold.

The mistress of the novices is a stern-looking woman with deep-set creases on each side of her mouth. She makes ragged, rapid cuts with the dull blade. I hear the scrape of metal around my ears, and I feel the fine strands tickle my neck and shoulders as they fall.

I do not know what to feel for only numbness fills me, as if I have crawled inside a womb where only beating silence can be heard. At dawn, the convent nurse lifted my son from my arms and brought him to the nursery, where the arms of a wet nurse from Dorsoduro are waiting to cradle him. An infirmary novice has helped me bind my breasts in linen swaths to stop the flow of milk.

The hair-cutting is the final step before taking my vows, the last renunciation of my own display of vanity, the death knell to any part of me that might be construed as an instrument of seduction. Any trace of my carnal past—from seducing a man to suckling an infant—is now erased. I am to be a bride of Christ.

The bell sounds for sext, the midday prayer that brings us all into the high choir of the church, where I sit among a handful of other novices in the long choir stalls and listen to the intoning of our confessor.

The mistress of the novices takes three final snips, then lays her shears on the wooden table beside us. With a loud grunt, she bends over and picks up the hair off the floor and places it in a basket. Unceremoniously, she plunks a small wooden cross on top of the pile of shorn hair, and places the basket on the table. I have been told by the other novices that the hair will sit outside the novice chamber at night, and will be burned publicly tomorrow along with the locks of four other girls who are set to take their vows with me.

"I have never heard of such a short period of discernment," one of the girls had said to me.

"I have nothing to discern," I replied numbly.

In my heart, I know they are right. My baby will have the best chance at life within these walls. And as for me, what other choice could I make? My father, my cousin, and my Cristiano have vanished from the earth. The possibility of becoming the wife of Pascal Grissoni was tenuous from the start, and I am not surprised how quickly it fell apart, under the circumstances. Where else would I find my place in this world?

I reach my hand to my head and rub my palm over my scalp. The ragged edges of my hair scrape across my palm and I feel hot tears sting my eyes. The mistress hands me a black cloth to drape across my head. Then without a word, she walks out into the corridor that leads to the church.

Chapter 44

Twenty-four eggs.

One by one, I count them as I crack the shells into the bowl-like circle of dough I have created with my hands. The clutches of eggs are still warm from where they have been pulled from under the birds in the great hennery alongside the northeastern convent wall. A few of the eggs still have downy feathers pressed to the sides of their smooth, speckled surfaces.

For days, I have learned nothing else but how to knead the dough. It is deceivingly simple, I am told, for there is an art to each step in the process of making the pastries that have made the convent of Santa Maria delle Vergini famous.

Mostly, I am grateful to have work to do with my hands, for it helps them feel less empty. The nuns have done their best to keep my every waking moment occupied, but my mind turns to my little Giuseppe all day long. I imagine him in the orphanage nursery, at the breast of his wet nurse. My hands and forearms are sore from days spent pressing the dough, but they still feel empty. I feel empty myself. I take solace in knowing that he is safe, that I will see him on occasion, and that he will have a better chance inside these walls than he would ever have outside of them.

Thanks to my aunt's influence, I have been placed in the kitchen as a baker's apprentice. Lauretta, a young girl with smiling green eyes and skin as plump and pasty as the dough I press with my hands, has been assigned to familiarize me with my tasks.

My aunt has also told me that the abbess has heard of my vocal talents, and that she has thought about having me work with the cantor to teach the orphan girls some of the liturgy. That will come in time, she says. For now, I must learn to work the dough.

Patiently, Lauretta recites the convent's secret recipe for fritters in my ear, and I cannot help but wonder what Antonella would sacrifice in exchange for this information. Six *libre* of goats' milk, fresh butter, sugar, rose water—that's the real secret, she tells me—finely sifted flour, a little salt, and a pinch of saffron. After everything is mixed in a large copper bowl, that's when the eggs are added, one by one. Let it rise overnight, she tells me, and only uncover it when the nuns outside the great doors to the orchard have the lard hot enough to make spitting sounds.

I hear the now-familiar din of chattering voices from the corridor. "Here they come." Lauretta presses her elbow into my side, then wipes her doughy hands on a rag.

Small fingers and wide eyes suddenly appear over the tall counter ledge. Orphans. On Sundays the nuns allow them to visit the convent kitchen, to peer over the counters and ledges into the cavernous, vaulted space with its flour-covered worktables and great brick ovens. Their eagerness brings a smile to my face, along with a sharp pang of loss.

Almond cakes. Jellied fillings. Egg glazes and sugar dusted on the top. Their excitement has been building all week. From the back worktable, the nun who oversees the Sunday kitchen brings a large wooden tray to the counter, and passes out the small delights into their pudgy hands. Their chattering falls silent, and all that is left are expressions of glee.

"*Bambini*," the nun in charge of the gaggle of children calls, "you must be grateful that you are housed in the convent with the most famous pastry kitchen in Our Most Serene Republic!" Her voice rises to a high, shrill octave, and the words come out like a song.

She is right. The pastry kitchen is a marvel. Much like our Republic's great shipyard, the Arsenale, the convent kitchen is staffed by specialists. Certain nuns concoct the dough, as much alchemists as bakers, calculating the right amount of flour, eggs, water, and sugar gauged through years of experimentation. The novices are tasked with breaking the eggs and kneading the dough until the right consistency has been reached for each type of sweet: almond cookies, jam-filled cakes, carnival twists, and an infinite variety of other treats. A brawny, ever-perspiring nun named Elisabetta manages the great brick ovens, and barks orders to two assistants. Along one wall are the finishing touches: pine nuts, raisins of purple and gold, shriveled cherries and plums. At the front of the kitchen large metal dishes hold finished pastries.

Just outside the kitchen doors rolled open on a track, two nuns are responsible for tending the fire underneath a great copper pan mounted on a metal tripod. There the *fritelle* and other sugar breads are fried into crisp, golden puffs. Another nun stands by, armed with a large metal sugar sifter and a small pitcher of honey.

Beyond the doors, the convent orchard spreads out to the limit of the walls. There are several tidy rows of grape vines for making wine, and several dozen neatly tended fruit trees now close to harvesting. These are the orchards of pear and plum trees where we make jellies, Lauretta has told me. Before the little sisters and cousins come to visit, the nuns press small cakes and cookies into the branches, and convince the wide-eyed visitors that the convent is a special place where such treats grow on trees. Too late, the girls discover that only the fruits grow on the trees, not the cakes, and that they are responsible for harvesting the fruits and making the cakes themselves. By then, their hair has been shorn and they too are closed behind the walls for the rest of their days.

My aunt has shown me the recipe books, the great leather-bound tomes thicker than many of the thickest liturgical books in the convent library. She has reviewed our nearly endless annual litany of sugary treats, a yearly calendar for the kitchen to follow that is as sacred as our own litany of holy offices observed in the church. Dry, hard almond biscuits to be dipped into sherry or *vin santo*; square-shaped *baicoli* flavored with pistachios; thumb-sized *essi*, small cookies shaped like the letter S; flat oval biscuits billed as the tongues of cats or mothers-in-law; weightless meringues the color of canal water; speckled ovals that resemble quails' eggs but are filled with jelly.

At Carnival, my aunt has told me, we pull in several apprentices from the bakers' guild to help us keep up with the volume of the crunchy slivers of biscuit called *galani*; oval-shaped fried dough studded with raisins; pastry dough filled with *zabaione*, custard cream.

"These are only for the personal family gifts of our most wealthy sisters." Then she showed me the recipe that called for small gilded stripes painted across the tops of the tiny cookies some of the sisters give their families on feast days.

My aunt's eyes lit up when she showed me the small pots of liquid, edible gold they kept in a locked cabinet. "For you," she said, placing a small paintbrush in my hand.

WHEN THE BELL rings for matins in the novices' dormitory, I hear the others stir, but I lie still for as long as I can. In those moments between sleep and wakefulness, my mind is filled with the world outside the convent walls.

The painter's gilded box. My father's house. My cousin's laugh. My lover's hands.

Has the painter's wife given birth to her baby? Has the painter returned from his excursion to terra firma? What chaos has he found at his home? Has the painter's half-sunken gondola been pulled from the water? What of my father's workshop? Does it stand empty and forlorn? Has it already been sold to the gilder down the alley?

These questions remain obscure and unanswered. Unless someone calls me to the visitors' parlor, I have no way of knowing any of it. I pray for the *gastaldo* to come and give me some shred of news, some information about my former life on the other side of the great wall.

"Wake up, *bellisima*." I feel Lauretta's hand give a gentle shake on my leg. "I have a gift for you."

I open my eyes to see her pudgy, eager face before me. In between my face and hers, she dangles a necklace with beads the color of fire, probably coral. I reach out and turn their smooth, round surfaces between my fingers.

"*Bella*," I say.

"It's yours," she says, wrinkling her nose. "My mother sent me others."

I sit up in my narrow bed and swing my feet to the floor. On the bed alongside mine, Lauretta has laid out several lovely necklaces with colored beads of glass, amber, and coral. Two other novices have come to sit on the other edge of Lauretta's bed, running the strings of colored beads between their palms.

They are only the latest baubles to catch the novices' attention. Across the dormitory, the girls have stashed gems, dresses, hair adornments, elaborate undergarments, and other treasures, pressed under their mattresses, in their sparse drawers, or in trunks at the ends of their beds. There is no shortage of wealthy daughters in the convent, I realize. Most of them are the unfortunate second, third, fourth, or fifth-born daughter, whose eldest sister was handed off in marriage along with a handsome dowry to secure the family's future in this world. The rest were promised to the convent along with more meager donations, where they secured the family's future in the World to Come.

The families, for their part, ring the bell to the visitors' parlor on Sundays bearing gifts for their daughters and nieces. Some of the women here, I am told, hold large collections of dresses and jewelry, wear fancy clothing under their habits, and exchange their expensive baubles in games of dice and cards, which are also smuggled in as gifts. I have even seen a few gilded boxes among the older nuns' possessions, though none as special as the one I copied in Master Trevisan's studio.

"You can hide it under your habit," Lauretta giggles.

I fish my habit from the meager trunk at the end of my bed, which otherwise stands empty. I place the coral necklace Lauretta has given me inside the barren trunk, and as I do, I think of another, more precious necklace I once hid between my dress and my shift.

A lifetime ago.

I pull my habit over my head, then follow the line of sisters filing from the nuns' dormitory to the church for the matins prayers.

An older nun shushes the chattering that echoes in the vaulted hallway. "Quiet, *ragazze!*" she whispers loudly. "We have reason to pray as well as give thanks this morning. Our confessor brings news that the pestilence is continuing to lift its mantle from Our Most Serene City."

A nun in front of me whispers to Lauretta. "My sister told me that they have removed the barriers in Cannaregio."

Lauretta makes a sharp turn backward, grasping my arm.

"Isn't that wonderful news, Maria?" Lauretta turns her smiling eyes on me. "Cannaregio! Isn't that your quarter? Did you hear? They are removing the barriers on the streets! Finally!"

"Thanks be to God," another sister says, clasping her palms together, then pressing her hands on my shoulders. "Our prayers have been answered!"

"Yes," I say, hearing the words but finding them strange, unbelievable. "Wonderful. Thanks be to God."

IN THE UPPER nuns' choir the air is stifling. We crowd together into the wooden stalls, our bodies sticky and warm under layers of black wool. Pale hands pass small fans from one sister to another. Small huddles form around whomever holds a fan in her hand, waving wafts of air in the faces of her sisters.

Each sister carries a different style of fan made of thin wood, paper, leather, or parchment. Two of the elderly nuns at the front refresh themselves with fans in the shape of flags, small wooden handles and leather flaps with stamped and gilded decoration. Another woman near me holds a fan with an exquisite ivory handle and a scene painted on the lightweight wooden paddle that reminds me of the engraving of Pyramus and Thisbe from the book of engravings in Trevisan's studio.

The priest's monotonous voice rises up from the altar below. I cannot see him, and can only hear his dull intoning of the Latin scriptures. Unlike many of these women, I have never had the privilege of learning Latin and it sounds strange to my ear. My sisters tell me that I will learn it in due time. We sit high in the nun's choir so that we are not visible to visitors who may be present below us. They have placed me in the back row with the other novices, most younger than twelve, whose families have bound them to follow this life.

From this vantage point, I can only see the top of the altarpiece that Master Trevisan, the journeyman, and I have made with our own hands. It has only been weeks since I laid the gold leaf on the poplar panels, to the glittering surfaces that appear luminous from where I sit. From behind, the nuns' heads look the same, but I recognize my aunt several rows ahead because of her diminutive size.

She seems happy and satisfied to have brought me here, having spread word of my talents throughout the community as if she herself might take credit for them.

The priest's dull voice stops, and along with the others, I lift my voice to sing. The chant transports me, and for a long moment I close my eyes and allow myself to be present in the music. Everything else falls away.

As I sing, I run my fingertips over the armrest of the choir stall. It has been rubbed smooth over the years by the many hands of sisters who have sat in this seat. I imagine that it may be gilded, and I open my eyes to look. I see that it was once gilded, but the gold leaf has rubbed off over many years. Only a light patina of gold appears, the red bole exposed by years of palms running over it. I imagine how the sheaves of gold were beaten, how the gesso and bole were laid down, how the leaf was laid on top.

I feel a pang in the pit of my stomach. The gold. I want to work the gold. I realize that as much as my heart and my hands long for my child, they long also to work the gold. I cannot imagine that I will spend the rest of my days here inside these walls, never again having the chance to work. It is what I am supposed to do, I realize. I do not know why it took me so long to accept it.

And the gold is not dead, a voice seems to speak to me from inside my own head, perhaps from somewhere deep inside my soul. *The gold is not dead.* It is still very much alive, perhaps always will be. The truth hits me as clear as the summer sky outside the convent windows.

With a start, I stand and press myself against the nuns beside me in the choir stall. "*Scusate,*" I say, pressing past their knees. As if she can sense my movement all the way from the front row, my aunt turns around. Seeing me pushing myself past the row of sisters, she launches out of her seat and rushes after me. Some of the nuns shush her and pull at her habit to make her sit back down, but her feet move swiftly to the aisle.

I am halfway down the stone spiral staircase when she catches up to me and reaches for my shoulder. I grip the iron rail to prevent myself from hurling down the stairs.

"*Tutto bene, cara*? You are not feeling sick, are you?" Her urgent whisper fills the stairwell. "Where are you going?"

I pause and meet her eyes. "I am leaving," I say.

"Leaving?" Her brow wrinkles.

"I am sorry, *zia*," I say. "I have changed my mind. I am grateful for everything you have done to help me. Truly, I am. But I cannot stay here. I have made a terrible mistake."

My aunt grasps the sleeve of my habit. "You cannot make such a rash decision, Maria. You are now a *novizia*. You are to be a bride of Christ; you cannot simply walk out the door. Let us get you some help. Our *badessa* will know what to do. Wait here."

I pull my arm away from her grip. "This is not where I belong, *zia*. I should have recognized it before. I belong in my father's studio. Everyone has tried to convince me that my destiny lay somewhere outside my father's house, that the gold was dead. They were all well-intentioned. You were well-intentioned, *zia*. For that I am grateful. But I was wrong to think that the gold was dead. And I was wrong to think that I was meant to do anything but continue my family's legacy."

My aunt's forehead forms deep creases. "You are not thinking rationally, Maria. How will you make it on your own?"

"I do not know. All I know is that I am going home."

Chapter 45

I hardly recognize my father's house.

In the weeks that I have been in the convent, the quarter of Cannaregio has begun to come back to life, but the house remains a silent shell of what it was. My father's worktable still stands under the window, and a few tools remain scattered across the surface, small pots overturned, the evidence of ransackers who came through in a haste and, finding nothing of value, left. The pillagers have taken what meager vegetables were put away in the root cellar. I stand alone in the middle of the barren room, the first day of the rest of my life, and I try to fathom where to begin.

A warm swath of sunlight pours through the open door of the workshop, and an orange cat tiptoes into the pool of yellow. It bends its body around the doorjamb and squints at me through orange eyes. After a moment another feline head appears in the doorway. The second cat, with stripes of grey and black, slips around the orange cat and trots across the floor toward me with its tail held high in anticipation. The striped cat weaves its way around my ankles, and I feel its skinny, warm body begin to vibrate against my leg.

As I make my slow inventory of my father's workshop, the cats follow me, the striped one eager, the orange one more tentative.

I suspect that they must be among the cadre of felines that once occupied old Signora Granchi's quarters upstairs. Bereft of their mistress, most of the ragged animals seem to have wandered off in search of better prospects, but these two, at least, have lingered. The cats leap onto my father's worktable and settle themselves there, watching me sweep grey ashes from the hearth.

The *gastaldo*, after recovering from the initial shock of seeing me back in my father's workshop, began soliciting help. He has already arranged for a boatman from the *traghetto* to fetch my trunk from the painter's house. The gondolier, an old man with a limp, helped me press the trunk—now holding all of my earthly belongings in it—against the wall where it always stood in the days before I left my father's house. This small gesture brings me some comfort, and I lift the lid.

On top of the small heap of clothing, I find a collection of tools that someone—perhaps Master Trevisan's journeyman—has gathered from my workbench in the back of the painter's workshop. There are also the tin molds that Trevisan taught me how to use on the gilded boxes. I remove them, running my fingers over their bumpy surfaces, then lining them along my father's nearly empty workbench.

I push the striped cat aside as I examine the small glass jars containing our powdered pigments lined up along the wall. The bench has been toppled over. As I return it to its proper position, an image flashes through my mind of my father sitting on this very bench, firing the bellows to melt gold and solder jewelry when our gilding work slowed. A small pot of gesso that we use to prepare panels is also left intact. I unpack my meager gilding supplies from my trunk and lay them out on the table alongside my father's. The orange cat paws at one of the palette knives, then stops to scratch his ear vigorously with a back leg, sending flecks of dust and orange hairs spinning into the wash of sunlight.

Earlier in the morning Signora Gardesano, the wife of another *indoradòr* across the alley, has stopped at my doorway to let me know that more than half of the neighbors on the street have gone to the World to Come. "Our guild will take care of us," she tells me. But I know that she is trying to make me feel better. The guild saves our dues for such unfortunate events, but its coffers have been depleted by the number of people who have perished in recent months, and the number of families that need assistance.

"My husband says that they have buried those of our guild— including your father and cousin—not in one of the mass pits for plague victims, but rather in the cemetery on one of the outlying islands where many of our fellow painters are laid to rest. Thanks be to God for that, *cara*. At least in that you may take some comfort." Signora Gardesano then pressed a meager stack of linens in my hand. "I embroidered them with my own hands," she tells me.

"I am grateful," I said.

She crossed her arms over her ample breast and continued. "The walls are chattering with the news, you know." Her eyes passed over my midsection, but she forced herself to return her gaze to my face. I resisted the urge to bring my hand to my stomach.

"I am prepared," I said. "I am going to be all right on my own." I do not tell her that even though I know leaving my baby in the convent is the best thing for him, it has taken everything in me to do it.

The *gastaldo* has told me that the guild will provide funds to help me buy what I need to replenish my father's house. It is meager but the bereavement payment is to be expected in such circumstances, he has told me. Beyond that, it is up to me now to try to reestablish our patrons and make a living for myself. If I am to make a life from this place and carry on my father's trade, it will be up to me.

THE NEXT TIME I hear a knock at the door, I am startled to see the painter's wife.

"There she is!" she exclaims, running her eyes over me up and down. "Look at her, poor dear."

"Signora Trevisan," I say. I put down the horsehair cloth I have been using to sand the new alder wood box on my father's worktable. Her midsection seems to have deflated, but her cheeks are still flushed with pink just as when she was with child. I cannot help but observe beautiful blue satin trim at her waist and neckline, and the pearls entwined in the fine piles of hair she has arranged around her face. She carries a brown woven bag under her arm.

"*Dio*, but you are brave!" says the painter's wife, stepping across the threshold and scanning the space with her wide eyes. "Having a child and then going back to reclaim your father's house! Where is the little one? I came to lay eyes on the baby!"

"He… He is with the sisters," I say, feeling my heart pound at the sight of her. "It seemed the right thing to do… under the circumstances." My eyes land on a pair of large dust motes in the corner and I wish that I had swept.

"Ah," she says, and I see her face fall. "A sensible arrangement, under the circumstances, as you say. Well, God bless him. And to you. *Auguri*."

"That is very kind of you," I say, watching the painter's wife's eyes scan the cramped room. She places her bag on the table, then runs her eyes from the low wooden beams on the ceiling to the worn desk under the window, to our modest hearth. I am acutely aware of the cobwebs in the window and our bare furnishings.

"Congratulations are in order to you, too, signora?"

Her face lights up. "A little girl," she says. "Benvoglio was perhaps disappointed, but no matter. She is healthy, as am I. That is what is important."

"Thanks be to God. I would like to offer you something to eat," I manage to say. "Forgive me. I would have been better prepared if I had known you were coming."

"*Figurati*, there is no need," says the painter's wife. "I am here to help you, my dear, not the other way around. But I will sit."

"Of course," I say, rushing to pull out one of our rickety wooden chairs.

The painter's wife heaves herself onto the chair and sighs audibly. As soon as she sits, the two cats, who seem to have taken up residence with me even though I have nothing to feed them, weave their way around Signora Trevisan's ankles. She ignores them. From a ceramic pitcher on the table, I pour well water into a chipped ceramic cup and hand it to her.

"I walked all the way from San Marco," she says. "And in this heat! But how else was I to get here? Who would want to ride in one of those filthy boats from the *traghetto*? Ha!" Signora Trevisan swallows the water in a single gulp. "When the *gastaldo* informed us that you had returned to your father's workshop, well, I insisted that we come to see you right away," she says. "I am sorry that my husband was not able to join me. He is occupied, as you know, with his many commissions." Her fingers fidget nervously around the cup.

I feel heat flash across my cheeks. The painter and I have not set eyes on one another since that night when I ran from him in the church and he left for terra firma. "Of course," I say.

"He asked me to convey his best wishes," she continues.

"Master Trevisan has returned home," I venture.

"Yes," she says. "He came back home as soon as he received word of the... surprising events... that occurred in our home."

I am not able to find the words to respond. I refill the ceramic cup with water, grateful to have something to do with my hands. Mercifully, the painter's wife continues to talk.

"We did not want you to go away feeling that we harbored any ill will," says the wife. "We did not hold you responsible for... the things that happened." She is looking at my stomach now, refusing to lift her eyes to my face. "What I mean to say is that what happened with our servants, well... none of it had anything to do with you. And the matter with the gondola... It is unfortunate that you were caught in the middle of such a turn of events." It is unlike the painter's wife to hesitate like this, and I wonder if her husband has planted the words in her head.

Finally, unable to restrain herself, the painter's wife throws up her hands and meets my eyes. "Antonella and that evil boatman seem to have disappeared off the face of the earth. I knew we were wrong to trust them."

"Master Trevisan's beautiful gondola," I say.

"The gondola maker and his sons from the Squero Vianello came to help us fish the boat out of the water," the painter's wife says. "By the time they arrived it had sunk nearly all the way to the bottom of the boat slip! They had to get the rocks out of it to pull it up," she says.

"What a shame."

"Now it is upside down on trestles in the boat slip. The gondola makers offered to repair it right away but my husband does not seem to be able to bring himself to do anything with it. A shame, you are right. It was a beautiful boat but I doubt that my husband will have it repaired, at least for now, for he is unlikely to hire a new boatman," she says.

"The boatman and Antonella..." I venture.

The painter's wife shakes her head vigorously as if to rid the image of her servants from her head. "At first he seemed to be such a capable young man. Almost too good to be true. But I knew it was a mistake to bring him back. I knew not to trust that boatman. He was marked by fire already, for the love of God! Surely Benvoglio should have heeded such a sign. But Antonella... That took me by surprise. I never would have thought of the two of them together. Such a transgression of my trust! I confided everything to her, even my own children."

"They have not been caught?" I ask.

The painter's wife shakes her head. "The *signori di notte* looked for them for a while, but never found them. Then my husband got word that they were seen on terra firma trying to pawn off the box to a second-hand broker."

The striped cat makes a tentative move to jump into Signora Trevisan's lap, but she stands. Thwarted, the cat rubs himself along my leg instead.

The painter's wife takes my hand. "But enough about us," she says. "You, my dear, look one step away from the pesthouse yourself, if I may say it! Have you nothing to eat? My goodness, a girl like you, all by yourself. How will you manage?"

"The *gastaldo* is helping to arrange my father's affairs," I say. "I will be fine."

"But how will you get along?" She gestures around the barren studio. "When we heard that you had left the convent... Well, we just could not imagine that you would try to come back to your father's workshop all by yourself."

"The convent was not for me," I interject, "and… well. It seems that neither was marriage."

The painter's wife examines my face. "The baby's father?"

I shrug. "He perished in the *lazzaretto* with my father and cousin. That is the only conclusion."

The painter's wife nods, and the two of us fall silent. Signora Trevisan's eyes scan the meager tools on my father's worktable. Finally, she says, "It will take some time for you to establish yourself."

"I know my father's patrons," I say, "though I must rebuild those alliances. It will take some time, but above all I want to carry on my father's legacy."

"Very honorable. That reminds me," she says, and I wonder if I see her eye twitch. "My husband has asked me to tell you that he will continue to send you gilding work as you are able to do it. Anyway, he has sent you something."

From the dark woven bag on the table, the painter's wife dumps some two dozen new metal molds onto my worktable. I gasp, then finger each one, examining the small forms of women, men, decorative designs, animals, and plants. I imagine the numbers of different gilded boxes that I might make with the molds.

The painter's wife then produces a leather book from the bag. I recognize the stamped binding immediately. It is the book of engravings that I thumbed through so many times in the painter's studio. The value of such a book might amount to two times what my father and I might earn in a year.

"Oh no!" I say. "I could not accept this, Signora Trevisan. It is too precious."

"It is the least we could do for you, *cara*. After all, it is thanks to you that my dowry has been preserved." She shakes her head. "If that boatman had made off with all of that gold... Well, I can hardly stand to think of it."

"I do not know what to say."

She waves her hand. "My husband insisted. He says that he retrieved the molds from his cousin's studio when he was visiting his ancestral lands near Padua. He has little use for them. He thought you might use them, and the book will help you get started," she says. "Benvoglio says that on terra firma they are successful in selling these gilded boxes to new brides. "Perhaps they will help you earn a living once you get a few of the boxes out there. Maria," she says. "This path you have chosen will not be easy for you. *Cavolo*, look at this place!"

I feel both insulted and ashamed, though she does not seem to notice. I pick up the orange cat and stroke the silky fur between its ears, as if this small act might soothe the affront. "It is not the same as your husband's workshop, signora," I say. "But it never was, even in our most prosperous time."

The painter's wife grasps my arm. "No. That much is true. And even so, I would change places with you," she says, giving me a thin-lipped smile. "I can see that you belong here with the gold, that you are strong enough to do well here in your father's studio on your own. Truth be told, I envy you."

Chapter 46

With each passing day, it becomes clear who is on my side and who is not. Signora Gardesana, in addition to bringing me two rickety chairs, has also brought me an onion pie and some asparagus and radicchio that she put away in the spring. I remove a few small pieces each day from the containers, making it last. She has also offered me some seeds for the garden. I have sowed them in the hard ground and wonder if they will last long enough to be nourished by the fall rains. The baker at the corner dispatches her son at the end of the day to bring me a loaf or two of bread left after the day's customers have finished their marketing.

A few of my father's guildsmen have appeared at our doorway to offer their condolences. On the surface it would seem a generous act, but I quickly realize that many of them are there to gawk at me and my meager workshop.

"Your father would not have wanted to see you in such a state," said the wife of one of these men, a woman who knew my mother long ago. I know she meant well, but I felt stung under her sharp gaze, and pulled at the linen wrap that I have fashioned to cover my shorn hair. "How will you get along by yourself?" she had asked.

"I will be fine," I said, but the more I am asked the question, the less I know the answer.

But most of the guildsmen and their wives have not taken the time to express their opinion to me directly, though I am certain that they whisper to one another at the market and the laundry well. Most have simply stayed away or kept their judgments to themselves.

Along my father's worktable I have lined up the rectangular wooden boxes, and placed their lids in a row along the dining table. The carpenter would not accept a *scudo* in return for making the boxes for me; not that I have any to offer. With sad eyes he said, "Keep them, signorina," before frowning and rubbing his gnarled hands together. I imagine that the carpenter must not have much to spare himself after feeding all of those children of his, and I feel grateful.

I have set aside the tin molds that Master Trevisan has brought me. For days, I have rearranged the figures into varying designs, referring to the book of engravings for inspiration. I have drawn numerous sketches of possible compositions and combinations, using some of the newfound drawing skills I have learned in Master Trevisan's studio. I have also put aside the precious pieces of gold leaf I have retrieved from the drawer of the *battiloro*'s worktable behind our house. I will need to count my money to see if I can afford to buy the *pastiglia* to mold the figures after I purchase some bread and gruel to eat.

After a few days, the stream of hat-holding guildsmen and curious wives dwindles, and I am left to my work. A hush has fallen over my father's workshop, replaced only by my singing.

WHEN THE *GASTALDO* appears at the door, I am affixing a newly formed figure onto an alder wood box with rabbit-skin glue. I am experimenting with the new molds that the painter's wife has brought me, and feel certain that no one else in Our Most Serene Republic will be able to produce such a box.

"Signorina *indoradòr*," the *gastaldo* nods his head. His bulky frame fills the doorway and I see his eyes crinkle as he gives me a familiar smile. "It smells like heaven in here," he says.

"It's the *muschio*, I say. "I am mixing it with the paste so that the boxes will be scented. The *vendecolore* told me that is how they do it in the workshops around Padua." The color-seller has given me much more than information. He was so full of pity at the loss of my father that he sent me home with two bags full of *muschio* scents, the rabbit-skin glue, and two additional adhesives to try, not to mention some of the gold-like alloy that I used in Master Trevisan's studio.

"I see that you have found your purpose."

"The colored pigments were not for me," I say.

"Your talents lay elsewhere," he says. A grin spreads across his face, then his brow furrows. "My dear, you are not eating?" the *gastaldo* gestures to my lean body.

"I am not hungry," I lie, pushing away the image of the empty root cellar from my head.

I sit on the small stool of the gilding bench. The *gastaldo* pulls up a rickety chair and removes his hat.

"You have everything you need?" He sets his blue eyes on me.

I nod. "Mostly. I will need more firewood soon." I do not want to appear needy, for I am desperate now to make it on my own. I do not tell the *gastaldo* that I am sleeping on a makeshift pallet on the floor, made with linens handed down from a neighbor. I do not admit that I have pulled apart the planks that formed the cross over the door and thrown them onto the fire. "The neighbors have brought me some food and there are onions in the garden that have resurged from last year."

"But you have little money."

I study the floor. "I have not sold any boxes yet. But Master Trevisan's wife says that there will be eager patrons once people have seen them. And soon I shall have my father's bereavement payment," I say.

"The bereavement payment," the *gastaldo* says, scratching the top of his head where the hair has disappeared. He takes a deep breath. "I am sorry to tell you this, Maria, but there is no other way around it. Your payment is, for the moment, in question."

I stand up, clutching my chest. "What?"

The *gastaldo* stands and begins to pace the room. "I am afraid it is not as simple as I thought, Maria. The guild statutes state that the written wishes of the deceased person must be followed to the letter. Now the marriage to Pascal Grissoni is out of the question."

"That was his choice!" I raise my voice. "It is not that I am disappointed; that must be clear. He was a logical choice for my father to make, I suppose, but I did not love him. You may have deduced."

The *gastaldo* raises his palms to calm me. "*Capito.* If it were up to me I would simply give you the payment, Maria. But there is some resistance from certain of our guild members. These are dark times. Our guild coffers are nearly bare. There is so much need and only so many resources to go around. The members... They are having trouble with the idea of a woman here on her own, having birthed a... child like you have birthed... under the circumstances... being part of us, a full member of our guild. No father, no husband." He pauses and waits for my response but I am struck dumb. The *gastaldo* continues. "I am looking for a solution that will satisfy everyone and allow you to get through this difficult time. I do not want to see you suffer."

"You and the others are trying to punish me for having a child with a man you do not accept, out of the bonds of marriage!"

"Maria." The *gastaldo* measures his voice. "I assure you that I am not trying to punish you. On the contrary, I am trying to help you."

"Then give me my father's share from the guild, as I am entitled. It is so written in the guild statutes. I am not stupid. You know that my father would have wanted that!"

"Maria, the last thing you are is stupid. I also know what your father wanted. He wanted you to marry a guild member, continue to work in our trade yourself as you have done for so many years, and for you to bear sons who could carry on our craft. That is the unspoken promise of each member of our guild. I am sure you know that. If we don't at least do that, our entire trade is in jeopardy." He clasps his hands and wags them in my direction.

"My father would not have promised me to Pascal Grissoni under the circumstances. All I ever wanted was to stay here with my family and our *battiloro*! I am sure that is no secret by now," I say. "Anyone who might have doubted that before certainly does not now."

The *gastaldo* opens his palms toward me. "Maria, I understand. The *battiloro* was a good man, a fine craftsman. I was the first of our guild to argue that he be allowed as a full member of the gold-beater's guild on the premise that his mentor was deceased and that he continued to work in the trade under your father's roof. Many opposed the idea, and it took work on my part with the *gastaldo* of the gold beater's guild. Even if he had survived and he had stayed under this roof, our guildsmen would have had trouble accepting it. You must understand that is the reality."

"We do not know that he is not still in the pesthouse!" I gesture to the doorway.

"Maria," the *gastaldo* says softly, "surely you must resign yourself to the reality that he perished with the others. There is no other answer. Otherwise where is he?" I look at a crack in the plaster wall and clench my throat, trying to push down the large lump that has formed there. The *gastaldo* continues. "In order to follow your father's wishes to the letter of the law and keep your workshop and position in the guild, you must marry a guild member. That is what the others are saying."

"Pascal Grissoni will not marry me!" I insist.

"Understood," he says, raising his hand. "Your father only had your best interest at heart back when he arranged your apprenticeship with Master Trevisan, and when he asked me to help select a suitor among our guild members. He was trying to secure your future. It would be difficult to do better than Pascal Grissoni. You have seen his house and his pictures yourself."

I nod. Of course I see the logic, but it does not account for the emptiness in my heart.

"Perhaps I should not tell you this, but Pascal Grissoni was not initially enticed by my insistence to pay a visit to Master Trevisan in order to meet you," the *gastaldo* continues. "After all, your father was not in a position to make him a compelling offer of a dowry. The guild might have scrounged together a meager one, as we do in cases like this where our guild members cannot. Still, such an amount would not be considered an appealing arrangement for a man like Pascal Grissoni. But fortunately," he says, a grin crossing his face, "the dowry seemed not to matter anymore once he laid eyes on you. I expected that might be the case."

I feel my face flush. "But of course he is no longer interested. And I am no longer... unspoiled." As I say the words I feel the pang of loss, and long to hold my son in my arms.

The *gastaldo* shrugs. "Pascal Grissoni is making a mistake, in my opinion, but I can only give my advice. I cannot force him."

"What do you suggest that I do, then?"

The *gastaldo* paces in front of the window for a few long, silent moments. Then he stops to face me. "Maria, you know that I have been a widower for many years. I do not know if you remember my wife, Gerita. You were a small girl when the fever took her from us. I have never seen a good reason to marry again. My sons are big and able. They carry the burden of work in my studio and I find myself idle more often than I would like to admit. One might say... free. In fact, apart from my role as *gastaldo*, which will only be for another season, I am freer than ever. Free to start a new journey in my life." His expression softens and he pulls the stool up close to sit in front of me.

I stare at him, unable to accept what he is suggesting.

"Keep your father's workshop," he says. "I am happy to work here with you. And I am certain that the guild would find the arrangement acceptable. Father Filippo would be overjoyed." He lets loose a quick chuckle. "And no doubt my sons would be happy to rid themselves of me." The *gastaldo* takes my hand and squeezes it gently. "The two of us together. Who might have foreseen it? I have known you since you were a little girl. I respected your father and knew him like my family. He respected me, too. You know that."

"My father trusted you more than anyone in the guild," I manage to say, but I cannot bring myself to meet his gaze now.

The *gastaldo* kneels in front of me and takes my hand in both of his. "*Cara mia*," he says, "I understand the passions of the heart. Your son was born out of love. I know that. I can restore your legitimacy within the guild, and you will not have to leave your home again. I can help you if you will let me." The *gastaldo* moves one hand to cover his heart and places the other on top of my hand. "I do not stand in judgment of you or your son," he says. "Perhaps he will join us here, when he is old enough. If he grows up to be like his grandfather then he will be a worthy addition to our clutch of *indoradòri*. He will continue our legacy—mine, yours, and your father's. Maria," he says. "Think about it."

I hear the *gastaldo*'s voice, but somewhere inside, a deep shudder runs unbidden through my body. My stomach turns, and I feel that I might vomit.

I finally manage to meet the *gastaldo*'s clear blue eyes, but when I do, I watch his expression transform from sincerity to concern.

"Maria. Are you all right?"

I nod, but a profound malaise has begun to creep into my bones.

"Of course it is a lot to consider," he sighs and stands. "*Bene.* You know where to find me. I shall leave you in peace, my dear."

After the *gastaldo* leaves the house, I return to my worktable and my boxes, but peace will not come. Instead, my heart races in my chest. By the time the sun has sunk below the still lagoon, I have begun to sweat, and no amount of well water will quench my thirst.

Chapter 47

The air has turned as heavy as a leaden blanket, still and moist, sweltering. Do the others feel it, too, or am I the only one who has soaked through my linens? I dip a small pail into the canal behind the house, and splash water on the dreary little patch of garden that I am trying to resurrect from having gone to seed, a hopeless exercise for the month of August. Soon enough, the stench of rotting vegetables in the canal and the row of latrines behind our block overwhelms my senses. Another wave of dizziness, and I feel I will drop to my knees.

I return to the dim stillness of the house and lie on the pallet I have made on the floor. The striped cat is already there, curled into a tight knot. When I lie down, he raises his head and peers at me through the narrow slits of his green eyes. Then he stretches and begins to gnaw at the fur on one of his hind legs. I place my hand on his scrawny back, and he settles into a curl again, uttering a soft murmur through his nose.

From my vantage point, I can see the wooden boxes that the carpenter has delivered to me. They are lined up on the table, waiting for the work of my hands. I must begin, I think, just as soon as I can drag myself from here. An unquenchable thirst has overtaken me, but I cannot imagine how I would walk all the way to the wellhead in the *campo*, much less walk back with buckets laden with water.

There are no more curious guildsmen or wives at my door who might bring me water. Even the *gastaldo*, who has shown more compassion for me than anyone might expect, has left me alone for two days. He knows that I know where to find him, and he has given me space to consider his proposal. I close my eyes, and in the silence, I do consider the *gastaldo's* request.

It makes perfect sense for me to accept his proposal. Of course it does. I would be well fed, well taken care of for the rest of my days. When my son comes of age, I can pull him from the convent as our apprentice, our heir. My father might even be proud of me, I think, if that is even possible under the circumstances. I cannot imagine that I would feel anything close to the fire that I felt with Cristiano, not with the *gastaldo*, not with Pascal Grissoni, not with anyone else. But in my heart I also know that when people say I cannot do this on my own, they are probably right.

Still, I have delayed my response. The hours stretch out. I know in my heart that the right thing to do is to go see the *gastaldo*, to accept his proposal. I cannot put it off much longer. I will do just that, I think, as soon as the profound ache in my head subsides.

I feel the chills come again, but there are no blankets. What has happened to them? I cannot seem to think straight. Has someone taken all the linens from the house?

I must ask my father or Paolo. Have they gone somewhere? I do not recall.

When I open my eyes I do not know if it is night or day, nor how much time has elapsed since I lay down with the striped cat, who has now disappeared.

At one point, I see the *gastaldo's* face float before me, his brow furrowed and his mouth pitched into a deep frown. I feel his broad hand brush across my forehead.

"Yes," I say to him, but I barely hear my own voice and he does not seem to hear me at all.

My head… My eyes close again.

The next time I open my eyes, I hear the soft, liquid voice of the *battiloro*'s mother. "Come back, child." Zenobia. Is she speaking to me or to little Giuseppe?

I feel her strong hands rub an oily substance on the soles of my feet. Her hands on my feet feel wonderful, but the concoction smells sharply of onion and vinegar and I press my hand over my nose. I want to thank her, to tell her how beautiful her grandson is.

My son. Where is he?

"Giuseppino!" I try to push myself up to sitting.

"Shhhh…" I hear Zenobia say, then her voice and her touch fade away.

The next time I open my eyes I expect to see my *gastaldo* or Zenobia before me again. Instead, it is Father Filippo, and he looks very sad indeed.

Chapter 48

In my bed lie an old woman and her daughter—at least I think it is her daughter, as the old woman calls lovingly to her through the day. The younger woman rarely answers, but the old woman keeps talking, whispering, singing, moaning. Sometimes the old woman turns toward me, her sour breath spreading over my face. I turn my back, but I still hear her whispered complaints, nonsensical words in a tongue I have never heard before. Her voice sounds like a song. After a while, I stop trying to understand the words, but lull myself into oblivion on the cadence of its strange, lilting melody and long sighs.

Why are they here? Are they waiting for a gilded box? I must get up and finish at least one. Surely they will be delighted with its beauty. Surely they have never seen one like it. If only my head would stop hurting, I could finish it. My cousin. Paolo. We can work on it together. He can help with the gilding so that I can fill the molds that Master Trevisan gave me.

Master Trevisan. Where is he? Has he returned from terra firma? I must ask his wife.

Darkness.

Long, silent darkness.

The sound of a bell tolling. The call of a ferryman traveling over the still water. The scrape of metal gates.

Darkness again. Merciful oblivion.

Then pain.

Suddenly there is nothing but sharp stinging in my armpit, so painful that white light flashes across my closed eyelids. I gasp and try to sit straight up in bed. I open my eyes to see two women dressed in white pressing my shoulders to the straw-stuffed mattress. A man with a black leather mask over his face leans over me. All I see are clear, green eyes.

He is the one causing the pain. I try to swat his hand away, but the women press my other arm to the mattress.

"Where is she?" I demand.

"Where is who?" one of the women asks. Her face is serene except for a birthmark on her cheek the size and color of a strawberry.

"My aunt!" I say.

They do not answer. I feel my eyes open wide, but all around me are shadows, darkness. Disoriented, I grasp for any familiar sight or face. I make out a long hall with wooden beams above my head, and a few windows open to the fading light of dusk.

"This is not the convent infirmary." My heart pounds in my chest and I struggle to sit up. The women beside me shift in the bed.

The *medico's* voice comes out muffled through the mask. "Lazzaretto Vecchio," he says, and I see his eyes crinkle with what might be a smile. "*Benvegnesta.*"

The pesthouse. I gasp for air and blink hard in the darkness to try to see clearly, to try to clear the clutter in my head. I struggle to push myself from the mattress, but the woman with the strawberry stain on her cheek pushes me back again.

"Be still, *cara*," she says. "Almost finished." Her clear, bright eyes are full of compassion.

I feel the sharp sting in my armpit again, and I wince. Then it spreads into a dull ache across my chest, and I hear the splash of liquid streaming into a metal container. The doctor stands. He looks down at me over a cup held with a bloodstained glove.

"Combative," the doctor says through the mask. "A good sign. I will check you again tomorrow," he says before he disappears from view.

Another woman in white brings me a cup and props me up to drink. She says nothing, but presses it to my lips. I take a sip, filling my cheeks with a foul mixture that tastes of urine and eggs. I retch over the side of the bed.

"You will get used to it, I promise," she says, then the women disappear and I fall back against the mattress.

Darkness again. Long, condoling darkness.

In the night, I hear the swish of silk robes and the voice of a priest intoning rites at our bedside. The old woman's whispers fall silent and I only hear the moans of others farther away.

Later, I hear my father's voice at my ear.

"*What comes next, Maria?*" I hear him whisper.

A challenge. A test.

I know the answer. Surely I do. In the fog, I cannot seem to grasp it.

Chapter 49

"It is good to leave the hall to take some fresh air," the woman with the strawberry birthmark tells me, lifting me by my shoulders and gently pressing the small of my back when I am upright. I sit on the edge of the bed and look at the glowing light of the doorway at the other end of the vast, dark hall. I cannot imagine how I would walk that far.

"Come," she says. "That's it. You have been in bed for a long time," she says. "You must get your legs under you again."

I do not imagine that I will be strong enough to bring myself to standing. But if I do not get to the doorway, if I fail to get up at all, then I do not live. That's what the women in white tell us, and I can only believe that what they say is true. All around us is the evidence.

How long have I been asleep? I feel as though I have awoken from a long, dark dream. Beside me in the bed, the two women lie ashen and still. The old woman's thick white hair splays out across the mattress, her fragile-looking freckled shoulders protruding over the top of the sheet. Next to her, her daughter lies frozen and staring at the wooden beams above us, a bony arm hanging over the edge of the mattress, covered in black bruises and boils.

The woman in white presses me up to standing. I feel myself totter unsteadily, my ankles weak. My head spins and I feel the sting under my arms again. What if I don't want to live? What is there to live for? My knees soften and buckle under me.

I feel for the edge of the bed with my hand, but the petite woman is insistent and stronger than she looks. She presses me forward, and I find my footing. I take one more look at the two grey women in my bed. They are no longer moaning, no longer whispering. Have they passed to the World to Come? I begin to shuffle through the dimness toward the light in the arched doorway.

"Your lesions are beginning to show signs of healing," the woman speaks softly in my ear as we take a few more steps. "The *medico* says that you may live," she says, "but only if you do as we say."

I shuffle down the aisle between the rows of beds. Each one is full, two, three, or four wretched souls to a bed. In the delirium of the past days, I have not grasped the great numbers of beds and sick people around me. I am one of so many. I am insignificant.

What kind of God do we have to bring such suffering upon us? What have we done to unleash this horror on Our Most Excellent Republic? Who would know if I perished here? And who would care?

Two large men bearing a stack of folded linens pass us in the aisle. *Monatti.* Corpse bearers.

Once a day, they pluck the dead from their beds, wrapping the bodies in linen. Each man grasps one end of the sheets, and they carry them out of the infirmary hall in a long, limp package. The nun acknowledges the men with a nod, then presses me more insistently toward the door. I turn my head, and I watch the *monatti* stop at the foot of my bed. They begin to unfurl the sheets. One of the men reaches for the dangling arm of the younger woman and tucks it in by her side.

Sooner than I imagine, we are passing through the door. I squint against the brightness, my eyes aching with the light. The nun leads me to a wooden chair tottering on a brick floor.

"There," she says, lowering me onto the chair. "I will return for you."

Once my eyes adjust to the daylight, I see a broad, covered portico overlooking a large, open field with a wellhead in the center. I had not realized that the hall lay on the upper floor, and from this vantage point I can see the great iron gates in the wall of the *lazzaretto*, and the docks beyond. I press my forearms on the parapet before me, and rest my chin on my hands.

Fresh air, the nun has said, but there is none here. The Lazzaretto Vecchio—even the outside of it—smells only of smoke and death. The high walls marking the edges of the island have been blackened with fire and the ground is covered in fine, grey ash. Small flakes of ash rise into the smoky air.

I hear loud rattling below me, and I lean over the parapet to see a wooden cart stacked high with bodies wrapped in white linens. I recognize the two men who I have passed in the hall. They strain against the weight of the cart, rolling its great metal wheels across the cobbles. Finally, the *monatti* and their grisly cargo move out of view. In my mind, I imagine them dumping the bodies in the great trenches along the waterside.

Suddenly, images of my father and my cousin appear in my head, and I realize that my mind sees with greater clarity than it has had since I fell ill days, perhaps weeks, ago. The reality that my father and Paolo must have occupied this same place twists in my gut. I press my eyes against my hands and wish for the cloud of delirium to overtake me again. Where did that woman with the strawberry birthmark go? All I want to do is return to my bed so that I can close my eyes and drift away for good. Surely it is simple.

The next noise I hear is the loud clang of a brass bell at the pesthouse gates and the call of the ferryman. The boats are coming to dock. From my bed, I have heard the shuffling of feet, the crying, the calls of the workers as they unload the sick onto this God-forsaken strip of land in the sea. Do any of these poor souls return to their homes from this hellish exile?

I lean over the parapet and, as if in direct answer to my question, I see some several dozen men and women filing into the courtyard below. It looks as though Hell has emptied its bowels onto the cobblestones. The skeletal figures, white and gaunt, spill into the square, pressing their way toward the gates and the docks beyond. They are a picture of the apocalypse—ragged, ashen beings, little more than walking death. But they push ahead with the force of a mob on the verge of bursting into chaos.

They are leaving this place, I realize, making their way to the next level of hell, the Purgatory that must be the Lazzaretto Nuovo. The Lazzaretto Nuovo occupies another island they call Vigna Murata on the other side of the lagoon. I wonder if the island where those who have shown signs of healing go can really be much better than this place, can be worth the pushing crowds. Whatever the truth, the pressing crowd of wretched patients makes a desperate push toward the next stop on their journey home.

And then, I see him.

From my vantage point, only the top of his head is visible in the swirling, ragged crowd. I recognize the tight curl of his hair, the broad forehead, the even features, the spread of his shoulders. He files into the bustle of ferry passengers, then reaches up to run his hand over the top of his head. I see his broad fingers and fore-arm then, his honey-colored skin sagging but still gnarled from a lifetime of beating gold into thin sheets. Now, there is nothing but absolute certainty in my pounding heart.

Cristiano.

My *battiloro*.

Chapter 50

Somehow, I find my voice. It comes out as squeaking and raspy as the rusted wheel of the corpse cart.

"Cristiano!" I clear my throat and try again.

His face. Suddenly it is there below me. He turns toward my voice. I grasp the parapet with both hands and pull myself up. I see his eyes grow wide, and his hands clasp his linen shirt in a ball around his heart. I lean over the parapet.

"*Dio Mio*! You are sick! No!" he exclaims.

"Yes," I say. "I went home. I was looking for you… But then I fell ill. I do not know how I got here."

Cristiano has broken from the mash of ferry passengers now, and pushes his way through the crowd toward the staircase. "Maria! Listen to me. There is nothing but death here. You must leave this God-forsaken place. Come with us! Get on the ferry! I will help you." He presses toward me.

"*Stilda*!" One of the corpse-bearers presses his palm against Cristiano's chest. "Have you lost your senses? She will only bring death to everyone else. Do you not want to live, man? Get on that boat, for the love of God!" He pushes Cristiano roughly back toward the crowd, and I watch him stumble backward into the wall of people waiting to board the ferry.

As much as I want to rush down the stairs into his arms, I know that my legs will not have the strength to take me. I lean over the parapet for support. "Please! Cristiano, you must save yourself. I will only drag you into the grave." I feel tears begin to spill onto my cheeks.

"You are strong," he says to me, pushing forward again, and I see his eyes glaze with tears, too. "You must fight!" He starts for the stairs, but this time two large men place their bodies in front of him at the bottom of the treads. He grasps the brick railing and pushes his body forward, but they push back, and I see that he is too weakened to overcome them. One of the men grasps Cristiano's arm and holds him tight.

I do not try to stop the tears. "Cristiano," I say pulling myself along the parapet to the top of the stairs. "We have a child. A son. Your son… I tried my best to tell you, but I could not find you. I could not get through the barriers. Now he is in the convent orphanage at Santa Maria delle Vergini. Please, save yourself. Go find him. My father's sister is cloistered there. You can trust her. She will help you, I am sure of it."

"Maria," he presses forward again, against the two men blocking the staircase. One of the men places both hands on Cristiano's shoulders and pushes him backward. Beyond, I see the last passengers boarding the ferry for Lazzaretto Nuovo, and only Cristiano remains in the courtyard.

"*Amigón,*" the man says to Cristiano, "unless you want to stay on this island for all eternity, you had better get yourself onto that boat before they close the gates! There will not be another boat for thirty days."

I grasp the railing at the top of the staircase and lock eyes with Cristiano.

"Giuseppe," I say. "Your son. He carries the same name as my father. He… he is beautiful."

Cristiano looks at me again for a long moment. "Maria," he says, stumbling under the pull of the two men, who are now trying to drag him toward the iron gates. "If we have a son then he is no doubt waiting for you out there," he says, gesturing toward the gates. "*I* am waiting for you!" He pounds his open palm against his heart. "For the love of God," he commands, "get yourself out of this place and return to your father's house!"

He shakes off the men's grasp and turns toward the pesthouse ferry. The men follow closely behind, shoving him through the gates and sending him stumbling forward onto the dock. They close them behind him with a loud clang.

Then my knees buckle and I feel the cool brick floor under my cheek.

Chapter 51

Sixty-seven days. I have marked off each one on the hem of my linen shift with a piece of coal that I found burned in the pyre. Each day I fold back the hem and count the marks over again, just to be sure. Sixty-seven days since I laid eyes on Cristiano. He is alive. And *I* am still alive. Nothing else matters.

From the creaking deck of the plague ferry I look beyond the broad back of an oarsman onto the emerging vista of Our Most Excellent Republic. The sun glints off the small peaks of water, its hot beams searing through the haze that has settled over the surface of the water overnight. As the white fog begins to clear, the walls of the Arsenale shipyard come into view, then two crooked church towers. A few small cargo boats make slow progress across the canal, their metal fittings flashing in the emerging white light.

And from here, the low, tile roofs of Cannaregio come into view.

Home.

The cloud that has hung over me for the darkest season of my life begins to lift.

Around me, several dozen people sit on benches or stand against the wooden handrails. Some press their backs against the railings, taking shade from the beating sun under a canvas cover that flaps loose on one side. Others mill around nervously, waiting to be released back into their lives from their journey to Hell and back. A heavy silence falls over the ferry, the weight and anticipation of it all beyond words.

There are women, men, children of all classes. A few of us have survived the Lazzaretto Vecchio, graduating to the Lazzaretto Nuovo for convalescence. Others—mostly family members of the sick and dying who never developed signs of the pestilence—have only sojourned at the Lazzaretto Nuovo until the doctors cleared them of danger. A handful of health officials and priests who have had contact with the sick have also been forced into quarantine. Most of them carry large sacks of linens, clothing, and other belongings that have been boiled in the steaming pots and aired out in the great fields of the *lazzaretto*.

As for me, I only have the dull linen shift that covers my depleted body. The orderlies gave me this shift when I disembarked from the ferry that carried me from the old *lazzaretto* to the new one. They herded us women into a large room where they gave us new gowns, loading the old ones onto a cart headed for the pyre in the center of a large *campo*. It was the last vestige of what we left behind at the Lazzaretto Vecchio.

Those few of us who were fortunate enough to have improved were sent on a dilapidated ferry across the lagoon to the Lazzaretto Nuovo on the island they call Vigna Murata. There we were freer to roam than in the old pesthouse, and I spent the days restless, wandering the open fields, the storehouses with their stacks of medicinal herbs and the closely guarded rows of goods offloaded from the merchant galleys that had been fumigated with smoke and pungent concoctions.

I did not wish to befriend anyone among the families of the infected. I sat on the far end of the great hall where they served our meals, listening to the strange tongues of the men from the merchant ships moored in the lagoon, who were, along with the rest of us, forced to share the same forty days of Purgatory while we waited to return to our lives.

I hear the rattle of the chain that secures the ferry's wooden gate. I look up to see a restless crowd forming around the quayside. I hear shrieks, laughter, cries of disbelief. There are joyous calls for those who have come home alive, tears for those who have not come home at all.

I feel my heart clench. All that matters is that I go home. Will he be there in my father's house, waiting for me as he has promised? I want to go back to Cristiano, back to my father's house, back to my work. It is all I have ever wanted.

The boatman pushes his way through the crowd to the side of the boat, lashing the encumbered craft to a piling at the quayside. I press into the mass of people waiting to disembark. A slight woman, little more than a waif, is the first to step through the open gate. Behind her, there goes another, then another is released into the crowd of people waiting for their loved ones. One by one, their sunken eyes search the *campo* for a familiar face. I hear shrieks and cries of relief.

Finally, it is my turn, and I step out into the blinding light.

Chapter 52

In my father's house, the cobwebs have been swept from the eaves and the stone floor feels cool and smooth under my bare feet. There is a new copper pot hanging from the chain in the hearth, and the comforting smell of boiled onions fills the house.

Zenobia begins to remove the plates from the table, and I stand to help her. "Sit," she says. "I will take care of it." She stacks the ceramic plates and walks to the back door to dump the pigeon bones into the canal.

Beside me, Cristiano presses back into his chair, satiated from the dinner his mother has prepared for us. He takes my hand and sets his brown eyes on me, the eyes that have been in my head every day. My heart is so full that I feel it will burst.

Somehow, Cristiano and his mother have managed to bring my father's workshop back to life. The room is still bare, but there are new things: a few ceramic plates and cups, linens on the beds, and a new cooking pot. In the root cellar, glass jars filled with the fruits of a summer harvest have begun to appear on the shelves.

"I still can't believe it. I can't believe all of this," I say, gesturing around the room.

He shrugs. "My mother brought her own things from the *pensión*. And her friends helped by giving us what they could spare. It is not much, but you will have what you need."

"*Madre di Dio*." I am overcome, pressing my eyes with the heels of my hands. "How did we make it back here? I spent all those months trying to get to you," I say, feeling a catch in my throat as the truth of all we have endured washes over me in a thundering wave. "I was at the monastery garden every Friday. Then I tried everything in my power to reach you here, but by the time I managed to get through the barriers to come here you were gone."

His face is drawn, his once strong body now lean, but with a spark to rekindle. I must hope that I too might recover from my own emaciated form, my grey, sagging skin, my ragged hair beginning to grow out from when it was shorn.

"And I tried my best to find you," he says, squeezing my hand and gazing at me as if he doesn't notice any of it. "Your father would only say that you were working for a painter elsewhere in the city. I knew that you were in the San Marco quarter, but I had no idea where to look. And your cousin…" He shrugs. "Then they erected the barriers near the baker's bridge and none of us could leave the quarter. We were well for a long time as others fell ill. But soon enough, your father and your cousin broke out in the black boils. Then I had to leave."

"Father… He sent you away sick!" I say, my eyes hardened.

"No, you don't understand," he says, grasping my arm, his brow furrowing. "I was still well even after the two of them had taken ill. I tried my best to bring them back to health. Your father kept begging me to leave the house so that I would not get sick. I stayed as long as I could. I tried everything I could to save them, Maria. I am sorry." He presses his palms to his face.

"You risked your own life for them," I say, pulling his hands away and looking into his eyes.

"For you," he says. "For your family, for this workshop. And for my own future. What else was I to do?"

"How did you leave?"

"One day the priest and the inspectors appeared at the door. They neglected to examine me, so your father insisted that I leave before the Sanità returned to nail the cross on the door. Even if I had never fallen ill, if I had stayed in this house it would have meant a death sentence for me, too."

"But where did you go? The Health Office had no record of you."

"When I left here I did not know where to turn. I tried to find my mother that first night, but she was not at the boarding house or at the laundry," he says. "And truth be told I was already not feeling well myself. By the time I had packed up my goods and left the workshop I felt the fever beginning to start. The last thing I wanted to do was infect my mother or anyone who had been kind to me. The old *battiloro*'s studio where I grew up had already been sold to another guildsman; I could not go back there."

I feel pained to think of him turned out on the streets, knowing that few would open their doors to a Saracen stranger, especially one who had fallen ill.

"The sisters at the almshouse at Santa Marta took me in," he says. "Where else was I to go? I was there for only a few days when the black boils began to appear under my arms," he says, gesturing to his armpits. "Then, well, they appeared here, too, just like they did with your cousin," he says, running his palms over the insides of his thighs where they meet the groin. "I felt nearly dead already. I could hardly lift my head."

"They put you in the infirmary?"

"Yes," he says. "The doctor and some other officials came to visit us there and they told me that I had to leave; otherwise they would have to put the institution under ban and I think the nuns wanted to avoid that at all costs. So, they boarded me on the ferry with a few other foreigners."

"But you are not a foreigner!" I insist.

"No. And once we were in the *lazzaretti* there was no difference between any of us. Surely you saw that yourself. There were people from every kingdom and state—rich, poor, black, brown, white, those from the ships out in the lagoon. Anyone who believes we are different, well, pestilence and death make no distinction between any of us."

I press my hands to my face again and thank God that I am free of the hellish pesthouse. I feel Cristiano's grip on my forearms, and he helps me to standing. He presses me in his arms, then he pulls me by the hand to my father's bed, where a new firm, straw-stuffed mattress has been placed.

I have never been so grateful for the soft cradle of a bed. I curl into a ball, and Cristiano wraps his body around me. For a few long minutes I bask in the feeling of his strong arms holding me, and I can hardly believe it is real.

Then the events of the past months begin flooding into my head.

"I went to the *lazzaretto* looking for you," I say, turning to him and looking in his eyes. "No one could tell me if you were there, and I was scared to death. I wanted to tell you that I was carrying your child."

"But Maria, I knew," he says softly. "It is the only reason I am still here walking this earth."

"You knew?" I gasp, pressing myself up to sitting.

"How do you think I recovered from that place?" he says, the corner of his mouth turning up. Then he draws me into his chest and closes his eyes. "A son. I could not believe it. But it is what made me fight for my life."

"You knew!" I exclaim again. "How?"

"One day I was working out there," he says, gesturing to the worktable on the other side of the room where my half-gilded boxes still stand. "It was before your father first fell ill. A boatman appeared in the canal. He slowed when he saw me, and asked if I was Cristiano the *battiloro*. He said that the gilder's daughter was sending me a message. It took me a moment to realize that he meant you."

"A short man in a fine gondola?" I say, grasping for the knowledge that the painter's boatman might have succeeded in reaching Cristiano, and wondering why that evil boatman did not share this information with me.

"No," he says. "It was a small skiff like the ones they have at the *traghetto*. The boatman was tall and as black as I am. He said that he had been paid to bring me a message. The message was that the gilder's daughter was well, that she was housed in the studio of a painter named Master Trevisan in San Marco, and that... that she wanted me to know that she carried my child." The *battiloro* pauses and huffs, reliving the scene in his mind. "And then he was gone, just like that. Unbelievable."

I marvel, realizing that my plan to get word to reach Cristiano had worked after all.

"For a long time after that boat disappeared," Cristiano continues, "I wondered if I had imagined the whole thing, if it was all just inside my head." He runs his palm over his scalp.

"It was real," I say in earnest. "I tried my best to get a message to you. It was the only way I could think of, but I did not think that the message reached you."

Cristiano continues. "What he told me... That you were safe, that you were carrying my child. That is what I kept turning over in my head while I was in the pesthouse. It was difficult for me to believe and surely impossible to verify. But as I considered it I felt in my heart that it was true."

For a fleeting moment, his face brightens and he places a tender kiss on my head. "Somehow I felt it here," he says, pressing his fingers to his heart, "that you were communicating with me from somewhere else in the city. Then your father got sick, I left, and within a few days I was on that ferry." A shadow crosses his face and he falls silent. Both of us had survived the pesthouses, and there was no need to say more.

"Maria," he says, "I swear the only thing that kept me alive, that gave me hope, was the idea that I might see you, that what that strange boatman told me might be true. That you were out there somewhere in the city carrying my son, and that we might find each other once this horrid thing was over. I am just sorry that your father and cousin did not come out on the other side." He grasps my hands. "I never saw them in the *lazzaretto*. They were just... gone."

Cristiano flips onto his back and stares at the wooden beams above our heads. We lay silent for a long time, our bodies pressed together in the hot air. I say nothing, but stare at his face, soaking up the knowledge and the realization that he is still here.

I hear Zenobia walk from the courtyard and into the shadows of the house. She takes the copper pot from the chain and returns to the courtyard with it.

Cristiano takes my hand and squeezes it between his palms. "And now it's your turn," he says.

"What do you mean?"

"You must tell me what you have been doing all these long months. How did you manage as a pregnant woman on your own in this Most Serene Republic of ours?" I hear the sarcasm in his voice. "And *Madre di Dio*, what has happened to your hair?" He laughs, a loud bark.

I run my hand across my shorn locks. "Let us say that things got complicated after my father turned me out."

"He was not trying to turn you out, Maria. He was trying to have you married."

I nod. "Yes. He almost succeeded."

"As much as your father's decision pained me," he says, "I know that he wanted you to prosper. He thought that the gold would die."

"But the gold," I say. "It is not dead. You shall see."

"I hope you are right," he says, "for I know nothing else."

"We have a lot of work to do, you and I." I prop myself up on my elbows and reach for Cristiano's hands. "Do not ever leave this house again."

He looks into my eyes. "Maria," he says. "The last thing I want to do is leave here. But what future can we have? Who will accept me?"

"You have been working here legitimately for many months," I say. "No one doubts your strength or your skill. They respected my father and me. They respect your work. Besides, you belong here with me. And our son," I say.

"What priest will marry us?" he asks.

"I do not care," I say. "We have been through too much to let them stop us from living here together."

The shadow that falls across Cristiano's face this time is profound. He sits on the edge of the bed, and from this vantage point, I see how frail his body has become, the outline of his ribs visible under his linen shirt. He presses his face in his hands, and I know that as much as we both want it, it will not come without a price.

Chapter 53

The air has turned crisp and leaves have begun to fade into pale shades of orange and yellow when I cross the bridge away from the ferry station. The plague ferries have disappeared from the lagoon, and the *traghetti* are operating regular passenger boats again. I have stepped off the ferry, placing a *bagattino* in the hand of the ferryman. It seems an extravagance, but I am feeling buoyed. We have sold three gilded boxes in the last two months.

I move through the maze of alleys toward the convent where my aunt is cloistered. I veer onto a street of fine shops, the domain of hat makers, tailors, and purveyors of wigs, all there to feed the appetite for self-ornamentation among our rich. Has it only been weeks since the barriers have been destroyed with hammers and axes? Our Most Serene City seems to have come back to life from the brink of death.

On a stand outside her shop door, a milliner assembles a display of felt and velvet hats, each festooned with combinations of bird feathers. She gives me a half-smile and looks down at the plain, brown grain sack in my arms. Little does she know that it conceals a small treasure.

In the convent visitors' parlor, I hear my aunt's leather soles slap on the marble floor as she rushes from the adjacent corridor. Then her wide smile appears through the wrought-iron bars.

"*Cara*! Thanks be to God!" she exclaims, pressing her hand through the iron toward me. I watch a tear escape the corner of her eye. "When they told me your name was on the plague registries I nearly died of anguish myself! What were you thinking? *Madre de Dio*! You were safe here, Maria! You were insane to have gone outside of these walls!"

"A miracle, *zia*," I say. "A series of miracles."

After her initial tirade, my aunt struggles to calm herself. "Santa Maria! How are you managing?"

I consider whether to tell her that many of my father's old patrons remain afraid to come to the quarter, and that, pestilence or not, many others would not patronize a workshop operated by a woman and a Saracen anyway. Our colleagues, our neighbors, our acquaintances, our patrons… They have all shown their true selves. We cling to the ones who continue to offer their steadfast support in spite of our unusual arrangement.

I am relieved to know that our *gastaldo* is one of them. We have not spoken again about his proposal of marriage. As soon as the *battiloro* and I both returned alive from the pesthouse, the *gastaldo* removed himself from my private business completely, speaking to me only of matters of our guild rather than matters of the heart.

"We are doing well enough," I say finally. It is not the whole truth, but neither is it a lie. "The Health Office provided some linens and a small stipend for new clothes, for I returned home with nothing," I finger the white trim on a *camicia* I have purchased in the market. "And the *battiloro's* mother is helping us."

The truth is that Zenobia has been a great gift from God, taking over the duties of the household while Cristiano and I work to get the gilding studio running again. Zenobia delights in the company of her son, and she has folded into my father's house as if she had been there all along. I have only known her a short time but already I feel a deep affection for her.

Over the course of the last weeks, Zenobia has told me of how she learned of her son's fate, and how she located me. "After you came to me at the laundry," she told me, "I tried to discover the painter's house where you were lodged. I finally got the information from one of the gilders outside the quarter. But when I got to the house the lady—she was heavy with child—said that you were no longer there. She looked down her nose at me and was quick to close the door."

The painter's wife.

"But then," she said, "as I was leaving, a young man came out. He told me that you had taken your vows at Santa Maria delle Vergini. But when I went there they told me you had left the convent to return to your father's house. But by the time I got here, *cara*, you were already one foot in the pesthouse."

In the visitors' parlor, my aunt sets her clear green eyes on me. "You have not changed your mind about coming back to the convent."

I shake my head. Of this I am certain.

She purses her lips together and nods. "Understood. But it will not be an easy time for you," she says.

"That much is clear." I manage a laugh. "But we have begun to receive commissions for our gilded boxes," I say. "Things are improving."

"And the painter and his wife?"

"They have sent us commissions for several boxes for their own patrons. And the gondola makers have brought us new lanterns. It is enough for us to have bought some gold ingots. It has also given me a chance to put into practice all that I learned in the painter's studio. The boxes are becoming popular as gifts for the newly married and the newly born. Word is beginning to spread. That reminds me," I say. "I have brought you something."

From my plain grain sack, I remove a small, beautifully gilded box. I have made a special one for my aunt, fashioning a scene of the birth of Saint Anne from the molds Master Trevisan left in my father's workshop. I have covered the entire box with pure gold leaf. "For you," I say. It will not fit through the iron bars. "I will make sure the sisters at the gate get it to you."

My aunt's hands fly to her mouth in appreciation. "*Che bella*," she says under her breath. "Fit for a bride."

"Even a bride of Christ," I say, and my aunt laughs and claps her hands. "At least now you will have a proper gift from your family like the other sisters. You must show it to Lauretta."

I open the box, and my aunt gasps at the purple silk lining. From the box I produce two small prayer books. "When I was cleaning out father's studio, I found these by Paolo's bed," I say. "They were left behind in the house. I do not know why they did not burn them or take them away. Perhaps the inspectors did not find them. Not even the looters found them."

"*O Grazie a Dio!*" she exclaims. "I gave him these prayer books when he was just a small boy. He took them with him from the convent when he came to live with you." Her eyes well with tears and I press the small books through the grate.

"I hope you understand, *zia*. I am happy in my father's studio. I am happy with Cristiano. I am happy working the gold again. It is what I was meant to do," I say.

My aunt nods. "I do understand," she says. "You were right to follow your heart. Now it is up to you to carry on your father's legacy."

I stand. "Forgive me for not spending more time, *zia*, but you must understand that I cannot wait another moment to go to the nursery. Today I am taking my son home."

Chapter 54

I am scraping golden flakes from a palette knife when the neighbor's boy knocks on our door to tell us that they are ready for us in the parish church. The knock interrupts my singing.

"Tell the *gastaldo* we are coming," I say, then set down my tools and pick up the verse of the song again. The melodies flow out of me unencumbered these days.

On the table before me stand several rows of gilded boxes, each adorned with molded decoration, each one scented. The entire studio is filled with the aroma of musk and civet. No two boxes are the same. We have created different compositions across the surface of each box, using the scenes from Master Trevisan's book for inspiration.

Zenobia has gotten involved in the production of the boxes, too, but only when she is not showering the baby with attention. She sits in a chair by the small wooden crib that a neighbor has brought to us, making careful stitches into a swath of purple silk. She has shown great skill with the fabric linings that go inside the boxes, as well as affixing the small locks that the blacksmith has crafted for us. While she works, she keeps her eye on Giuseppe, looking for any sign that he is stirring awake.

I take a moment to stop and appreciate the surprising bounty in our house over just a few short weeks. I survey our production on my father's worktable, and I realize that all of the boxes are already spoken for. The money we earn from selling the boxes will fill the root cellar for the winter. More patrons have heard of our unusual scented boxes with the gilded relief decoration, and they are coming to place their requests.

We have placed one of the boxes on the meager mantel above our hearth, and I have begun to collect sheaves of gold leaf inside it. It is a paltry sum compared to the dowry box on Master Trevisan's mantel, but day by day, our material wealth increases. No matter. Now I know that as long as my new family is by my side—Cristiano, the baby, and Zenobia—my treasure lies inside the walls of my house and nowhere else.

I push the back door open, into our canal-side courtyard. The now-feral cats have disappeared, and, under Zenobia's care, the small garden has begun to show signs of life. Best of all, Cristiano has returned to the goldbeating table. Through the day, we hear his hammer ring on the gold, but sometimes I must go out to see him, just to make sure he is really there, that he is not part of some fantastic dream that lives only in my head.

I come up behind him and lace my arms around his waist. He lays his hammer down, then turns to me. Thanks be to God, Cristiano has regained his strength. The dark circles under his eyes have disappeared and the color has returned to his cheeks. He is still thin as a poker but is eating like a horse. I too feel myself returning to health at long last.

"They are ready for us." Zenobia appears in the courtyard holding her grandson in her arms. She looks beautiful, her skin oiled, her new dress hanging elegantly from her tall frame. Zenobia holds little Giuseppe, freshly awake, in her arms, joyfully nudging his cheeks with her nose.

As content as he is with Zenobia, as soon as Giuseppe sees his father he begins to squirm. Cristiano lifts the boy into the air, then clutches him to his chest with his broad hands. The baby presses his face into Cristiano's linen shirt and settles into the crook of his arm. In return, he gives his father a smile that would melt the most hardened heart.

"Look at these two beautiful ladies we have the privilege to escort to the guild meeting," Cristiano whispers to the baby.

I have done my best to look presentable. I have put lemon juice on my hair to brighten it, and have soaked it in boiled water infused with rosemary and lavender so that it smells good. My hair has begun to grow, and I have woven some strands of gold that I have fashioned with my own hands into it. I have aired out my new dress and have even woven some of the gilded threads into the neckline.

Together, the four of us pour into the alley and make our way toward the *campo*, where, not long ago, our neighbors' belongings were burning on the pyre. I have seen the neighborhood representatives with their iron crowbars, removing the wooden crosses from the doors at last. The winter has returned but the pestilence has not. For now, all of us are well.

Near the square, market sellers have begun to lift the canvas covers from their tables, to unfasten the iron locks and open the battens that have covered their shop windows for several long months. The cool air has brought in fresh relief for those of us in the quarter who have suffered unthinkable trials.

The few of us who have returned healed from the pesthouses have formed our own odd community. It is among those neighbors—bound by our shared experience—that Cristiano has found supporters. A few of them have whispered to us that they accept our strange union, even if most do not.

Today's gathering is important, one of just two that will take place all year. Right now, each one of Our Most Serene Republic's painters and gilders is preparing to assemble in the guild chapel inside the church of San Luca. Today, the men will install new officers they have elected by popular vote. All of us expect our *gastaldo* to be reelected for a fourth time.

Shoulder to shoulder, we follow one of the narrow, parallel canals for San Luca, the official meeting place of our guild. We move into a more haphazardly laid-out neighborhood to the south, which teems with merchants of all stripes. In addition to the small storefronts spilling over with goods from fruit to birdcages and leather belts, some of the boats docked along the quaysides have pushed back their covers to sell spices, dishes, rugs, and medicinal plants. The quarter has finally come back to life.

In the square before the church, I recognize the familiar faces of our fellow guildsmen. A knot of men pushes into the portals of the church, their voices and laughter echoing off the stones. Near one of the doorways, I catch sight of Master Trevisan and his wife along with their new baby girl wrapped against her mother's body, the two younger children hanging onto their mother's skirts. I reach out and caress the head of our baby, still settled happily in his father's arms. My beautiful boy. My heart swells. I wonder if Signora Trevisan's heart is as full as my own.

Across the square I recognize the elegant figure of Pascal Grissoni. At his side is a young girl, the wide-eyed daughter of another one of our guildsmen, who stands protectively on her other side. Pascal and the girl are engaged to be married, I am told. I watch her with some fascination for a while, marveling at how dramatically all of our fates have shifted over the past months.

Then the *gastaldo*'s face appears before me. He grasps my *battiloro*'s shoulder, then gives me a smile. "The heir to the gilder's workshop!" the *gastaldo* says, running his hand across Giuseppe's little head of fuzzy hair.

At the meeting, the *gastaldo* says, he will ensure that my bereavement payment is arranged so that it goes to Giuseppe instead of me. "No one can argue that your father's workshop—and everything else that is rightfully his under the law—cannot go to his grandson." He smiles. "It is clearly written in our rule book. Our little Giuseppino is the rightful heir."

"It is thanks to you that we are here today. I am grateful," I say. In the past month, the *gastaldo* has worked with his counterpart in the goldbeating guild to ensure that Cristiano is considered a full member, not as one of the *lavoranti* or *garzoni*, but as a full *maestro*. Nowhere else in the city are the members of two trades housed under the same roof, he has told us. An unconventional alliance, to be sure. We are unusual in more ways than one.

"I have something for you," the *gastaldo* says. He pulls a small, paper-wrapped package from the front of his doublet and hands it to Cristiano. Cristiano tears the paper. Inside there is an exquisite gilded rattle fashioned into the shape of a gold-beater's hammer. He picks it up and it makes a pleasant rattling sound.

"Pebbles from the beach at the Lido," the *gastaldo* laughs. "It seems you have inspired me to improvise, Maria."

I gasp. "It's beautiful, *gastaldo*. I have no words."

Cristiano places the hammer in the baby's hand, and Giuesppe's pudgy fingers grasp the handle. He holds it up to the sky, and his eyes grow wide. He moves the hammer around. His lips part and his eyes squint, and then he makes the most beautiful smile I have ever seen.

The *gastaldo* throws his head back and laughs.

"I think he likes it, *gastaldo*," Cristiano says.

"Of course he does. How could he not?" says the *gastaldo*, ruffling the boy's hair again. "He has gold running through his veins."

Author's Note

THE BUBONIC PLAGUE is spread by fleas. As a waterlogged city and a gateway to the world, Venice was especially vulnerable to outbreaks. Over many centuries, smaller and larger epidemics terrorized the city. The 1510 plague portrayed in this story took the life of 32-year-old Giorgione, one of the most celebrated painters of the Venetian Renaissance.

To see pictures and learn more about the research behind this book, visit www.lauramorelli.com/TPABonus. There you will find videos, images, and in-depth background research on:

- The bubonic plague in Venice
- Locations and vocabulary used in this book
- Saracens in Europe
- The *lazzaretti*
- Gilding in Venice
- Gilded boxes like the ones Maria makes in this story
- Painting in Renaissance Venice
- Suggestions for further reading
- And much more!

And, if you would like to recommend *The Painter's Apprentice* to your book club, you will also find a book club guide there.

> **Visit:**
> **www.lauramorelli.com/TPABonus**

FREE DOWNLOAD

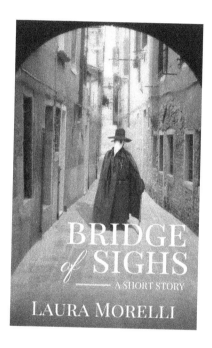

Join my Readers' Group and get a free copy
of my Venetian short story, "Bridge of Sighs."

To get started visit:
www.lauramorelli.com/bridge-of-sighs

Acknowledgments

I HAVE ALWAYS been fascinated by the Black Death but writing this book during a time when my own father was suffering and lost his life to cancer—the plague of our own times—brought the context of this old disease into sharp focus. I was forced to confront the depth and universality of physical suffering, as well as the profound helplessness that goes along with the realization that there is nothing you can do to save someone you love. I honor those who suffer, and the ones who love and sacrifice so much in such circumstances. The emotions around losing someone dear to a horrible disease could not be any different in the sixteenth century than they are today.

My parents read to me long before I could do it myself, then instilled the value of stories over five decades of telling them to me. Without their love and guidance I may have never begun to put words on the page.

My husband and our four children have endured my long vigil at the computer with patience and understanding. Dixie, my lapdog extraordinaire, has clocked many hours of high-quality REM sleep during the making *The Painter's Apprentice*.

My fantastic production team helped turn this tale into a book. I entrusted my editor, Jessica Hatch, with all the vulnerability and self-doubt of a first draft, and I am grateful for her excellent suggestions and unflinching dedication to the heart of the story. Special thanks to my group of eagle-eyed beta readers for spotting mistakes and helping to keep me honest. Kerry Ellis created the beautiful book cover design and revised the cover of *The Gondola Maker* to match. Shannon Bodie of Bookwise Design worked her graphic magic inside the book.

I am grateful to my art history mentors, professors, colleagues, and students, with whom I have shared many years of excitement around the history of art. Surely the subject of painting in Renaissance Venice is one of the most exciting of all.

Thanks especially to readers of *The Gondola Maker*, who urged me to keep writing about sixteenth-century Venice. Their anticipation and encouragement kept me going through the long winter of writing this book, and I am extremely grateful.

Did you enjoy *The Painter's Apprentice*?

Would you take a minute to leave an honest review?

For authors these days, online reviews are the lifeblood of our careers. Readers make decisions based on them. Online book retailers determine whether or not to show a book in search results based in part on the number of reviews. And, behind the scenes, we authors only have access to certain advertising and promotional opportunities if our books have a minimum number of reviews. A book with few reviews—even they're all positive and the book is fantastic—has little chance of being discovered. So, thank you for your time in reviewing this book. It really does mean a lot!

And, if you email me a link to your review(s), I'll thank you personally and add you to my Readers' Group. You can reach me at laura@lauramorelli.com.

Post your review with your favorite online book retailer:
www.books2read.com/PaintersApprentice

About the Author

LAURA MORELLI holds a Ph.D. in art history from Yale University, has taught college students in the U.S. and in Italy, and currently produces art history lessons for TED-Ed. She authored a column for *National Geographic Traveler* called "The Genuine Article" and has contributed pieces about art and authentic travel to CNN Radio, The Frommers Travel Show, and in USA TODAY, *Departures*, and other media. Laura is the author of the Authentic Arts guidebook series that includes the popular books *Made in Italy* and *Made in Venice*. Her fiction brings the stories of art history to life. Her debut novel, *The Gondola Maker*, won several literary awards including an IPPY for Best Historical Fiction and a Benjamin Franklin Award.

the
GONDOLA MAKER

By Laura Morelli

I chew my lower lip while I wait to see my father's gondola catch fire.

Beneath the boat, a pile of firewood is stacked so high that I find myself in the odd position of looking up at the underside of its black hull. A meticulous servant or day laborer has split the logs and arranged them into neat stacks, then pressed dried brush into the spaces between the wood, with the intention to start an impressive blaze. The gondola has been lashed to the largest logs of the pyre, yet it remains skewed at an angle. From my vantage point, I cannot help but admire the craft's flowing lines, its elegant prow reaching toward the sky as if to defy this injustice.

My father had nothing to do with the crime committed in this boat, of course. I feel certain that none of the onlookers has any idea that my father, our Republic's most renowned gondola maker, and I, a young man barely worthy of note, crafted this gondola with our own hands. Surely no one has noticed our *catanella*, the maple-leaf emblem we carve into the prow of each gondola that emerges from the Vianello workshop.

I stand in a crowd of bakers, clockmakers, tailors, housewives, fishermen, and merchants, all hungry for a fiery spectacle. I cast my eyes to what must be hundreds of individuals gathered around me. No, not one of them is thinking of my proud father or myself, even though I helped my father craft this fine boat just two years ago in our family boatyard. The only man on people's minds is the one who threw the rock that started this humiliating affair.

I hear murmuring behind me, then the crowd parts in unison. I scramble to the fringes just in time to feel the swish of a silk robe as a man strides purposefully by me, ignoring my presence as if I were a mere bird fluttering out of his path.

"The Councillor," I hear someone whisper beside me. My heart begins to pound.

Beneath the clasp that holds his garment closed, the man's chest protrudes. His brow pulsates at the temples, and flecks of gray dust his otherwise slick head of black hair that shows beneath his close-fitting cap. A perfectly straight nose and an even, thin-lipped mouth define a regal profile. Silently, the man circles the doomed boat, turning his piercing dark eyes into the depths of the pyre as if he can see through to the other side. He looks up at the great black craft, and everyone in the circle follows his gaze, shifting from foot to foot in anticipation.

The man in the silk robes completes his circumnavigation of the pyre. Finally, he addresses the crowd, which has grown silent over the course of the man's dramatic entrance. A shadow darkens his face, and his mouth forms a scowl as the deep cadence of his voice reverberates through the air:

"The Lords of our Most Excellent Council have ruled in the case brought against Bonito Banfi, boatman of Cannaregio, so that justice may be served in a manner proper and fitting to any individual who would seek to disrupt the peace and stable government of our Most Serene Republic. Accounting for the harmful scourge that irreverent boatmen bring to the peace of Our Most Excellent State, Bonito Banfi has been sentenced to ten years of service on the convict galleys."

By now all of us have heard the story of Bonito Banfi, the condemned gondolier whose boat—the same one that launched from our boatyard ramp two years ago—will burn on the pyre.

The tale has spread across the Venetian Republic for nearly ten days. As with so many crimes in our city, this one began with a family quarrel so old that no one remembers how it had started. Banfi had been making his rounds of the ferry stations when he spied his archrival, another gondolier called Paolo Squeran. Squeran owed him money, Banfi said, to settle a gambling debt. The two men commenced a shouting match, their foul words echoing across the canal waters from one gondola to the other. The verbal insults escalated and began to draw crowds of onlookers to the edge of the quay.

Banfi didn't know it, but the passenger riding behind the curtains of Squeran's gondola happened to be the French ambassador, returning to the embassy after a meeting at the Great Council. Banfi lifted a large rock that he had been carrying in his gondola just in case he happened to cross paths with Squeran. Instead of hitting Banfi's rival, however, the rock rang against the ambassador's passenger compartment. The curtains parted and the enraged ambassador emerged from his peaceful retreat to hurl insults of his own, in French, at the offending gondolier. The ambassador then ordered Squeran to ferry him directly to the Council of Ten, where he lodged a formal complaint with the body of justice-makers.

Banfi's sentence, so it has been recounted, is to serve for ten years on the convict galleys. Banfi's ankles were shackled, and he has been escorted to the state shipyard, where he will be chained to a crew of prisoners forced to row one of Our Serene Republic's sailing ships, part of a fleet that embarks each day for Crete, Corfu, Acre, and other port cities of our colonies in the eastern Mediterranean. To be sure, the convict galleys mean a sentence for Banfi that is worse than prison, perhaps even than death. A host of ills awaits him, seasickness and diarrhea the very least of his worries. All of us have heard the stories of dysentery that make you vomit blood, scurvy that causes pus-filled wounds to emerge across your thighs, and gangrene that turns your feet black. This is all on top of falling victim to whatever tribulations one's fellow prisoners might inflict under cover of darkness.

A modest state pittance will be provided to feed and clothe Banfi's wife and four small children, who watched tearfully as six of the state night-guards, the *signori di notte*, seized the gondola. Within hours, the boat was sentenced to this fiery doom. The intent, of course, is to set an example for the notoriously foul-mouthed gondoliers whom everyone in the crowd already considers the scourge of the city.

Before the pyre, I watch the man in the silk robes, himself surely one of The Ten who received the complaint lodged by the French ambassador. I see his lower lip twitch, an almost imperceptible, involuntary spasm that seems at odds with this otherwise well-composed official. It vanishes as quickly as it appears. He continues:

"Today, it is both my obligation and my privilege to oversee the public disgrace of this boat, as an example and a symbol for any boatman who would seek to act in any manner against Our Most Excellent Government. The greatest weight shall be placed against those who would seek to disrupt the peace of Our Most Serene Republic. So decreed on this four-hundred-fifty-first day of the reign of our Most Illustrious and Benevolent Prince Doge Nicolò da Ponte."

He turns and nods to a servant hanging on the edge of the crowd. I draw my breath now and watch a lean, muscular African dressed in a pair of drab breeches and a short-waisted jacket step forward into the circle. The crowd presses back to make room for the Councillor, who stands to face the prow of the boat. The servant approaches the pyre with a lit torch, which he begins to swing, igniting the wood prepared beneath it.

Small flames dance inside the pile of brush and logs. Within moments, flames climb, rapidly reaching up to lick the bottom of the great black craft. With a crackle and a whoosh, the gondola is engulfed in a blaze. I suck in my breath, but soon smoke assails my nostrils and the heat tightens the skin on my face. As the wooden planks begin to crack and char, I recognize the same malaise I have experienced at public executions—an incongruous mix of fascination and revulsion that forces me to freeze in place, incapacitated.

My feet feel glued to the cobblestones, yet I need to avert my eyes. I look beyond the pyre where the gondola now stands ablaze and cast my attention past the square and into the Grand Canal. Cargo boats, private gondolas, and public ferries traffic the great basin that extends between the Piazza San Marco and the island of San Giorgio Maggiore. What must amount to more than five hundred gondolas bob in the vast expanse of glittering water, more than I have ever seen assembled there in all of my twenty-two years on this earth. The boatmen and their passengers are gathered there for just one reason: to watch this boat burn between the great columns of justice that mark the gateway to the city. I gaze skyward now at the tall, white columns, one topped with a shimmering, gilded, winged lion, the other with Saint Theodore treading on a crocodile. These two statues are the symbols of My Great Republic, My Most Serene, my home, the city of my birth, the only place I have ever known.

Of course, this gondola-burning isn't the first public humiliation that I have witnessed on this very spot in my life, but I am certain that it will be the most memorable. Nearly every day, on the platform between the columns of justice in the *piazzetta*, the smaller square off our main Piazza San Marco, some poor wretch is clapped in the stocks for cursing in public, snitching an apple from a fruitseller, staggering drunkenly into his parish church, or committing crimes much more serious.

A few times, I have seen rapists and thieves dangling by their necks from a rope suspended between the columns. Their bodies hang for days, sometimes weeks, to decompose before our eyes, their cheeks bloated and black, their eyes bulging as if they were watching the crowd below in a frozen expression of horror. A few of my braver childhood friends hurled rocks and sticks to make their doll-like bodies swing and spin, then ran off laughing as armed guards from the nearby Doge's Palace chased them until they disappeared into the shadows of the arcades lining the square. I had never had the nerve to do it myself. My father would have seen me hanged, too.

When I was a very small boy I even saw someone—a man who had murdered eight people, they said—tied with ropes to four horses by his wrists and ankles between the columns. When slaves whipped the horses, they galloped into four different directions. The man's body exploded, and as long as I live I will never forget the sound it made, something akin to a ripe melon bursting from the inside out. I watched, frozen, as a flock of shrieking seagulls descended to fight over a feast of entrails. At the sight of it, a woman standing beside me vomited on my shoes. All of it was meant to uphold the just and civilized society of Our Great Republic of Venice, so it was explained to me.

None of those public spectacles, however gruesome, compares with this one, at least for me. My father will not leave the boatyard today. He could not bring himself to watch one of his own creations so publicly disgraced. That is because this is not just any gondola. It is one of the most perfect boats we have ever made. Although I am proud of how I shaped the prow, I know I will keep my pride to myself, as my father will not permit me to show it.

The sound of crackling fire snatches me from my thoughts, and I turn my attention back to the burning boat. It has disintegrated even faster than I could have imagined. The flaming craft remains little more than a skeleton now, like the bones of an enormous fish. Curls of black smoke rise into the gray sky. My eyes follow the black embers upward, where they seemed to take flight, dancing crazily in the haze.

The spectacle nearly over, onlookers scatter away from the square to resume their lives as if nothing of significance has happened. Their voices echo through the narrow alleyways that snake away from the Piazza San Marco. Beyond, in the wide expanse of the Grand Canal, an eerie light makes shimmering patterns on the water, and the dark gondolas crowded there begin to disperse without a sound down the smaller rivulets and watery passages that pervade our great city.

I cannot seem to move myself from the spot where I have stood transfixed. The flames of the burning boat are dying now, but the embers glow, making wavering reflections in the water. Overhead, a bird coos. I watch it hop from its perch on the stones of a building facing the square and sail gracefully to a fluttering landing. Birds begin to gather and peck at detritus left behind by the crowd. Two gray birds squabble over a crumb lodged in the crack of a cobblestone. I take one last look at the pyre and then force myself to leave the square.

The harsh stench of burning lacquer lingers in the air long after the crowd has dispersed. The smell of scorched paint stings my nostrils, yet I feel incited to inhale this aroma. It is repugnant and yet at the same time strangely comforting. I sense that my clothes and even the dark locks of hair that fall across my cheeks are impregnated with the smell. I feel my head reel and my stomach turn. Of course. I don't know why I did not recognize it before. It is my family's secret recipe for boat varnish, a special lacquer we use to protect the boat keels from the lichen that collects on them in the canals. The origins of the recipe were lost even to our own boat-making ancestors, but we continue to mix it in the jars of my father's workshop every day. The smell grips me, haunts me as I quicken my pace, eager to find my way through the narrow alleys leading back to my neighborhood in Cannaregio.

When at last I reach the fish market near home, I find that Signora Galli, the fishmonger's wife, has already set aside something for me. I approach her stall as she plunges her arm into a bucket, scooping out a writhing handful of eels trawled from the sea this morning, and plunks them on the scale.

"Tell your sister to make everyone a nice *risi e bisoto* for the midday meal," she says, wagging a pudgy finger at me. "Good for the baby."

"Thank you," I say.

It looks as if someone has dumped the entire contents of the Venetian lagoon onto a wooden table before me. From this bounty, the fishmonger's wife selects a few small fish and presses them into my satchel.

"She's a bit old to be birthing a baby, your mother," Signora Galli continues. "But a woman must accept children from God no matter when they come." She puts her hands on her hips and nods.

"*Santo Stefano*, let the poor boy go home," says Signor Galli the fishmonger, slapping his wife's backside affectionately with a rag as she accepts my coins. "He has no time for your opinions. The boy has a full day's work ahead of him in his father's boatyard."

"*Salve.*" I salute the fishmonger and his wife.

It is true, I am eager to reach home now. We are waiting for the baby.

Keep reading at:
www.books2read.com/GondolaMaker

CPSIA information can be obtained
at www.ICGtesting.com
Printed in the USA
FSHW010737100920
73679FS